Susan Sallis is one of the most popular writers of women's fiction today. Her Rising family sequence of novels has now become an established, classic saga, and *Summer Visitors, By Sun and Candlelight, An Ordinary Woman, Daughters of the Moon, Sweeter than Wine, Water under the Bridge, Touched by Angels, Choices* and *Come Rain or Shine* are well-loved bestsellers.

D0528692

Also by Susan Sallis

A SCATTERING OF DAISIES
THE DAFFODILS OF NEWENT
BLUEBELL WINDOWS
ROSEMARY FOR REMEMBRANCE
SUMMER VISITORS
BY SUN AND CANDLELIGHT
AN ORDINARY WOMAN
SWEETER THAN WINE
WATER UNDER THE BRIDGE
TOUCHED BY ANGELS
CHOICES
COME RAIN OR SHINE

and published by Corgi Books

DAUGHTERS OF THE MOON

Susan Sallis

CORGI BOOKS

DAUGHTERS OF THE MOON
A CORGI BOOK : 0 552 13934 3

Originally published in Great Britain by Bantam Press,
a division of Transworld Publishers

PRINTING HISTORY
Bantam Press edition published 1992
Corgi edition published 1993

7 9 10 8 6

Set in 11pt Linotype Sabon by
Phoenix Typesetting, Ilkley, West Yorkshire.

Corgi Books are published by Transworld Publishers,
61–63 Uxbridge Road, London W5 5SA,
a division of The Random House Group Ltd,
in Australia by Random House Australia (Pty) Ltd,
20 Alfred Street, Milsons Point, Sydney, NSW 2061, Australia,
in New Zealand by Random House New Zealand Ltd,
18 Poland Road, Glenfield, Auckland 10, New Zealand
and in South Africa by Random House (Pty) Ltd,
Endulini, 5a Jubilee Road, Parktown 2193, South Africa.

Printed and bound in Great Britain by
Cox & Wyman Ltd, Reading, Berkshire.

Prologue

The gallery was so crowded that people were being admitted at intervals. It was unusual to find such a quantity of work in a retrospective exhibition but when it became known that the proceeds were going to the disaster fund, owners brought their pictures from far and wide. Over three hundred paintings were hung on the dead-white walls of the Bond Street gallery, and the queue of viewers moved very slowly indeed.

An old man, sitting opposite the group of portraits corporately titled 'Girl with Red Hair', watched and listened avidly as people came and went.

'Amazing.'

It was a word used often when all the jargon of the art critics failed to describe the dozen portraits in the collection.

'Look at this one! It's as if he painted each individual hair separately!'

'And what about this one? It's the same girl. But it's so . . . *erotic*!'

'And this one could be called "Chastity". There's a purity about it—'

'The one on the end . . . she's not hiding behind her hair any more. He knows her now. Completely.'

'Amazing.'

A woman, obviously alone, stood for a long time in front of the pictures, then looked round, saw the sofa and sat on it in evident relief.

'Feet,' she explained to the old man.

'Quite,' he nodded sympathetically.

She said, 'Have you seen the seascapes?'

'Yes.'

'Amazing, aren't they?'

'Amazing.' He nodded.

'But it's this girl. She must have had a dual personality. I had to come back and look at her again.'

They sat quietly, examining the twelve portraits, listening to the comments, smiling occasionally in agreement.

And then another man arrived: tall, powerful-looking, with a face that seemed to have lived several lives already, though its owner could not have been fifty.

'We've got the car outside, Edward,' he said in a low voice to the elderly man.

'Fine.'

The man stood up with difficulty and leaned on a walking stick. He smiled a farewell to the woman and then hesitated and leaned over her.

'Actually,' he said quietly, 'the portraits are of two girls. He knew them both. Very well.'

She stared after him and then looked back at the pictures.

'Amazing,' she murmured after a while.

One

Even if Terence and Amy Patch had lived to maturity, they would never have been in the Donald Wolfit class. But they did have their own repertory company and they kept going all through the war, doing performances of Shakespeare in village halls and school classrooms; on village greens in the summer and barns in the winter. They took the Wessex Players all over the lower third of England, from desolate Exmoor to lush Wiltshire, bouncing over the dusty roads of Dorset in their converted charabanc, finding suitable lodgings in places that had never heard of theatrical digs. They believed in themselves and the importance of what they were doing and they gave performances in spite of bombing raids, food shortages and freezing venues. They never had to contend with apathy. The quality of their performances, the tattiness of their costumes, the shakiness of scenery and props, mattered little to their audiences. Winston never actually used the words 'The show must go on'. But it had to, and to the best of their ability the Patches made sure it did.

The twins were born in war-torn Plymouth at two-twenty on October the thirteenth, 1944. The European campaign was going well, and Eisenhower's smile, avuncular, reassuring, seemed to hang over the country, disembodied, like a Cheshire cat's. Amy, most definitely a woman of her time, smiled similarly with closed lips for courage. She had taken two weeks off before this birth and intended being back on the boards again in another two weeks. She had been furious to discover she was pregnant, but once reconciled to it, had found endless possibilities in imminent motherhood. And now, unexpectedly, the possibilities were doubled.

She sat up in the narrow hospital bed just a few hours after the delivery and said proudly, 'I'm a real traveller. Could have had them by myself behind a hedge if Terry wasn't such an old fuddy-duddy!' As Terry was sitting on the end of the bed at that precise moment, in full Hamlet make-up – and the Patches were heavy on make-up – the term fuddy-duddy cut no ice with the other visitors. They laughed, as they were meant to. Terry's middle-aged brother, Cedric, slipped an affectionate arm around Amy's shoulders and told her she was marvellous. Terry's middle-aged sister, who was the only one to have looked in on the babies in the nursery, smiled uncertainly and wondered what their future would be. The female members of the cast, who had a concerted thing about Terry, kept looking intensely right at him. The male members, who were either too old for the war or had bad hearts, tried not to look at Amy's distended breasts and thought their own thoughts.

It was Terry who said, 'What are we going to call them, darling? Are we sticking to half of what we said?'

They had decided that a boy would be Orlando and a girl Ophelia. They had to bear in mind that whatever sex it turned out to be, it would certainly go on the stage and they had wanted it to have a flying start.

Amy said, 'If only they'd been a boy and a girl we could have stuck to the whole thing, sweetheart. But what goes with Ophelia, for God's sake?'

Terry racked the brains behind the carefully coiffeured hair. 'Octavia?' he hazarded. 'Antony and Cleo if I'm not

8

mistaken.' He knew very well he was not mistaken so they all forgave him for sounding smug.

Amy was appalled. 'Darling! Imagine being lumbered with a name like Octavia! Anyway the phonics are all wrong. I mean O-phelia. And Oc-tavia.'

Cedric settled himself more comfortably on the pillow so that Amy was practically engulfed in his large frame.

'How about Mary and Margaret?' he asked. 'After dear old Ma and Maggie here,' he nodded towards his sister. Margaret, who hated being in the limelight, coloured slightly and made murmuring noises.

Terry was adamant. 'No offence intended, Sis. But listen to it.' He dropped his voice to a dull monotone. 'Mary Patch. Maggie Patch.'

One of the girls laughed with her mouth slightly open. Amy said quickly, 'I like Margaret. And we've always said the family name could be slightly lengthened.' She lifted her voice and spoke musically. 'Margaret Passmore.'

Cedric's appreciative squeeze dug uncomfortably into the bandage-things they'd strapped around her till her milk came in. She sighed and dropped her voice again. 'Darlings. Do you mind? I'm so frightfully tired.'

Terry was up like a shot. 'Anyway we're on stage in an hour, everyone!' He put his forefinger on Amy's full lips and pressed slightly. He would not risk his make-up with a proper kiss and anyway did not want to be seen competing with Cedric.

However, Cedric did a proper job and Amy did not object, because for the last three months she'd been playing dame roles while the girl with the laugh did Viola and Hermia and Portia – Amy had refused to allow *Romeo and Juliet* to be performed until she was able to resume her Juliet to Terry's Romeo. Therefore she allowed Cedric's kiss to come to its end and patted his cheek as if she'd actually enjoyed it.

9

'Farewell, Thespians all!' She extended her arms in an adieu which effectively removed him from her neck area. Terry paused at the door of the ward and made an elaborate bow before disappearing. The others drifted out, already thinking of other things. Margaret said, 'Will you be all right, Amy? Is there anything you want?'

Amy suddenly felt like crying out, 'Yes, I want my mother!' But of course her mother was long dead, so she smiled and shook her head charmingly. Cedric said, 'We'll see you tomorrow then.' He looked very serious. 'Take great care of yourself now.'

'And the babies,' Margaret said.

Amy maintained her smile. 'I will. I will.'

The door closed and she fell back on the pillow and spent ten frantic minutes trying to get beneath the bandages for a good scratch. Then she composed herself, crossed her hands on the bed covers and looked saintly. She did that for all of another ten minutes. Then she looked at her watch. Six o'clock. She was convinced it was an hour since Terry had left, which meant that he'd been lying: because of double summertime they didn't go on until seven o'clock. And if he'd been lying it followed that he wanted to get away from her.

She turned her head and wallowed in self-pity, then the door flew open and the first cot trundled in, closely followed by the second. She was surprised; rather alarmed. For a moment she had forgotten that at lunchtime she had given birth to twin girls.

'Hello, Mother!'

A buxom nurse, older than Amy, parked one of the cots and took up her station at the side of the bed. The other nurse said, 'And he said to me – all Americans aren't the same, honey.'

The first nurse pushed Amy forward, pulled up her nightie and began to undo the bandages.

She said, 'Don't trust him. My sister believed every word—'

'What are you *doing*?' Amy bleated.

The bandages were released and she fell back on the pillow; two surprised faces came into view.

'Teatime, Mummy,' explained the buxom one.

'I had tea with my visitors! Surely it's supper—'

Both nurses threw back their heads for a hearty laugh.

'*Babies*' teatime!' they said practically in unison.

Amy was absolutely horrified. 'But there's nothing there! It said in this book – and anyway the doctor told me—'

'They have to learn to suck, dearie.' The buxom one stuffed an extra pillow behind her head. Pillows appeared at her elbows. She was trapped by pillows. It was like a nightmare. 'And you have to learn how to handle two babies!' The laughter grew to mammoth proportions.

But it was not funny. For one thing the small moist objects wedged into Amy's arms reminded her forcibly of piglets; and for another she did not take kindly to the nurses manhandling her poor breasts in quite such a businesslike way.

'Oh dear,' said the buxom one when she began to cry. 'We'll have to take them one at a time. It'll take ages, but—'

'I have to get off at seven-thirty sharp.' The other nurse looked at her fob watch, no longer amused at the situation. 'My boyfriend is picking me up at eight.'

The buxom nurse removed one of the piglets who let out a wail of distress, and fixed the remaining one firmly in position. The baby sucked mightily; the pain was intense.

'I told you, don't trust them. Not any of them,' said Buxom. Her tone altered to one of doting admiration.

'Look at this one – she knows which side her bread is buttered on.'

'It hurts,' Amy bleated. 'And she's getting nothing.'

The other baby continued to wail like a lost soul.

'I haven't got to – I can't – no, really—'

'Just a few minutes. On the other side.'

But the second twin wasn't a quick learner and could not manage to connect. Amy sat forward to be rebandaged, then sank among the pillows thankfully.

'Aren't you going to take them back to the nursery?' she asked above the wailing as the nurses made for the door.

The buxom one showed her teeth professionally. 'Just an hour with Mummy!' she trilled and was gone.

Amy stared at the two cots, both vibrating as their inmates brought the house down. After a while her own tears dried on her face. She pushed back the bedclothes and very cautiously swung her legs to the ground. The edge of the bed was hard and she pulled a stitch somewhere down there and gave a yelp. But then she stood up and felt better. She held on to the cots and stared into them, appalled and revolted. The babies were wrapped like mummies, just their heads showing. They had fronds of hair sprouting here and there from large scalps. The hair was pink. Both sets of eyes were lost in folds of loose flesh. The noses were buttons, the mouths holes. She could detect no difference between them. But then one of them – the one she had fed – suddenly gave a Sir Toby-like belch and shut up. And then the other produced a shoulder and an arm from its swathings and reached for something only she could see.

Amy leaned closer. 'You can be Margaret,' she said softly. 'You might not always get what you want, but by golly, you'll keep trying!' She turned to the other cot which no longer trembled passionately. A kind of smile hung on this baby's mouth. Amy found herself smiling in return. 'Yes.' She nodded as if in congratulation. 'You're like me. You'll always get what you want.' She thought of Terry and made a moue. 'It's finding just what you do want, isn't it, little one?' She actually laughed at that. Because of course she knew what she wanted. Fame. Just fame. And Terry too if he could get it for her.

She said, 'You shall be Miranda. Margaret and Miranda.'

Margaret reached again, with desperation, and yelled lustily and Amy's laugh died.

'But I can't be doing with either of you,' she mused. 'This feeding . . . the whole thing. It's one enormous bind.'

She was still staring at them when the door opened and supper arrived. The trolley was pushed by a squat girl with greasy hair. Amy turned on her charm.

'How heavenly! But I simply cannot eat anything in the midst of this frightful din!' She leaned towards the girl and smiled. 'Do you think you could possibly trundle the darlings back to the nursery for me?'

The girl was mesmerized. 'You'm that actress. Married to that bloke what looks like Tyrone Power.'

Amy maintained her smile with difficulty. 'Yes,' she cooed.

''Sever so romantic, innit?' The girl left her trolley and stared down at the children. 'An' you 'avin' to give it all up cos o' these little dearies.'

'Give it up? I wouldn't dream of giving up the stage.' Amy put a hand to her throat, another to her forehead. 'The show must go on, you know!'

The girl's face sharpened. 'Then you'll have to send 'em off by themselves like. Wun't you?'

'Send them off?' Amy had had visions of nannies.

''Vacuate 'em. Eff you don't go with 'em, they'll 'ave to go by theirselves. Can't keep 'em 'ere. Not in wartime.'

She glanced up from the cot and ran her gaze over Amy. 'Wun't want to feed 'em neither. So you'll need a safe place and someone 'oo knows what they're doin'.'

Amy met the calculating eyes and said, 'I suppose I shall. Pity you don't live in the country, isn't it?'

'My auntie do. She were a nurse. Takes in chillun for the duration.'

'Fosters them?'

'No.' The voice was almost scornful. 'They'm billeted on 'er like. It's all official. She 'ad a letter from the Queen congratulatin' 'er on 'er war work!'

'Did she now?' Amy murmured.

She sat on the bed and did not notice the pulling stitch. She arranged her face in a half-smile.

'You're right, of course. We play in a lot of cities as well as . . . yes, you're right. Children must come first. It wouldn't be fair to drag them along with us.' She met the girl's dark eyes and put a hand to her head again. 'Oh dear. Oh dear. I don't know what to think.'

'En't goin' to faint, are you? Look, I'll take 'em down nursery now. Then I'll give you the name o' my auntie. She d'live in Keele. Right down there by Land's End. They'll be safe there. An' she'd put you up for a weekend whenever you wanted to see 'em.'

Amy watched through her fingers as the girl manoeuvred the cots through the door. She liked the idea of quiet Sundays by the sea. A wonderful excuse to get away from the others. She smiled down at her knees and thought that she would ask Cedric to go and give the place a recce. Yes, he'd like that idea. And it would get rid of him from the side of the bed.

Her smile widened. She stood up quite briskly and went over to the trolley. There were ten plates of limp salad stacked there, each with its single slice of Spam. She picked on one and shovelled its contents on to another.

She was suddenly ravenously hungry and after all she needed to eat for two, she was probably the only person in Plymouth to have had twins that day.

She tucked in with a will.

Keyhole was a tiny village huddled around one of Cornwall's coves to the south of Land's End. The harbour was almost landlocked by the two jutting arms of its piers, and within their protection two small girls could play in the pools at low tide without supervision, with a glorious sense of freedom, and the instinctive knowledge that everything they saw, touched, smelled, belonged to them.

Mrs Roe, known locally as Mrs Hitler, adored small babies. She had doted on them until they could walk and talk, and then, quite suddenly, like a mother bird, she wanted them out of the nest.

The war was over, but there was no place for Miranda and Meg with the Wessex Players. Amy and Terence visited them often in the winter, hardly ever in the summer. Amy taught them to swim – they were never allowed to forget that – Aunt Maggie taught them to read and arranged which school they should attend when they were five, but mainly they were educated by the place itself: shouted at by Mrs Hitler, fussed over by older girls who earned sixpence by keeping an eye on them, knocked by the sharp rocks around Lannah Cove, soothed by the salt water and foamy surf of the Atlantic.

They needed no friends: they had each other; they complemented each other. Miranda would tackle anything, surging into the next experience like the Cornish luggers breasting the swell of the sea. Meg was not so much cautious as curious. She wanted to look, to touch, to explore. She was always turning pebbles over to see their undersides; and she would put them back as she had found them.

Miranda laughed at her carefulness but understood it.

'You gotta put 'em back like they was,' she explained to her sister as if Meg did not know why she was doing these things. 'Cos that's the side for our foots.'

Meg, fitting her instep around a smooth pebble, nodded in perfect agreement. The girls often spoke each other's thoughts; mostly they did not need to vocalize them, they were simply shared wordlessly.

The harbour walls were steep, the boats moored to the rails by long ropes, some fitted with pulleys. When the tide was in, the men would often use these pulleys to coast down to their craft rather than use the steps. There were accidents and Meg never watched them do it. Miranda watched and yearned to try it herself.

Terence and Amy had been down the week before to tell them about boarding schools and how they would be expected to behave: the need to wear shoes all the time, to eat with a knife and fork, to speak 'properly'. Aunt Maggie had talked to them before about school and told them they would manage very well because they could write their names, speak poetry by the ream and had each other. They had understood and appreciated that. Amy's adjurations were more difficult to accept and she had implied that they might not see Keyhole again. Ever.

Miranda stood by the harbour and watched the tide flood the cove and imagined herself as Amy.

'Farewell, and then farewell!' she murmured, unconsciously placing a hand on her heart.

A voice said, 'You're the tadpole kid, aren't you?'

The voice was different, not local. She looked up and saw a boy who was obviously a 'visitor'. Open-necked shirt, khaki shorts, dark hair falling into one eye.

She said, 'None of your business.' And resumed looking out to sea. He did not know much because she wasn't the tadpole kid at all, she was one of the tadpole twins.

The boy said, 'I asked about you when I saw you swimming at Lannah. They said you were called the tadpole because you swam like a tadpole.'

Miranda was not quite five and ostensibly a child of nature, but she was also a child of Amy and Terence Patch, so she said precociously, 'How obvious.'

The boy grinned appreciatively and Miranda almost smiled back.

He said, 'You'd like to go down one of those ropes like a commando, wouldn't you?'

'What do you know about the commandos?' she asked, still truculent.

'More than you do. I can remember them when they were stationed at St Ives. They used ropes to go up and down the cliffs.'

'How old are you, then?'

'Fourteen. How old are you? Three?'

She was so angry she almost hit him. But then she was glad she hadn't because he said, 'Come on. Let's have a go.'

She swallowed. 'Now?' She looked around. No-one was about.

''Course. I go home tomorrow.'

'I go to school,' she said sadly. It was a bond between them.

They walked along by the rail and chose a boat low in the water, well ballasted, steady. The boy took hold of the pulley with both hands.

'See. It's like a bosun's chair. You've seen them practising from the lifeboat, haven't you?'

She nodded, trembling with excitement. It looked a hundred miles down to the lugger beneath them. They'd crash on to its deck and be smashed into pieces.

'Well?' said the boy. 'You scared?'

'No.'

But she was. She had difficulty in fitting her hands between the larger ones of the boy. Then they had to clamber over the rail and position themselves so that she was standing between his legs and he was crouched to match her height.

They might not have launched themselves off even then, but someone shouted at them from the window of the Lobster Pot and, startled, the boy turned too quickly and the next minute they were soaring down towards the all too solid deck of the lugger.

Their lack of expertise was their salvation. The boatmen swung themselves over the last few yards of slack rope; the boy had not seen that. They hung suspended over the sea on a rope which now climbed upwards towards the lugger.

Furious shouts came from above. Miranda waited no longer. She dropped like a small pebble into the water with hardly a splash and swam beneath the boat to emerge unseen at its stern.

The boy, floundering in full view, was the one who got into trouble. The furious voice belonged to his father who said very loudly that if they had not been going home tomorrow they would certainly have been going home tomorrow! The boy's shorts were hung with seaweed as he was dragged up the steps by this very angry man. But he was smiling. And Miranda never forgot that he did not mention his companion.

The strange thing was, that Meg met her at the entry to Mrs Hitler's house with dry clothing.

'How did you *know*?' Miranda asked, fumbling her way out of her sundress and into the glorious warmth of a jumper.

Meg said, 'Well, I just knew. But more than usual.

18

There was a boy. And you were very happy and very excited.'

Miranda said, 'Yes. Yes. Yes.'

And then they started to laugh because for the first time they realized and fully appreciated their connection.

Meg and Miranda sat in the taxi on either side of Uncle Cedric. They had been to Plymouth every school holiday since leaving Keele two years ago, but they knew it wasn't really 'home'. It was where Amy and Terence were based but, as Terence frequently told them, the world was their home. Roots meant loss of freedom. So the idea was not to stay long enough anywhere to start growing them!

They'd laughed at that because they laughed at most things their father said. Miranda had wrinkled her nose and said, 'Anyway, I wouldn't want to grow in Plymouth! It's too noisy!'

Amy kissed the small face that reminded her so much of pictures of Ellen Terry, then spread her arms wide and said, 'Doesn't it make you tremble inside to think of Plymouth being reborn after the Blitz?'

And this time they did not laugh because the pneumatic drills did indeed make their stomachs vibrate inside.

They had talked about their parents in bed that night – actually only four weeks before – marvelling that they were called Amy and Terence, never Mummy and Daddy, and that they were 'citizens of the world', which made it handy for something called income tax and something else called rates.

Meg had said, 'Keele was digs too, was it?'

Miranda nodded. 'Yes. Like Plymouth. And that place before . . .'

'Exeter.'

Miranda said, 'Wherever Amy and Terence get a job they have digs.'

'We didn't have a job at Keele.'

'No. But it wasn't home.'

'That was cos of Mrs Roe.'

Miranda brought a strand of frizzy hair to the front of her head and arranged the end beneath her nose. She deepened her voice to a growl. 'You vill do exactly vot I tell you!' she intoned.

Both girls were convulsed with giggles. Then Meg said, 'But I liked the place in spite of Mrs Hitler.'

Miranda dropped her plait. 'You mustn't! You might start growing there like Terence said!'

Meg nodded in agreement. Then she said sadly, 'We've got nowhere to ask anyone for the holidays.'

Miranda was unworried. 'We've got each other. We don't need no-one else.'

They snuggled down in bed. The sheets were not theirs. Neither was anything else in the room. But then it had always been like that. Mrs Roe had told them often, 'You take care of my things, you girls!'

Meg said sleepily, 'You said that all wrong.'

Miranda, who had hoped her error had gone unnoticed, sighed deeply and corrected herself. 'We don't need anybody else.'

Meg murmured, 'Or – "we need no-one else".'

She got her thumb ready to insert in her mouth and added, 'D'you want to sit in my lap tonight?'

They arranged themselves accordingly and in two minutes were fast asleep.

But sitting either side of Uncle Cedric only four weeks later, removed abruptly from school in mid-term, with Amy and Terence suddenly called 'your dear parents', their rootlessness was a great disadvantage. And the pneumatic drills that were everywhere, that spring of

1951, made them shake inside with sheer terror. Because hadn't Uncle Cedric explained that a pneumatic drill piercing a gas main had caused the explosion which had killed Amy and Terence?

The cast gathered round them. Without a script they did not know what to say. A girl whose mouth seemed unable to close cooed, 'I was there the day you were born. Terence did not know what to call you. You were nearly Octavia and Ophelia.'

Miranda said, 'Yes. Amy told us. She chose our names. Margaret is *Henry the Sixth*. And I'm *The Tempest*.'

The girl with the open mouth laughed as if Miranda had made the best joke in the world, then sobered suddenly and said, 'You were marvellous. Both of you. Coming to the funeral. Bearing up.'

Meg said, 'Amy said religion was just drama. We were in a play.'

'Oh my God.' The girl turned away. Meg glanced at Miranda, asking a silent question. Miranda murmured, 'Not yet. Wait till Aunt Maggie comes.'

They had already decided they wanted to spend their holidays with Aunt Maggie. But Uncle Cedric said it was difficult because she wasn't married. Mrs Roe/Hitler hadn't been married either, so that made no sense, and they assumed it was an excuse Aunt Maggie was using to get out of having them.

They drifted across the hotel room towards the buffet. They were always hungry and did not realize that grief was supposed to make food unacceptable. Someone said, 'Look at them! It's the hair perhaps? Or the way they do everything in perfect unison.' The owner of the voice bore down on them. 'Listen, darlings. I am going to absolutely insist on you eating something. How about a nice salmon sandwich?'

They looked surprised. Then amenable.

'Such brave girls,' said the voice as they crammed sandwiches and cakes into their mouths as fast as they could.

And then Aunt Maggie came in and stood in the doorway, looking down at them. They stopped chewing and let their eyes fill up with tears. Then they turned towards each other and the crinkly red hair mingled. They spent a concealed moment swallowing desperately, and then they began to sob.

But Maggie had been going to do her duty anyway and offer her nieces a home with her. And now, suddenly, it wasn't such a duty. She had only half-known her baby brother; his theatrical ambitions had been a mystery to her. And Amy had not been the sort of wife to keep his feet on the ground either. But now, seeing the theatrical tears of these two small girls, she understood her brother and sister-in-law better than she had in life. She saw that part of their aim had been to have fun – and they had succeeded in that.

So when she crouched before the twins, she was laughing.

'Meg. Miranda. I gather from the tears at my appearance that either you loathe the sight of me or you want to come and live with me. Which is it?'

The girls were flabbergasted. Neither their acting nor their twinship had blinded Aunt Maggie. She talked to them as if they were grown-up, honest, and reasonable.

The tears dried up magically. Miranda glanced at Meg who was cautious, and saw her own thoughts mirrored in the sky-blue eyes. She said, 'We'd like to live with you, Aunt Maggie.' And Meg, unexpectedly, added, 'Very much. Please.'

Maggie said, 'Well, I'd like that too. But there might be snags. I'm single, you see, and I live in a flat. Quite a small flat.' She stopped smiling and looked thoughtful. 'There is a man I could marry. He's a solicitor. With a house.'

Miranda said, 'Is he nice? Do you like him?'

'Yes, but not enough to share our lives with him. I'll have to think of something else.' She stood up. 'Listen. I'm going to load some plates with food and we'll go to my place and have a conference. Is that all right with you?'

Miranda smiled and Meg said lovely. If Aunt Maggie hadn't been using both hands, they would have held one each. As it was they kept very close to her until she asked someone to call a taxi.

They solved the problem by sharing Uncle Cedric's house. It wasn't ideal because Uncle Cedric had been in the Navy and had been invalided out with a dicky heart. They had to be quiet and they had to be cuddled. Uncle Cedric was a great cuddler. Many of the elderly gentlemen who called on him were cuddlers too. They grumbled about noise; about the house being overrun with women, Miranda's declamations as she learned lines for the latest school play, Meg's painting things in the attic, even Aunt Maggie's books which crept from her room into the study and from there into every part of the house, even the bathroom. But a cuddle, a kiss on the top of a bald head, and all was well. It was when the girls were discussing Uncle Cedric one night that Meg discovered the very first difference between herself and her sister.

Miranda was laughing about the sudden increase in their allowances. Every holiday it was the same: he would listen to their pleas for more money, glance at Maggie who kept her gaze studiously on whatever she was doing, and shake his head.

'You girls cost me a fortune as it is. When I was a boy I was lucky if my uncle slipped me a sovereign once a year! Everything is provided for you at that posh school of yours! You get more money than my mess allowance before the war! Not a penny more, my dears, and that is definitely that.'

Aunt Maggie invariably cut short further pleas by a firm 'Having got that little matter out of the way, shall we eat up. Mrs Marks has made one of her steak and kidneys specially for your first day back, my loves!'

No-one liked Mrs Marks's cooking, but Aunt Maggie's school broke up well after the twins' so they had to put up with it for a few days until she could take over. Anyway, they recognized their aunt's ploy. Whatever rise they needed in their allowances would be made up by her. She hated haggling about money.

But there was never any real need for Aunt Maggie to bale them out. Because whenever Miranda needed a sub, she would take Uncle Cedric his hot toddy before she went to bed, and sit on his knee.

'It's killing!' she chortled to Meg. 'He knows what I'm after and he says – "it's no good you trying to get round me, young lady" – ' she deepened her voice to a very near semblance of Cedric's. 'But after half an hour—'

'Half an hour!' Meg sounded horrified.

'Well, it's not much to give the old darling, is it?' Miranda replied, making Meg feel mean. 'You could take over half of that if you like!'

'No thanks!'

'Quite, absolutely quite.' This time Miranda sounded exactly like Amy, only neither girl knew that. 'It's because I know you're not keen on the cuddly bit that I take it on! You should be grateful!'

'I am.' Meg was suitably contrite. She imagined at that moment that she and Miranda were still tuned into each other. If she hated Uncle Cedric's cuddles, then so did Miranda and she was being self-sacrificing. She laughed at herself. 'It's the way he calls me Nutmeg that really finishes me off! If I'm a nutmeg then he's a grater!'

They were convulsed at this. Then Miranda spluttered, 'The best of it is, when he agrees to up our allowance, he always begs me not to mention it to Aunt Maggie! So of course I promise that I won't if he won't!' She spread her hands and used the latest term they'd learned in physics classes. 'Ergo, we get two rises for the price of one!'

And suddenly Meg felt the schism between them. They weren't really cheating Uncle Cedric; he was cheating himself. But they were cheating Aunt Maggie. And Meg loved Aunt Maggie who treated them with respect as well as love and never asked for anything in return; not even cuddles.

But Miranda did not see or feel the schism and Meg said she had to go to the lavatory and made a quick exit. She couldn't bear the thought that there was even a moment when she was not in tune with Miranda. She pulled the flush vigorously, then realized she was cheating again and sat down to spend a penny. And tried to forget it all.

Cedric had enough of Terence in his blood to enjoy the role of beleaguered male. He loved being cajoled by the two small editions of Amy. He never noticed that Meg avoided being alone with him, and he continued to call her Nutmeg and snatch a kiss whenever she passed. He grew fat and ruddy-faced and could not wait for the holidays to come round.

They were happy, all of them. Maggie felt like a career woman instead of a spinster schoolteacher, the girls brought their friends home and wondered what Terence had meant all those years ago when he had said something about never putting down roots. Putting down roots was fine. Absolutely fine. That first year, 1951, Uncle Cedric took them all to London to see *Swan Lake* at the new Festival Hall, then on to the Tate to see some of the Hepworth sculptures. Two years later he managed to get a 'window' to view the Coronation and he bought them a camera each so that they could take their own photographs.

Miranda said, 'Sometimes I feel quite, quite dreadful about enjoying everything so much since Amy and Terence died.'

Meg thought about it carefully. 'We didn't know them that well, did we?'

'No. But they were our *parents*!'

'They were very ambitious. I don't think they wanted to be parents.'

Both girls were aghast at this mutual discovery. Meg had voiced it, but it was one of their shared experiences. They stared at each other, their pale blue eyes wide. Meg said slowly, 'They wanted to be actors first. That's all I meant. That was why they sent us to Mrs Hitler.'

'Yes. I know. Of course.' Miranda nodded quickly. 'Well, that's OK with me. I mean, I feel the same way. About acting.'

'Do you?' Meg looked doubtfully at her sister. She knew that *she* wasn't very pretty with her funny apricot-coloured hair and fishy eyes. And everyone said she and Miranda were identical so that must mean Miranda wasn't very pretty either.

Miranda got the message. 'I know Amy was beautiful. But acting is about making people believe lies.'

'I wasn't thinking . . . that.' But Meg flushed guiltily because obviously Miranda was privy to most of her thoughts. 'I was thinking it's nice being private. Like those painters and sculptors and all. Nobody knows anything about them. But they're acting in a way. They're making people believe things that aren't true.'

Miranda nodded. 'All right,' she said comfortably. 'You be a painter and I'll be an actress.'

Maggie, coming in at that moment, said humorously, 'Doesn't anybody want to be a schoolteacher and have piles of books to mark every night and go to camp with the first years?'

They laughed and Meg said, 'We'll make lots of money and you can stop being a teacher and live with us.'

'Darling, the best thing about being a teacher is that I get a pension. And I shall be retiring in two years' time and living on it. Won't that be marvellous?'

The girls applauded frantically.

So Maggie retired and things got even better. She could come to all the plays and events at school. She brought Uncle Cedric in her new car and all the girls thought he was a 'pet'. They were a bit wary of Maggie, but when they came to stay in the Plymouth house they appreciated her much more. In large doses Uncle Cedric could be a crashing bore and Aunt Maggie knew this and made certain the doses were quite small.

In 1956, after the Hungarian débâcle, she insisted on housing a couple from Budapest. They had the dining room and downstairs bathroom and the back bedroom above. It meant that the girls moved into the attics, which they loved. But it also meant that for a year there was no room for their friends. What was worse was that Maggie took the brunt of the refugees. She drove them to other houses to keep in touch with fellow refugees. She was always cooking them meals and trying to teach them English. She found them jobs and eventually a flat. Then she went to the doctor.

She never told anyone what he had said. But her loss of weight soon made it obvious anyway. She died in the late summer of 1958, just before the twins' fourteenth birthday.

Uncle Cedric, suddenly old and frail, got a housekeeper with a small child. Mrs Jenkins was a good enough cook and a good enough cleaner, and there it ended. The house was not the same; there was no more laughter, no more treats, no more anything much. Maggie had left her money in trust for the girls when they became twenty-one and Cedric missed her domestic contributions. There could be no summer holiday this year; he suggested that they should invite a couple of friends and show them Plymouth.

They invited one friend. Her name was Pamela. She was one of the girls who had called Cedric a pet. She was blonde and pretty and she had definite breasts so she thought she was one up on the others.

'I'm going to bring happiness into this household!' she announced at supper the first night. 'Life must go on – you two should know that after losing your parents.' Pamela did not believe in dodging issues. She often referred to the twins as 'the orphans'.

She lifted her glass of water. 'Come on! Let's drink to happiness!'

It sounded marvellous somehow, like a rallying cry. Miranda drank her water in one gulp and suddenly turned round and threw the empty glass into the grate. Pamela gave a shout of laughter and did the same. After a startled second, Uncle Cedric followed suit. Meg put her glass back on the table. The set had belonged to Aunt Maggie. She glanced at her sister and forced herself to laugh with her. But it was perhaps the second time that she had recognized a difference between them.

Uncle Cedric did not come with them on their tours of Plymouth. So every evening Pamela would insist on going into his room to tell him exactly what they had done and how wonderful it had been.

'We stood where Drake stood. I mean, we actually stood on the same spot! Can you imagine it?'

Cedric looked up at her as she paused in her constant movement around his room. She was vibrant with life; just like Miranda and Nutmeg had been before Maggie . . . he swallowed fiercely and held out his glass for her to fill it.

'You old drunkard!' she said fondly, in the frank way she had. 'What are we going to do with you!' She danced back to the desk to replace the bottle. 'You sit here all by yourself all day long wallowing in misery! Yes, I mean it!' She shook her finger under his nose. 'Wallowing!' She danced away again and went to the darkening window. 'Why don't you come with us?' She peered briefly into his telescope. 'Oh, I suppose you can see it all from here—'

He said mournfully, 'Dear Pamela. I'm nearly seventy, child! It was different when Maggie was here to drive me around the place—'

'There you go again!' She was back, behind his chair this time, her fingertips glancing off his polished pate. 'Self-pity! That's what it is, you know!'

He felt tears on his cheeks. 'You don't understand, child. I hope you never will understand!'

She was wonderfully contrite. She cupped his head, moved around the chair, held him against her gingham shoulder.

'I do understand. I feel I can be honest with you, Uncle Cedric. Because I'm so close to the whole family, I can say exactly what comes into my head. It's a compliment, you know. My father says I'm very mature for my age and I think that's why I can say the things I do.'

He snorted a watery laugh, but she was insistent.

'I mean it!' She took the glass from his shaking fingers and sipped delicately. It was revolting but she managed to control a shudder.

'You see?' She put the glass down on a side table very quickly. 'Anyway, if I can say anything to you, surely you can say things to me? Talk to me about your feelings. Your real feelings.'

It was better than Truth and Dare really. She could be rude to him and he had to respond by telling her his innermost thoughts. She slid round on to his lap.

He said hoarsely, 'The girls aren't close to me any more.'

Pamela nodded. She had noticed that Meg and Miranda had gone into themselves since the bereavement. It was all right for them, of course; they had each other.

She said, 'Listen, Uncle. I have come here to make things all right for all of you.' She saw herself as a light brightening their darkness. 'I am close to you. Can't you see that I have been trying to make it up to you?'

He sobbed suddenly and put his forehead down again on to her frail shoulder. Her bones were like a bird's; like Miranda's; but he knew that both girls were as strong as horses in reality. Stronger than he was. Certainly stronger than poor dear Maggie. He put his arms around Pamela's waist and held on to her as if he might drown.

She felt a wonderful sense of power. She was standing in for Meg and Miranda in their hour of need. She was comforting this poor old man, who surely did not have much longer to live. She'd already saved him from the demon drink by sipping at that glass and then removing it. She held his head hard to her chest and kissed the awful sweaty baldness on the top and thought she must be quite saintly. And his right hand moved down from her waist.

Meg and Miranda were sitting with Mrs Jenkins's small boy while she was at the pictures. In spite of the heatwave, he had a cold, which meant that when he tried to suck his thumb he was unable to breathe. Meg was rubbing his chest with camphorated oil while Miranda read to him from one of her own nursery books. They too were in role; Meg had cast young Adrian as neglected semi-orphan, herself and Miranda as fellow orphans in a cruel world. Miranda saw them as a combined Florence Nightingale and hardly noticed the snuffling patient.

His eyes were beginning to droop when Pamela's screams thrust up from Uncle Cedric's room. He sat bolt upright and joined in. Miranda dropped the book and said, 'It's Uncle Cedric!' And Meg continued the thought, 'He can't have died too!' And they left Adrian to his screams and ran out on to the landing to meet a sobbing Pamela climbing upwards.

Probably if Maggie had been there it would never have happened; but if it had happened, she would have smoothed everything down. Neither Miranda nor Meg, nor for that matter Uncle Cedric, knew what the fuss was about. When Pamela's father arrived Uncle Cedric wept again and said, 'But all I did was cuddle the child! She was comforting me and—'

'That's how you cuddle a child, is it?' Pamela's father was coldly furious. 'You put your hand on her bare buttocks, do you? Is that your usual—'

And Miranda, thinking she was helping Uncle Cedric, cried out, 'But he does that to us, doesn't he, Meg? It doesn't mean a thing! We don't mind!'

Pamela's father was horrified. He said no more but he insisted on taking the twins back home with him that night and he rang the Welfare people the next morning.

Two

It was Mr Bracknell who came to the rescue.

Uncle Cedric died quite suddenly in the middle of all the 'fuss' as the girls called it afterwards, and it seemed Mr Bracknell was their sole remaining trustee. He and Uncle Cedric had been in charge of Aunt Maggie's bequest, and now Mr Bracknell took on Uncle Cedric's last will and testament too. And that was that after the house was sold and everything paid up, the girls should have what was left when they were twenty-one. Mr Bracknell made it very clear that it would not be a great deal, there might be as much as fifteen hundred for each of them. But, added to Aunt Maggie's bequest, it would certainly be enough to 'set them up' in some way. He assumed they were too young to imagine just how they would like to set themselves up, but of course they weren't. They knew exactly what they wanted to buy with their money. Miranda wanted a course at drama school. Meg wanted to buy a little house in Keyhole where they had been so happy, and paint pictures all day.

Meg was shattered by the 'fuss', Miranda defiant and angry. They were to be in the care of the local authority until they were sixteen, and the social worker who took them under her wing believed that twins should seek their own identity as early as possible, and should therefore be separated; different homes, different schools. Mr Bracknell could do nothing to dissuade her from this course, but he arranged for Meg to go to a hostel in

Higher Compton, run by a fairly philanthropic couple called Dora and Matthew Penwith. From there she could go to an elderly grammar school where she stood a chance of winning a scholarship to Plymouth Art College. With such a carrot ahead of her she settled down immediately to blend into her background. She was good with the smaller children, totally reserved with the older ones. Dora looked on her as a daughter; she never ever looked on Dora as a mother.

Miranda presented a harder problem. There was something wild and wayward about her which defied Mr Bracknell's common sense and outraged his dignity.

He visited three possible foster homes on her behalf and suggested to the social worker that a couple who lived near the theatre might be suitable. The wife was a cleaner in the theatre and the husband took a turn at the stage door.

The social worker reported back tersely. 'She told me to stuff it. Says she wants to be an actress not a skivvy.'

Mr Bracknell went to see Miranda in the council's children's home in Stoke.

'Be reasonable, Miranda. Meg is quite prepared to make the best of things in Higher Compton with a view to getting into art college later—'

'Let me go to Higher Compton with Meg then,' Miranda said swiftly. 'You know I'll be OK if you let me stay with Meg.'

'My dear, the authorities have a point. When you two are together you don't make other friends—'

'We had Pamela and look where that got us!' Miranda interpolated bitterly.

Mr Bracknell said unhappily, 'You know very well what I mean, child. I have told Meg that if she works hard she will get a place at art college. I am telling you that—'

Miranda's interruption was passionate this time. 'I cannot *wait* that long, Mr Bracknell! You don't understand! Amy – my mother – left school at fourteen and joined a theatre company immediately! My father—'

'Miranda, I know about your parents.'

He had known Cedric and Maggie very well; Terence had been much younger. The black sheep of the family really. The wild and wayward one. Mr Bracknell sighed deeply, recognizing the connection and not knowing how to deal with it.

'In your mother's day everyone left school at fourteen—'

'And I am fourteen now!'

'And in the care of the council.'

'You are my trustee!'

'I am entrusted with your inheritance, Miranda. I have a certain influence which I have used in your case.' He dropped his voice deliberately, remembering dear Maggie and how much she had loved these girls. He must not sound even faintly irritated. 'Listen, child. Just try to settle with the Brimmingtons. The fact that they are connected with the theatre will be a bond between you.'

'I cannot stick living with strangers until I am eighteen!'

'Will you stick it until you are sixteen?'

Miranda stared at him mistrustfully. 'What will you do then?'

'You will have taken your end-of-school examinations. There are courses at some of the technical colleges—'

'Technical colleges!'

The words were spoken with disgust.

Mr Bracknell waited silently, he had shot his bolt, but he did not enjoy watching her as she searched her mind for other possibilities and found none.

And then she did something which upset him a great

34

deal. She smiled quite suddenly, perched herself on his knee and kissed his cheek.

'All right then. Till I'm sixteen. Then I know you'll think of something. I could come and keep house for you.'

He stood up, almost spilling her to the floor. He knew now how it had happened for Cedric. Poor Cedric. And poor Miranda. It would never have happened if Maggie had been alive, of course. Poor Maggie.

He said, 'Make the best of it, Miranda. As Meg is doing.'

She walked to the door with what dignity she could muster. He and Uncle Cedric had served in the Navy together, but he wasn't like Uncle Cedric. He wasn't going to help her any more. She was on her own. And how could she be like Meg if she wasn't with Meg? None of them understood.

She slammed the door fiercely as she left. And immediately began to make plans to manipulate the Brimmingtons.

But the Brimmingtons had no feeling for the theatre. Ernest had come out of the army in 1946 and taken a job in the dockyard. Unskilled labour was easy to come by, but the drudgery of it had eaten into Ernie Brimmington's soul and when he heard of the theatre job he took it to get away from the welding yard. He liked the unsocial hours of the theatre, the feeling of being almost his own boss. He liked it better still when Elsie took the cleaning job. It meant he hardly ever saw her; she worked during the day and he worked in the evenings. By the time he got home she was too tired to nag him about starting a family and they'd been told three years ago they were too old to adopt a baby.

Fostering was different. It was lucrative, and if they

fostered a school-age kid, Elsie could keep on her cleaning job too.

Miranda was their first and last foster child.

She did her best. When Elsie plaited her frizzy orange hair into two plaits, she put up with it. After all, Meg wore her hair in a plait. But when Elsie then plaited her own greasy black hair, stood next to Miranda's mirrored reflection and said, 'Anyone would think we were sisters, wouldn't they?' she had gone too far. Miranda unplaited her hair then and there and smiled at Elsie.

'I don't think so.'

Her voice was quiet and pleasant enough, but Elsie recoiled as if Miranda had spat in her face.

As if giving her a chance to recoup, Miranda then suggested – kindly – that Elsie might 'get her in' for a performance of *Romeo and Juliet* which was being put on by the Northcott the following week.

'When you're a bit older, perhaps, dear. Some of the things they put on are a bit . . . well, you're not old enough yet.'

Miranda knew already that Elsie was narrow-minded, she now knew that Elsie was going to insist on treating her like the ten-year-old she really wanted. Miranda decided to tackle the silent, morose Ernie as she had tackled Uncle Cedric.

'Let me make you your cocoa,' she insisted on Saturday morning when Elsie had gone to work. 'I know how you like it. Milky with two sugars.'

Ernie stared at her suspiciously.

'Thought you was anxious to get up to see your sister?'

'I am. I want to give her a treat. A surprise.' She set the cocoas on the table and drew up a chair next to his. 'She's doing Shakespeare at school. Well, we are too, but she goes to a good school. You know, posh.' She hated herself for talking like that; she was acting a part, that was all.

'Stupid, I calls it.'

'What?'

'Shakespeare. They does it down the theatre. Can't understand a word.'

'Well, there you are. If I could take her to see the play it would help us both to understand it.'

'You? Go to the theatre?'

'Yes please!' She sparkled at him, put her knee against his, lowered her lashes.

'Not on your life, my girl! You're in our care, you are! I won't say no to the pictures, but the theatre – never!'

His reasoning – if he had any – escaped her. She was baffled and frustrated.

'But – it's important. Exams. Shakespeare—' She was stammering with temper. She had forced herself to sit by him, make his damned cocoa and she was getting nowhere. 'It's such rubbish at the pictures—'

'It's not real people. That's the thing. Theatre people – they're all no better 'n what they should be! I know. I was in the Army for four years—'

'What the hell has the Army got to do with *Romeo and Juliet*?'

'Don't you swear at me, my girl!'

'But I can't get through to you any other way! You're not listening to me! My sister and myself – ' she enunciated very clearly, 'are doing Shakespeare at school and need to see a proper—'

'I've had enough of this. Fluttering your eyelashes at me. *You're* no better 'n what you should be either! Wait till I tell Elsie what you been up to!'

She was so angry she nearly hit him. Instead she smiled right at him and said softly, 'Wait till I tell her what *you* been up to, Mister Brimmington!'

But even the dawning realization and horror on his face did not console her. She went up to Higher Compton and spent the rest of the day with Meg, fuming furiously about the Bloody Brimmingtons. Meg, white-faced and introverted, told her to stick it out somehow. But Miranda could not. She knew that once Ernie and Elsie had talked together she would be out, and working on the principle that it is better to leave under one's own steam rather than wait for the sack, she set fire to her bed that night while Ernie was still at work. She thought of it as going out in a blaze of glory, but it wasn't easy; she used a whole box of matches on the blankets and still produced mere scorch marks. But then, halfway through a second box, she decided to slit the mattress. Inside was a wodge of horsehair. It crackled delightfully as it burned. She wandered into Elsie's room and said brightly, 'I say, did you know the house is on fire?'

Rena and Paddy Barnes were next on the list. Mr Bracknell had thought them too rough and ready for Miranda, but after the psychologist had dithered about a 'treatment centre' both Bracknell and Miranda gladly accepted the still-open offer of a home for her, and she moved into the cramped terraced house in North Street during the spring of 1959.

Rena and Paddy had six children of their own and envisaged this new teenager as an unpaid baby-sitter and washer-up, contributing in many ways to the family besides being the reason for the monthly cheque from the Children's Department.

Miranda tried her Uncle Cedric approach with Paddy, only to be smacked hard on the bottom and told to 'wait another year or two, you saucy bitch!' Paddy told Rena openly what had happened and Rena shrieked with laughter and said that perhaps later they could share him between them. There was never any acrimony in the house. There were rows known as 'shouting matches' thoroughly enjoyed by both parties, but if Miranda tried to get out of a chore by outrageous behaviour or by conniving with one against the other, she was usually greeted with gales of laughter or a suffocating hug and a promise of 'a nice cup of tea' to make her 'feel better'.

It was like punching a pillow. She tried arson again and was abetted by Rena who said they could get a new mattress out of the insurance. She demanded her own room.

'Why?' Paddy was astonished.

'I'm nearly fifteen! I get periods!'

Paddy raised his brows at Rena and said, 'Course you do, stupid bitch! We'd have you at the doctor tomorrow if you didn't. What's that got to do with having your own room?'

'I need the privacy!' Miranda could have wept at their joint obtuseness.

'But you only got the two babbies in there! Christ, you couldn't get more private than that! Think they watch you when you change your towel?'

The fact that Paddy spoke those words rather than Rena nearly crucified Miranda. However brazen she was, he could always outdo her.

That night she ran away and shared Meg's bedroom. She turned up at North Street for her breakfast and was galled to discover neither of the Barneses realized she had been missing. Piqued, she said nothing, but continued to sleep with Meg for two weeks until her absence was discovered by the social worker who called one evening in response to a report from a neighbour.

'They're not fit to have me,' Miranda said scornfully. 'They think in a year or two I'll share their bed!'

The social worker was horrified and there was a big meeting with Mr Bracknell, the child psychologist and the head teacher of her school besides the bewildered Barneses and Miranda herself. Unfortunately, Meg was not invited.

'We was joking!' Paddy explained.

'We thought she was joking too!' Rena enlarged.

'She is of course emotionally disturbed by what has happened in the past,' said the psychologist.

'D'you mean the Uncle Cedric fuss? Because if so just say it straight out.' Miranda wished she had the strength to bundle them all out of the oh-so-cosy private room in the council offices, down to the Hoe and into the sea. 'If you think I was worried about Uncle Cedric – Christ, he was a poor old man—'

The Head got his oar in quickly. 'Her language is what worries the staff most at school—'

'Paddy says Christ all the time,' Miranda explained.

Mr Bracknell looked at her. 'Obviously you wish to leave North Street, Miranda,' he said quietly. 'In which case I think your alternatives have run out.'

She saw the pit she had dug for herself just in time.

'I don't want to leave North Street at all!' Her voice rose childishly. 'I just want everything sorted out a bit! I have to see Meg more often—'

'Christ, you can go up there every day if you like!' Paddy said. 'She can come down to us. If that's the only problem there's no problem!'

Mr Bracknell said incredulously, 'You're still willing to foster Miranda, Mr Barnes?'

''Course we are. Aren't we, Reen?'

'If she's willing to be one of the family, then . . .' Rena hadn't yet told Paddy but she was almost sure she was pregnant again. She would need Miranda.

'I'm only baby-sitting once a week,' said Miranda as if she could read Rena's mind. 'And you should pay me, really.'

Paddy was shocked. 'If you're one of the family, Randie, you do things like that for love.'

'But I don't love you,' Miranda said, her voice well under control again. 'So once a week. And don't call me Randie!'

Mr Bracknell spoke to the psychologist. 'Perhaps a quiet word between the four of us while Miranda and the Barneses work things out between them?'

And in the end Miranda got her own room and did some grudging but unpaid baby-sitting, and for a whole year she put up with Rena and Paddy and they did not even realize how hard it was for her.

She could have left school at fifteen but if she had done that she would have had to take a dull job somewhere, or stay at home and help with the new baby. So she stayed on, though there was no hope of getting any of the new O levels. She enjoyed history lessons and the newly qualified history teacher; her favourite class was English Drama. She could quote yards from Shakespeare plays in spite of Ernie Brimmington's discouragement, and declaimed Portia's and Miranda's speeches to the goggle-eyed Barnes children instead of reading them stories. At weekends she went up to the hostel; the social worker drew down her mouth sadly. It was obvious there was no separating these two.

And then in the early summer of 1960, Miranda's enforced patience was rewarded. A note was sent from school to say that on Wednesday of the following week the top class would be taken to see an outdoor performance of *A Midsummer Night's Dream*. A packed lunch was required.

All forty-five of them were herded into a bus at Lara and taken to nearby Newton Abbot, then marched in a ragged crocodile on to the moor. Natural outcrops of rock made a rough semi-circular arena; the backdrop of branches hung with ivy, the cubes of packed straw, the carefully arranged logs were all the scenery necessary.

It was a ragged, fey production, performed with a great deal of dramatic gesture. But nobody forgot their lines and every word could be heard.

They called themselves the Arbitrary Group and as Miranda watched she had an enormous sense of *déjà vu*. Perhaps her mother had been almost sixteen when she saw the Wessex Players for the first time. Whatever it was, Miranda knew that destiny was on the move; the Arbitrary Group was practically heaven-sent. She recognized the various types from faint memories of the Wessex Players of long ago. There was a Terence, adored by the female cast, seeing himself as another Sir Laurence Olivier, never knowing when he was acting and when he was not. She could not pick out an Amy-type; the girls who took the parts of Helena, Hermia and Titania were too subservient to Lysander, Demetrius and Oberon. Amy had made certain in all her performances that she was the leading lady.

Miranda, hanging around for her turn to talk to the actors afterwards, chewed her lip thoughtfully. If Amy's position was vacant, could she fill it?

The girl who had played Puck, still plastered with real leaves and twigs, gave a little jump and landed in front of her. She waved her hands in the air and pushed her face towards Miranda's.

'"How now spirit! Whither wander you?"'

Miranda felt like saying in Amy's disgusted tones, 'Oh for God's sake!' but she had got right out of the habit of showing her real face in public. Instead she too looked coy and quoted, '"Over hill, over dale, thorough bush, thorough brier . . ."' She stopped, crestfallen, and added, 'Sorry, I don't know any more.'

But Puck was amazed. 'Hey! You listened. You actually

listened!' She turned her head. 'Lysander! Over here!'

Lysander, definitely a Terence-type, detached himself from a small knot of girls with autograph books, and, blowing kisses at them, moved away calling, '"I will be with thee straight!"'

Puck grinned puckishly. '"Follow me then to plainer ground."' She bowed low. '"One of the fairies I will swear."' She laughed up at Lysander. 'Honestly, Brett, don't scoff. This child – this nymph – actually listened to the play!'

Lysander–Brett looked at Miranda while hugging Puck to him very hard.

'Really? What makes you think so?'

Puck nodded violently at Miranda and without thinking she said, '"By my modesty, the jewel in my dower, I would not wish any companion in the world but you."'

He stared, nonplussed for just a moment, then he said slowly, 'That is not from the play we have just performed.'

She blushed furiously. She knew lots more dialogue from *Midsummer Night's Dream*. What had possessed her to quote from *The Tempest*? Then she knew why.

She lowered her aquamarine eyes – she always thought of her eyes as 'aquamarine' – and looked at the toes of her scuffed sandals. 'Sorry, sir. My name is Miranda, you see.'

If he didn't pick that up, he was no Terence and she did not want to know him; she made the bargain with herself in the pause that followed.

Then he said haltingly, '"The very instant I saw you, did my heart fly to your service."' He laughed. 'I'm sorry too, I can't go further with that unless I look it up.' He put out his free hand and took hers and drew the three of them away towards the rock which hid the dressing tent.

'Well, Miranda, you know that I am Brett St Clare. And this is Olwen Pugh-Davies. You know we are actors, and the Arbitrary Group is our company. All we know about you is your name and that you know your Shakespeare.'

This was marvellous. Miranda let herself be drawn close to his side. She could smell his armpit. She wondered fleetingly whether Olwen Pugh-Davies was Brett St Clare's Amy, then decided not.

She said, 'I want to be an actress. My father ran a company like this called the Wessex Players. He and my mother were killed ages ago, but they wanted one of us to act.'

'My God.' He released her in sheer surprise. 'You – you're not Terry Patch's daughter, are you?'

She too was amazed. Things were getting marvellouser and marvellouser. She nodded vigorously.

He actually slapped his thigh. 'By all that's holy! Ollie, have you ever heard of a coincidence like this? Terry Patch gave me a walk-on part right at the beginning of the bloody war! I would have stayed with him when he formed the Wessex, only I was eighteen and had to do my bit!' He stared at Miranda, still staggered by this real-life drama. 'I can't believe it! You're not like him except that you can quote Shakespeare at the drop of a hat!'

She smiled. 'We're like Amy. Our mother.'

'We?'

'There are two of us. Twins. Miranda and Margaret. Meg is going to be a painter and I'm going to be an actress.'

She felt easier standing free of his bear-hug. She was conscious of her slimness, alone beneath the huge rock. She put her hands on her hips and lifted her head and the Dartmoor wind blew tendrils of hair into an aureole around her face.

Olwen said grudgingly, 'Christ. She's a natural, Brett. Look at her.'

'Yes. Ye-es.' He did indeed look, intently. 'I never knew this Amy. Were they married?'

Miranda was indignant. 'Of course! They were joint partners in the company!'

'And you were born . . . 1942?'

Miranda was thrilled that she looked older than her years.

'Yes. Almost.'

'Liar. These kids are in their fourth year at school.'

She blushed. 'I said almost,' she brazened it out. 'Actually I'm sixteen.'

'So you could leave school now?'

'I could have left last autumn. But I was waiting for you.'

Olwen Pugh-Davies laughed briefly, but he took her as seriously as she was taking herself.

'It certainly seems as if fate is taking a hand here.'

He glanced at Olwen and she put a hand to her mouth to stop the laugh, then said, 'I'm sure when you are a bit older, you will follow in your mother's footsteps.'

'And in her father's footsteps.' Brett let his gaze rise above Miranda's head to the clear sky. 'He was a wonderful man.'

He held the reverent moment while Miranda counted four, then clapped Puck on her leafy shoulder. 'Off you go, Ollie! Conjure up some tea from fairyland, there's a dear. I need to get a few things straight with our shipwrecked heroine.'

Miranda smiled, delighted. Not only with the prospect of a conference with Brett St Clare, but also because it was obvious Olwen Pugh-Davies was no Amy.

*   *   *

45

That evening Meg arrived in North Street on her bicycle. Miranda had been pressed into baby-sitting for
the second time that week. Paddy and Rena had discovered the delights of bingo.

'Am I glad to see you!' Miranda said fervently. 'See if
you can get Dominic and Francesca off while I heat up
this bottle. Smother them if all else fails!'

Unusually, Meg delayed climbing the stairs to the
squawking children.

'Something happened to you today.' She spoke as she
tore off her school beret and blazer. 'Something to do
with Terence.'

Miranda was startled out of her usual sang-froid.

'My God! You tuned in properly, didn't you?'

'It stops me feeling lonely. What happened?'

'It was that drama group. Remember I was going with
the school to see *Dream* today? On the moor? They call
themselves the Arbitrary Group. The bloke who runs it
knew Terence.'

'He what?' It seemed too much of a coincidence. Meg
took nothing at face value any more.

'I know. Absolutely incred.' Miranda shook the bottle
over her hand. 'That'll do, still on the cold side but better
than too hot. Meg – I'll tell all when you've settled
those *bloody* kids! The best of luck!' She disappeared
into the front room where the pram and baby were
kept almost permanently. Meg ran upstairs and confronted the seven- and eight-year-olds with the expertise
gained from helping Dora Penwith.

It was getting dark before the twins could sit together
in the kitchen. Meg had no lights on her bike but could
not tear herself away; it really was 'incred', as Miranda
put it.

'I suppose when you think of it from the beginning –
I mean Terence must have known heaps of actors and

it was likely that one of them would want to form his own company. And this Brett St Clare did. But me sort of bursting in on him in the middle of the act, as it were – well, absolutely incred!'

'And he really does want to take you on?'

'So he said. I told him about you. And I told him we were in council care because Amy and Terence were killed and then Aunt Maggie and Uncle Cedric died . . . he wasn't very happy about that. I got the feeling that he doesn't like the council people at Plymouth – something about a grant. So then I said Mr Bracknell of Bracknell and Passmore was our trustee! Oh, that made him sit up and think!'

'Why?' Meg asked innocently.

Miranda laughed. 'Well, if you've got a trustee it means there's some money in the future. And theatre companies always need money!'

'How do you know that?'

'Terence and Amy were always after backers. Uncle Cedric and Aunt Maggie put money into the Wessex. I heard them talking about it when the Wessex affairs were being wound up.'

'Eavesdropper,' Meg said without criticism. She frowned and went on, 'Doesn't it worry you that this Mr Sinclair might be after your money rather than you?'

'Worry me? I couldn't care less! All I want is to join the company. Get away from here – ' she swept the tiny kitchen with a large gesture. 'I want to start to live, Meg!' She put her hands back on the table. 'And by the way, it's Brett St Clare. Not Sinclair.'

Meg felt that was another black mark against the man but she said temperately, 'I know this is a difficult time for you but—'

'And for you! You could come with me! Design sets and things.'

'No. I know what I'm going to do, Sis. In two years I'll be at the art college. And when I'm twenty-one I'll have got my diploma and we shall have some money, and *then* I can start to live!'

'Oh, Meg. You're so patient. I can't be like that. I'll have to go. Will you mind?'

'Yes. But if you get the chance, I know you have to go.' Meg looked at the piled sink. 'Darling, it might not be a certainty. Mr Bracknell is such a steady man—'

'You mean a boring old buffer!'

'He might well think you are too young to go off by yourself—'

'I'll go and see him. I'll threaten to kill him if he doesn't try to help me!'

'But you do realize he can't do more than try? That social worker—'

'He's got a lot of influence with her – with all of them in the department. And I think he – and the bloody department – would like to get rid of me.'

'I wish you wouldn't keep swearing! And for goodness' sake wait and see. Don't get too excited.'

'All right, Aunt Maggie!'

Meg smiled at the enormous compliment then said briskly, 'Come on, let's do that washing-up.'

Miranda made a hideous face but took the tea towel and waved it like a banner.

'We're going to win through, Meg! I feel it in my bones!'

And Meg, thinking of her lampless bike and being on her own in Plymouth, had to force a smile.

Three

Miranda skipped school on Thursday and went to see Mr Bracknell. Her explanation, entailing as it did a great deal of parenthetical urgings – 'I've got to do it!' – 'I'll curl up and die in North Street if I don't do it!' – took him some time to unravel and comprehend. But when he did, Miranda was surprised – almost piqued – when he did not immediately give her the thumbs-down. Then she saw a possible advantage and seized it quickly.

'Of course if I was the responsibility of Mr St Clare, I'd be out of your hair, wouldn't I?' She laughed at the unintentional rhyme and stored it away for future giggles with Meg.

Mr Bracknell did not laugh. He took his quasi-guardianship very seriously, feeling it was a bequest from Maggie Patch. Miranda's volcanic eruptions were a disturbance in his life, of course – he related more closely to Meg who was 'making the best of things'. But he accepted them because Maggie and Cedric had accepted Terence. He recalled discussions with them when they had baled out the Wessex over and over again – against his advice.

'It's more important than money, old man.' Cedric had been a sentimental old buffer but Maggie had had a very clear head which she had nodded in agreement. 'It's his way of life. He's a throwback. Somewhere along the line we've got connections with Sarah Siddons, y'know,

Edward. Wrong side of the blanket – that kind of thing. Terence would probably take to drink if the Wessex folded.'

Mr Bracknell remembered that now as he stared at the pale yet vital being on the other side of his desk. He had a very large desk. Edward Bracknell needed plenty of space. It was something Miranda refused to give him. If she went off with this . . . lot . . . there would be space. She was right to an extent; she might always be his moral responsibility – because of poor old Cedric and especially because of Maggie – but at least there would be the equivalent of a very large desk between them.

Not knowing whether his motives were good or just selfish, he agreed to meet this man with the pretentious name.

'Make an appointment with my secretary, Miranda. I will at least talk to him.'

'He'll pop round to your flat tonight, Mr Bracknell.' Miranda was overjoyed. She clasped her hands beneath the desk to stop them fiddling with her hair and revealing her tense excitement.

'Tonight? At the flat?' Already Edward Bracknell felt put out.

Miranda smiled beguilingly, remembered his reaction last time she'd tried that, and straightened her face. 'Don't forget he is working each afternoon. They rehearse in the morning, so that's no good either. I told him to give you a day to think it over, then call round.'

'I see. I'm surprised you didn't call round yourself last evening.'

'I wanted to. But I had to baby-sit for the rotten Barneses.'

'They've been kind in their way, Miranda. And wherever you went, you would have rebelled.'

'Not if you'd got me in with Meg,' Miranda said stubbornly.

'You could not have borne the hostel. And you would have ruined it for Meg too.'

Miranda was standing, already on her way out, but that halted her in her tracks.

'Am I really so . . . disruptive?' The word had been used a great deal in her Personal Reports.

He instantly regretted hurting her; it was like dismembering a butterfly. He smiled and shook his head in what he hoped was a gesture of resignation, then went to the door to open it for her.

He watched her as she swept through. It was true, all she could do was act. Maybe that was all she would ever do. Which was terribly sad.

He closed the door. Disruptive was the only word for Miranda. But she was the other side of Meg; and Meg was so like her aunt. And he had loved Maggie. If all this actor-chappie wanted was Maggie's legacy, he was in for a big disappointment. Space or no space, Edward Bracknell was committed to the Patch girls.

That Thursday evening Brett St Clare arrived at just the right time; after dinner but before the port. Mr Bracknell gave him a mark for that and indicated the deep leather chair opposite his own. As he opened the preliminaries he studied the man covertly but minutely.

'I understand you have offered some kind of apprenticeship within your company to Miss Patch—'

'I understand you are connected with Miranda Patch—'

'And that you knew her father—'

'And that she is in the care of the council after the sad death of—'

They both said their pieces carefully to avoid all suggestion of fencing for supremacy. The result was a tie.

They sipped their port while Mr Bracknell inserted several questions disguised as comments to test St Clare's knowledge of Terry Patch himself, the Wessex Players generally, and his own place with both.

St Clare had had nothing to do with the Wessex Players; he had known Terry before the company had been formed. He had been eighteen when they met; Terry had a small part in a slick modern comedy touring the Midlands. They were friendly enough for Terry to get St Clare a tiny walk-on part. Apparently that gesture had cemented a friendship. But that was more or less all there was to it.

Mr Bracknell put his glass down and watched St Clare do the same. He was very good-looking; too much so for everyday life. But there was something likeable about him. He had the same absurd sense of mission that Terry had had. As if the country was waiting for him to bring them Shakespeare and Marlowe and Sheridan and Wilde.

'And you think Miss Patch will fit in with your – er – company? She is still so young. No experience.'

'I could tell instantly that she could act. And when I heard she was Terry Patch's daughter, I needed no further recommendation.'

Except that you probably also know she has some money coming to her, thought Mr Bracknell cynically.

But he said aloud, 'Look. You'd better tell me exactly what you have in mind. Exactly. I shall need to know what to tell the authorities and what to keep to myself.'

Brett smiled with conscious boyish charm – yet if he was eighteen in 1938 he must be forty now – and quite suddenly Mr Bracknell knew that Miranda would be absolutely safe with him. It must have been Maggie's shade somewhere reassuring him. Or maybe his years in the navy and practising the law had given him some kind of key for opening the minds of people like this Brett St

Clare. Unusual people. He remembered an Americanism Miranda used about poor Ernest Brimmington – oddballs.

Brett St Clare took a long time about being 'exact', yet at the end of his speech it seemed that he was offering Miranda very little – but not much less than the rest of his cast.

There was no money for proper salaries; the cast took a cut of whatever takings there were. In the winter Miss Pugh-Davies's aunt housed them all in Exeter and from there they did pantomime and made costumes and props and rehearsed their summer repertoire.

'I should like to see the books,' Mr Bracknell put in.

'Books?'

'You must keep some kind of record of what comes in and what goes out.'

'Oh. I see. I thought you were referring to scripts. Yes, Olwen – Miss Pugh-Davies keeps an account of the finance. But of course theatre is not about money.'

'No. So I gathered from my connections with the Wessex Players.'

'There are times during the winter when members of the cast are able to take outside work to supplement our income. I explained this to Miss Patch and she found it reasonable.'

'Did she?'

'She understands how a small theatre company works, of course.'

'She was barely seven years old when her parents were killed.'

'Yes. Quite. In her blood, however.' St Clare cleared his throat. 'I take it there was compensation for their tragic ends?'

'They were taking a short cut to their digs. The area was clearly marked.'

53

'I see. How . . . appalling.'

'Miss Patch has inherited money from her father's family. There is no question of it being touched – or used as collateral – until she is of age. You understand that?' Mr Bracknell had been told he could look menacing on occasions and he was pleased to see St Clare's throat move convulsively.

But the man spoke with dignity. 'I am not after Miranda's money, sir. She has the potential to be a first-rate actress. And the connection between us . . . I look on it as my duty to help her in any way I can.'

Mr Bracknell surprised himself by saying after a protracted pause, 'I believe you.'

He would not allow Brett to present himself to the child care people because he knew they would never see what he had seen. He prepared his 'case' thoroughly, first of all visiting Miranda's school, bypassing the head teacher who had made such a bad impression at the last meeting, and interviewing the woman who taught Miranda's favourite subject. He received cautious praise for her knowledge of Shakespeare and a promise that some kind of testimonial would be provided.

Quite by chance he met the history teacher in the corridor and enquired whether Miranda was a good pupil.

'Miranda Patch?' The young man blushed enthusiastically. 'A wonderful student. Such flair. She has a feeling for the Elizabethans and Plantagenets . . . and such a vivid person. She will go far.'

'Quite.' Mr Bracknell remembered that awful scene in his office when Miranda had been only fourteen. He had assumed she inherited that minx-like quality from Amy; since meeting Brett St Clare he wondered whether it might come from Terence.

'Would you be happy to provide her with a reference? She has applied to a repertory company to be trained as an actress. I am her solicitor and need to put forward a good case to the Children's Department.'

'Her exams . . .' the young man began, then remembered other remarks from the staff regarding Miranda Patch and her chances of success. 'Yes, well, it's what she is best at. Certainly. Anything I can do. I shall be sorry to lose her but can quite see . . .'

So Mr Bracknell eventually presented himself at the Department decently armed with evidence of Miranda's reformed character, and was not surprised to obtain what amounted to a pardon for her with the proviso that he should keep an eye on her until she received her inheritance. As he intended to do this anyway, there were no more problems.

This separation, however, was greater than anything the twins had known before. And it was Miranda's choice. Neither of them could fight it.

'Don't feel you've burned your bridges,' said cautious Meg. 'I think if we made enough fuss, Mrs Penwith would put up another bed in here and let you stay. You're at least free of the red tape now, I suppose.'

'Darling, I couldn't come here. Old Bracknell was right when he said I'd spoil your life—'

'He said what?' Meg put in angrily.

'Not exactly that. He implied it. And he was right. I couldn't stick this place. It's the same as the Barneses except that you can't shout at Dora Penwith!' She hugged her sister. 'Anyway, darling, it's going to be all right! Can't you just tell that things have all been arranged by Amy and Terence? It's heaven-sent, that's what it is!'

Meg nodded. It did indeed seem as if someone 'up there' was arranging things for both girls. It was just that this long period of marking time would have been so much easier if she could have seen Miranda most evenings.

Miranda looked at her and hugged her passionately.

'Meg. I'm a selfish beast. I'm so excited about what is happening, I'm not too worried about our separation.' She leaned back, eyes shining with sudden tears. 'You'll tune in to me when you can, won't you?'

'Our twinship link, d'you mean? I can't *make* it happen, Sis . . . It just does. And not often.'

'You could do it if you tried, I'm sure!' Miranda jumped up and went to the window, turning her back on her sister. 'Listen. Concentrate on me. What I'm thinking.' She paused. 'I'm going to think a special thing. Something to do with what I see out of the window. Try to pick it up.'

Meg was not fooled by this attempt at comfort. 'Miranda, I *know* what you can see out of that window. I sit and stare out of it for yonks.'

'Shut up. I'm thinking.'

Meg shut up obediently and relapsed on to the bed, closing her eyes. There was silence in the bedroom. The smell of dusty curtains and mothballs seemed overpowering. Then Meg opened her eyes, stared at the ceiling, and said wonderingly, ' "I know a bank whereon the wild thyme blows." '

Miranda's crow of delight could be heard all over the house. Dora Penwith came running; the foster children of the moment could be heard crying downstairs as the bedroom door opened violently.

Miranda danced across the room. 'It's OK, Mrs Penwith! We're both fine – absolutely fine! We're twins! Did you know that?'

Dora looked at her and was thankful that Meg was the one who lived here.

'Someone screamed,' she said.

'It was me.' Miranda could not stop laughing. 'I was looking out of the window at your herb garden. The thyme – that's all it was. The thyme.'

Rena Barnes would have scolded vociferously; Paddy would have shouted with either anger or laughter. Dora primmed her mouth and withdrew.

Miranda joined the Arbitrary Group at their winter quarters in Exeter and was billeted with the others at Miss Pugh's tall old house near the river.

Miss Pugh was built like a carthorse and in any case was no actress, but her theatrical aspirations were as strong as Miranda's. She had done everything in the theatre except act: cleaned the auditorium, mended costumes, sold programmes and ice-creams. When her parents died she had a house and became a theatrical landlady; she had discovered her niche at last. Her visitors' book was filled with names, some of them well known, and comments such as 'home from home' followed most of them. She would point proudly to the signatures of Jeanne de Cassalis and Tommy Handley. On Miranda's first night there, she was given a conducted tour through the book.

'See that?' Miss Pugh trained a magnifying glass on a scrawl. 'Donald Wolfit, that is. And there's Sarah herself.'

Miranda was agog. 'Not Sarah Bernhardt?' she whispered.

'And that is Ethel Barrymore,' declared Miss Pugh, turning the page quickly.

Miranda looked at the enormous horse-face above her with adoration. 'You've known them all, Miss Pugh.'

'Every one of them, child.' Then she won Miranda's heart. 'And now I can add you to the list.'

Even when Miranda knew that many of the names were forged, she never forgot that Miss Pugh had recognized her immediately as an actress.

Naturally, Brett and Olwen were also staying in the tall house by the river; Olwen slept with her aunt and Brett had the big bedroom over the hall with a view of the weir and the swans and the cathedral rising solidly from the jumble of red sandstone buildings. Miranda spent a lot of time in that room hearing Brett's lines and reading all the other parts. This was her 'training'. The other juveniles – both in their twenties – resented this and tended to cold-shoulder Miranda. She was unworried. She had coped with the Barneses and their brood, she could cope with a pair of histrionic actresses. She had a bed of her own plus a chest of drawers and a wardrobe, she had plenty to eat in return for helping Miss Pugh lay tables and wash up, and she was going to be acting.

Meanwhile she concentrated on knowing the rest of the cast thoroughly.

The two girls with whom she shared were called Jennifer and Janette. They would also have liked to be called Jones and Scott like the film stars, but as that was much too obvious they settled for Jennifer Patterson and Janette James. Two other women completed the female cast: both were in their forties, both were married. Marjorie was married to Elliot and had been in what she scathingly called 'commercial theatre' until she saw Brett's light and moved in with the Arbitrary. She had soon realized that Brett belonged to Olwen and had married Elliot Markham who was next best. They believed in being unashamed of their love and held hands across Miss Pugh's breakfast table in a very annoying way.

Caroline Decker was even older than Marjorie and

specialized in being Mistress Quickly. She was married to someone who was supposed to be waiting for her in London. Jennifer informed Miranda that he had installed his mistress in their flat on the Embankment and Caroline had moved out. Olwen once said bitterly that if he spent as much on Caroline as on his woman, none of them would be forced to wait on tables or wash up in café kitchens again. But legally he was free to do as he liked: Caroline had left him.

Three men completed the Group: Oliver Freres, James Cotton, and Joseph Lanham. Oliver seemed to be a permanent fixture. He was not a brilliant actor, but capable of some very quick changes and could manage as many as four parts in one play. The other two disappeared after a very short time and were replaced by other 'Jims' and 'Joes' fresh from various drama schools, soon to try their luck with television or film. They saw the Group as apprenticeship-time. Until Miranda arrived, the core Group numbered ten. They used other actors as and when they were available, but when they crammed into Miss Pugh's there were always ten of them. There was not an eleventh chair for Miranda around the big dining table; Miss Pugh brought in a stool, forever to be known as Miranda's perch. Everyone else had a chair; Miranda had a perch. It made her special; she was like the Group's mascot, and she was determined to bring them luck.

During that autumn Brett and Olwen worked up a pantomime for the local schools and organizations. It was a blend of Goldilocks and Snow-White. Olwen was the prince who wandered through every scene, slapping his leg and yearning for a princess. Brett was the dame in full regalia, in charge of the three bears, roaring like a bull one minute, slapping sloppy meals about the next. Jennifer was Goldilocks who tried to take over from

Brett in looking after the bears. Janette was the wicked stepmother. Miranda was the baby bear.

At first she thought the whole thing was rubbish, but at the first dress rehearsal – in Brett's room – she was completely drawn in. She remembered a lop-eared teddy she and Meg had shared in Keele, and she walked with a limp and held her head at an angle and peered around at the audience with exaggerated coyness.

'She's got it!' yelped Miss Pugh from her seat in the window. 'They'll love her!'

And 'they' did. The opening night was in mid-November at a village hall near Tiverton. There were plenty of spare seats because the locals considered it decadent to think of Christmas until mid-December, but the children who were there were captivated by Miranda's teddy bear. When one of them began to scream in terror at the wicked stepmother and her poisoned apple, Miranda made an unrehearsed entrance at floor level, lolloping past the front row with a bag of sweets and calming the child down instantly.

Olwen called it hogging the limelight, but Brett grinned widely and patted her furry head and told her again she was a natural. Miranda glowed. She loved him as she would have loved Terence, seeing all his weaknesses and not caring because he was an actor.

They got a proper booking in the draughty pier theatre in Weymouth to open on Boxing Day. It meant that she did not see Meg at Christmas and Meg's plans to travel to Weymouth to see the pantomime were shelved because the Penwiths needed her help with the little ones.

The cast ate their Christmas dinner on stage on 25th December: sandwiches and Thermos flasks; a bottle of something-or-other passed between the men. Then there was the final rehearsal. On Boxing Day they played to a packed house and everyone loved them. But nearby Bournemouth featured Norman Wisdom, and numbers dropped drastically at the pier theatre. Brett said it was all good publicity and even better experience. But Miranda was bitterly disappointed. She hopped and skipped and twitched and lolloped to no avail. She needed a full house to stimulate such improvisation and there were no more full houses that winter.

They went back to Miss Pugh's and began to prepare for the summer season. There were no Shakespearean parts for Miranda; the cast had been fixed last year and there were no gaps. Brett suggested she visit the Labour Exchange and try to get some work.

She was so disappointed she became aggressive. 'I'm supposed to be having training, you know!' was the best she could manage.

He smiled. 'This is training, Miranda, dear.' His smile became kinder. 'I did warn you right at the beginning. On that first day—'

'I thought most of the cast would get jobs! Not just me!'

'You feel put upon?'

'Yes!'

'You cannot see it as a privilege? Helping to keep the boat afloat while there is no work?'

'We made pots of money at Weymouth! And before that!'

'There are ten of us to keep. Eleven including you.'

'But I pulled my weight in the panto. You said as much yourself. I don't see why I can't have a part. You've all got to double up, so it's not as if—'

He moved into his room and for a dreadful moment she thought he would shut the door in her face, but he made an arch with his arm and she went through. He shut the door carefully.

'Miranda.' He went to the window and stared down at the river. 'Surely you can see what a difficult position I am in here?'

'No,' she said stubbornly, though she guessed what was coming.

He sighed. 'Nobody here gets special treatment except you. And it isn't as if that old lawyer chappie of yours is paying me any fees. Nothing like that. As far as the girls can see, you are a special case for no special reason. I've explained that I knew your father, but I'm afraid that doesn't cut much ice.' He turned to look at her. 'The men can see what I can see. Olwen too, sometimes. Your father's enormous talent. The other girls cannot. Or will not. And neither will Olwen if I fit you into the summer schedule.'

She said, 'You don't have to pander to them all the time, surely?'

'I never "pander" to them, Miranda, as well you know. I pander to you.' He glanced round again, saw her face and said quickly, 'Pander is not the right word at all. But I do arrange certain things for your sake. Now I am asking you to do something for my sake.' He turned and held out his hands. 'Is that very difficult for you, my dear?'

She went to meet him. Her hands which had been icy cold were suddenly sweatingly hot. She could not look at him, just to feel his unaccustomed touch was almost more than she could bear. Tears made her throat ache.

She coughed and said hoarsely, 'Sorry. Of course I'll . . . of course . . .'

'Take your time, child. Think about it and if it still seems unjust to you, talk to me again.'

But of course she went out immediately, grabbing scarf and gloves from the jumble on the hall stand, anxious to get to the Labour Exchange before they closed. She ran past the old red walls of the city as the first flakes of snow began to fall. And before she reached the Labour Exchange, she saw the sign on the shop door: 'Help wanted, mornings only'. It was a greengrocer's. The girls were already carrying in the baskets of potatoes and turnips from the front of the shop. They carried them ungracefully, leaning far back, balancing the edge on protruding stomachs. Miranda saw herself lifting the baskets on to her hip and swaying into the shop; even taking them in on her head, straight-backed, with an ineffable dignity.

She got the job because nobody wanted to work in an open-fronted, unheated shop in the snow. Miranda certainly did not enjoy it; within the first two days she had a heavy cold and chilblains, but it was her act of love for Brett and she stuck it out. Her popularity with Jennifer and Janette took an upward turn. She brought them home damaged bananas and oranges, and, once, a huge pineapple for Miss Pugh. Her fingers were too sore to take on the interminable costume repairs, but she listened to lines and went to the matinées at the various schools in Devon and when Easter was over and the summer season began, Brett told her to give in her notice at the shop as he was going to try her as Puck.

Olwen was furious; it had been her part for three summer seasons. They were in the big front bedroom, all three of them. It was raining relentlessly and the river was flooding gently into the water meadows, making them feel trapped inside the tall house. It was the dead hour between lunch and tea; filled with activity when there was a school matinée, filled with ennui when there was not. Miranda felt none of this. She had spent a very damp morning bagging potatoes in the back of the greengrocer's, and Miss Pugh's seemed warm and welcoming. It had been extra wonderful to be summoned to Brett's room for 'a conference'. She sat on the windowsill gently massaging her red fingers, and when Brett made his announcement she was still, breathing ecstatically, 'Oh, Brett . . . really?'

'Of course. It will be a try-out only. But if you can cope with it—'

Olwen's fury burst its banks at almost the same time as the River Exe.

'Sorry, Brett! That's not on! Puck is mine and Miranda is not going to have him and that is that!'

Brett smiled, maddeningly. 'This is a conference. You're entitled to put your views, Olwen. But I am the manager of this company and I will now put mine. As manager.' He paused and looked at Olwen. Her gaze dropped before his but her body was still rigid with anger.

He said slowly, 'I could give Miranda another walk-on part. She could be a messenger. Anything. But I want you to be Helena. And Jennifer is too . . . developed . . . for Puck.'

Olwen was stopped in her tracks. Miranda held her breath. She knew she could do Puck; she was still as flat as a pancake and with her hair in a cap of leaves and green tights . . .

Olwen said, 'I'll think about it. I'm not absolutely sure of the lines.'

'You'll learn them in five minutes,' Brett said.

'Probably. Oh God, I need a cup of tea. Miranda, pop down to Aunt Gladys and see if you can rustle something up, will you?'

Miranda glanced at Brett who inclined his head. She left. Outside the door she paused, listening. Olwen said, 'Look here, Brett. You might be manager, but I've got a big stake in this company. It's in my aunt's house we make our headquarters and believe you me, she wouldn't have us if I didn't ask her nicely.'

'Don't remind me.' There was a pause. His voice dropped and became muffled. As if he were kissing Olwen's hair. 'You know I rely absolutely on you.'

Olwen answered decisively, 'Yes, I do. And you know that I'll only take so much.'

'Darling girl. Listen. Miranda's been working at that bloody awful shop since January. What do you think Bombastic Bracknell would say if he knew? We need to keep that girl and her unofficial watchdog very happy for the next four years.'

There was another pause, then Olwen said, 'All right. But I don't like it.'

He laughed. 'At least you don't have to be jealous, darling, do you?'

She spoke quietly and seriously. 'No. I think I'm probably the only person in the world who understands you, Brett.'

Miranda crept away. She had always guessed that Olwen and Brett were lovers, but she had chosen to see it as a superficial thing, the Amy role still vacant. It hurt to realize the seriousness of their affair.

She ran down the stairs as lightly as she could and comforted herself with the knowledge that by the time she was that magical twenty-one, Olwen would be into her thirties and over the hill. And if it was Aunt Maggie's money Brett was after, he could have it and welcome. At a price.

She went down the dark tiled hall towards the kitchen and grinned suddenly. It seemed she needed to mention Mr Bracknell's name now and then to get what she wanted. And she was certainly not going to give up Puck's part now that she'd got it. No question of that.

*   *   *

That spring she met John Meredith for the first time.

His name cropped up occasionally as one of their very few backers and Miranda associated it with some undercurrent of . . . unpleasantness? Difficulty?

If Brett and Olwen were having one of their spats about new costumes or sets, Oliver might say, 'We can always turn to Meredith, of course.'

The spat would end as if a magic word had been uttered. Oliver would raise his brows quizzically; Brett would say irritably, 'We can manage without resorting to that.' Olwen would change her tone to one of conciliation and suggest that last year's crinolines would be sufficient to make this year's Regency high waistlines; the argument would be over.

But that summer their Arts Council grant was cut by half, and 'Meredith' was invited to a performance as a preliminary to a request for funds. Jennifer and Janette seemed unimpressed by his imminent arrival, unaware of anything special about him. Miranda elicited from Jennifer that he lived in Cheltenham, represented St Paul's ward on the town council and had indeed stood as an Independent candidate in the election after the Suez fiasco three years before. He was a man of substance, a public figure, yet obviously mysterious too.

Unfortunately on the day of his visit the weather was atrocious and they had to perform in a local village hall just outside Newton Abbot.

Brett cornered Miranda outside the gents' toilets, rehearsing her lines with eyes tightly shut.

'I'll try to keep you in the background after the performance, Miranda.' He did not say 'excuse me' or attempt to explain what he was talking about. Of course, she knew. 'But if I have to introduce you, eyes right down and quick march as soon as possible. Got that?'

Her face opened wide at him.

'Why? I'm not going to let you down, you know, Brett!'

'Of course not, child. But your Mr Bracknell entrusted your welfare to me.'

It was further proof that he took his unofficial guardianship very seriously and she was thrilled. But intrigued too.

'Is he very wicked?' she asked, blue eyes glowing greenly in the half light of the dusty passage.

'He's . . . unsavoury,' Brett came back thoughtfully and turned on his heel.

It was a well-chosen word. Wicked she might have wanted to know more of. Unsavoury suggested body odours and nasty habits. So she went through her part without flicking one of her quick glances around the audience. It would have been so easy to pick him out too in the muddle of schoolchildren crammed into the hall. She resisted the temptation.

Afterwards, with teachers barking orders about silence and single file – how thankful she was not to be part of that any more – a man detached himself from a seat at the back and made his way through the mass of bodies to the front of the stage. He was tall, thin, old – well, as old as Brett anyway – but he did not look unsavoury and she was too far away to extract information from her long sniff.

Oliver, already on hands and knees gathering leaves from the 'forest floor', leaned forward.

'Nice to see you again, Meredith. How are you?'

Olwen passed Miranda on the steps leading to the toilet and hissed, 'Come *on*!'

Miranda let her go ahead.

Meredith's voice was without timbre; the sort of voice interrogation officers had in films.

'All right. And yourself and your love?'

Oliver said quickly, 'We're all well. Colds and so on throughout the winter. But all present and correct as of now.'

It was not like Oliver to be so chatty. And who on earth was his 'love'? He seemed to be trying to keep the man at bay while appearing to welcome him. Miranda pretended to catch her heel on the step. She stopped, sat down and rubbed it.

'And who is the new Puck?' The voice was amused, somehow challenging.

Oliver ignored the question. 'I'll fetch Brett. I expect you'd like a chat with him.'

'By all means. You always did fetch things didn't you, Freres? Fetch and carry.'

Oliver ignored that too and went to the back of the stage. Just for a moment no-one was around. The body of the hall was almost empty. Miranda, watching covertly, saw the silhouette of the tall man turn, lean itself against the edge of the stage and apparently watch the last departures. The big fire doors were closed with a bang; silence.

'Well, Puck. Had you better bring that heel for me to see?'

He was back to using the amused voice and she realized then that it had been for her ears all the time. He had not been one whit amused by Oliver.

She emerged from the darkness of the wings and limped forward.

'It's not too bad,' she said, standing above him – not *that* much above him, he was very tall. 'I caught it on the step.'

'I saw.' He turned and looked up at her and she blinked and looked back. He said, 'How old are you, Puck?'

She meant to say seventeen. She would be seventeen in October after all. But she said, 'Sixteen and a half.'

'And have you got another name?'

'Miranda. Miranda Patch.'

And that was as far as it got because Brett practically leapt to her side and said, 'Off you go, Miranda. We have to be out of here by five o'clock as you very well know!' He turned her forty-five degrees to her right, pushing at the same time. Suddenly Olwen appeared back on the steps and received her just as ungently. She was bundled off like any naughty schoolgirl but not before she had registered quite a lot about Mr John Meredith. Tall, sandy-haired, pale grey eyes, pale skin, he warranted Olwen's furious description – 'like a long piece of rhubarb forced under a dustbin!' But there was something else too. A waiting stillness. An intensity of being. A hypnotic quality that made her think of Svengali. And, yes, she could imagine being Trilby.

The years passed. It was never boring with the Arbitrary Group. They lived on the edge of bankruptcy the whole time, begging for Arts Council grants to fund school Shakespeare in the winter, doing free outdoor performances in the summer and sending Miranda around with the hat afterwards. John Meredith came to no more performances but she gathered from overheard remarks that he was contributing occasional cash without being asked, which was interesting. She never quibbled again about taking outside work and indeed most of the cast had their regular part-time jobs in shops and restaurants around the city. She was rewarded with better parts and an indefinable but accepted place next to Brett. Olwen might be his right-hander, but Miranda was always on the left. The side of his heart, she told herself.

In 1962 Janette married that season's juvenile lead and they left to try their luck in the world of film. Caroline returned to her husband on a temporary basis. They were not replaced and Miranda doubled and trebled up like everyone else and thoroughly enjoyed herself. She was eighteen, a seasoned pro; she was over-confident, almost overbearing. When she heard that they were to do *Hamlet* in the new Civic Theatre in Cheltenham during the dead month of February, she said flatly it was about time she was Ophelia. Olwen practically blew a fuse but unexpectedly Brett was silent.

'We'll see,' he said, giving Olwen a look from his dark eyes.

She said, 'Brett, I've had enough! She wants taking down several pegs, does that young flibbertigibbet! You let her do Ophelia and she'll think she can get her way with you all the time!'

Brett said heavily, 'We'll talk about it, Ollie. Over Christmas.'

'Around the tree? With fairy lights making her ghastly pink hair look auburn?'

Miranda did not protest, she smiled. It nearly drove Olwen mad.

Brett said, 'Ollie. Please. There's more to this than you realize. I told you – we'll talk it over. It can be your decision.'

Miranda stopped smiling.

She spent Christmas with Meg at Higher Compton. She could not imagine how Meg bore it all. The Penwiths had come to rely on her as they would have done an older daughter, and Meg did not seem to mind. She had been at the art college for one term and was happy.

On Boxing Day they caught a bus to Newton Abbot and walked on the moor. It was bitterly cold; the early snows had reached Plymouth and up on Dartmoor everything was solidly white. They managed to get some lunch at a farmhouse and caught the bus back to Plymouth where they walked the deserted streets rather than return to the hostel. Meg talked about her course at the art college. Miranda talked about the wonderful opportunity about to happen to her.

'He said it could be Olwen's decision. Well, obviously she'll choose to be Ophelia. Yet I can't help feeling Brett has something up his sleeve. Keep fingers crossed for me, Meg!'

'Are they secretly married?' Meg asked in her innocence.

'No. They're secretly something else though. But he doesn't love her. Not properly. I think she must put some money in now and then.' Miranda sighed theatrically. 'We're always short of money!'

Meg swung her college scarf over one shoulder. 'You'll have to be careful when we're twenty-one, Sis. I reckon Mr St Clare will expect you to pay for all your training then.'

'I don't mind putting money into the Arbitrary. But on my own terms, of course,' Miranda said airily.

'Quite,' Meg came back doubtfully. 'Well, I haven't changed my mind. As soon as I've got my diploma I'm going to buy a house in Keyhole and try to be a proper artist!'

Miranda made a face.

'That dump!' she said scathingly, thinking of Weymouth and Cheltenham and Worcester and Exeter and all the places she would live in. 'I know now what Terence meant about roots!'

But then they began talking about it and it was a safe subject. They had been childishly happy in Keyhole, properly together then. They laughed and chattered like magpies all the way up the steep and slippery Plymouth streets to Higher Compton. Their twinship was renewed and when they reached the hostel, Miranda hugged her sister's arm close to her side.

'I wish you could come and see me next year. In Cheltenham.'

There was no hope of that however and even when Olwen caught a cold – and it was a proper cold and not a ploy to save her face – and Miranda definitely had Ophelia's part, the snow was too thick for a special trip from Plymouth. It did not matter too much. Brett was Hamlet. Everything was perfect. She wished she could do something to show him how she felt. What she wanted to do was to sleep with him; the thought made her body tingle. But not only was there Olwen, there was something else. Brett looked on her as a child. He was her trustee just as Mr Bracknell was trustee to Aunt Maggie's bequest. She smiled at her reflection in the dressing-room mirror: in just over two years Mr Bracknell's trust would end. And, she was fairly sure, so would Brett's.

Four

It was the best part she had had so far and she knew she was good. She had been practically typecast as Puck; mad Ophelia was a natural progression. She wound artificial flowers in her hair and wore silver lipstick and tore her dress from neck to waist for the crazy scene. Olwen would have been furious if she had known. But, on the first night, as if to punish her for her overacting, the snow kept theatre-goers away and they played to a house of perhaps thirty people.

She spotted John Meredith immediately. He sat in the stalls, tucked away behind a pillar, but her swift glance around as she made her entrance connected with him magnetically. And she understood why Brett had wanted to talk to Olwen about who should play Ophelia. With an electric thrill Miranda knew that the mysterious Meredith had arranged this whole thing. The Cheltenham theatre, the choice of play, and the actress for Ophelia. He had waited for two years . . . bided his time . . . for what? She forced her gaze up into Laertes' face and leaned more heavily on his arm as she uttered her first undistinguished words.

' "Do you doubt that?" '

Laertes had all the best bits in this scene, he held her at arm's length, twirled her, then hugged her while his long speech wound itself to an end. But when she had the chance to get something in, she turned from him and stared directly down to the pillars supporting the balcony as she declaimed, '"Do not, as some un-gracious pastors do, Show me the steep and thorny way to heaven . . ."'

Yes, there was definitely a connection between them. She was reminded again of Svengali and Trilby. She let it happen, let him dominate her performance. And . . . she knew she was good.

Afterwards there were flowers sent round to the old-fashioned greenroom for 'Miranda Patch, the most beautiful Ophelia I have ever seen'.

He was there again on the second night. After a terrific review in the early edition of the *Echo*, the house was suddenly full of people fed up with snow and television and themselves. This time the flowers were handed up on to the stage. Miranda smiled into the auditorium and blew a kiss. She felt wonderful; as if she could conquer the world. Even after the final curtain when Brett took her arm and piloted her into a corner of the greenroom and told her not to be a little fool, she was unscathed. Usually her happiness depended on Brett's look, Brett's smile, Brett's unspoken approval. Now, be-cause of Meredith, she could rise above Brett. It gave her an enormous sense of power.

She said pertly, 'I don't think *I'm* making a fool of myself, Brett! Perhaps you should have a word with someone else?'

He said directly, 'Miranda. That man is after you. You're old enough – and with what has happened in the past, surely wise enough – to know what I mean and what it can do to you.'

She almost laughed. It could do nothing to her – she had proved that. Uncle Cedric's attentions had never bothered her. Meg maybe. Yes, Meg certainly. But *she* had been unscathed. Frankly, it had been poor old Uncle Cedric who had come unstuck.

But she held back any further ripostes. She hoped – expected – Meredith to appear at the stage door that night. He did not.

When the following night brought no flowers and no sense of electrical connection during the performance, she was ridiculously deflated. All right, the weather was appalling and driving practically impossible, but Svengali would not have kept away from his Trilby.

Brett said, 'That was good, Miranda. I felt your real grief – your bewilderment and uncertainty – coming across. You've been declaiming to the audience – tonight you were inside the play. Excellent.'

And still she was not comforted, in fact she really did feel uncertain and bewildered; almost bereft.

That night when they all sat around the big dining table for their late supper – all except Olwen who was still nursing her cold – she had to take a lot of fairly good-natured teasing about Meredith.

'Did he come to see you, Miranda? Perhaps the close-up put him off?'

'Or the fact that there was nothing inside the ripped bodice!'

It was a perennial joke that Miranda could never take full-bosomed parts.

Marjorie patted her arm comfortingly and said, 'Perhaps it's as well. We've all heard about stage-door johnnies.'

Brett said quietly, 'I had a word with him actually.'

Everyone was surprised; she was outraged, touched, furious, pleased.

'I can't understand you, Brett!' She was stammering with all these conflicting emotions. 'He's a backer! We should be encouraging him—'

'It is awkward, I agree. I need your co-operation.'

Jennifer, sensing a conversation in which Miranda was

75

the sole topic, said, 'For goodness' sake, let's ask the land lady for hot-water bottles. My feet are about to drop off.'

But Olwen had the only hot-water bottle.

Brett said, 'If you would go up and put the gas fires on, it would help.'

There was the usual quibbling about shillings for the meter, but eventually they all stood up and edged their way around the table. Brett put out a hand and detained Miranda.

'A quick word before you retire, Miranda.'

She subsided. So. He needed her co-operation, did he? She tightened her mouth, propped her forehead with one hand, fiddled with the cruet with the other. Oliver closed the door with unnecessary force and the chimney belched smoke into the room.

Brett got up and put the fireguard carefully in position.

'Meredith *was* there tonight, Miranda.'

'Was he? I didn't see him.' She forgot her pose and turned on the leatherette seat of her chair to stare at him. Not only hadn't she seen Meredith, she had not felt him either.

'No. He did not wish to be seen.'

'Why not?'

'It would have been his third visit. People – local people – notice things like that.'

'Oh.' She turned back and shook some salt on to the tablecloth. She wanted terribly to giggle with a kind of triumph.

'He had a word with me after the performance.'

'I thought you said you had a word with him?'

'Stop imagining this is a play, please, Miranda. Try to see yourself as a very small mouse and Meredith as a very large cat.'

'Oh, for goodness' sake, Brett!' She rubbed the salt into the linen threads with her forefinger.

He sat down again and leaned back in his chair wearily. She was suddenly conscious of his age.

'Listen, Miranda. He expressed an interest in the Arbitrary a long time ago. He saw a performance of *Merchant* on the green in one of the Cotswold villages. There were two girls – not much older than you are now – Marguerite and Sally – doing Portia and Jessica. Sally left with him that same afternoon. He put some money into a production we did in Worcester and we all thought he was God's gift to us – though Ollie always reckoned it was some kind of pay-off for Sally. After one or two extravagant gifts, he asked Marguerite to go to London with him – said he'd try to get her into television. He knew someone. We never saw her again. But then we heard Sally was in hospital in Gloucester. Ollie went to see her just before she died. She'd been in an accident – horse riding.'

'What are you saying?'

'I'm telling you what happened. Olwen was convinced he had beaten the girl. She was worried sick about Marguerite and managed to trace her eventually. The girl was down and out in a squalid house . . . well, to use a Victorian term, she was ruined.'

Miranda tipped out some more salt.

'So on the strength of that Olwen thinks John Meredith is a murderer and rapist?' she asked conversationally.

'Not quite.' His voice hardened. 'She thinks he uses young girls for his own pleasure, then discards them.'

'And what do you think, Brett?' She looked up and smiled. 'Do you think that he . . . "ruined" . . . two of your company and paid for it by backing you?'

Brett flushed darkly.

'I know. It's collusion. If he is immoral then I am worse.'

She was remorseful. 'I didn't mean . . . what I meant

77

was, you can't possibly believe what Olwen is suggesting Otherwise it would be impossible for you to accept his money.'

He nodded. 'Yes. That's what I tell myself. But I'm not going to risk you, Miranda.'

She brushed the salt away and smiled at him. 'Oh, Brett. You – you're so . . . sweet and protective. But please don't worry about me. If John Meredith secretly fancies young actresses—' she giggled. 'Preferably with ripped bodices and flowers in their hair—'

'Please don't talk like that, Miranda!'

'We're living in the 1960s, Brett! D'you think I don't know about – ' for a moment she could not remember the word then said emphatically, 'perverts?'

For some reason he flinched as if she had hit him, then seemed to collapse into himself.

He said tritely, 'You're so young.'

'I'm an actress, Brett. And there was my Uncle Cedric. Nothing shocks me.'

He glanced at her. He really did look old.

'He offered me a great deal of money, a hundred pounds, if I would persuade you to spend a night with him.'

In spite of herself, she felt immensely flattered.

'I told him to clear off, of course.'

'Oh, Brett! It was sweet of you. Protecting my honour and all that sort of thing. But a hundred pounds for one night!' She shook her head as if regretfully, but her mind leapt ahead. This was her chance to prove herself a woman of the world; to get hold of some hard cash to keep the Players going for another month or two; to get Brett . . . well, in her power. Besides, the excitement was fire in her veins. She could hardly wait to see John Meredith again: Svengali and Trilby.

She put a hand over his. He became very still.

She said, 'Brett. Dear, kind Brett. My honour disappeared when I was fourteen. And I'd do more than this for you and for the wonderful Arbitrary. Surely you know that?'

He said, 'Just be on your guard, Miranda. If he approaches you, turn and walk away.' He withdrew his hand and stood up. 'It's not a question of honour, my dear. It's a question of danger. All right, nothing can be proved against him. But the circumstantial evidence is there. We cannot risk ignoring it.'

He checked the fireguard and went to the door.

'Put the light out when you go upstairs, Miranda. Good night.'

She was furious with him. He had made her feel young and cheap. But she knew what she was talking about because Uncle Cedric must have been a pervert if everyone made such a fuss about it. And Uncle Cedric's attentions had been nothing. Just a way of getting extra pocket money. Where was the difference? If she had to let John Meredith make love to her properly, well, that was all right too, wasn't it?

She went to bed simmering. And then, in order to forget Brett, she deliberately conjured up an image of the elusive John Meredith. She remembered him well; she had stood above him and he had looked up at her. During that encounter, she had obviously enslaved him. He must be quite passionately in love with her. Just like the old-fashioned stage-door johnnies, as Marjorie had put it. And he was rich.

It was rather marvellous really. And she longed to 'show' Brett. Though she was not entirely sure just what she did want to show him.

She saw nothing of her admirer for the next two nights,

but on Saturday night, as she struggled through the snow which had banked against the stage door throughout the performance, he was suddenly at her elbow.

'I've got my car here. Can I give you a lift?'

She looked up and around, startled in spite of all her fantasizing over the past three days. He wore a black homburg and a black overcoat – she hated hats on men and thought black fit only for funerals. But his voice was so clipped and definite. A bit like James Mason's.

She faltered, 'I didn't see you tonight.'

'I was there.'

The electricity had let her down; she wondered if that was an omen and looked around for Brett or Jenny or Marjorie. There was no-one else visible in the driving snow; her footprints were already filling up.

He took her arm and suddenly there was the current again, tingling along her elbow, making her legs buckle at the knees.

'Come on,' he ordered and led her into the road and around the bonnet of a car. She slipped and almost fell and he held her up while he opened the passenger door and thrust her inside. The door slammed shut again. She told herself not to be such a fool, he was giving her a lift home, he was one of their backers, there was nothing to worry about. She wasn't exactly burning her boats. And it was warm inside the car and away from the accursed snow.

The car rocked as he climbed in beside her and immediately started the engine. Lit by the street lamp outside, his face turned towards her, smiling. She had forgotten his amusement; as if she were a child to be indulged. It put her on her mettle.

'A quick getaway I think, don't you?'

'From what?' she asked tartly.

'The guardian angel. Or chaperone.' He laughed. 'Chaperone, I think!'

She could not let him mock Brett.

'My trustee has put me in Brett's care. He takes that very seriously.'

'Well he would if there's money in it!'

The car ground along the Bath Road. It was fitted with chains and went very slowly. Hardly a quick getaway. She smarted on Brett's behalf, though she had always suspected that part of his concern for her was because of possible future cash 'injections'.

She said stiffly, 'Second on the left. Opposite the pub.'

'Don't be ridiculous. I've borrowed a friend's house. Top of Leckhampton hill. It's ours till the morning.'

She gasped. 'You said a lift – I thought—'

'No you didn't. St Clare has told you how I feel about you. And you know it anyway. You feel the same.' His white face flashed round at her again and the tingle was an automatic reflex. 'We have to be together, Miranda. You knew that two years ago in that dump in Newton Abbot.'

She gasped again.

He said, 'Well? Can you deny it?'

She did not know what to say. If she denied it she would betray the electricity. But what did he *mean* about being together? Was he asking her to marry him? Was it just a night of love and nothing else?

He breathed a laugh at her silence. 'You see?'

She gabbled, 'I don't know. I – I'm not nineteen until October—'

The laugh escalated slightly; his left hand released the steering wheel and alighted on her thigh. The tingle became a shock. He registered that with a final snort of triumph.

He spoke reasonably enough even if his words were outrageous.

'That's why it has to be now, my love. My Ophelia. Next year you will no longer be a virgin. I'm interested only in virgins.'

In the welter of sensation into which she was falling, Miranda looked for a life raft and grasped at a familiar spar. He had called her his Ophelia. She was still Ophelia. Playing a part. In thrall to Hamlet. Miranda was safely somewhere else.

Her leg relaxed tremblingly into his hand – after all, she was wearing a thick coat and stockings and he was wearing leather gloves. Mixing her roles absolutely and nervously, she giggled.

'Svengali didn't care whether Trilby was a virgin or not!'

He was not thrown by the non sequitur. 'You see me as Svengali? Do I hypnotize you?'

Her giggle died as his hand moved.

'Almost.'

'Good.' The car bucked over a ridge of ice and she gasped again in spite of the thicknesses of material between hand and leg.

'That's the best of actresses,' he said with satisfaction.

She made a vain effort to regain her own self.

'You'll have to be very nice to me if you want to stay in this particular performance.'

It sounded a clever sophisticated remark, but it made him laugh again.

'Oh, I'll be nice to you. Very nice indeed!'

And while she was thinking about that and trying to control her thumping heart and her legs which had started trembling again, the sound from the manacled tyres changed and they turned through ghostly gateposts and into a sweeping drive. Through the snow she could see the dark mass of a large building; no lights, no staff. It could have been Daphne du Maurier's Manderley; even Dracula's castle. Her heart changed pace and the thump became more pronounced.

He said, 'This is it. Thank God, it's empty. Hang on, Ophelia. I've got a key. I'll open up.'

She continued to quake in the passenger seat while he struggled invisibly inside what must be a porticoed entrance. Then a light sprang up, making her gasp again, and he appeared, beckoning her inside. She was annoyed; he should have come out and opened the door for her and ushered her through the snow. If this was being very nice she did not think much of it. She scrabbled out and slammed the car door on her coat and had to reopen it. He almost pushed her into a large hall.

'For God's sake – take your time, won't you? The whole countryside will see us at this rate.' And he went to the light switch and plunged them into darkness again.

She spluttered furiously, 'I thought – when you said you were going to be nice – there might be a fire and a supper. Or something. And here we are in total darkness, freezing cold, wet—'

'Stop moaning and come here.'

He did not wait for her to move. He was with her, arms around her, mouth over hers. The sensual electricity was switched on full force. Physically he was as cold as she was, but her temperature soared nevertheless. He engulfed her; absorbed her into his being. By the time they stumbled up the stairs and searched for a suitable bed, she really was in the trance-like state of a Trilby.

The strange thing was he did not speak another word. She called his name often – never John, always Meredith – but he did not reply with words and often his response was so brutal her calls became whimpers and once a scream. He stopped her mouth with his, very quickly, and for a while he was almost tender with her. He was a sadist but as Ophelia or Trilby she did not mind that. Only when the pain pushed her out of role did she have to be restrained. Most of the time she possessed her Hamlet or was hypnotized by her Svengali and could respond as savagely as he.

How long the strange and perverse love-making lasted, she did not know. When he eventually rolled off her he must have been almost instantly asleep. She lay waiting for him, her overheated body cooling rapidly in the icy bedroom. And as she chilled so she came out of role and realized what she had done. Not what Meredith had done; not what Ophelia/Trilby had done; what she had done.

When it became obvious that there was to be no more of it, she sat up slowly and pulled her clothes around her and bowed over her knees with a physical weight of shame. And it was then, in the middle of the night, that she knew Meg was with her. The shame compounded a hundredfold. Meg knew what had happened. It was the most terrible moment of their young lives. She heard a strange keening sound; it was herself, weeping.

After a long time she became aware of the cold again and the smell and her own damp body. She stood up and made for the door. She could just see; the uncurtained windows showed white with the snow outside which reflected along a landing lined with doors. She found a bathroom and used the lavatory. Then she ran a bath; it was not very hot but she lay in it for a long time, scrubbed herself with a nail brush, used the enormous towels on the rail. She dressed again and plodded like an old woman along the landing, opening doors and looking inside bedrooms, cupboards, another bathroom. When she found a child's room, the bed made up with huge eiderdown and embroidered pillows, she went in and crept beneath the covers and wept agonizingly until she fell asleep.

He woke her while it was still dark.

'Get dressed. We have to be out by seven. You shouldn't have come in here.'

The electricity was not working. She hardly knew how to speak to him; but more than anything she was hungry. She'd had no food since her bread-and-butter tea yesterday. She wanted breakfast and there was to be none. Just as there had been no supper.

They ground back down the hill. Neither of them spoke. There was nothing between them any more and she wondered how she could have let him manhandle her as he had done. Her legs ached, her pelvis was a throbbing mass, she thought there must be bruises on her shoulders and small breasts. It was horrible; she felt sick at the thought of it.

This time he took her to the digs, got out and opened the door for her. She would have walked away without a word but he caught her shoulder and turned her to face him.

'You'll never forget tonight. You're mine now.'

Just for a second there was the echo of a thrill. Then she walked away from him. She glanced back and saw him standing there, his white face stretched with surprise. Well, after her performance last night she supposed he had a right to be surprised at this rejection.

She said in explanation, 'I have to go to Plymouth. It's Sunday. I have to see my sister.'

He did not understand that Meg was her better half. That she was turning her back on her wicked half. That it was over.

Brett held her and she wept into his neck.

'I'm sorry . . . sorry . . .' she sobbed helplessly.

He was terribly distressed. 'My fault. I should have

stayed with you. I waited for the blasted box-office receipts.'

'I wouldn't have listened anyway.'

'Has he hurt you?'

'I don't know. Not really. I'm so ashamed. I thought – ' she tried to laugh. 'I thought I was Trilby and he was Svengali.'

'Oh my God. Oh Miranda, I've been frantic – we must get you to a doctor—'

'*No!*' She was horrified. 'I – I'm not – *damaged* – or anything!' How could she tell him that she had – had – *responded* – probably encouraged the violence. Shame swept her again. 'I'm sorry – so sorry – ' she sobbed. 'I did not mean to betray you. You are the only person in my life – in that way – I admire you and respect you and love you—' She tried to lift her sore mouth to his but he held her hard to his shoulder.

'Listen. Miranda. You are a child. Especially to me. A – a trust, if you like. From your father. Do you understand that?'

She tried to nod against the tweed of his jacket.

'Try to think of me as Pygmalion. You are my Galatea and I am your Pygmalion.'

It sounded wonderful. Svengali and Trilby indeed! She needed no crazed hypnotist to bring her to life, but a sculptor – a Pygmalion – to mould her and train her in his ways. Just like Galatea. She wept anew.

'Oh, Miranda. What can I do?' he asked.

'Nothing. I must go to see Meg. Can you get me to the station and find out about trains and things?'

'Of course. And stay with her for a while. Forget *Hamlet.*'

That made her lift her head convulsively. 'Certainly not! The show must go on. I am an actress first and a person second!'

His dark Tyrone Power eyes looked into hers with a kind of sadness.

'Aren't we all, Miranda?' he asked.

She arrived in Plymouth some time during Sunday afternoon and walked to Higher Compton. Meg must have been watching for her out of the window and ran down the drive to meet her, weeping, flinging her arms around her and holding her as if she wanted to blend their bodies.

The pain mingled. When Miranda tilted her head at last she could see the agony of last night's coupling in Meg's clear blue eyes and it stabbed through her anew. It was like a wound. In her mind she thought of it as 'a knife entering my heart', and though she was aware of the melodrama of the phrase, nevertheless that was how it was. She put her face to Meg's again and let their twinship assert itself like a fortress around them.

She was by now terribly tired. There had been no snow in Plymouth but it was bitterly cold, and they walked along the Hoe staring at the iron-grey sea and capitulating to melancholia.

Meg said, 'I am so *glad* to see you! I was going to wait until it was dark and then phone that number you gave me. But I knew if you didn't come, you no longer wanted me as a twin.'

Miranda said, 'How do you work that out?'

'You knew that I knew. We had to share that. Or let it separate us.'

'We'll never be separated by . . . secrets . . .' Miranda's head buzzed. 'Because we know each other's . . . brains. There can be no secrets between us.'

'But they must be shared. Don't you understand?'

'I think so.' Miranda shivered convulsively. 'I hardly slept last night. I'm feeling rather strange.'

Meg was instantly contrite. 'Of course you are – I should *know* that!' She hugged Miranda's shoulders, feeling the thinness of her coat. 'Listen. I'm being paid now for the jobs I do around the hostel. Let's go and have some tea, then I'll smuggle you back in like I used to, and we can have an early night. How's that?'

Miranda started to cry.

'Oh, Meg . . .' The thought of a decent night's sleep, curled up by her sister as if they were children again, was sheer heaven.

She left just before nine the next morning as if she were Meg going to college. The Penwiths never even knew she'd been in the hostel. Meg insisted that she should wear her own thick duffle coat and leave the leaf-green mini in its place. Miranda snuggled into the hood as she waited at the station for the Penzance train. She was all right now. Herself. It had been an experience and in a strange way she was glad she had had it. Or at any rate, glad Ophelia/Trilby had had it. She was smiling as she got on to the packed train. Immediately someone stood up and gave her a seat.

Two years passed and she did not see John Meredith. In a way this was not surprising, as Brett had refused his money and told him to clear off otherwise certain facts would be put before the police. But in spite of that Miranda felt piqued occasionally. That shared intensity of sensation had been swept under the carpet almost too efficiently. Several times she dreamt of him and the next day felt shame and guilt in equal proportions.

But the Arbitrary went from strength to strength and so did she. She was most definitely Brett's protégée, even Olwen accepted it now. People who had come to see Brett came to see her too; it was suggested to Brett that he might take on other pupils. He was an excellent Pygmalion. Brett said she had brought them luck.

She bloomed with happiness. Her hair took on a life of its own; it was fashionable to have long, straight hair, unconfined in any way. The other girls managed a gap of a few inches between the obligatory curtains, through which they peered provocatively. Miranda's apricot locks strayed across her face like a constantly shifting veil, and had to be tucked behind her ears with one of her special, personalized gestures, from where it would explode like a dandelion clock, strand by strand, and begin its seductive drifting again. Her complexion was flawless, her strange eyes opaque and often more green than blue. She might have lost her virginity, but not her innocence. She believed in Brett and her own talent; she believed in their ultimate success together both professionally and personally.

She and Meg celebrated their twenty-first together. Meg had been awarded her diploma and was only waiting for the precious cheque from Mr Bracknell before she began to look at possible houses. Miranda was impatient for her money too; they had a booking at a small theatre not far from Miss Pugh's for a two-week run of *Lady Windermere's Fan*, and even Olwen knew that the part of Lady Windermere would be going to Miranda in return for a 'cash injection'.

When the cheque came the day after the celebration, Miranda banked it immediately, waited the mandatory four days and wrote Brett a cheque for one hundred pounds.

'Darling girl. We'll get some new costumes for *Lady W*. You shall have a genuine Edwardian décolletage. I can see that milk-white neck of yours arising from a froth of lace.'

'Let's have a party for the first night, Brett! I'll ask

Mr Bracknell and Meg and we can go somewhere really plush.'

He smiled. 'Why not?'

They started rehearsals. Meg telephoned often. She was down in Keyhole of all impossible places. She was house-hunting and seemed to think Miranda might join her there occasionally. Miranda tried to let her down gently. She thought the tiny village around the damp harbour was a hole. But Meg did not seem to pick up this particular message. And, unaccountably, Miranda became irritated.

And then, in the middle of rehearsals, when Miranda had had a barney with Brett and Olwen had smirked triumphantly, Meg phoned again. She had tuned in to Miranda's mind; she knew that Miranda intended to buy the Arbitrary and Brett with it. And this time her anxiety for her sister was an intolerable burden.

'Darling, do you have to keep ringing with these dire warnings?' Miranda knew she was being unfair. 'I am not throwing my money about as you seem to think. And if you are implying that I bought the part of Lady Bracknell—'

'No such thing, Sis!' Meg was horrified.

'Let's be clear about this, Meg. I am not criticizing you for using your legacy to buy a house. But I intend to use mine to buy happiness. That's what your jaunt into my private thoughts seems to have missed entirely!'

It wasn't a row and if Meg chose to interpret Miranda's sharp words as such, then she'd have to get on with it. But Miranda replaced her receiver first and told herself that in a way Meg was no less than a voyeur. She wished she had thought of the term when she was speaking to her.

And then there was a long silence. No phone calls, no letters, nothing. Miranda never bore a grudge where Meg was concerned, and she promised herself that she would telephone long before the first night of *Lady Windermere* and Meg would come up to Exeter and they would talk nonstop. But when she did telephone Meg was out. She rang the next day and the landlord of the Coastguards again disappointed her.

'Two days running?' Miranda was unaccountably annoyed.

The landlord sounded portentous. 'She is out with a local artist. They are great friends.'

Somehow this piece of information was disconcerting in itself. Meg 'going out' with an artist and not letting her know? She left a message for Meg to ring her back but Miss Pugh reported no phone calls and she was hurt and put out. She was determined not to ring again. She got through to Mr Bracknell instead and asked him to come to the first-night supper. He was delighted.

'I'll get in touch with Margaret,' he offered. 'We can come together.'

'That would be fine.'

'Why don't you make it just the four of us?' The old man was surprisingly sentient at times. 'You and Mr St Clare. Margaret and myself.'

'Well . . . yes. It would be nicer. I'll see what I can do.'

She thought about it a lot. A foursome. It was the ideal time for herself and Brett to announce their love. Their engagement. And the ideal place would be the intimate Marquis.

She told him that Mr Bracknell insisted on an intimate dinner party.

'I think he wants to ask your intentions, Brett!' She dimpled at him and tucked her hair behind her ears. 'Don't worry, will you? He'll drone on about the uncertainty of an acting career. Oh, and your age!' She laughed. 'I've always said I would put money into the Group, and I'll stick by that, whatever he says!'

Brett did not laugh. 'I think our age difference stands us in good stead, Miranda,' he said seriously. 'He cannot see me as a threat – after all we have been together now for five years and I've never taken advantage of you, have I, my dear?'

She knew what he meant and shook her head and her hair flew everywhere. 'I think somehow Mr Bracknell has always trusted you, Brett. I can remember being so surprised when he agreed to me joining the Group.'

'He understands.' He spoke very quietly, then coughed and resumed in a stronger voice. 'As for your money . . . it is up to you. You know yourself about the difficulties—'

'I can put us on a proper footing, Brett!' She smiled. 'Let's make everything quite clear to him at supper, shall we?' It would be a good time to make everything quite clear to Meg too. She would not be at all happy about Miranda tying herself to a man old enough to be her father and putting her money into a struggling theatrical company.

He nodded. Olwen came into the room and Miranda left. She was no longer jealous of Olwen. She thought over what had just been said; she was convinced that Brett would announce their engagement during the supper.

They were starting their run on a Saturday in the hope of having a gala first night. Mr Bracknell and Meg did not appear in the big communal dressing-room before the play, and Miranda felt unduly nervous as she waited on stage for the curtain to go up. There was that long hiatus before the action started during which she fiddled with some flowers and let the audience enjoy the sight of her long neck emerging from the low bodice of the promised Edwardian gown. She was still full of confidence, Wilde himself would have adored her, but Meg had seen her only in Shakespeare plays and never a leading role; and the trouble with Wilde was that he was so . . . so theatrical. She knew that they would both be embarrassed by her solo opening; as the curtain went up she had to force herself to stay at the small table front stage, arranging the flowers. It seemed eternity until Jack appeared; she couldn't be arranging flowers for ever; she stepped back and put her hands behind her back, surveying the vase critically. And, thank God, he was announced and she could go forward with outstretched hands. And after that, she forgot that somewhere in the darkness, Meg and Mr Bracknell were watching. Not until she took no less than three curtain calls did she remember and smile blindly into the circle especially for them. Afterwards it was a terrible disappointment when he appeared alone with an enormous bouquet.

'Meg? Is she waiting outside?'

'Dear child. You were very good. I was most impressed.' He beamed at her and shook her free hand with unwonted enthusiasm. 'I am so sorry Margaret is not with me. How she would have enjoyed it.'

Miranda stared at him above the massed gladioli spearing their way through a froth of gypsophila.

'She's ill,' she said flatly.

'Not very.' Mr Bracknell smiled his congratulations at this latest evidence of their 'telepathy'. 'She has the most frightful cold. I simply refused to bring her.'

'But she's all right? I mean, it's not serious?'

'Oh no. It's just that she would have coughed and spluttered all through the play and she could not bear the thought of that. She wanted to come and wait in the foyer, but . . . well, as I said, I couldn't allow it.' He looked at the opaque eyes, made agate with shadow. 'I knew you wouldn't want that,' he added quickly.

Miranda swallowed her disappointment somehow. She would have wanted that; it would have been wonderful for Meg to have heard the applause without the embarrassment of seeing the play.

'It'll spoil our foursome,' she said in a lost voice.

Mr Bracknell, however, seemed completely undismayed by everything.

'I telephoned and cancelled her booking. This is my treat, Miranda. Don't argue. And it will be better. Just the three of us.'

'Better? Why?'

'I think Mr Sinclair has something to tell us, hasn't he? And it might have made Margaret feel a little. . . left out perhaps.'

Miranda could not believe her ears. He knew. And his acknowledgement that he knew was a tacit acceptance! Her heart leapt into her throat then settled back, beating hard. Oh, she dearly wished Meg could be there. Of course she would not feel left out, Miranda would not have allowed it.

She gulped. 'I did not realize you were so – so sentient, Mr Bracknell.'

He smiled at her. 'You are so like your mother, Miranda. And Maggie – your aunt – explained her to me often. You want to be like her – a partner in this company of players?'

He was amazing her. 'I . . . yes,' was all she could manage.

'I hope you will continue to want that. It would not be a bad thing.'

'I am so surprised you see it like that.'

His voice became more weighty, more Mr Bracknellish. 'So long as it's entirely a business arrangement and you are certain it is a worthwhile venture.'

They took a taxi to the Marquis and were ushered to a table in a corner well away from the dance floor and the band. Miranda wore an emerald green frock that presupposed green eyes with her red hair. Her eyes did indeed look green; not agate, clear, sparkling emerald green. Her hair was still arranged on top of her head; she wore no jewellery whatsoever, not even a watch. She thought Brett looked incredibly handsome, more like Tyrone Power than ever. She loved him so much she could hardly look at him without feeling her eyes fill with tears.

Mr Bracknell was full of compliments for the night's performance.

'Five years, Mr Sinclair,' he said in his pompous way as they opened enormous menus. 'Five years' tuition you have given Miss Patch, and I saw tonight how well you have taught her.'

Brett nodded, accepting the compliment.

The elderly man swept on, 'Obviously I knew I could trust you, Mr Sinclair, and I knew that dear Margaret would be able to tell me if anything was wrong . . .'

Miranda was appalled. Had he asked Meg to spy on her through their telepathy? Anyway it was obvious Meg had done no reporting. But what a crafty old so-and-so he was.

Brett said, 'Miranda is a great asset to the Group, sir. There will be a place here for her . . .' Miranda barely listened.

He didn't have to toady any more and neither did she. Bracknell was – amazingly – on their side.

Mr Bracknell turned to her.

'Well, my dear? Would you like me to draw up some kind of agreement? On the lines that you are sole proprietor of the Arbitrary Group?'

He was going too far. She shook her head quickly. 'It won't be like that, Mr Bracknell.' She smiled at Brett. 'We shall be equal partners. Obviously.'

'Ah.' Mr Bracknell raised his brows, surprised but

pleased. 'You are not putting all your money in, then?' He turned to Brett. 'You do have some assets. That is excellent. A partnership. I see no reason why it should not work. After all you have proved over the past five years—'

Brett cleared his throat. 'I have no assets as such, of course. My arrangements with the schools . . . funding from the Arts Council . . . goodwill . . . that kind of thing.'

'Then I do not quite see . . . the company will be Miranda's.'

Miranda looked at Brett, agonized. Why didn't he tell the silly old buffer that they would be getting married? He nodded, apparently agreeing with everything that was said.

Miranda said rather loudly, 'The partnership is marriage, Mr Bracknell. Brett and I will be getting married. Everything that is mine will then be his.'

There was a silence. Miranda knew suddenly what the phrase 'pregnant pause' meant. Then Mr Bracknell said blankly, 'You do know . . . Mr Sinclair has told you . . .'

And Brett said, 'No!' as if there were a rifle at his throat.

Miranda thought with terror that it was Olwen. Olwen and Brett were secretly married; had been married all this time.

Mr Bracknell said, 'We'll discuss this presently. Here is the waiter. What shall we start with?'

Miranda looked at Brett and saw that he was staring fixedly at the cover of his menu. Her heart had not actually started to break yet; it was pounding and she was angry, not believing anything any more. Surely it had always been understood between them that once she had her money they would be together? Was it marriage itself? Was he frightened of being tied?

Mr Bracknell was saying, 'Poached salmon, I think. And green beans. Yes, salad would be very acceptable.'

She said, 'I'll have that too.'

Mr Bracknell said gently, 'I was ordering for you, Miranda. I will have an underdone steak with mushrooms. And Mr Sinclair?'

Brett looked up, almost startled. 'Yes. The same,' he mumbled.

Miranda's anger grew. How dared old Bracknell order for her and how dared Brett choose the same as the old buffer? When the food came she changed plates deliberately.

'Brett prefers fish,' she explained to Mr Bracknell.

'Ah.' He smiled at her and his hand touched hers. She wanted to have it out now, but something stopped her. She had to wait for Brett to explain; somehow she had taken on the role of Lady Windermere again; she felt powerless.

The steak was awful, bleeding as she stuck her fork into it, practically impossible to swallow. In an effort to take control of things again, she summoned a waiter and asked for a bag.

'For the cat,' she smiled at him. 'They do this in America all the time.' She looked at her two companions, both satisfyingly embarrassed. 'Miss Pugh has got the most wonderful cat you have ever seen! He's black and ginger and tortoiseshell. And he smiles.'

Brett looked ready to die, but Mr Bracknell suddenly rose to the occasion.

'Let him have some of mine too. I was reading an article only the other day that red meat is bad for the heart.'

She was angry with Brett for accepting her salmon in the first place and then for flushing as if she were a recalcitrant child. Angry with Mr Bracknell for coping so well. He was acting just as Aunt Maggie had always acted; as if everything and anything that happened was perfectly normal.

She snapped, 'I'm surprised you've got a heart, Mr Bracknell!'

He looked at her, eyebrows raised. 'How did you know?' he asked inexplicably.

'Know? Know what? What are you talking about?'

'That I gave my heart to your Aunt Margaret many years ago.'

She felt her mouth open. His heart? To Aunt Maggie? She vaguely remembered a reference to some solicitor-admirer.

He smiled. 'Sorry. I've embarrassed you. It's hard to realize I ever had a heart, I expect. But I think she's given it back to me, Miranda. That was how I knew it was all right to entrust you to Mr Sinclair.'

She could think of nothing nasty enough to say and watched him while he tied the top of the bag and placed it alongside her foot.

He went on very blandly. 'I could see he had a genuine interest in you. Mr Sinclair had known your father. And there was affection too. Because of that.'

Brett said, 'Please, Mr Bracknell.'

Mr Bracknell looked across the table and he was no longer smiling. 'The child deserves to know the truth, Sinclair. You have not made your position clear. I am going to the lavatory. By the time I return you will have explained it to her.'

He stood up and walked across the restaurant. He was elderly. But he walked quickly and his back was very straight.

Miranda said, 'What is happening? Brett, I don't understand.'

Brett kept his eyes on the table. 'Your father. Terry. He was a wonderful person, Miranda.'

'Not so wonderful. He drove Amy mad sometimes. She told us so.'

'Probably.'

He had never been interested in Amy; of course he had never known her.

Miranda said impatiently, 'Never mind my father. What is Mr Bracknell talking about?'

'Me. Terry . . . your father.' Brett kept his dark eyes on his fork, apparently mesmerized by it. 'I loved him, Miranda.'

'So you've always said—' She stopped herself and stared at the thick hair which was all she could see of him. 'You . . . *loved* him? You mean, you *loved* him?'

'I was called up before . . . we could . . . it's possible that if the war hadn't happened you would not have been born, Miranda. We were very close.'

'Oh . . . my God!

Suddenly words poured from him. 'I heard he'd got someone. I tried to keep away, told myself I was doing the honourable thing. And then when he was killed in that bloody gas explosion I wished I'd gone straight to him after my demob.' He gave a kind of dry sob and turned his fork over to score the starched tablecloth. 'I didn't know about you, of course. I didn't know he'd married your mother. It was ghastly. Death . . . no more opportunities. I cannot come to terms with death.' He looked up and past her as if actually seeing Father Time in Mr Bracknell's seat. Then he looked back down and pressed hard with the fork. 'Thank God I met Oliver. I told him about Terry. He understood of course. Has always understood.'

She drew a sharp breath. Oliver? Oliver Freres, the one male member of the cast who never left them.

Brett went on, his enunciation perfect as usual but his words coming fast now that the floodgate was open.

'We set up the Arbitrary. As a kind of memorial to

Terry Patch. That's how I thought of it. Oliver went along with me, though he had never known Terry. Miss Pugh took us in and looked after us. She knew about us. When Olwen gave up dancing and joined us, she knew too. They've kept their counsel.' The fork pierced the linen and he pulled it out and moved to the left. 'Otherwise we'd be in clink, I suppose.'

There was a pause. Miranda said stubbornly, 'I don't understand.'

He said, 'There will never be another Terry Patch. But I love Oliver and he loves me.'

She breathed, 'Oh my God!'

He went on fast. 'You think of me as being unfaithful to your father, Miranda. Maybe I felt the same way. That was why your . . . advent . . . seemed like a benefaction from him. A forgiveness.'

But she was following her own train of thought. 'You and Oliver . . . That's the hold Olwen has over you!'

'Quite.'

He glanced up briefly again. 'I thought you'd get to know gradually. The others – they can't be sure of course, but they probably guess. I thought you would too.'

She shook her head, not so much in negation as to clear it. She said in a high voice, like a plea, 'You said you loved me! I thought – once I was twenty-one – we would be together!'

'I do love you. But not . . . I think of you as a precious gift, Miranda. Terry's gift to me after all these years! I've done my best – my utmost – to protect you and look after you. That was why . . . oh God, it was so awful when you went to that Meredith. He was an unnatural bastard.'

'*He* was unnatural?'

Colour came into his face then receded. He put the fork down very slowly.

'You hate me. I can understand it. But *you* try to

understand, Miranda. I've never given you reason to think there was anything more than friendship between us.'

She racked her memory. There must have been something.

He went on again. 'It was such a spiritual thing.' He looked up at her properly, his dark eyes watering sentimentally. 'A message from heaven if you like.'

'I don't like, actually.'

'You're disgusted with your father too. Of course you would be. You idolized your parents and the thought that your father loved someone before your mother—'

'I hardly knew my father. I don't care about any of that. It's you – you – ' She gave a dry sob. 'Oh, I thought it was my money you wanted – as well as me, that is. But I didn't care! I knew you loved me. You said you loved me! You said we were going to be together—'

'No!' His voice was stronger. 'No, Miranda. I have never suggested anything like that. Think back carefully.'

She did so, but repeated helplessly, 'Well, you let me think . . . you must have known how I felt—'

'I was standing in for your father, child!'

'It wasn't like that!' She was very close to tears. She must not cry. Whatever happened, she must not cry. She said brightly, 'So. It's all over, is it?'

'It need only be starting, Miranda! If you are willing to invest—'

'Don't be absurd, Brett! I've invested more than money in the Arbitrary and seen it disappear. D'you think I'm going to waste my inheritance in the same way?'

He was silent. She swallowed desperately.

'Well. It has been . . . an education. Quite an education.' Her voice sounded light, almost amused; she was deeply grateful that her acting ability was standing this test.

'Miranda—'

'Here comes Mr Bracknell. We'd better get back to

Miss Pugh's. I've got a feeling this bag of steak is leaking.'

He stood up as she did. He looked helpless, his eyes still wet with tears. Well, she wasn't going to sink to that level of bathos.

Mr Bracknell said briskly, 'All sorted out? I've ordered a taxi for eleven. There's a train from St David's at quarter past. Perhaps I can drop you at Miss Pugh's?'

Brett was incapable of replying. Miranda said, 'That would be marvellous.'

'Allow me.' He helped her with her coat, pressing her shoulders through the sleeves. She refused to acknowledge such unspoken sympathy.

'You can carry the bag of leftovers,' she said and swept out of the restaurant without waiting for either of them.

Five

The cheque arrived in the post the day after their birthday meal.

Meg handled it almost reverently. It marked the end of that long waiting time between Uncle Cedric's perfidy and living properly again. It seemed incredible that such an enormous sum was symbolized by a mere scrap of paper with the briefest of covering letters from Mr Bracknell. It all seemed something of an anticlimax.

Meg rang him to thank him for the cheque but he still sounded very formal. She said a cautious goodbye. She intended going to Cornwall as soon as she had cleared out her room at the hostel.

Keyhole had not provided many memories of home for either girl, but once out of the cramped cottage of Mrs Hitler they had been happy enough. In retrospect, it seemed to Meg that it had been an idyllic time of sunshine and shell collections. And there had been artists there too. Keyhole was obviously the ideal place for struggling artists. Cheap cottages, wonderful light, no distractions . . . there was enough money to live on for quite a while. She could buy precious time for herself; time in which she could find out whether she could earn a living by her brush.

As the train jolted from station to halt between Plymouth and Penzance, she forced herself to remember, dredging up half-thoughts, half-pictures, in a wonderful montage of colour and sea-sounds. The big, clumsy-looking boats had been called luggers. They had been linked to the high harbour wall by lines with pulleys . . . why pulleys? And there had been flights of stone steps cut in the harbour wall down to the stony beach. She could remember the feel of those steps beneath her bare feet; and those feet had moulded themselves to rock surfaces too. Like limpets they had clung and gripped and sucked themselves free again. And then the freedom of the sea. She and Miranda had swum before they could walk, taught by an enthusiastic Amy on one of her rare visits. They had been expert swimmers too. They had earned a special nickname for their swimming; what had it been? She racked her brains all through the two-hour journey and as she lugged her cases on to the platform it came to her. The tadpole twins. It did not surprise her when she phoned Miranda from the Coastguards Inn that night to hear: 'I've been thinking of Keele all day. D'you remember they used to call us the tadpole twins?'

Meg laughed. 'And until I arrived at Penzance I'd forgotten they called Keyhole, Keele!'

'You've got a lousy memory!'

Meg laughed again. 'It doesn't matter. You've got a good one. I can always tune in to yours!'

Miranda was suddenly and unexpectedly petulant. 'It's not fair, Meg! You can tune in to me all the time. I never tune in to you!'

'But you have been – today!'

'No. I have been thinking of our time together and you tuned in to *me*.'

It was the first time Meg had realized this. Oddly, it was comforting. She did not really want to give Miranda the freedom of her mind. Miranda didn't mind. Or at least she hadn't minded till the awfulness of that man, Meredith.

But there was nothing she could do about it so she

said consolingly, 'We share everything, Miranda. Just wait till I've got us somewhere down here to live and we can share properly again.'

She had forgotten – chose to forget – that Miranda professed to dislike Keyhole.

'Darling. I don't want to be mean and of course I'd love to put in my five cents' worth, but I'm still of Terence's opinion. About roots, I mean. You do understand, don't you?'

'Of course. But you will come and stay whenever you can, won't you? In between times.'

'Oh darling. I'm so sorry . . .'

'Shut up, idiot! This is my idea entirely. Anyway cottages are so cheap here it's unbelievable!'

'But I might not . . . I mean . . . supposing I marry?'

Meg's eyes opened wide at her own reflection above the phone.

'You've met someone?'

'No. But . . . you don't know? I mean, this particular . . . thing . . . isn't getting through to you?'

Meg said cautiously, 'I know you're happy. I've known that for ages. But . . . a specific person . . .'

'Thank God!' Miranda laughed. 'Sorry, darling, but I do need *some* privacy!'

'I know. I'm sorry.'

'It's just that – I might do an Amy. You never know. Marry someone in the profession. Which would mean I wouldn't see a great deal of you all the way down there.'

'You're so mysterious! I can tell something is happening – no, I don't want to know, don't tell me! You're right, you need your private world.' She tried to laugh above a sharp anxiety. 'And anyway, if you follow in Amy's footsteps, maybe I'll be like Aunt Maggie and you can come to me for holidays and things.'

Miranda made cheering sounds and then changed the subject completely and talked about the rehearsals for *Lady Windermere*.

Meg replaced the receiver carefully and went downstairs to dinner. She was still glad she was here, still determined to put down her roots. The trouble was, all the memories she had of Keyhole included another figure: Miranda's.

Meg wrote in her diary: 'Keyhole is a symmetrical semicircle cut out of the cliffs by nature on the south side of Land's End, and enclosed by man within two granite jetties stretching their arms across the entrance, almost touching, never quite. The huddle of cottages around this natural harbour are twenty feet above the sand, reached by three sets of steps cut into the rock. Along the harbour rail mooring ropes are tied at regular intervals and the fishermen get on to their boats by coasting down these ropes commando fashion.'

She looked through the window at the winter view. Of course, that was why the pulleys had been there. Hadn't Miranda used one once and nearly drowned herself? Meg smiled, knowing that she was still in touch with her sister; Miranda must have sent her that particular memory.

She scribbled some more: about her train journey down and the bus from Penzance to Keyhole yesterday; about the Coastguards Inn and her view of the lifeboat house; about her feeling for the place. Yes, this was where she would start growing those roots.

She closed the diary and glanced at her watch. Eight o'clock and barely light. She decided to go outside and look at the place before breakfast.

It was a typical November day. She surveyed the swoop of the harbour with satisfaction; she had been unable to see it from her room, and last night it had been dark when she arrived, but she had recalled it perfectly in her diary. The tide was in and most of the boats were being made ready to go out. She walked over the road and leaned on the railing, wondering if the fishermen still went aboard so precipitately. It seemed she was too late to see them even if they did; a boy of about ten years old was going from rope to rope tugging at the rolling hitch knots, throwing the freed ropes down where they were coiled neatly as engines were started.

The air was damply cold, sea and sky uniformly grey, but neither the solid ceiling of cloud nor the surface of the sea appeared to move. It was a terribly nostalgic moment; Keele had always been empty in November, wrapping itself in mists, apparently enjoying its privacy. In the summer its beauty was obvious to everyone; in the winter it needed a longer look. Meg gave it that longer look and breathed deeply of its smells. She had forgotten the smell of having the sea on the doorstep. In Plymouth the seaweed, spume, and fish smells had been filtered through civilization before they reached Higher Compton.

She waited until the last of the luggers wallowed between the jetties, then turned back to the hotel reluctantly. The scent of breakfast bacon drowned everything else, but she was still breathing deeply as she went into the dining room of the Coastguards.

'Ah. Olfactory delights as my old grandad used to say!'

She guessed that the landlord was in his fifties, not a Cornishman, far too eager to please. Meg smiled.

'Sounds Edwardian!' she commented, following him to her table by the window overlooking her bedroom view: the sea and lifeboat station.

He pulled out the chair, rearranged the cruet.

'Well, I suppose it was.' He leaned on the back of the other chair. 'Let's see. I'm talking pre-war. And I mean the Great War.'

Extrovert Miranda's words came into her head and were spoken before she could stop them.

'Good Lord. You don't look old enough to have been born pre 1914!'

He smiled, well pleased. 'I'm as old as the century, my dear. Sixty-five.'

She was genuinely surprised and glad that those coy words had turned out to be sincere. But after he'd turned away to relay her breakfast order to the kitchen, she spoke silently to her sister. 'No more putting words into my mouth, Miranda!'

However, the landlord had already been flattered into near servility and appeared by her side every time she came and went that day. She was to call him Arthur – in fact call him at any time of the day or night. He was there to look after her. That was his job. And it was no hardship either, it was a pleasure.

It seemed as though Miranda was well and truly banished, because she could think of nothing to say to him. It was quite a relief to be able to ask him the times of the buses to Penzance the next day.

'May I give you a lift?' He looked like a dog waiting for her to throw a bone.

'No, really. I'd prefer to . . .' to what? Be on her own?

'Ah. You're going shopping! My late wife could not bear me to be with her when she was shopping!'

'Actually I want to call on various house agents.'

'You're looking for a property?' He was delighted. 'Go no further, my dear Miss Patch. I simply mention it over the bar this evening—'

'Please don't do that!' Meg was serious. 'I can remember how it was when a foreigner wanted to move in. They'd put the price up astronomically just to keep them out. I'd rather do it through official channels – honestly, Mr . . . Arthur.'

He nodded judiciously. 'Your word . . . and so on.' He reached towards a pile of information leaflets on the desk. 'Timetable . . . timetable.' He produced one and handed it to her. 'You were down here before then, my dear? You lived down here?'

'I was evacuated here when I was a baby. At the end of the war.' Meg spoke briefly, flipping through the tiny figures and finding suitable services.

'Then you must have contacts? You're no foreigner.'

She tucked the timetable into her bag. 'We made no friends.' There had been no friends at boarding school, until Pamela. She smiled brightly. 'I'm one of twins. We've always had each other. And we left when we were five years old. Mrs Roe would be dead by now, I'm sure.'

The idea of twins captivated him anew and she had difficulty in getting away. He enquired further of Mrs Roe and nodded. 'Yes. She died. The kiddies used to call her Mrs Hitler but they tell me she was good with babies.'

'Yes. She was. We've always been very healthy. She must have given us a good start.'

At last she was sitting on the bus lumbering its way along the narrow cliff road. She wondered if it was odd that they had no 'contacts' down here; no friends in Plymouth. Perhaps it had not been so odd in Keele all those years ago. They had combined forces anyway against the dominance of Mrs Hitler; other children had steered clear of the house in case they were caught up in the constant battle that always seemed to rage within its walls. They had never gone to school there – that might have made a difference. Certainly there had been other children during those beachcombing sessions, but no-one strong enough to break through their one-ship. And once back with Amy and Terence, they were always moving from theatrical rooms to theatrical rooms. Perhaps that was why it had been so delightful at school.

She remembered the outings with Aunt Maggie and Uncle Cedric before . . . the fuss. There had been friends then; friends who wanted to enter their charmed circle, friends who loved Aunt Maggie and thought Uncle Cedric 'a darling'.

She let her mind make the accustomed leap between Pamela's scream and the hostel in Higher Compton. Miranda had still been around then, at least for the first awful year. They had met on the Hoe, or in the little lanes of the Barbican. Sometimes Miranda had played truant and come to the hostel and Meg had smuggled her in so that they could hang on to each other and weep and eventually sob themselves to sleep.

And then Miranda had left school and joined the Arbitrary Group. Meg frowned, wondering why the Juvenile Department had permitted that. Miranda was entitled to leave school at fourteen, certainly. But she had still been 'in care' until she was sixteen. It must have been that Brett St Clare – ostensibly trustworthy – had taken on her care. Meg shivered at the thought; where had he been when Miranda was practically abducted by that dreadful man? She recalled her own nausea that night; how she had woken suddenly, her whole body wrapped in pain; how she had run for the bathroom.

She never ceased to worry about Miranda since then. It would not happen again, of course – Miranda had sworn to that. But Miranda's personality made her so vulnerable, so terribly vulnerable. And now she was obviously contemplating marriage.

'Noolin post office!' yelled the conductor, turning momentarily from his conversation with the driver of the bus. 'Anyone for Noolin!'

A woman stood up and the conductor concealed his impatience with difficulty and followed her as she struggled between the seats and stepped off the end platform.

He banged the bell forcefully with his palm and they pulled away from Newlyn. Before them swept the glorious curve of Mount's Bay with St Michael's Mount rising out of the November greyness like a mirage. Meg felt unexpected tears in her throat; she had been unconscious of unhappiness when she'd been here before, which must mean that she had been happy enough. Anyway, whatever Terence had said in the old days, she had put down roots. She could feel them physically tugging now. The sights before her were amazingly familiar: the bulk of the Scillies ferry rising above the harbour wall, the jagged-tooth-like silhouette of the parish church and the huddle of houses. Cornish settlements were always a 'huddle'. Her smile came again, no longer rueful. Everything was going to be all right now. Miranda had promised a long time ago that she would never sell herself again. She had kept that promise; Meg knew that. Meg would always know if she kept her promises. Everything was – most definitely – going to be all right.

The agents had almost too much to offer. Cornish tin and copper were on the wane, it came much cheaper from South America, miners were moving again to the States and Australia.

'I need something in Keyhole itself,' she protested, thumbing through leaflets hopelessly.

'It's known locally as Keele, Miss Patch,' the agent said indulgently. 'It's such a close community, I wonder if you would be quite happy there?'

'I lived there as a child. I want to paint.'

His face became longer. 'So many people have that idea. The days of the St Ives and Newlyn Schools are really over—'

She said desperately, 'I have a small income. I need

somewhere with an attic – skylights – I need a view of the sea.'

He picked up another leaflet and thrust it at her.

'Eureka! Prospect Villa. Facing the sea. Detached. Private steps to Lannah Cove.'

She took it doubtfully. Did she want to be detached? The huddle-instinct was in her too.

'Thank you.' She glanced at the price. 'Is there anything else? Possibly something I could have converted?' She pulled a paper out of the pile in front of her. 'Now this one—'

'Shop premises.'

'So it has a very big window—'

'On to the harbour front.'

'That was exactly what I had in mind.' She wondered if he had been listening at all.

'Are you going to be living alone?' he asked repressively.

Miranda would have said 'What earthly business is it of yours?' She nearly did say it. But Meg prevailed. 'Most of the time. My sister will be with me occasionally.'

'Noise. All through the summer months. Especially when the Coastguards and Lobster Pot turn out. Not much better in the winter, I understand.'

'May I look at it?' She set the leaflet aside and went on. 'And this one—'

'Away from the harbour. You stipulated the harbour front.'

She could have screamed. Prospect Villa was halfway up the cliff. And hadn't he said the harbour was peopled by drunks?

'Fish Street isn't so far away. I'd like to take a look at it if I may.'

'Naturally. That's why I'm here. To help you.' He was checking reference numbers and searching in a drawer.

'The keys to Fish Street are out at the moment. But I can take you over the shop this afternoon if that would suit you.'

'Perfectly.'

He glanced at the Fish Street details and saw the price. 'And tomorrow for this one,' he added hastily. 'As soon as Mr Snow returns the keys.'

Miranda might have said, 'Is that Peter Snow, the artist?' But Miranda knew nothing of painters, so Meg was silent.

The shop would be ideal once she'd had it converted. There was room in the loft for a studio, one of the two bedrooms could be made into a bathroom, the kitchen and living room on the ground floor could be knocked into one.

'Fine when you are on your own.' The agent felt duty bound to object. 'But when your sister comes, you will have to turn out of your bedroom.'

'I shall sleep in the studio all the time.' Meg was surprised. 'I need to sleep with my work otherwise it goes away.'

The agent did not meet her eyes. 'And, um, the house in Fish Street? That is much bigger, of course. The attic has two skylights. And there is the fish cellar too.'

'It would be lovely. But this is fine.'

He looked crestfallen. The shop was just under £2,000, not much commission to be had there.

She said, 'I'll go and look at that and Prospect Villa, just to make sure.'

He gave her a set of keys. 'I'll leave you to do Prospect Villa when you feel like it. And as soon as I get the other keys—'

'No hurry.'

*　　*　　*

Arthur at the Coastguards was delighted. 'I can keep an eye on you if you take the old shop.' He led her to the window of the public bar. 'See? It's right across the harbour. Faces north, mind.'

'That's all right.' She stared at it. Was this really where she was going to put down roots? The single front window glinted at her as the riding light of a boat caught it in the dark November afternoon. There was a lot she'd have to do to it and she wondered whether she could cope with recalcitrant Cornish planners and builders.

Arthur said, 'What will you call it? Harbour View?'

'It's called the Old Shop,' she explained carefully.

He guffawed appreciatively. 'Oh, I like it!' He pulled the curtain cord and the curtains glided closed. 'The Old Shop! Very good!'

She went upstairs to wash for the evening meal. She couldn't see the joke but knew it wasn't important. After dinner she would come to bed early and make some sketches which she could take with her when she went to see architects or solicitors or whoever she had to see. She swilled soap from her face and looked at her reflection in the mirror above the basin. What a strange, nothing sort of a face she had. She tied her bushy hair back in the nape of her neck as she'd done since school and wondered whether she should outline her eyes as Miranda did. They were so pale and the lashes were ginger like her hair. Miranda's eyes were one of her striking features, yet they were identical to Meg's own. She smiled, her usual rueful smile, and turned away. Miranda was, after all, an actress. Meg was just herself.

The next morning it was raining and visibility was down to about ten yards. Arthur was nowhere to be seen at breakfast-time and the girl who brought her tea and toast looked harassed and unhappy. Meg heard her grumbling to someone in the kitchen; it seemed Arthur was 'sleeping it off'.

Meg donned boots and a mack and went outside. The wind seemed to be blowing from all directions at once; dimly she could see a tangle of seaweed and lobster pots on the slipway. Presumably it was too rough for fishing; the luggers tossed sullenly at their ropes. No-one was about.

Bent double, she walked around the harbour to the Old Shop and peered through the big window. For some reason it looked much smaller than it had yesterday and for the first time she noticed the gas bracket on the wall. Surely there was electric light somewhere? She climbed the alley at the side, the wind pressing hard against her eyeballs and ballooning inside her hood. The tiny back yard was filled with junk. She leaned over the wall and peered down. Because the cottages were in steep terraces the yard would always be dark and cavernous; no light in the kitchen at all. There was a dripping tap to one side of the back door. Was that the only water supply? She racked her brains and could not remember whether there was a tap above the shallow yellow stone sink in the scullery. Yesterday, everything had seemed so predestined. Today it did not. It was, of course, just the weather; even so she felt horribly depressed.

She could not face Arthur's possible hangover so she went in to the Lobster Pot for coffee and then, thoroughly at a loose end, decided to look at the outside of the Fish Street house and Prospect Villa. The streets ran roughly parallel to the curved harbour and climbed like giant's steps to the cliff top. They were connected by cobbled alleys which were hard on cars but easy for pedestrians, with steps slotted into the pavement and a metal handrail along the sides of the houses. Meg decided to do the long climb first and set off at a brisk pace in an effort to shake herself out of her grey mood. This slowed down quite quickly, and by the time she had left the huddle of houses and was walking along a sandy unmade road between damp bracken she was down to half a dozen steps and a pause for breath.

The agent had been right; the view was enormous from up here. The cloud had lifted off the sea and let in some light and she could see beyond the opposite headland into Penzance itself. Probably the back of the villa would have views stretching down to Land's End. She began to wonder whether this might be her answer; right away from the huddle, glorious isolation. Rather like Uncle Cedric's house overlooking Plymouth.

But she was disappointed. The road ended abruptly with the promised flight of steps going down to the next cove. It was an unprotected drop and quite dangerous; it would have to be fenced. And of course the road itself would be her responsibility. She came to a sagging gate, almost invisible between dripping fuchsia hedges. She had difficulty with the gate and when she got through she saw the path to the front door needed urgent repair and the whole house was neglected. It had obviously been empty for some time, brambles had grown over the front window. She pushed her way between them and peered inside. It was a beautiful room, square and spacious; but the paper hung damply in pleats and the ancient linoleum was cracked here and there as if the floorboards themselves were giving way.

She needed to look no further, but she did walk the fractured path to the back. The cliff rose perpendicularly six feet from the windows. No more room than the little yard down at the Old Shop, and the rock face was pouring water. Darkness and damp. She went back to the gate understanding why the house was so reasonably priced and still so empty. She stood for a moment, staring around her. Even allowing for the November twilight, it was an eerie sort of a house. She did not like it.

She hurried back down into the village as the clock was striking twelve. She'd ring Miranda at one. Just before lunch. They would finish rehearsals then. She'd ask her to book a seat for *Lady Windermere*. It would be good to have something to look forward to.

She swung down into Fish Street determinedly cheerful, and was immediately confronted by a 'For Sale' poster hung like an inn sign above a front door. No-one was about. She stood with her back to the wall on the opposite side of the tiny road and surveyed the front of the house. Steps led up to the door, sash windows either side like a children's drawing; the fish cellar was below, a squat door, a single window; above was a line of bedroom windows and jutting from the roof was an enormous dormer. It was wonderful. A dream house. She went up steps to the street above and saw that it had skylights opposite the dormers and a yard big enough for flower tubs as well as washing. She felt breathless with sudden desire; Miranda was forgotten. She went down to Fish Street again and stood with her back to the door of the fish cellar. There was a glimpse of harbour between two rooftops. There would be a better view from the next floor. She climbed the outside steps to check on it. Yes, both the sash windows would look over and between chimneypots to the twin jetties of the harbour.

Suddenly the front door opened. She nearly jumped out of her skin; she clutched the metal banister around the top step and turned at the same time. It wasn't the agent; presumably the house was lived in, though she thought that at some time he had said it was empty. The man standing there, eyebrows raised, hand impatiently on the doorknob obviously wanting to close it, was probably about thirty, though she wasn't sure because of his beard.

He might be a Cornishman; he wore a filthy fisherman's smock and rubber boots over ancient trousers.

She said, 'I'm so sorry. I understood the house was empty.'

He nodded once. 'It is. D'you want to see round it?'

'Well . . . yes. But . . . is it convenient?'

'Perfectly. The agent sent me. And I know about you. Miss Patch, isn't it?'

'Well, yes.' She despised herself for prefacing every remark with well. She straightened her shoulders and walked past him into a decent square hall with a passage beyond. Stairs ran up ahead of her. He closed the door and she had a sense of the house enfolding her protectively. It was absolutely wonderful.

She pushed back her hood and turned to the man, smiling. 'You are looking around too?'

He did not respond to the smile. 'Yes. Obviously. I thought I was going to buy it until last night.'

'Oh dear.' She wondered what snags he had discovered. She wouldn't care if there was worm and dry rot everywhere. She loved the place.

'Yes, it is a pity, isn't it?' His suddenly sarcastic tone surprised her, but she was already through the door on her left into what must be the sitting room. It was nearly as big as the one at Prospect Villa, the ceiling lower, the window smaller. And there was a glorious view of the harbour.

She was so excited she almost brushed past the man into the hall again and through the other door. This was the dining room, small, with dressers either side of the fireplace. She remembered to look at the floor. Wide splintery knotted boards, but surely no rot?

He said with exaggerated aplomb, 'And the kitchen is through here, madam.' He indicated a door facing the window. 'Or it can be reached via the passage of course.'

She spared him a laugh over her shoulder and went through to the kitchen. It was awful; an ancient gas stove, another of those shallow yellow stone sinks, a soggy wooden draining board, a smell of wet wood. This then was the snag. She went through the other door into the passage and was halfway down the stairs to the fish cellar before he knew it. She wished he would leave her alone; she wanted to explore every corner of this marvellous place.

The fish cellar was amazing. The enormous floor space was interrupted here and there by granite pillars which presumably supported the rest of the house. There was an old press in the corner, a rusty range on one wall. The smell of pilchards still hung in the air. The two tiny windows, one to the street, the other to the yard, made it permanently twilit. She imagined it warmed by the range, glinting with pans and glassware.

Behind her he said, 'That kitchen's frightful, isn't it? Damp as hell. Cost hundreds to do something about that.'

She said breathlessly, 'I'd leave that. Have the kitchen down here. And eat down here too.'

'No dampcourse, obviously. Mouldy clothes. You can't keep anything decent in these old cottages.'

'No.'

She was thrilled. He was going to turn the place down because of a bit of damp! He must be mad.

He said, 'You don't want to see the bedrooms then?'

'No. Not really.'

It didn't bother her if they were falling to bits. She had to have this house.

Suddenly he smiled. His teeth glinted in the bush of beard and she saw that he had blue eyes and a predatory sort of nose.

He said, 'Right. Then you can go out of this door if you like.'

She too smiled full at him and saw him blink.

'Thank you so much for showing me around, Mr . . .'

'Snow. Peter Snow.'

Her mouth was open. He took her hand and pumped it with a kind of relief. His hand was like sandpaper. She looked down at his wrist; of course there was paint everywhere; on his protruding shirt cuff, all over the blue smock.

She swallowed. 'You're the artist. You work in Newlyn. I've seen your stuff in the gallery there.'

'Hey, nobody's ever heard of me before!'

He was ingenuously pleased and pumped her hand again.

She said shyly, 'I liked the picture of the miners. At Geevor.'

'Thank you. Thank you very much.'

She removed her hand from his and opened the little door. She had to crouch to go through it. He crouched too, his hand on the lintel, the smile, which had developed into almost a schoolboy's grin, disembodied in the darkness of the cellar.

She said hesitantly, 'I'm surprised . . . I should have thought this place was ideal for you.'

'Oh, it is,' he said immediately. 'I don't care two hoots about the damp. But the agent told me you would offer five hundred more, so I had to put you off somehow!'

He laughed, then said abruptly, 'You know, you've got a very interesting face. I don't do portraits, but I'd like to paint you. If you're here for any length of time.'

She stared at where his eyes must be. She felt a disappointment out of all proportion to the loss of the house. She said, 'Yes. Well . . . perhaps.' Then she swallowed and straightened. 'I have to go. I have a phone call to make.' And she turned and walked into the rain, not bothering to put up her hood.

Six

She skipped lunch and went to her room to stare out of the window and fill in her diary. Unaccountably the depression was back; she couldn't find the will to ring Miranda until almost three o'clock, by which time she felt chilled and had a headache.

Miranda sounded as out of sorts as she was herself.

'Oh. Hello, Meg.'

'How are you?'

'How is anyone this weather? I bet Keyhole really is a hole, isn't it?'

'Well . . . it's rather lovely in a way.'

'A damp way.'

'Yes, I suppose so.' Meg felt as if she was batting a ball against a stone wall. 'You sound as if rehearsals are going badly,' she ventured.

'Mm. I'm having difficulty with Olwen. Can't say too much, she might be listening at the door.'

'Oh, Sis.'

'What about you? Found somewhere yet?'

'Actually, yes. But there's something else. Bigger. Nicer. Quite a bit nicer. But someone's after it.'

'Offer more money. You've got the money, darling, use it. If you want it, go after it!'

'This buyer – he got in first. I can't do that.'

'Don't be crazy, honey! If it were an auction you'd think nothing of trying to outbid a rival.'

'Yes, but it's not an auction. And he's a painter.'

'I bet if you'd got in first he'd outbid you. Men are like that.'

Meg noted the cynicism. But, remembering Peter Snow's ploys yesterday, she thought Miranda was probably right.

'Perhaps I won't give up on it just yet,' she said.

'Good for you! Remember I shall be spending *some* time with you! I'd prefer not to sleep in a bag on the floor of a cellar!'

Meg tried to tell Miranda that the Old Shop wasn't like that, but Miranda said quickly, 'She's just gone out. Honestly Meg, she accepts that I've got Lady Windermere – after all she's Mrs Erlynne which is a great part – but she keeps needling me about it!'

It was then Meg said anxiously, 'Listen, Miranda. Be careful with Aunt Maggie's money, won't you?'

There was a brief silence then Miranda said, 'What on earth d'you mean?'

'Well. You know. The Arbitrary are always short of cash and they must know you have it—'

'Hang on there, Meg!' Miranda's voice had sharpened angrily. 'First of all, it's not Aunt Maggie's money now, is it? It's yours and it's mine. I'm not telling you what to do with yours, am I?'

'Sorry. Sorry, Sis. I didn't think what I was saying.'

'No. Well. I don't like the implication that I wouldn't be Lady Windermere if I didn't have the cash. That's all.'

The receiver clicked in Meg's ear. She removed it and stared disbelievingly at it. Had she implied that Miranda was buying herself good parts? Surely not.

Carefully she hung the phone on its hook.

She would not let herself think. Instead she went to the desk in the foyer for more pennies for the phone and got through to the agent.

'I'm very interested in that cottage in Fish Street.' She was about to explain that she had seen round it, then decided to keep quiet about that.

The agent made encouraging noises and she went on, 'As you offered to take me round, do I gather it is definitely on the market?'

'Certainly. I have an offer but nothing in writing. If you could name a better price—'

'How much have you been offered?'

'Two and a half thousand.' The agent's voice was alert with interest.

She said, 'Yes. I think I can make it two thousand seven fifty.'

He was thrilled. 'By all means, Miss Patch. And that is a firm offer?'

It was over a thousand pounds more than the Old Shop and still a lot of work to do to make it habitable, but she nodded at the flock wallpaper. 'Yes. It's exactly what I want.'

'Right. The next step is for your solicitor to get in touch with me. Have you got a solicitor in Penzance?'

'No. We have a family solicitor in Plymouth.'

'Ah. I was hoping we could have started the ball rolling immediately. You could change to a local firm, you know.'

'I'll stick with my old one.'

'Fine. Fine. As soon as he has instituted searches and so on . . .'

He said more but she hardly listened. She deliberately forgot Miranda in a surge of nervous excitement. She was getting the house she wanted, but she was out-bidding someone she admired very much. However, he had almost tricked her out of the house in the first place, so, just as Miranda had said, she was practically entitled to put in another bid.

She spent the rest of the afternoon as close to the fire in the lounge as she could get, doing sums on a piece of paper. She would need six or seven thousand pounds of her inheritance to live on while she was establishing herself as a painter . . . if she ever did. If she invested that wisely it should bring in £700 each year which was ample. How much was that a week? She did tortuous sums. Probably about £14. Rates were . . . she didn't know what the rates were. Coal, gas, electricity . . . she didn't know about those either. She could manage on a fiver a week for food. But canvas and paint were expensive.

It was dark when she decided to take a walk to the top of the cliff and look down on the sea. Her head throbbed, the excitement had gone but the nervousness remained. She would walk it off, come back to dinner and have an early night.

Arthur was doing a stint on the desk as she went past. He looked tired but perfectly normal. He shivered dramatically as he glanced at the window.

'Raining cats and dogs,' he observed. 'There's a fire in the lounge. I could bring you some tea.'

She explained that she had been in front of the fire all afternoon and needed fresh air, but as she pulled up the hood on her still-wet anorak she had to admit the great outdoors lacked attraction that night. She picked her way carefully over the road and stood by the sea rail, staring down at the black water filling up the harbour. And after a few minutes the rain, cold and unwelcome at first, seemed softer against her skin. She lifted her face and let it fall on her closed eyes, then licked it from her mouth. Miranda had done that as a small girl. She remembered her shrill voice calling to Meg, 'Taste the rain – taste it!' And she had never done so. Until now.

She walked through the town, feeling the unease of

her foolish quarrel with Miranda like a weight on her shoulders. She ducked under the canopy of the town hall, rubbed a hand over her wet face and stared through the rain at the line of masthead lights trailing from harbour to open sea. When she was small she had always thought the link between herself and her sister was wonderful. She had never felt lonely, not even when they were separated and she had gone to the hostel in Higher Compton. Miranda had felt the same way; they had talked about it often. But then had come that vicarious yet internal sharing; the awfulness of Miranda sleeping with a man for money. And suddenly the link had become a chain and something to be feared. Meg understood only too well how Miranda felt about it.

She blinked away more rain, tightened the drawstring on her hood and thought of Aunt Maggie and her enormous common sense. Dear Aunt Maggie. She had not tried to comfort the girls that day of their parents' funeral. She had said, 'When things get tricky, all you can do is get on with the next job. So, if you're hungry, tuck in.'

Meg smiled a mental salute to her aunt and stepped out into the rain.

She was on Sunday Street, one level above Fish Street, and had to pass the back of the house to get to the next level. She smiled again into the rain; it was going to be such fun renovating that big cottage and making it into a home and then letting her roots grow down through the living rock. She glanced to her left at the retaining wall of the back courtyard and was surprised to see the skylights glowing in the near-darkness. Was Peter Snow looking around for the last time or something? She went to the wall and heaved herself on tiptoe to see over it. Of course he did not yet know that she was buying the house, so probably thought he was entitled to be there. She felt a pang of guilt, then hardened her heart. The agent had offered her the place; she had not even known anyone else was interested.

She dropped back down on her heels. The skylights were being sluiced by rain and were probably frosted glass anyway. She could see nothing inside. She turned and went on along the winding roads until she passed the dead end to Prospect Villa and tramped on to the very top of the cliff. Here the tiny road connected with another; left for Lannah, right for Penzance. She crossed it and climbed on to the Cornish stone hedge. And there it was beneath her, almost twee in its miniature prettiness, a picture she had to make in her mind from the wavering pricks of light coming through the rain. She smiled yet again; it was like the pictures in their old nursery books supplied so regularly by Aunt Maggie. 'Find the picture by joining the dots.' How she had loved that. The slow discovery of an image that had been there all the time. And how they had bored Miranda!

In a kind of compensatory gesture she lifted her head again and tasted the rain, then jumped down and began to walk back gingerly. In the two-mile clamber to get here she had met not a soul and it occurred to her that if she fell and twisted an ankle she would have to stay put until Arthur missed her at dinner and organized some kind of a search party. Even the thought of her own embarrassment was enough to make her cringe inside her anorak. She almost crept down to the unmade road to Prospect Villa, pausing there for breath and a glance around her. It was then that she saw the light inside the house. The house had been obviously empty for ages when she'd peered through the windows the day before yesterday, so whoever was there was unofficial, to say the least. She hesitated, wondering whether she should investigate, then decided that discretion was definitely the better part of valour in this case. She would call into the police station next to the town hall. And even as she made that decision, the light went out.

She half-convinced herself it was a reflection from the Land's End lighthouse, except that the beam would not hit that particular window. But it could be the lights of a car, or a boat. Or anything. She decided against the police station and continued the steep descent with less care than before. Imagination told her that she was being followed, common sense said that was nonsense. Nevertheless it was a relief to reach Sunday Street and lamps shining on the wet cobbles and door knockers within easy reach at every few steps. She took another break; she was hot. She undid the drawstring of her hood, pushed it back and lifted her hair to let the air get to her neck. Then she crossed the road and hoisted herself up by the wall to look down on the skylights of Fish Cottage. They were dark this time. She leaned further over the wall. The tiny yard was visible in the nearest street light; four wooden half-casks were lined up beneath the kitchen window. She stared at them. They were full of earth. Were they planted with bulbs for next spring? Had he done them? Was he staking some kind of claim to the place?

The hand on the small of her back was not exactly rough but it was not gentle either. She practically fell off the wall, heart hammering frantically, scream only just stifled. It was, of course, Peter Snow again.

She looked at him and drew a shuddering breath to tell him what she thought of men who crept up on girls in the pitch dark. But she was too late.

'Not content with gazumping tactics, you decide to trail me all over the bloody town!' His face, which she remembered as tanned, was white in the lamplight and distinctly furious.

He went on, 'What the hell d'you think you're doing? You told me earlier that you weren't interested in Fish Cottage. Then, this afternoon, when I went into Penzance with my sodding solicitor, it was to be informed that you had topped my offer! What d'you think this is, some kind of bloody auction?'

Her breath was taken away. She had not heard so many swearwords in one sentence since the old days of Amy and Terence. And yes, she had thought it was like an auction.

She bleated, 'I didn't say I wasn't interested in the house—'

'You didn't even want to see the blasted bedrooms, for God's sake! I was all set to outbid you, but my solicitor told me to hold my horses. He thinks what you are doing is illegal. So don't think you've won, will you? I've got a bed in there and I'm planting shrubs and going into the business of squatters' rights!'

Still she couldn't speak. It was all so awful. She had thought he might be disappointed; very disappointed. But she had not thought he would be so angry and she had certainly not imagined she was doing anything dishonest.

Her silence seemed to madden him further. 'Well? Haven't you got any feeble excuses?'

'No. Of course not. I . . . Mr Allen said . . . I thought . . . How can it be illegal?'

'Don't know. It's bad practice anyway and Allen ought to be shot at dawn for agreeing to it. I made an offer and it was accepted. You led me to believe you didn't want the place. That should have been that.'

She stood there, much as she had stood before Mrs Hitler so long ago. She knew exactly what she should do. Protest her innocence, talk about an open market, upbraid him for nearly frightening her to death. Miranda would have done all those things. She said not a word.

It seemed to take the wind out of his sails. He breathed heavily, then spoke with renewed violence as if he'd had to wind himself up.

'I told you the bloody place was practically uninhabitable. I should have guessed you were after it when you took that on the chin. But you looked so damned innocent, all eyes and hair, I didn't dream you were able to pour money into the place!'

At last she spoke. 'I can't. It just seemed . . . perfect.'

Another pause. Then he said, 'Well, it is for me. But it's hopeless for a holiday cottage. Too much upkeep – it needs someone to live in it all the time.'

'Yes. I know.'

'You mean . . . you intend to live here?'

'Yes.'

He changed tactics, his voice became persuasive. 'It's a hell-hole through the winter. Oh, OK, I know this misty rain . . . probably seems romantic to you now. But day in and day out. The locals aren't friendly, you know. By February you'd be in hospital.'

She said, 'I lived here when I was a child. I know what it's like.'

'Ah. You've got friends locally. I see.'

'No. Actually Mrs Hitler is dead and we never made friends. We had each other.'

'We?'

'My sister and I. I was only five when we left.'

'Mrs Hitler?'

'She was called that. She took in evacuees.'

He seemed to have slowed right down. His face changed shape; he might have smiled.

She said quickly, 'Look. I'm sorry about this. I'll withdraw my offer, of course. I'd better go. They'll wonder where I am.'

'You're staying here – in Keele?'

'At the Coastguards.'

There was another pause and she said, 'Goodnight then, Mr Snow.' And turned to go.

He moved alongside and said abruptly, 'I'll walk you back. You shouldn't really clamber right up to the top of the cliff in weather like this. You could fall and no-one would hear you.'

They came to the end of Sunday Street and took the steps down to Fish Street.

She said, 'It was you in Prospect Villa. And you followed me down.'

'Yes.' He did not apologize.

'I wondered . . . I thought it might be reflected light. Imagination.'

'I frightened you. I thought I might. Sorry.'

They came out on to the harbour. It seemed light here after the small streets. She glanced at his face and saw she had been wrong about the smile or any kind of lightening. He looked grim.

He said, 'I know. It was a sadistic thing to do. I was angry. I saw you peering into the cottage. And that shit, Allen, had given me the keys of Prospect Villa. He can't get rid of it, that's obvious. Anyway, I followed you up as far as the road that leads to it, guessed you were going for a walk, and went to see it. It was chance I left just as you were coming back down. Sorry.'

Suddenly, inexplicably, she smiled. 'That's twice you've apologized. Did it hurt?'

And just as suddenly, his face creased and shortened and he snorted a laugh and said, 'Yes!'

It was ridiculous that they both thought it was so funny. They hung on to the harbour railing laughing helplessly, and it was as if all the ill-feeling washed away with the rain and ran into the harbour.

At last he said, 'You're getting soaked. You should

130

have kept your hood up. You looked like a medieval nun going up the hill just now.'

She put up a hand. Her hair was sleek to her head on top, rats' tails from the clasp at her neck. It was glorious not to care. She said, 'We used to love the rain. My sister used to drink it. Like this.' She lifted her face to show him and when she looked at him again there was no responsive smile any more. He was still, watching her.

He said, 'I'd like to paint you, actually. I've never seen anyone so . . . empty . . . before.'

She was astonished and he said quickly, 'I don't mean empty-headed. I mean . . . waiting. For something to come into . . . oh God, I'm making it worse.'

Her astonishment turned into a kind of bewildered acceptance and she shook her head slowly. 'No. You're right. I have been waiting. For ages. But I think . . . things . . . are starting now.' She wanted so much to explain. She added helplessly, 'I am there. Somewhere.'

He said, 'I know. I'd find you when I painted you.'

She swallowed the rest of the rain. 'Like joining the dots.'

'What do you mean?'

'Nothing. Childish things. I must go.'

'I feel awful now. About the cottage.'

'Oh, please don't. I wasn't going to bother to look at it even! I'd viewed the Old Shop and it suited me, and then I saw Fish Cottage and fell for it.'

'So you've got somewhere else?'

'Yes. Let me show you – come on—'

Without thinking she seized the sleeve of his duffle coat and drew him back along the harbour. And with natural companionship, he tucked her hand over his elbow and came with her. She lengthened her stride to match his; there had never been an 'outside' friend like this, but it seemed perfectly natural to hold his arm and match her steps to his.

She hauled him to a stop in front of the tiny shopfront. 'This is it. I'm going to leave the window and make that into a big living room. And have the attic converted into a studio.'

He gripped her arm. 'My God. You're an artist! That's what it is, of course! I knew there was an affinity! How could I have been so dim? What do you do? Paint? Clay? Wood?'

'Paint.' She was shy. He was a 'proper' artist and she hadn't even started.

'What's your name?'

'Margaret Patch. You won't have heard of me. I finished college last summer.'

He was full of enormous enthusiasm. 'I'll help you with the attic! It will make me feel less . . . you know.'

'I'd like that. D'you mean it?'

'Of course. We'll talk about it. Tomorrow. It will be great! And you can come and help me sort out Fish Cottage.' He shed several years and became a schoolboy. 'I say, this is fun!' He paused and looked closely at her. 'It is, isn't it? You're not too fed up about—'

'No. It's just that . . .'

'What?'

But she couldn't very well say 'I've never had a friend before.' So she laughed again and shook her head. 'Cornish workmen. Expense. That kind of thing.'

'I know. But I've been working in Newlyn for ages now and there are some good blokes there who know just what a painter needs. We'll see them together.'

She felt a surge of pure joy. This was what it meant to look outside her twinship at other people. Let someone in. Someone other than Miranda. Perhaps it would not have happened if she had not alienated Miranda.

Perhaps there would have been no room for anyone else.

She was still smiling when she went into the Coast-guards again. Dripping wet, boots muddied almost to the top, but smiling.

It was as if the weather was in the same mood. Next morning the harbour rails were covered with rime and the sun came out of the sea beyond St Michael's Mount, pale but determined. Before Meg had finished her breakfast Peter Snow appeared in the doorway, his duffle coat still heavily wet but a woollen hat and gloves giving him a winter-sports look.

'Sorry. I forgot you'd have a proper hotel breakfast.' But he did not retreat into the foyer and Arthur was not yet around to suggest he did.

Meg said, 'Sit down. Have some toast. I'll get them to fetch another cup.'

He beamed and repeated last night's words. 'I say. This is fun, isn't it?'

She nodded, grinning foolishly. 'The meals here are very good. Mr Bowering has someone in from the village and she doesn't try to be clever. Just good.'

He buttered toast industriously and quoted, ' "Be good, sweet maid, and let who can be clever." ' He folded the triangular toast in half, put it all into his mouth and spoke through it. 'A bit of Shakespeare I believe.'

Meg wanted terribly to giggle. 'Charles Kingsley.'

He swallowed with difficulty then narrowed his eyes. 'I didn't have you down as a bluestocking, Miss Patch.'

She could no longer hold back her laughter. 'I'm no bluestocking! Amy and Terence Patch – my parents – ran a travelling theatre group. Shakespeare for Schools. That sort of thing.'

'God. I remember a group like that coming to my

school in Exeter. They were terrible. I forget what they called themselves . . .'

'The Wessex Players?'

'The Wessex Players! That's it!' He stopped buttering and folding another piece of toast and looked at her with sudden apprehension. 'Not . . . don't tell me . . . Amy and whatsit—'

'Amy and Terence. My parents. They were the Wessex Players. With various hangers-on.'

'Oh, Margaret! I'm so sorry. Promise you won't ever tell them what I said.'

'They wouldn't have minded. They totally ignored adverse criticism. They thought what they were doing was a sort of calling.' She pushed across the marmalade. 'I couldn't tell them anyway. They died ages ago.' She smiled reassuringly. 'It's all right. Don't look like that. Miranda and I were down here till we were five – only saw them now and then. Then we lived with our Aunt Maggie and Uncle Cedric. Terence's older sister and brother.' She looked past Peter Snow's head. 'That was lovely. While it lasted. Then they died and it was awful for ages. In fact till I decided to come down here.'

He did not put the toast in his mouth this time. He was staring at her as if fascinated. At last he sighed sharply. 'God, I really do feel rotten. You must have Fish Cottage, Margaret. I mean it. I can go anywhere and do my lousy painting. But it's important for you to . . . to . . .'

'Put down roots.' Her smile was back, wide and warm. 'I couldn't really afford Fish Cottage, you know. The Old Shop is ideal. I don't need all those rooms.' She nodded at his hand. 'Eat your toast and have some tea in my cup. You can drink from the other side.' She poured and pushed the cup and saucer at him. 'You can do me a favour if you would, though.'

'Anything. You know that. We're friends already. Didn't I know your parents before you were born?'

She felt warm all through, glowing, happy.

'Not before I was *born*! Anyway . . . will you come with me to the hateful Mr Allen? Get the cottages sorted out once and for all?'

He munched contentedly. 'I wanted to suggest it. But it sounded as if I was coercing you into . . .' he held up his hand as she began to protest. 'Of course we'll go together. Then we'll come home via Newlyn and see a chap I know who does loft conversions for a song. Then we'll have some lunch and go round both houses again.' He took a swig of tea and added, 'And Margaret, please try to call me Peter.'

She said breathlessly, 'I'm known as Meg, actually.' She laughed. 'Can you spare the time? I mean – your work—'

He said, 'We can work together.'

He noted her startled look and said, 'Friends do things together, you know, Meg. Sometimes they do everything together!'

'Do they?' She spoke with obviously genuine surprise and he laughed as if she'd said something really funny.

The weather lasted exhilaratingly until mid-afternoon, then it became iron cold as the daylight faded. They got the ubiquitous George Allen off their list immediately, and were both amused by his blandness which refused to recognize any kind of sharp practice or take any kind of blame.

He saw them to the door, beaming happily. 'So glad to have been of service to you both!' he said, reaching for Peter's hand, then thinking better of it. 'May you be happy in your houses.'

As they swung down Market Jew street, Meg said helplessly, 'Perhaps he isn't such a bad chap after all. He's fixed us up all right in the end. And I suppose it was up to him to get as much money as possible for his client.'

Peter was less forgiving. 'He doesn't give a damn about any of his clients. It's his commission he's thinking of.' He took her arm as he had done last night. 'Are you sure? Absolutely certain sure? About the Old Shop?'

'Yes. Certainly I am.' She remembered the large rooms of Fish Cottage. 'I can't think what possessed me, wanting such a big place. I'd have rattled around it like a pea in a drum. Even when Miranda came it would have been too big.' She glanced at him anxiously. 'Will you be able to afford to heat it properly? It could do with a good Aga in the fish cellar and central heating running off it.'

He was delighted. 'That's the sort of practical advice I need, Meg! I could enlarge that cellar window and eat down there. Sleep too. And if I've got pipes running up to the attic I won't be too cold there either!'

She asked again, 'Can you afford it? It will cost a lot of money. I was doing some sums – when I thought I was going to live there. And I think it would have used up all my money.'

'Oh, Meg . . .' He gripped her arm against his smock. 'I wish we could have shared it.' He brightened suddenly. 'What am I saying? Why can't we? Dammitall, let's buy the house between us, Meg! We can share the studio – share everything – it's big enough! What do you say?'

She did not take him seriously but she answered straightly just in case. 'No!' Then she looked up and saw the dark face drop with disappointment. 'Don't be silly, Peter. We're individuals. I couldn't work with anyone, let alone someone who has already made a name for himself! And you must have been planning to have people to stay—'

'I was. But I wouldn't if you didn't want me to!'

'You see? Already you're starting to limit your plans.' She shook her head decisively. 'I can't believe you're that serious, Peter. But don't think about it any more. You – you're so bull-headed. You rush into things. It's all right with me, but you should be careful with other people.'

He pulled her round to the railing that guarded the high pavement from the road. 'Oh, Meg! I love it when you button up your mouth and give me your granny-advice!' He stopped laughing and looked over the tops of the shops on the other side of the road. 'Meg . . . if I hadn't gone into things bull-headed I wouldn't now have you for a friend. Would I?'

'I don't see why not.' She felt herself pulling away from him mentally. 'No doubt we would have met before you actually got me into a court of law—'

'And weeks would have passed. Time would have been wasted.' He transferred his gaze to her and sighed. 'I'm much older than you. I can't afford to waste my time.'

She met his brown eyes and relaxed suddenly. 'Oh, you – you – charlatan! You *actor*!'

They were both laughing again. He suggested coffee at a place he knew in Chapel Street. It turned out to be the Admiral Benbow where everyone knew him and accepted her as his 'friend'.

'My friend, Meg,' he said largely to the bar staff and a small knot of men who had arrived at opening time. 'We'll have a pot of strong coffee in the lounge please, Bill.' He grinned, they all grinned back. Meg wondered if it was one of those male conspiracies dealt with in magazines and pastoral-care talks by her old housemother. But he had said 'friend'. Always he had talked of 'friendship'.

Afterwards they took the bus to Newlyn and went into the little gallery on the front. She discovered two of his pictures with audible cries of recognition.

'This one – the man who took us for portraiture had a print of this! He was fascinated by the way your figures emerged from darkness. Sort of loomed out of the frame.'

He laughed but was pleased. 'They're not portraits as such. I wanted to get back to Stanhope Forbes – that school. That man there – ' he pointed at the picture – 'was climbing out of a dinghy – down there by the steps. It was about four years ago. He suddenly emerged from the darkness just like that. He'd been there all the time . . . oh you know, I can't explain.'

She nodded. 'Like the dots.'

'Tell me about the dots for Pete's sake.'

She told him and he didn't laugh. 'Yes. Like that. I did a series of girls looking over their shoulders. Their faces had been invisible behind their hair. Then something caught their attention and they looked round. Amazing.'

'What are you doing now?'

They came out into the crisp air again and walked down the steps.

'People. People about their business – like Forbes.' He led her over the road to the row of eighteenth-century villas facing the sea. 'My studio is up here. Come and see.'

He unlocked one of the doors and picked his way past a bicycle and a baby's pram. 'They let out the attics all along here. Some of them allow you to sleep in them too. Not Mrs Pascoe.' He turned on the stairs and winked, nodding his head into the depths beyond the passage.

A raucous voice responded immediately. 'Got three kids of me own! Can't do with fosterin' another!'

He laughed. 'Just taking a fellow painter up to see my stuff,' he called.

'No hanky-panky, mind!' she yelled back.

He lifted his brows at Meg. 'How did you know she was female?' he shouted curiously.

'What other kind are there?'

He laughed good-temperedly and without embarrassment, and continued up another two flights of stairs. And Meg followed.

The studio was enormous but at least two-thirds of its area was too low for more than storage space. It was used to the full; Meg estimated that there were over a hundred canvases stacked there. In the higher area beneath the dormer, he had his easel and a trestle table cluttered with pots, brushes, palettes. The floor was bare boards, the ceiling – incredibly – bare rafters with the slates lying precariously on laths that looked like firewood. The roof supports were enormous lumps of timber peppered with wormholes, sprouting out of the floor at all angles and places. And everywhere there was dust; on the bare board flooring, hanging from the rafters and laths, over all the canvases.

Peter went to the easel and removed a swathe of cheesecloth.

'This is the latest. I haven't told her but it's actually Mrs Pascoe coming out of her frying pan!'

'What?'

'Honestly. When she cooks it's always in a frying pan. And she gets right down over it to see through the smoke. Then she looks up. Like this.'

Greasy apple cheeks were highlighted beneath small deep-set eyes. Hair, damp with sweat, curled over unexpectedly small neat ears.

He said lovingly, 'Notice the ears. And the chin – sorry, chins – are so – so vulnerable.'

She said, 'It reminds me of Hals. Somehow.'

He was enormously flattered. 'Really? I know the one you're thinking of. The gypsy girl. Yes, Mrs Pascoe has something of the gypsy in her.' He covered the picture again. 'Let me show you some of my abstracts. D'you like abstract painting?'

'Some of it.' But she watched him as he displayed each canvas. She wondered about him. And what he meant by friendship. And what she meant by it too. When he straightened and cracked his head on one of the supports, she longed to soothe the incipient lump with her fingers.

He said, 'Don't worry. I'm probably concussed. But for God's sake don't you worry!'

And she could laugh again. That was what friendship must be.

They were eating bread and cheese on the heights above Keyhole when the weather began to change imperceptibly. Meg felt her ungloved fingers stiffening and blew on them as she bit into her bread.

Peter nodded. 'I'm numbing too.' He looked at his watch. 'Half-past two. We'll walk back down to your pub after this and call it a day. Tomorrow we'll see the chap about the loft conversion. How's that?'

'Fine.' She was grateful. She felt she had been at a party for the past six hours and longed to be alone. Obviously this friendship business had its limits for him too, and she was grateful for that. Perhaps he was not quite so precipitous as she'd thought.

She said, 'I'll phone Bracknell too. I'd like to do that today.'

'Bracknell?'

'The solicitor who dealt with Cedric's stuff.'

'I want to hear more about Cedric. And Amy and Co. And your sister. I want to know all about you.'

She did not mind the odd anecdote, but she could not tell him about Cedric. Nor Miranda.

She said, 'There's no more to know. I'm what you see. I've done my training and I want to make a home. I don't want to be judged by my background.' She smiled to take the harshness out of her words. 'I want to be judged for myself, Peter.'

'OK. OK.' He tipped up the wine bottle they had shared. It was empty. He levelled it at her and looked through it as if it were a telescope.

'I shall paint texture when I paint you. I want to find a way of painting every strand of that apricot hair. And I want to get into those translucent eyes somehow.' He lowered the bottle. 'How do I do that if I'm not allowed to talk about you?'

'You talk *to* me, I suppose.' She shrugged. 'Come on. We shall get pneumonia sitting here. That's what my housemother used to say.'

'*House*mother? Hey, hey, what's this? You were wicked. You were in a reformatory—'

'Have you got digs or something? If Mrs Pascoe doesn't let you sleep in the studio where *do* you sleep?'

He turned his mouth down at the obvious change of subject, then said good-naturedly, 'I did have digs. I gave them up a week ago. Tell you the truth, I really have been squatting in Fish Cottage. George Allen would have had a fit if he'd known, wouldn't he? But I wanted the place to grow around me—'

'It'll be so cold – no heating.'

He stood up and pulled her to her feet and did not let go of her hands.

'Will you come and keep me warm?' he asked seriously.

If there had been any coquetry in his voice she would have walked away. But he asked her a straight question and she gave him a straight answer.

'No.'

'Fair enough. I agree it's beyond the call of friendship.'

He released her and began to giant-stride down the field. 'Don't worry. I connected the gas illegally. I light the stove and stick my feet in the oven!'

She did not know any longer whether he was serious. But she could not worry about this last, obviously dangerous, ploy. She was too worried about whether she had just evaded a much more dangerous situation. Or whether he had been asking her to cook him a meal, or light a fire.

The air was so cold it hurt her nostrils and lungs. But she didn't care about that either. She felt she was establishing something. Exploring something important. The meaning of friendship? He must know now that she wasn't like the other girls he took into the Admiral Benbow or upstairs to see his paintings. She was a true . . . friend.

Seven

Everything went well after that first day. Peter did not come with her to see Mr Bracknell in Plymouth. The old man was cautiously delighted that she was 'settling down' and very encouraging about the Old Shop.

'We'll have to wait and hear what the surveyor says and what the searches bring forth, but situated right on the harbour like that . . .'

'There was another one – bigger. But someone else got there first.'

'If it was bigger it was more expensive. You have to consider reselling prospects, my dear. Smaller, cheaper properties move very much more quickly.'

She smiled. 'I think I'm there for life. Especially now that I've made a friend.' The insouciant phrase had slipped out and she blushed.

'Ah. A special friend?' Mr Bracknell looked away from her and tried not to sound coy.

'*Just* a friend. An artist. You may have heard of him. Peter Snow.'

Mr Bracknell managed to watch her reflection in the glass-fronted bookcase.

'I think I have. One of the Newlyn bunch?'

She was surprised. 'I didn't realize you were interested in painting.'

'I never was. But since . . . I know quite a lot about the theatre too.' He turned and looked directly at her, smiling. 'It's good for me to take on fresh interests in my old age, Meg. I think your aunt would be pleased.'

'Yes. Of course.' Meg was puzzled and said more than she'd intended. 'Peter is very good. Some of his stuff is quite outstanding.'

Mr Bracknell nodded. 'Has Miranda met him?'

'No. Miranda isn't keen on Keele at all.' Meg did not want to remember the quarrel; she had heard nothing of Miranda since. 'Anyway she's busy with the rehearsals for *Lady Windermere*.'

'Quite.' Mr Bracknell was delighted. Meg needed a little space to develop this friendship of hers. Miranda would have put the kibosh on it: he would have taken a bet on that. He doodled a note on his blotter to remind him to fend Miranda off for a while. Perhaps a call to the landlord of the Coastguards requesting a spot of privacy for Meg?

'What is this hotel like – where you're staying?' he asked Meg as he poured the coffee brought by his secretary.

'Very nice. Homely. Warm. Mr Bowering is quite old, and . . .' Meg laughed '. . . most attentive!'

'In other words he has taken you well and truly under his wing?' How could he not? It was so obvious to Charles Bracknell that Meg needed a wing.

'I suppose so. Anyway he is really helpful.'

'Jolly good. Pity you didn't bring Mr – er – Snow with you. I'd have been most interested to meet him.'

But she was glad she hadn't. Mr Bracknell might not be their guardian but he was the nearest thing to it, and Peter would have sensed that and taken it as some kind of . . . official acceptance. Friendship, as she understood it, was absolutely informal.

After that first day, Peter seemed to know that she needed to make a new start; he never asked again about her reference to a housemother. When she said how enormous and unfriendly Plymouth had seemed to her, he nodded. 'It's the same with big cities everywhere. Except Florence.' He smiled. 'We'll go to Florence one day, Meg.' Then before she could express doubts about that he went on quickly, 'I want to be a part of your new life. Not your old. Nothing to do with your old life.'

She glanced at him and saw him watching her again. Artists did that, of course; but it was peculiarly unnerving at times.

She said, 'Is that why you did not want to come to Plymouth with me?'

'That was why I didn't come. I wanted to come very much.'

She met his eyes properly and with surprise. 'Why?'

'I want to find out about you. All about you. So that this portrait can mirror everything.' He smiled. 'You're a mystery, you see.'

She was still surprised. 'I'm not. Not at all, Peter.' She was half laughing in protest. 'You know about me – there's nothing else. My sister and I were boarded out with Mrs Hitler down here and in one way it was harsh, in another way it was idyllic. Then we lived with our uncle and aunt. Then they died and we were boarded out again. Then I finished training and inherited my half of their money and came down here. That's all. No mystery, I do assure you.'

He said sombrely, 'Everyone is a mystery. Everyone lives inside their heads – a life quite apart from the outside events. Sometimes the outside events are reflections of the inner life. That's why we tell each other about what happens to us. We lay a trail of clues.'

'Oh, Peter!' She laughed again. 'How complicated you make things sometimes!'

'That's because they generally are complicated.' He

smiled suddenly. 'It's all right. I don't want to pry and become part of whatever makes you unhappy—'

'For the millionth time, I am *not* unhappy!'

'But there's something – something you don't even recognize – that has made you this woman of mystery!' He was laughing now, teasing her. 'I feel sometimes as if there is only half a person behind those transparent eyes of yours.'

She was suddenly shocked. Of course he was right. She was half of a pair. Nothing could change that. Even if the strange telepathy between herself and Miranda had gone, nothing could change that.

It occurred to her, long after their abortive conversation, that she had never told him that her sister was also her twin.

He began the portrait.

He was still squatting in Fish Cottage while all the legalities were arranged, and Meg joined him for an hour each morning when the light was at its best. She was used to posing – they had taken it in turns at college – but she was still grateful that he preferred her to read a book or even knit. She sat on a stool under one of the skylights, the grey winter light encapsulating her; beyond, the rafters and tiles blended into the dark. He sketched quickly, roughly, and the third day blocked in the canvas with a smoky brown, a cobweb here and there, an uneven slate, the darker line of a beam. He did not work for long; immediately the light shifted, he would clean his brushes meticulously and talk about where they would eat their midday meal.

He told her about himself, where he had gone to school, the Cornish holidays with his parents when he had known that he wanted to paint. He spoke of his brother who was – of all things – an accountant. And he told her briefly about his parents' divorce and how it had split the family in two.

One day he left the easel and moved towards her slowly, looking at her from all angles.

'Stay still . . . don't move a muscle,' he ordered when she turned with him. 'I need to see the hair loose.' He reached out a hand and undid the clasp of the old-fashioned slide that nipped her hair into her neck. Then he lifted the hair from both sides and let it fall around her face.

She wanted to run and hide. Uncle Cedric had always played with their hair, smoothing it, brushing it, even pulling it quite hard. Somehow she stayed still. This man was an artist, he needed to 'see' his model in a particular way. Even when he pushed it back behind her ears and cupped her face, she stayed still.

Suddenly he said, 'No. Not yet. Nothing there yet.' And went back to the easel.

She made no comment at all. She knew her pale skin was bright red. But he did not seem to notice that.

They walked a great deal, striding over the brown-brackened headlands and down into neighbouring coves. It was the time she liked best, when an unspoken companionship grew between them.

One day, he wanted to go to St Ives to see a retrospective exhibition of someone called Gerald Scaife who had died some years before. She thought they might take the bus, or the train. But they walked over the hump of moors that separated south from north coast, along footpaths which were probably invisible when the fern was high in the summer, ignoring the easy route from Halsetown, striking across country again to Knills Monument and approaching the town from the other side.

It was midday, mild with the watery sun trying to break

through the cloud ceiling. He dragged her to Porthmeor Beach where the rollers pounded relentlessly up the shelving sand.

'Let's swim! We're hot and sweaty and we need to be part of the place – come on—' He began to struggle out of his smock.

'We haven't got costumes! Towels! Peter – we can't possibly—'

But he was down to his underpants, kicking off his socks, laughing like an excited schoolboy.

'Stop being such an old maid! Just for once in your life do something mad! Come *on*!'

He did not wait for her. She watched him pound down to the shallows, pause at the iron coldness of the water, turn to her helplessly. She began to roll up the legs of her jeans and move slowly towards the sea.

He yelled again, 'Come *on*!' and began to swim out strongly to where the waves were swelling while she gasped in the shallows. He came in fast, body-surfing right up to her and landing like a beached seal almost at her feet. He spluttered, stood up, wiping the sea from his eyes.

'Don't tell me you're scared of the water! You've changed!'

'I'm not afraid of the water! I haven't changed a bit!' she protested, wrapping her arms around herself. It was absolutely freezing and the sight of Peter in some very skimpy wet underpants embarrassed her more than she would admit to herself.

'Come on then!' He came towards her with outstretched hands and she squeaked and retreated.

'Get off – you're wet – Peter, stop it!'

She ran, splashing her clothes, suddenly annoyed with him for behaving so childishly. He caught her easily and tried to pull her in.

'Peter, I'm serious – stop it!'

He released her, surprised.

'You – serious! What's happened to the old spirit? What about the time you skidded down one of the mooring ropes?'

She didn't know what he was talking about for a moment, then remembered a time when Miranda had arrived home wet and secretive. He had heard about Miranda's escapade somehow and thought it applied to her!

'You've been listening to local gossip!'

'Oh no I haven't!' He began to advance again with mock menace. 'I don't need to listen to gossip!' He was laughing even as he grabbed her. He was horribly wet, horribly real and physical. All she wanted to do was to get away.

'You were fully clothed then – you might as well go in fully clothed now!'

He *had* heard about the time Miranda had fallen in and she had smuggled dry clothes out under Mrs Hitler's very nose.

She screamed in earnest. 'Peter! I've no more clothes – let me go – you idiot!'

And he stopped, turned her towards him and kissed her full on the lips.

She was horrified. She wanted to fight him off, but she remembered from Uncle Cedric days that if you stayed very still it would soon end and you would not lose face. She stood very still.

He released her and looked into her face.

'Meg?'

She said very brightly, 'Have you finished your swim? We could run across the beach. You'd dry off then.'

His hands dropped to his side. He said hopelessly, 'Meg – please come in with me. Please. It's . . . rather important.'

She laughed. 'It's also rather cold. I'm going for that run!'

She turned and began to jog along the wet sand towards Clodgy; she was not cold at all now, her body seemed to be on fire with something worse than embarrassment. A kind of terror. If he didn't join her it would mean that the kiss was serious. The friendship was over.

She turned at the rocks and almost sobbed with relief to see him loping towards her. She joined him; he grinned and she thought everything was all right.

'Nearly dry,' he panted as they jogged back towards the pile of his clothes.

'Jolly good!' She sounded like Joyce Grenfell.

A dog bounded up, jumping at his bare legs. Its owner panted along behind it, apologizing breathlessly. She was a middle-aged woman muffled in scarf and gloves.

'Sorry – heel, boy – so sorry!' She dragged the dog away. 'My goodness, you are brave. Wasn't it cold?'

And Meg caught Peter's glance and held her face still when he said, 'Not really. Quite warm at times.'

'You're marvellous, quite marvellous.'

They loped on. When they reached the pile of clothes he said seriously, 'Look. I'm sorry. Can't we forget it?'

She felt her face flame; she hadn't wanted him to be so open. She could not face talking about how she felt.

He was impatient now. 'For Pete's sake, Meg! This is 1965. I kissed you. What's there to forgive?'

She had her back to him, rolling her damp trousers over damp legs. She forced herself to say, 'Nothing. Of course – nothing. We'll forget it.'

In silence they walked through the tiny cobbled town to the gallery. He did not take her arm. She was suddenly so tired she hardly knew how to put one foot in front of the other. He was as fresh as a daisy.

The paintings were enormous and for her inexplicable.

She stood almost stunned before a twelve-foot-high oil-on-board entitled 'Headlands'. A black wavy line cut the picture in half diagonally; one half was green, the other blue.

Peter roamed restlessly from painting to painting and at last stood by her.

'What do you think?' he asked.

She shook her head. 'I can't – somehow – take them in.'

'Their size?' He said, 'You must see that they would be nothing in miniature.' He drew an audible breath as if tired at the idea of explaining it to her. 'He painted landscape. Landscape is large. He was large. He painted love. Love is large too.'

She was so tired, so bewildered, she thought she might weep.

He went on, 'It's too phallic for you, Meg. You can't bear it because it's talking of love – the love of land for sea and sea for land and man for woman and woman for man.'

She suddenly saw it: the headlands entering the sea and the sea allowing that. She did not move a muscle.

He said, 'When he painted this he knew his wife was dying. She had a brain tumour. Probably they weren't sleeping together any more. Not in that sense. It was a fierce, angry declaration of love.'

She felt her eyes fill. He was right, she could not bear it. The whole aggressive business of sexual love was too enormous for her.

He waited for a long moment, then asked, 'Aren't you going to say a word about it?'

She turned so that he could not see her face and spoke in a high voice that rose above her full throat.

'It is too painful. I don't want to think about it.'

She could feel his anger; it emanated from the whole of his body.

He snapped, 'Time we were going. It'll be dark before we get back. We don't want to get lost on those moors.'

She was appalled. She had fondly imagined a cosy tea somewhere and a Penzance bus along the A30. She thought of the huge hump of the moors in the winter twilight and shivered. People like Gerald Scaife had stood out there and seen the whole business of life in the lonely sea-bound land. He had found roots, unhappy ones, but roots. Her way was . . . domestic. Small, maybe petty in the eyes of some people, but it was her way.

She felt a streak of stubborn pride stiffen her spine. She knew Peter was waiting for her protest and she refused to make it. Beneath her jeans her legs were already salt-stiff from this morning's walk and their immersion in the sea, but she continued to turn almost casually on her heel and make for the gallery door.

'Yes. You're right. We'd better step it out,' she said.

He trailed behind her up Virgin Street and along the top of the cemetery to Ayr. Already lights were twinkling and the smell of soot from the chimneys intensified. They plodded slowly up the hill to Halsetown and took the first of the footpaths. And right on the crest of the spine between the two coasts, they both forgot their anger and stood together looking forward and back, amazed at the view of lights from St Michael's Mount on one side and St Ives Bay on the other.

He asked suddenly, 'What are you thinking?'

She glanced at him and smiled involuntarily. She loved him; it was the kind of love he could not understand but that was not his fault.

She said softly, 'It's like standing on a whale's back.'

He looked at the twin views again as if disappointed. Then he took her arm and they started to walk more

152

slowly, companionably, limping slightly. She said, 'What were *you* thinking?'

He paused, then sighed. 'The same as you, I suppose.'

They tramped down to Gulval and waited for the Newlyn bus and he added almost sadly, 'But Gerald Scaife would not have seen it like that.'

It was nearly midnight when she got into bed. And quite suddenly on the edge of sleep, it happened again. She was filled with Miranda's unhappiness. And more than that, bewilderment, anger, damaged pride. Something was happening to Miranda. She switched on the light and sat up in bed, wild-eyed, terrified. Her body was aching from the long trek, but this was a separate ache. Unbearable.

She slid out of bed, found her purse and went downstairs as quietly as she could. Slipperless and without a dressing gown she shivered in the hall while the operator connected her with Miss Pugh's in Exeter. She could hear the telephone ringing at the other end; she counted up to ten rings. They were in bed. Of course! It was the first night of *Lady Windermere*. Oh God. She'd forgotten about *Lady Windermere*. She should have telephoned, sent flowers. It had been a flop and it was all her fault.

And then a voice said anxiously, 'Hello—' and the operator said, 'You're through.' And Meg said, 'I'm so terribly sorry to worry you at this hour! Is Miranda there? This is her sister.'

And the voice said, 'Oh yes. Margaret, isn't it? Miss Pugh here. Miranda and Mr St Clare are having a late supper with the solicitor man.'

'Mr Bracknell?'

'Yes.'

'And she is all right?'

'She had a wonderful first night. It's good of you to phone. Wait a minute, this could be them now. Yes, it is—' the voice went away and mumbled some explanations. And Miranda's voice came crisply across the wires. 'Sorry about your cold, Meg. You missed a really good evening.'

'Cold?' Meg frowned. Then said, 'Are you all right? I had a feeling—'

'For goodness sake! I thought you'd given up that sort of thing!' Miranda laughed. 'I'm perfectly all right. It's you who is ill!'

'I . . .' Mr Bracknell must have lied for her. She said, 'I'm OK now. I'd better go. Just so long as you're—'

'I'm fine. I'll be down to see you at the end of this run.'

'Oh. That would be marvellous. Really marvellous.'

'Right. 'Night, then.' And the phone went dead.

Meg was exhausted the next day. Too tired to walk or even talk. She spent an hour in the afternoon sitting for Peter, her knitting idle on her lap. He stood before his easel, dabbing paint in what seemed to be an ineffectual manner. She stared into the darkness of the roof eaves and tried to think of things outside this friendship which had become so claustrophobic. Suddenly she saw that since she had known Peter, she had been out of touch with Miranda. And yesterday when the escapade into the sea at St Ives had escalated into intimacy, she had drawn far enough away from Peter to allow the essence of Miranda to return.

She continued to stare into the darkness of the roof, wondering if she could be imagining all this. Was it possible that the intensity of her friendship had pushed out the closeness she had always had with her sister? If so, then that intensity was over: she could think of nothing and no-one save Miranda. She longed to see her. She imagined her with her mass of hair on top of her head for her part in *Lady Windermere's Fan*. Miss Pugh had said the first night had been a triumph. If only she'd been there. She should have been there instead of gallivanting across Cornwall with Peter Snow.

Peter said abruptly, 'I've had it, Meg. I need to sleep. Sorry. I feel completely empty and useless.'

She was glad to be able to show genuine concern.

'It's so cold up here, Peter. I know you don't want to light any fires, but perhaps one of those oil convector heaters would be safe enough—'

'Sod the cold,' he interrupted rudely. 'It's nothing to do with the temperature of the studio! It's you. Cold. A cold fish.'

Her own chill disappeared on the instant; she felt a flush go from neck to face as she laid aside her knitting and began to struggle into her coat. He cleaned his brush and cursed because the turpentine bottle was empty.

She edged past him, turned to say goodbye and saw the picture. It had changed in that last hour. The face was still an indeterminate blur, but he had been painting her hair. She stood still, staring.

'Well?' He sounded unbearably sardonic. 'I suppose you hate it?'

She did not know what to say. The hair was as long as Rapunzel's, twice as bounteous, it looked as if he had painted every hair separately.

'It's not meant to be realistic,' he went on in the same tone. 'It's stylistic. Do you understand that word? Stylistic?'

She swallowed. 'Of course.'

'I can't get the face,' he went on. 'The owner won't let me see it. I refuse to paint the buttoned-up features she is showing me. But the hair . . . she can't do much about the hair, can she? When she let it loose that day . . . when I felt it . . . I knew she was hiding something marvellous. So I've given up on the face. This picture is going to be called "Hair". Like the musical running in London. Only not like that.'

She said in a low voice, 'Please don't, Peter.'

He seemed to slump. His brushes were lying in a fan shape on the paint-stained table he always used. He looked at them and said sadly, 'Don't you love me, Nutmeg?'

She could not believe it. She stared at him as if he had produced a knife. Nutmeg. The pet name Uncle Cedric had used.

She turned and went down the steep stairs to the bedroom landing, then on down into the living room, down again to the cellar which might one day house an Aga and be cosy and warm and impregnable. But not for her.

She almost ran back to the Coastguards Inn. It must have been obvious she was crying, but Arthur chose to put her wet face down to sea spray.

'Been standing on those rocks again, haven't you?' he asked jovially. 'Get changed and I'll bring you some tea in front of the fire. How's that?'

It was exactly right. That was the sort of person she was. Tea by the fire; safety.

Eight

Miranda did not know what to do next. The adage 'the show must go on' was deeply ingrained in her and she felt she had no choice but to stay with the Group until the two weeks of *Lady Windermere* were over. The telephone call from Meg was salt in the wound. It was obvious Meg had had no cold and Mr Bracknell had had to lie to cover her desertion. Miranda was absolutely determined that Meg must never know the truth about Brett.

Meanwhile she had never felt so alone in her life. Even in that first terrible foster home with the Brimmingtons she had not felt like this. Then she had been able to take some control of the awful situation, even if it had been by setting fire to her bed.

Now, not only was there nothing she could do about anything, she could not show her true feelings either. She considered talking to Olwen but could not quite descend to such depths of disloyalty to Brett.

The quality of her performance on stage changed. She saw parallels between herself and the foolish young Lady Windermere. She stopped overacting for the first time in her career and gave a subdued, frightened performance that made even Olwen congratulate her sincerely.

That would have pleased her at one time. Now it did not. She would not care if she never acted again. Her world was turned upside down; all her old ambitions were gone. She had no guidelines for the future.

If it had not been for Meg's indifference, she would have gone to Keyhole at the end of the following week and thrown in her lot with her sister. But apparently Meg was otherwise engaged. Miranda gave a wintry smile at her own thought. She probably was engaged. And knowing Meg it would all be so proper. He would be eminently suitable, have money of his own. And moreover be entirely heterosexual. That was a term she had just learned. She got a book out of the library and tried to understand Brett. And failed.

During that next week she read books, she thought about Oscar Wilde himself, she got into the skin of foolish Lady Windermere and she felt worse and worse. Unusually, she was sharing a bed with Jennifer, so could not even cry herself to sleep at night. Not that she would cry about Brett St Clare. Of that she was determined.

She spent Sunday as usual helping Miss Pugh. This carthorse of a woman was dearer to Miranda than anyone had been since Aunt Maggie, and the only thing that made Miranda regret having to leave the Group was the thought of also leaving Miss Pugh. She wished she could tell her everything but somehow Miss Pugh did not converse; she told anecdotes, she made statements; she did not encourage confidences.

So it was like a bolt from the blue when she paused in slapping some dough around an enormous pastryboard and said directly, 'Your perch will always be here. You know that, don't you?'

Miranda looked up from peeling a pile of Bramley apples. Her eyes were no longer blue; they stared at Miss Pugh with a peculiar drowned look that made the older woman cluck comfortingly.

'It's not the end of the world, you silly girl!' She turned the dough on to its other side with a slap that sent loose flour flying. 'You've still got your acting. And after you've had a nice rest with your sister, you'll see that. And you'll come back. And there – ' she jerked her chin towards the end of the table – 'there will be your perch. Ready and waiting.'

All Miranda could manage then was, 'Oh, Miss Pugh.'

Miss Pugh seized the rolling pin and attacked her dough. 'Cut the apples a mite smaller, will you, my dear? We'll get half a dozen pies out of this dough if I'm not mistaken.'

Miranda said, 'Oh, Miss Pugh.'

'An' you'll be a famous actress one day. Never fear. And that's what you really want, isn't it?'

Miranda chopped apples and thought about it. She shook her head sadly. 'I don't know what I want any more, Miss Pugh.'

'That's why you need to get away for a bit. Five years you bin with this lot. No break, no nothing. Get right away and look back at it and see it proper-like. For what it is.'

Miranda quoted something she – or Meg – had said ages ago, 'Making people believe lies.'

Miss Pugh cackled hideously. 'An' that's not easy!' she commented.

'No,' said Miranda, and sighed.

But that night she was conscious of an area of quietness around the core of pain. She lay very straight on the edge of the bed until Jennifer fell asleep. Then she slid carefully away from the sheets and padded barefoot to the window. She lifted the edge of the blind and stared out at a typical winter moon, small and harried by racing clouds. The river glinted to her left in the darkness but ahead, a fluorescent orange umbrella hung over the heart of the city from the street lights. Exeter was home to her now, she had never hankered after Plymouth, and Keyhole was just somewhere falling off the end of the country. She shivered at the thought of leaving Miss Pugh's and shivered more at the thought of the tiny cove in Cornwall. She had no wish to go down there and witness Meg's happiness. And, as if in contradiction of that, came the essence of Meg. Miranda stood by the window and felt Meg's being flow into her. She was transfixed by this sudden invasion of her mind. It had not happened to her before. It made a definite physical movement inside her head, then throbbed through the rest of her body. It was pain, strong enough to make her gasp and then stand rigidly, trying to control it. And then it ran from her. She felt it go through the soles of her feet. From head to toe she had been washed by Meg's pain. And after it had gone she stayed where she was, weak, shaking, understanding at last how Meg had felt during her sudden connections with her sister. It was not an experience to be courted; it was – literally – shattering.

After a while she got back into bed, trembling with cold and emotion. Jennifer groaned and rolled towards her and Miranda turned her back and let some warmth from her companion flow into her bones. She tried to think what could be happening to Meg. A long unhappiness; at least a week. Miranda thought back; yes, it had happened just after the supper party. That was when Miranda's own pain had doubled without her realizing it. And it must be to do with Meg's friendship with the artist . . . what had Meg called him? Peter something. Peter something was making Meg unhappy. All Miranda's stubborn pride vanished that night. She would be going to Keyhole, not for her own sake, but for her sister's.

The next day began the last week of *Lady Windermere*. Miranda did not know how she was going to get through it. The need to be with Meg was overwhelming; she almost forgot Brett's presence and went through that

Monday night automatically. Afterwards, at supper, she was able to tell the rest of them with perfect truth that she had to go to Cornwall the following Sunday morning, on the first possible train.

'My sister is in some kind of trouble,' she said briefly.

Olwen, who had always been fascinated by Miranda's twinship, said, 'I know your sister sometimes has sort of premonitions about you, Miranda. Is this the same kind of thing?'

Miranda nodded, surprised and thankful that her departure was going to be so readily accepted. Perhaps it was only Miss Pugh who realized what had happened to her.

She said, 'I intended to go down there soon anyway. Spend Christmas with her. But this is more urgent.'

'How interesting!' Olwen, bright-eyed after her success with Mrs Erlynne, seemed to have some leftover kinship with Miranda from their roles. She patted her hand. 'It must be a wonderful feeling. You don't really know what loneliness means, do you?'

'Well . . .' She did not want to enter into a discussion about being a twin, but somewhere Olwen was wrong. Perhaps it was simply that when she did cut herself off from Meg, the loneliness was more intense than normal?

Brett said, 'Leave her alone, Ollie. She's tired.'

Miranda glanced at him, something she rarely did any more. She saw that he too was tired; exhausted. She saw other things now; that he invariably sat opposite Oliver at the table where they could exchange smiling glances. She tried to whip up a scornful picture inside her head: they sat opposite each other so that they could play footsie under the table? But even as the idea formed it fell flat. She could accept that Brett had really loved her father; therefore she must accept that he really loved Oliver. She let her gaze slide sideways to the man she had hardly noticed all these years. Oliver Freres; always there. It was a kind of rhyme. It was sordid, horrible, unnatural. But it no longer broke her heart.

Brett said, 'Would you like to go tomorrow, Miranda? Jennifer could take on your role.'

It was another knife wound. They could do without her. But she grabbed at the chance anyway.

'Yes please,' she said very definitely.

Meg had cancelled all negotiations on the Old Shop and was packed and ready to leave Keyhole – probably for ever – by that Sunday. She had phoned Dora Penwith and though her old room was filled with two new foster children, Dora had offered her the small room downstairs which Matthew used as an office.

'I can put the folding bed in there.' Dora sounded almost enthusiastic and Meg realized that she had been missed. It was slightly warming. 'Matthew uses the room for about an hour in the afternoons. That's all. You're welcome to stay as long as you like, Margaret. As our guest, of course.'

Meg nearly said, 'My God!' but checked herself. She might not be paying any cash for the room but there would doubtless be payment in kind.

She said, 'Thanks so much, Dora. It will be temporary. Things haven't worked out down here and I need to think what I'll do next.'

'I'm sorry. But you mustn't sound so defeated, my dear. You've only been gone a month. It will take you longer than that to be independent, you know.'

Meg passed on that one; she had been independent ever since Miranda joined the Arbitrary.

'Actually, I want to get up to Exeter next week to see my sister in a play,' she temporized. 'So Plymouth will be a good halfway house.'

'How nice. Perhaps you could take our new girl with you, dear? She is going through a very rebellious stage and I'm sure a really nice treat would help her to settle down.'

Meg smiled at her own reflection in the hall mirror as she'd done so often during her five weeks at Keyhole. Trust Dora to seize every opportunity. And why not, if she was doing it on behalf of one of her fosterings?

'Of course. I'd be only too pleased.' She knew that Miranda would not be only too pleased. But then, things were a bit tricky with Miranda anyway lately; perhaps a third party might not be a bad thing.

Her plans – negative though they were – had been made the week before. When she told Arthur that she would be leaving on Monday he expressed regret then said, 'Wait and see, my dear. You might change your mind, eh?' She knew what he meant. He thought she was having an affair with Peter Snow and there had been a lovers' tiff. The fact that Peter did not appear during the following week seemed to rattle him. He made a point of serving her breakfast on Sunday morning, though he had his usual hangover. He said very little and when she asked him to let her have the bill, he shook his head mournfully.

'I can't believe it's all come to nothing, Miss Patch. That Old Shop as you called it . . . and everything.' He did not venture to mention Peter's name but she could imagine what the behind-bar gossip had been like. It *had* seemed ideal: two artists, a house big enough for them to start a family . . . they probably thought Peter had jilted her. And he had in a way. But she knew it was her fault.

'It wouldn't have worked out, Arthur,' she said just as ambiguously. 'D'you realize I haven't done one painting since I arrived? Obviously it's not the place for me.'

'Rubbish. You were almost born here. It's your place right enough.'

She did not argue and after gazing over her table at the lifeboat station shrouded in misty rain, he left her to it and ambled off to the kitchen like a grizzly bear.

After breakfast she went upstairs to finish packing. She had hardly been outside the hotel in the last week, terrified she might bump into Peter. It would have been good to have had a last walk around the harbour, but after peering at the rain she decided against it. The morning stretched ahead endlessly; then lunch, then an endless afternoon. She sat in the windowseat and watched some boys clambering over the rocks below the lifeboat house. What on earth was she going to do with her life? If every man in the world was going to remind her of Uncle Cedric, then marriage was out. And she could not seem to get started on a career of her own. It was ridiculous.

She opened her handbag and took out her diary. What a complete waste of time the last five weeks had been. She read her first impressions of Keyhole: the meeting with Peter, the furore about Fish Cottage, the sittings, the long haul into St Ives, Gerald Scaife's enormous and terrifying pictures, and then that last day in the studio when Peter had finally shown his hand. Friendship could not stay at the level of their companionship . . . why not? Why did it have to become so suddenly an invader? She leafed back through the diary. She must be honest, he had always wanted more; he had always tried to find out what made her tick.

She closed the diary and laughed without mirth because, after all, there was nothing else to find out. She was as she was. No mystery. She put the diary away and looked at her watch. It was an hour since breakfast. She felt near despair at the way time was crawling, then she got up and shook out her heavy tweed skirt, pulled her jumper firmly over the waistband and made for the door. She would ask Arthur for the Sunday papers and have coffee in the lounge and perhaps a sleep after lunch.

Arthur was on the phone when she went through the hall. She waited by him and he said quickly, 'Well, that's it then. Must go,' and replaced the receiver.

She apologized. 'I was only going to ask for some coffee and newspapers in the lounge – no need to hurry your call.'

'It wasn't important. You go on in then. I'll be right with you.'

He no longer sounded depressed about her imminent departure. That was also depressing. She settled herself in a corner of the sofa and stared into the fire and sank a notch lower .

It was after lunch – roast beef and Yorkshire pudding – when she was about to go upstairs again to try for a nap, that Peter arrived.

Arthur had been invisible since he brought her coffee, but she saw his face momentarily behind Peter's and guessed he had instigated the visit. She began to get up, then sat back in her chair again. The coffee pot was still half full; she poured some into her cup and pushed it towards Peter as he arrived at her table.

He ignored it. 'You're leaving?'

He looked angry about it, which confirmed her decision. She had to get away. There was no solution to this particular problem and if he had come with promises not to pester her, she could not believe him and she must still go. Yet she liked him . . . she loved him . . . and it was going to be hard to stand against his blandishments.

'Yes.'

He did not sit down. 'I would have gone. I *will* go. There is no need for you to give up all your plans just because – because – you find me so unbearable.'

She replied in a low voice, 'You know I am not going because of that.'

'At least be honest, Meg!' He leaned on the back of the other chair and stared at her. 'You are to unpack. Do you hear me? I shall go back to Newlyn. We shall never meet.'

'I am needed in Plymouth. I mean it, Peter. And I have to go to Exeter this week too.'

'Rubbish!'

'It's not rubbish. Whether you go or stay I am leaving Keele. That is not rubbish.'

His impetuousness was checked by her calm voice. He hung fiercely on to the chair back, then said slowly, 'No, it's not.' He blinked and looked at the table. 'Is that coffee for me?' He pulled out the chair, sat down, and fingered the cup uncertainly. 'Meg . . . you can't go. I cannot let you go.'

She said very steadily, 'It is decided. I leave tomorrow.'

'We must at least talk about it, for God's sake! What did I do?' His voice began to rise. 'I showed you I loved you. Is that a crime? Is it a bloody crime to fall in love with someone now?'

She almost smiled at his hectoring aggrieved tone. He was like a child justifying himself.

'Of course it's not a crime. It's simply . . . I cannot deal with that kind of thing, Peter. So I am leaving. That is all there is to it. You will have to accept it.'

'Listen. All I ask is that you talk to me. For God's sake let's go for a walk – go somewhere private – talk—'

'Drink the coffee. And I will come for a short walk.' She looked him in the eye seriously. 'Don't get ideas, Peter. I would like to leave here knowing we were still friends. I want no quarrel with you. Ever.'

He stared again, then gulped the coffee and stood up in one motion. She collected her outdoor things. Outside, the rain clothed them instantly. She thought of herself showing him how to drink the rain . . . such a short time ago. She could almost have been angry with him for spoiling that wonderful new discovery of friendship except that she knew it was her fault.

He went ahead of her and took the slippery steps down to the gritty sand of the harbour. The tide was right out and he strode between the leaning boats until he came to West Pier. The sand was full of pebbles here, with pools of water between them. He did not look round to give her a hand; he picked a way beyond the pier and squelched over seaweed beds towards Pezazz Point and the lifeboat house. She followed willy-nilly, her brogues filling with water almost immediately, the hood of her anorak obscuring her vision, forced on by the same stubborn pride that had driven her on the walk back from St Ives.

She caught him up at the jumble of rocks the other side of the slipway. The boys had gone and the sea was moving inexorably in, claiming each pool, swelling menacingly around each rock pinnacle.

She gasped, 'Where are we going? It's dangerous here!'

He said over his shoulder, 'Calm as a millpond.'

She found a secure niche and leaned on her knees. 'I've got the most awful stitch. You went so fast.'

'Good for us. Gets the blood circulating. Quickens the heartbeats.'

'I thought we were going to talk.'

He stopped right above her, got on his knees and reached down a hand. 'Come on. Come up here and look at eternity.'

She took the hand reluctantly. It was only just over a week since she had looked at Gerald Scaife's idea of eternity and the experience had been frightening.

He jerked really hard and she almost leapt up beside him. He put an arm around her shoulders to steady her and then did not take it away. She stayed rigidly within it.

'If that sea was rough, we'd be drenched here,' she panted, looking down at the swell heaving and retreating six feet below them.

'But it's not, so we're comparatively dry.' He laughed and pushed back her hood with his free hand. 'That's better. D'you remember how wet your hair was when we met first?'

She also remembered that he had compared her with a nun or a monk climbing up Sunday Street in her habit.

She said, 'Things were different then.'

'How?'

She had known he would ask that, and she had no answer. But it was true. Things had been completely and entirely different then.

He answered for her, 'They were different then because you did not see me as a threat. Now you do.'

She cried out in negation but he continued inexorably, 'Can't you understand that life – if you live it and don't just exist within it – is always a threat! It's always dangerous! You knew that a long time ago when you wanted to go down that rope. You've forgotten it now. That's why I keep digging at you. I want to know why you've forgotten it. I want you to face it again!'

She tried to whip up more anger against him and produced only a dry sob. 'I don't know what you're talking about. Let's go back.'

'Not yet. If you're determined to leave Keele we've got to thrash it out. Why are you frightened of me? Do you think I will seduce you?'

'No!' She turned within his arm and tried to force herself free. He would not let her.

'No, I think you're right. You wouldn't allow it to happen, would you? Are you frightened I will rape you?'

She almost screamed at him.

He said, 'I've considered it. At one time I thought it was the answer. That was why I walked you back from St Ives. I thought I'd tire you out and your resistance would be nil!' He laughed but she knew he was serious. She became still again; she could hear herself sobbing.

'That's why I tramped you round here today. There's a place on the other side of the slipway. A bit of a cave. But the fates were with you because the tide has already covered it up.'

She summoned enough strength to try to free herself again. He released her so suddenly she almost fell into the sea and took his outstretched hand of her own free will.

He held it so gently. And then he said, 'It's all right, Meg. I know now how conventional you are. We'll get married. No seduction scene until the wedding night, OK? We'll live together in Fish Cottage and have four babies quite quickly and everything will be fine.'

She looked at him for the first time since he had jerked her up on to the rock. Her expression of incredulity stopped him in his tracks. She said, 'Is that what you thought I wanted? Marriage?'

He slackened his fingers. Their hands fell apart.

He said, 'I thought . . . there was something between us. Something special.'

'You told me it was friendship!'

'It was that too. It was . . . everything. I thought.'

'What you are saying . . . you are accusing me of a kind of blackmail!'

'Meg! You know I didn't mean . . . Meg, I love you! I want to be married to you! Please believe that – I've been clumsy and stupid!'

She nodded once. 'Yes.' Then quite suddenly she sat on the rock and slid down to the next. She felt the rough, limpet-covered surfaces tearing her stockings and cutting her hands. She did not care. She jumped on to the pebbles of the exposed beach and sank almost to her ankles in the saturated sand. She turned. 'Please don't come after me,' she called back, her voice amazingly composed. 'I am going to finish packing and I shall leave tomorrow as planned.'

He did not say a word. He watched while she slipped and scrambled around the pier head. Then very slowly he started to follow her.

She finished her packing, drank tea, ate dinner and saw nothing of Arthur. She thought her composure was total, but when she switched off the light and waited for sleep, sobs racked her body. She got up and looked through the window at the moon and thought that she could not bear it. But she was not quite certain what it was she found unbearable.

Miranda could not believe she had gone and Arthur could not believe this was the twin he'd heard of.

'It could be Miss Patch come back!' he repeated for the third time, and Miranda, bewildered and cross, snapped, 'It is Miss Patch and I have come back – I was here in 1949!'

'Certainly. I know, I know. It's just that . . . my God, you really are twins, aren't you?'

Miranda had left off her make-up and tied her hair in the nape of her neck, and the long and tedious journey had probably washed her out. If this was how Meg had looked there really was something wrong.

She said, 'She left yesterday, did she?'

'Yes. She was going to Plymouth, then coming on to see you in some play. Is that right?'

'Probably.'

Keyhole and its inhabitants were all that Miranda had feared. And now the whole purpose of her visit was gone. Trust Meg.

Arthur said, 'How about a nice cup of tea by the fire in the lounge? You can have your sister's room and settle in afterwards and I'll tell you about the Old Shop and Fish Cottage if you like.'

Miranda looked at him properly. He wasn't local and he wasn't the bumbling fool she had at first thought.

She said, 'I'd like.'

Arthur was a good raconteur and Miranda picked up a great deal of background information during their talk. She went upstairs to unpack and looked around the room curiously. This was where Meg had spent the last six weeks; this was the view she had seen daily, the window seat where she'd probably sat and filled in her precious diary. Miranda stared out at the grey sea and the lump of rock which protected the lifeboat house and the slipway. She was unimpressed. Her memories of Keyhole were shrouded, but as far as she could tell there was no nostalgia here for her. Probably Meg had found the same thing. Probably there had been no *grande passion*, no pain, no awfulness whatsoever. She had simply discovered that Keyhole was a dump and she had left it. Oddly enough this thought brought Miranda no relief; she felt merely irritated with her sister. As if Meg had actually summoned her down here on a wild-goose chase.

She glanced at her watch. Four o'clock. It would be dark soon and she'd done nothing with her day. She unlocked her case, tipped the contents on to the bed and selected a pair of jeans and a sweater from the jumble. She changed quickly, tucked some stray tendrils of hair

171

behind her ears and left the room. Arthur, still bemused by her appearance, bobbed out of the kitchen.

'What about dinner?' he asked as he might have asked Meg.

'What about it?' Miranda resented his proprietorial attitude.

'You're the only guest. What time would you like it?'

She shrugged. 'I'm not used to dinner. Might get some fish and chips. Don't do anything for me.'

Arthur fell back frustrated, and she went outside. She wanted to see the Old Shop before it was completely dark. She might walk around the place a bit; have a look at Mrs Hitler's cottage, a drink at the Lobster Pot. Then she'd phone Mrs Penwith from a kiosk. She wasn't going to talk to Meg from the Coastguards. She might not even mention where she was. What a mix-up it was. How typical. How infuriating.

The harbour was full of lapping water. She stared at it morosely, then at the line of boats bobbing on their mooring ropes. What had the two of them done down here for the first five years of their lives? Surely they had been bored to the point of madness? She recalled wanting to make things happen. Swimming too far out to sea so that the lifeboat would put out to rescue her, handling the biggest crabs she could find to show the local boys she was as brave as them. The lifeboat hadn't arrived and the boys had ignored her. It seemed to be the story of her life.

She said aloud, 'The girl who never made an impression.'

She looked up, conscious – as an actress – that someone was watching her. Twenty yards away around the curving harbour rail, someone else was leaning. She stared, frowning. It was a man dressed as a fisherman in a smock and rubber boots; no hat; very dark, bearded . . . yet she knew him. She went on staring, trying to see him without the facial hair, trying to strip him of fifteen years as she might have cleaned off somebody's stage make-up. He too was watching her, perhaps doing exactly the same thing. And then, finally, she had it. Her face split into an unaffected grin and she lifted a hand involuntarily and began to walk towards him.

He stayed where he was, obviously still puzzled, though she was certain he recognized her. That pleased her too; she must have made an impression on someone, at last, because fifteen years was a long time.

She halted a yard away. His eyes hadn't changed. Not at all. He was still capable of being absolutely mad.

She said directly, 'Shall we have another try? The tide's right in again so if we fall we'll have another soft landing. And this time perhaps your father will let us make our own decisions!'

He continued to stare as if he couldn't believe the evidence of his own eyes. She reminded him briefly.

'It's Tadpole.'

Then she reached over the harbour rail and held up one of the heavy pulleys.

He said, 'Did you remember all the time or has it just come to you?'

She grinned. 'Only just. When I saw you standing there, I knew who you were.' She began to clamber over the rail. The drop to the grey water made her feel dizzy and she turned.

'Come on! I can't do it without you!'

Instantly he swung a long leg over the metal.

'You trust me now, then?'

'Of course. If I could trust you when you were twelve or whatever, I can certainly trust you now!'

His laugh was one of pure joy. He put his hand above hers on the pulley and tugged it forward so that she was pressed against him. She felt wonderful. She forgot Brett and Oliver Freres and the sordid business of her own father; she forgot she wanted to be an actress even. All that mattered was being with this boy, holding this pulley, about to do something foolish and exciting with someone who understood exactly how she felt.

He said in her ear, 'Remember. When the rope slackens we swing forward . . .'

She nodded. 'That's where we went wrong before.'

They launched themselves into space. The years rolled back as they soared down the mooring rope, the solid deck of a boat coming towards them much too fast. And then exactly the same thing happened as had happened in 1949. The weight of their bodies pulled the boat towards them, making an enormous loop in the rope. Together they swung forward, but their impetus was not enough to carry them upwards. She screamed a laugh that held fear and he shouted, 'Drop! We'll have to drop!' And they dropped.

The water was colder than it had been in the summer all those years before, and then they had not been fully clothed. She rose, spluttering, already feeling the weight of her boots dragging like an anchor. He bobbed up after her. Incredibly, he was laughing.

She gasped, 'You silly fool! We're going to drown!'

He reached out a hand, grabbed at her sweater and shoved her unceremoniously towards the wall. It was barely eight feet away. He kicked himself after her and heaved her up on his shoulder.

'Grab that ring!' He could hardly speak for laughing.

She grabbed obediently and swung from one arm, her soggy clothes dragging at her. Her lungs were heaving, her heart pounding. She hung there, a dead weight, feeling him pulling her left leg sideways until he must surely tear it off.

'Steps!' he panted. And she felt her foot on something solid. She edged along the wall with her fingers and found the steps cut into the granite wall. She knelt there, forehead on her hands, trying desperately to get control of herself.

He was behind her.

'Tadpole! Are you all right?'

'Just.'

'Are we ever going to get it right?' He had checked his laughter; it was a serious question.

She said, 'We're not going to try again.' She was breathing properly. Her clothes embraced her horribly, but at least she could speak.

'Don't say that. Please.'

Surprised, she looked down at him from under her arm. There was some seaweed caught in his beard. She pumped out a laugh.

'You haven't changed. You really are mad!'

'Only where you're concerned.'

She felt a renewal of the excitement; this was wonderful, the absolute opposite of that cold-blooded affair which was her only experience of so-called romance.

She kept her head down, staring at him; it was getting dark already.

'Have we got an audience up there? I can't bear it if everyone is watching. This is not my idea of a starring role.'

He tipped his head back and scanned the crescent of the harbour rail.

'Nothing. No-one. It's teatime. Kids watching telly. We're OK.'

She lowered her voice, 'What are we going to *do*?'

'Now? Or later?'

'Now, you idiot!'

'Let's go home, get out of these wet things. I've a couple of oil heaters in the cellar. We can dry off.'

'Sounds marvellous. Far to walk?'

He laughed again. 'Get a move on! I'm getting chilled. You don't want to nurse me through pneumonia, do you?'

She clambered upwards with difficulty and together they squelched up into Fore Street, then climbed more steps. She saw a sign, Sunday Street, and vaguely remembered it, but when he opened a gate in a wall and led her down steps into a yard full of flower tubs, she had no idea where she was.

'We'll go in the back way,' he fitted a key into a lock. 'I'm still not supposed to be here so it would be better to avoid any unnecessary publicity.'

It was all delightfully mysterious. He led the way into total darkness and she stood shivering and remembering another similar, cold experience, while he lit candles and revealed a long, bare, but homely cellar. There were sacks at the windows, a table in the middle of the large undefined area, a mattress on the floor. She surveyed it suspiciously, then said, 'Are you married?'

He laughed again and came towards her.

'Are you schizophrenic or something?' He took her hand and led her to the table. 'Look. I'd just been out to buy provisions. Bread. Cheese. Pickled walnuts. Tea. Milk. Buns. We can have a feast.'

Her sense of *déjà vu* disappeared. A feast. It was all such fun. She kicked off her boots while he lit two oil heaters and put a kettle on one of them.

'Come on. Don't be shy.' He dug into a tea chest in the corner and came up with a fisherman's sweater in oiled wool. 'Put this on like a good girl. Here's a towel. You can have this heater, I'll have the other. Back to back. I know you.'

'I've changed since then.'

But she turned her back obediently and stripped off her soaking clothes. They lay in a spreading pool of sea water. She towelled herself and slipped into the sweater. It came to her knees; longer than some of her minis.

She laughed. 'You gave me this deliberately. It tickles in all the vital places.'

She looked round to find him dressed in dungarees, staring at her surprised.

He said slowly, 'You *have* changed. You would have never said that before.'

She laughed again. She was warm, dry, almost fizzing with excitement. She said, 'You don't know me. I am a woman of magic and mystery.' She glinted at him provocatively. 'You don't even know my name!'

He smiled. 'All right. I'll play this game.' He came close. 'May I call you Tadpole?'

'Yes please. And you're Mister Shark.'

He looked almost warily at her, then leaned forward and kissed her on the mouth. She looked at him, her eyes dancing.

'Are you going to eat me, Mr Shark?'

'I think . . .' He cleared his throat. 'I think first of all we'll have some tea. We've both had . . . a shock.'

That was all right with her. She was tinglingly aware of him, but she could wait. She hacked bread while he made a pot of tea. He was still wary; she was conscious of being in total control of the situation, able to call the tune.

He did not say a word as he poured two mugs of tea and gulped at his. He kept flicking glances at her as if he expected her to disappear at any moment. She met his eyes each time and smiled demurely and sipped as if she was at a vicar's tea party. When she saw he had finished his, she put her cup down still half full and said, 'Well?'

'My God.' He made no move. 'I can't believe this.'

She smiled. 'Don't be silly. We're very old friends, surely? We've faced death by drowning twice in . . . um . . . sixteen years? Surely we can dispense with a few preliminaries?'

He leaned forward and very gently touched her bare knee. She did not move.

'You know I'm frightened, don't you?' he said quietly.

She put her head back and laughed.

'You? Frightened? Of me?'

'Yes. If I do the wrong thing I know you'll be up and off. Just like the other times.'

'Other times? What are you talking about?'

He frowned. 'Perhaps you really are one of those people with split personalities.' He shook his head as if to clear it. 'I don't care. I love both of them.'

She caught his hand and put it back on her knee.

'No-one has told me that before. My aunt . . . my sister. No other man.' She leaned forward and kissed him, then said against his mouth, 'Don't be frightened, Mr Shark.'

He drew her to him, held her like a baby while he smoothed her wiry hair and kissed her face and eyes and ears. When he paused for breath, she sat up and slid out of the big jumper. And they lay on the mattress and made love.

Miranda knew she had never been so happy in her life. She had a suspicion that she might never be so happy again. She lay supine, her energy drained from her, and only just found the strength to lift her arm and look at her watch.

'Eight o'clock. I must go,' she said, making no move.

'Why?' He rolled over on to his elbow and kissed her.

'They'll send out a search party.'

He too squinted at her watch.

'Can't be eight o'clock. Your watch got wet. It's not working.'

She took him seriously. 'It was three-thirty when I left the inn for my walk. Then I saw you. Then we fell in the water. Then we came back here . . . no, it can't have taken us that long to – to—'

He laughed, kissed her again, and said, 'Three times.' The kiss developed and she knew it was going to be four times.

And then he said, 'Oh Meg, Darling. I do love you so.'

She stared at him through the candlelit darkness, her eyes black with pupil. Somehow she moved her arm again and put her fingers over his mouth.

'Did you . . .' Her voice was a hoarse whisper and she lowered it fiercely. 'Did you call me Meg?'

He bit her forefinger gently. 'Sorry. Tadpole. I meant Tadpole.'

She squeezed her eyes shut very tightly. Suddenly it was all so clear. So sickeningly clear.

'Is your name Peter Snow?'

He laughed. 'Not tonight, my darling. Don't you remember? You have to call me—'

She pushed and rolled and was on her knees by the side of the mattress pulling frantically at her clothes. She wanted to scream and drum her heels and swear and scratch his face.

He said, 'For God's sake, Meg! What is it now? Are we back to yesterday suddenly?'

She stood up, pulling pants and jeans with her.

'I'm not Meg.' She spoke in a tight, barely controlled voice. 'Meg is my twin sister. I am Miranda.'

'You are who?' He still thought it was some misunderstanding; he sounded almost indulgent and she wished she could kill him.

'Miranda. Miranda Patch.'

'But . . . you knew about the rope? We got wet . . . together. For the second time!'

It was getting through at last.

'Yes. I was the one on the rope. Meg waited with dry clothes for me so that Mrs Hitler wouldn't find out. I'm the one who gets into scrapes and Meg is the one who saves me.'

He got to his feet slowly as she tugged on her boots.

'Hang on. I've talked to you – Meg – hell's *bells*! I've talked about . . . it. The rope. Before.'

'You mean you've talked to Meg about us sliding down the rope when we were kids and landing in the water?' She pushed her arms into her coat; she was shaking. 'And what did she say?'

'I . . . can't remember. Nothing. I don't know.'

'That's because she didn't say a thing. She didn't know what the hell you were talking about.' She walked quickly to the door and pulled back the bolt. It caught her finger and she jumped, but the door swung open. 'Doesn't sound as if you communicate very well at all, does it?'

She took it out on the door. The whole house shook as it slammed shut. And then she ran down Sunday Street and back to the Coastguards. She avoided Arthur Bowering's fussy approach and took the stairs two at a time. Her finger was bleeding profusely and stained the sheets as she clutched them in bunches and screamed into her pillow.

Nine

If Meg had dared to believe her own perception that night, she would have known exactly what had taken place between Miranda and Peter Snow, but she told herself that it was too fantastic. Her twin-telepathy had let her down at last.

Then, the next morning, Mr Bracknell telephoned.

He said without preamble, 'Miranda is at Keyhole, my dear. She has just contacted me to know if you are in Plymouth. She wants to come to you. How do you feel about that?'

Meg stared at the bottle-green wall. 'How did you know I was here?' she asked just as directly.

'If you weren't at the Coastguards, where would you be? Miranda phoned from the Coastguards.'

'Ah.' Meg closed her eyes momentarily. She did not know how it had happened, or why it had happened, but she knew now that it had happened. Peter had made love to Miranda.

She said, 'I'll get in touch with her. Thank you – thank you very much for . . .' for what? '. . . for your intention.'

Mr Bracknell spoke hurriedly. 'Perhaps I had better mention, my dear . . . Miranda is under the impression you had a heavy cold last week and could not come with me to the performance of *Lady Windermere*.'

Meg digested this, then said, 'Why did you tell her that?'

'I – herm – the thing is, Meg, when you came to see me about the house . . . it seemed you needed time to – to – cement – your friendship with . . .' His words fizzled to a stop. For once in all the time Meg had known him, Mr Bracknell was lost for words. Meg felt as if she were staring down a vista of his past understanding. She smiled tightly at the bottle-green paintwork, then said, 'I shall be getting somewhere to live. Soon, I think. I've sent a load of work off to agencies in London and if I settled up there, I'd be able to freelance. Perhaps.'

That would tell him that it was all over at Keyhole and that she was not going to hang around living off her legacy indefinitely. And though her words were mostly bravado, she made up her mind that she would do exactly as she had just said. Even the thought of Miranda was almost too much to bear. She must get away and she must work. And first she must make sure that she and Miranda did not meet.

When she got hold of Arthur Bowering at the Coast-guards, however, Miranda had already left. Meg quelled a moment of sheer panic. If she could have spoken to Miranda on the telephone she could have forced the conversation the way she wanted it to go. 'Sis, I've got a chance in London. Won't see you for a while but I know you won't mind . . .' If they came face to face, that would be very difficult.

But when Miranda arrived, Meg was bowled off her feet. Miranda's remorse was so intense she could not stand against it. She could not even pretend it did not matter. It mattered terribly to Miranda. She had betrayed her twin; not deliberately of course, but it had happened. She repeated over and over again, 'I can't live with myself, Meg! I simply cannot bear it!'

Meg had to cope with getting her away from the interested ears of the Penwiths and trying to control the floods of tears and histrionics which intrigued everyone in the house to distraction. The awful issues underneath all that were forced into second place.

'No, Dora, honestly, she's OK. She's not having a nervous breakdown. No, really, if you could just leave us . . .'

Then, 'Miranda. Darling, just let me go for a moment. No, I'm not angry and I'm not going to throw you out . . . Sis, *please* . . .'

And Miranda wailed, 'Meg, do you realize what has happened? Have you understood what I have said? I have *betrayed* you, Meg! My own sister – twin – peas in a pod – and that's the trouble! If we weren't peas in a pod, this would never have happened!'

'Sis, will you listen to me!' Meg had to speak angrily at last. 'I have told you a dozen times since you arrived. Peter and I were finished! It was over! There is no question of betrayal!' She drew away sufficiently to stare into Miranda's drowning eyes. 'Now let me go down to the kitchen and make us some tea. You can lie on my bed and try to relax. I'll ask Dora if you can sleep here tonight—'

'Where else can I go?' Miranda threw herself back on to the pillows. 'My God – I'm homeless! Rootless! I've thrown in the Arbitrary and wrecked it for you at Keyhole – my God, Meg, we're back to being orphans!'

'We're together and we're independent – that means we're free. Think about that, Sis. And stop acting!'

She was glad to go to the kitchen and talk to Dora and make tea. Do normal, everyday things. She wondered if it would be possible to live with Miranda any more. There was a gulf between them; they could throw bridges across it, but could they actually live on the same side of the gulf? It was a moot point; already Meg felt exhausted and drained by her sister.

They were at Higher Compton for five weeks. Mr Bracknell helped them through it, taking them out for meals at weekends when the foster children were home from school and life in the hostel became unbearable. Christmas came and went and Meg heard that the managing director of a publishing firm called McEvoys would like to see her. When she read his signature on the letter – Charles Kovacks, himself a writer and illustrator of children's books – she was excited for the first time since leaving Keyhole. She caught a train at six in the morning, lugging an enormous portfolio of suitable sketches. The train drew into Paddington at ten o'clock and she sat, for two very long hours, in the foyer of the Royal Hotel where they had arranged to meet. She knew what he looked like; he had lectured once at her art college. When she saw him hovering at the desk she bounded out to meet him and almost immediately asked if he would excuse her.

'I've had six cups of coffee.' She could not be shy with him, he was enormous and shabby, like a very old but much used cuddly toy. 'I didn't want to leave my stuff. Could you possibly . . . ? Just while I . . . ?'

He looked at her schoolgirl's duffle coat, the long fraying plait and the strangely reclusive face, and smiled suddenly. 'If you could train yourself to like gin. Or whisky. Or vodka. It has a much better effect.'

She was uncertain about that remark. The gossip at college had been that he didn't have much of a liver left. But there was nothing to do but grin and make for the stairs to the extravagant powder room overlooking Praed Street. And when she came back down he had a taxi waiting outside and the portfolio under one bear-like arm. They lunched at a dark Dickensian restaurant in Soho and then looked at her sketches, and he talked about his own work and then asked about hers.

'Well . . . actually I haven't done any.'

He laughed and looked at the portfolio.

'That's stuff I did at college. I was going to get a little place in Cornwall and work from there. But it didn't work out. In fact I don't think I did anything in Cornwall at all.' She realized that again with surprise. She had sat for Peter, admired his stuff, looked at the work from the Newlyn school . . . and done nothing herself.

'Good, good.' He nodded approval. 'After college you need a fallow time. Most people pitch right in, desperate to get started. You've got all those impressions now. Most of them fey and interesting I expect.' He leafed speedily through a sketchbook. 'Yes, you do specialize in the fey. I can use that, of course.' He looked up suddenly. 'I'm not offering you a permanent job. You know that?'

She hadn't known he was offering anything. But she nodded, swallowing.

'I'll buy the ones you sent me through the agency. And I'd like more of the same. Rossetti stuff. Goblin markets. Standing stones and elves asleep beneath them.' He went back to the sketchbook, pausing now and then to discuss aspects of her work. She nodded, the excitement growing.

'I've got a bit of money. I could get a place up here. Small. I'd be on the ground then, wouldn't I?'

He looked up again. 'I can't offer you a living, Miss Patch. I'll mention your name, of course. Freelancing is a precarious business.'

'I know. Of course, but . . . you see, I haven't got a home. Or anything. There's just my sister and me. And I want to settle somewhere. So . . .'

'Is your sister working? How old is she?'

'We're twins. She's an actress.' Miranda would adore to live in London. It would be a new beginning for both of them.

185

He made a face. 'My God. Neither of you are in very secure professions. But who am I to judge?'

She knew from the college hand-out that he had arrived from Hungary when the Russians had entered Budapest; that he had gone back for his wife and returned only with his mother. That had been in 1956. Only ten years ago. She tried to guess his present age: nearly forty? That would mean he was still in his twenties when he arrived in this country, penniless, bereaved and with a mother to support. Yes, he had been in a precarious position.

He went on talking about money, telling her how much she would get for the stuff he was buying; it sounded an enormous sum.

'I'll send you a script, Miss Patch. And one of our annuals. See what you can come up with. No promises at this stage. You do understand that?'

'Of course. I can't thank you enough—'

'I'd prefer you not to try. I am a businessman before I am an artist. We are doing business together and that is a mutually advantageous affair, calling for no thanks on either side.'

She looked for a smile and saw there was none. Of course he would have to be hard to have been so successful. She nodded as briskly as she could.

'Well then, I feel it's a good bargain,' she amended.

'And so do I.'

He replaced her sketches and handed her the portfolio. The interview was at an end.

Miranda was oddly unresponsive to all her news.

'Yes. It would be lovely. I might get television work. Yes. I can quite see . . . it would be grand.'

'What do you mean "would be"? This is going to happen, Sis! I've left our name with a couple of house agents and I'm going to work like mad so that I can take some stuff with me when we go to view—'

'I think you'd better look for something quite small. I don't know quite . . . I mean I suppose I could be wrong . . . and anyway I might be able to find someone who would help. I think dear old Gladys Pugh might know someone—'

Meg felt an appalling foreboding starting in the pit of her stomach.

'What do you mean?'

The dreadful thing was, Miranda wasn't as devastated as she pretended. Meg knew this too.

'A baby? How can you know? It's only been five weeks—'

'One knows these things.' The tone teetered on the edge of smugness. 'My breasts hurt. And I'm being sick. And anyway I just know.'

'But – but – it's *impossible*!'

'Why? You know what happened! I've not tried to hide—'

'But it was only once!'

'I rather think that's how you and I came along. Remembering some of the remarks Amy made to Terence. And knowing . . . what I know.'

Meg ignored that, hardly noticed it, she felt physically ill.

Miranda was suddenly remorseful. 'Darling, don't look like that! I'll go and see dear old Gladys. I'll get rid of it. No problem – honestly—'

'You can't do that! You can't possibly do that!'

'Why not, for goodness' sake? It's nothing yet. A sort of amoeba thing—'

'It's Peter's baby!'

'He doesn't want it! Neither do I!'

'That's got nothing to do with it! Nothing at all! Don't

you see – you've created something and you can't kill it!' Meg was almost weeping.

Miranda sat down on the edge of the bed they shared and patted the eiderdown. Their roles were completely reversed and she was the comforter.

'Look. Sit down. Let's talk about this calmly—'

'Didn't Mr Bracknell say there had been enquiries about us? We both knew it must be Peter! He wants to see us—'

'And we don't want to see him.'

Meg suddenly fell to her knees. 'Miranda. You must want to see him. You must have loved him! And now – now he has a right to see you! Can't you see that?'

'Frankly, no.'

'Sis. Listen to . . . yourself. Tune in to your real thoughts. Not the acting ones. The real ones. You love Peter. Don't be afraid to say so – to admit it – because of me. I want to know that you love him. I *need* to know that you love him! You must love him—'

Miranda said calmly, 'Shut up, Meg.' She stared at the ravaged face on a level with her own. So much like her own. She said quietly, 'I must love him, because you love him? Is that what you mean?'

'*No!*' Meg sat back on her heels. 'I don't count any more. Not in this. We have to be separate in this. You have to love him. For your sake, not mine.'

Miranda closed her eyes. 'I don't know. I was so angry with him – felt he had duped me – us – led me into betraying you – I don't know.' She opened her eyes. 'But . . . yes. I did love him. And I suppose . . . I might still love him.'

Meg stood up. 'I'm going to phone Mr Bracknell. Now. Tell him to get in touch with Peter.'

'Hang on, Meg. Doesn't this have something to do with me?'

'Yes. You phone Mr Bracknell.'

'No.' Miranda's voice was flat but definite.

Meg stood up. 'You're quite right. Phone Peter. Of course. I've got his number. In my bag.' She rummaged fiercely. 'Here it is. Go and do it now.'

And after a long pause, Miranda did.

They were married in Penzance a month later. Peter was white-faced, bewildered, completely out of his depth. Miranda was all smiles, suddenly delighted at being married to an almost-famous artist, to be going to live in a charming cottage in Cornwall. Meg was calm, serious, very helpful.

'No. I won't come to stay. But I'll come when the baby arrives.' She spoke to them both, making a point of looking at Peter. 'By then I hope to be settled in London somewhere. It's going to work out very well. I'm really pleased about you two.'

Miranda went to change into another outfit for their honeymoon in the Scillies. Peter said, 'Meg, what must you think of . . . everything! My God, when I remember how we were—'

Meg was frank and straightforward. 'Peter, can't you see that this is ideal? There is something wrong with me – you always knew that – you could never find what it was and neither can I. But there was no future for us and that hurt you. Now you have a future with the part of me that is not damaged, that is not half hidden and peculiar. Can't you see that? Miranda is warm and wonderful and all the things you deserve to have—'

'I don't know what to think – oh God, Meg—'

'Don't think. Just get on with your work, Peter. Please. And be happy.'

Miranda came back, stunning in beautifully cut slacks and a Guernsey. 'Do I look suitable for St Martin's in

March?' she asked, striking a pose.

Peter stared at the wild hair and the aquamarine eyes. He said suddenly, 'I'd like to paint you, Miranda.'

Miranda made a face. 'I take it that is the ultimate sign of approval?'

Neither Peter nor Meg replied.

The slip of a house in Kilburn had been part of a doctor's residence before the war and consisted mainly of the old waiting room and surgery. There was no hall, the wrought-iron spiral stairs took up a lot of floor space in the middle of the waiting room and the surgery-cum-kitchen was a big glass verandah jutting from the back of the terrace. It was ideal for a studio and Meg soon learned to close her mind to the sounds of drumming rain on the glass roof and the constant roar of the Northern Line at the bottom of the garden. Mr Bracknell, on one of his rare visits, told her what a wise move she had made in buying a house in London.

She laughed. 'This is Kilburn you know, Mr Bracknell. Some way from the West End.'

'It's on the up-and-up,' he replied staunchly.

'It suits me here.' She took him up the staircase rather apprehensively. He must be well into his seventies by now. 'This is the bathroom and my bedroom. Of course they couldn't very well build over the verandah, so it's quite small.'

He would not hear a word against it. 'Ideal. Ideal.' He beamed at her. 'As an investment I can assure you it's a better deal than the property in Keyhole.'

He saw her face and wished he had not spoken.

Charles Kovacks became a friend. He adopted a rather stern, avuncular role which was an extension of Mr Bracknell's. The two met once and got on quite well.

Charles Kovacks was built like a 1940s charabanc, huge and bulbous with dark eyes that peered out from an overhanging forehead. By the time she was established in the Kilburn house, he was supplying her with regular work and had introduced her to other regular contributors.

He came to inspect her 'retreat', as he called it.

'You should get a phone installed,' he greeted her, holding out a hand like a bunch of bananas.

Because he was so ugly he did not pose the kind of threat that worried Meg, and she took the hand and said, 'Why?' in a puzzled way that made him smile.

'To spare me that awful cab ride. So depressing. I think hell might look like Maida Vale. Respectability gone mad.'

She laughed and ushered him past the obstructive staircase and into the kitchen. He stood in the doorway, looking around, smiling his sudden pleasure.

'You must have a house-warming. Important for your contacts to know where you are.'

She protested automatically. 'You can see it's much too small for a party. And I know hardly anyone up here—'

'The whole point of having a party is so that you get to know people!' He smiled. 'Can't you see you must meet friends, socialize . . . it's only by sharing ideas, observing, that you will get fresh ones!'

'Yes, I do see that, but—'

'And you can invite the neighbours in – how will you get to know your neighbours otherwise?'

'Well, gradually one makes acquaintance—'

'Gradually! You might need to know them next week or next month! They might need to know you! Let's see, today is Wednesday. We'll do it tomorrow!'

She bleated, 'There's no furniture in the living room! And I haven't got any food in! And—'

'Never mind the furniture. Open those doors and we can go into the garden. Everyone must bring a deck chair. I'll see to the drink. You get food – you'd have to buy it anyway. I'll bring my ma and the two illustrators you've already met. You must know someone in London. And what about your sister?'

'She's having a baby in about two weeks. I'm going down to help—'

'Good job we thought of this first then.'

She was terrified but in the end it was delightful. She got hold of two people from her college days and Mr Kovacks brought Jill Forsythe and her husband, both illustrators. The elderly Mrs Kovacks turned out to be as gentle as her son was aggressive. She spoke in charmingly accented English of her native city on either side of the Danube; of her schooldays in Vienna. Meg did some more of her sums and worked out that Mrs Kovacks had been sixteen at the outbreak of the Great War. When she remarked on this much later to Charles Kovacks he said, 'Yes. She hates to name-drop but you should know that she met Ferdinand at Sarajevo.'

'The *Archduke* Ferdinand?'

'Yes. And one of her other boyfriends was the Greek shipowner. Androulis.'

That meant nothing to Meg, and anyway she had liked Mrs Kovacks for herself. Very much. They became friends too.

In the middle of a very hot August Miranda gave birth to an eight-pound boy and she and Peter called him Alexander. They begged Meg to be his godmother, and rather than let any atmosphere build up, Meg agreed.

It was a difficult week. Fish Cottage had been renovated but was still the place she had loved so much. Peter took care never to be alone with her. Miranda was noisy and vivacious. Meg was thankful to return to Kilburn and her increasingly busy life there.

By the time Miranda produced Katie in December of 1968, Meg was a regular contributor at McEvoys and could have afforded a bigger house. But she did not move. Instead she had a phone installed and talked to Miranda on it every weekend instead of writing the careful letters that seemed to push them further apart. And she went down to help with Katie. It was easier than last time. Alex, two and a half and suddenly pushed out to the edge of the nest, adored his aunt. And she loved him. She began to adopt the role of maiden aunt; at twenty-four it might be a premature position to occupy, but in the circumstances it seemed ideal.

After Katie's birth there was Sebastian. Meg did not wait for his birth to go to Keyhole again. She spent a long summer holiday there in 1969 and took over most of the housework so that Miranda could rest. Sebastian arrived at the end of November, and at home. It was a wonderful time. Meg and Miranda felt that they had bridged the unbridgeable gulf. Meg was definitely part of the family now.

And then there was a long period of quiet. Miranda came to stay with Meg and told her Peter was looking for a London base and then Miranda could get back to acting. She showed Meg her Equity card, kept in an inside compartment of her handbag next to her driving licence and kidney donor card.

'I keep my hand in with the Newlyn Players,' she confided. 'Only am-dram of course, but it's good practice!'

Meg looked at her; the old Miranda was coming back. She wondered what would happen to Peter and the children in the future. Suddenly, surprising herself, she put her arms around Miranda and hugged her. Miranda looked up, near tears.

'That's the first time you've done that since . . .'

Meg said steadily, 'I know.' And told herself that after all, time *did* heal everything.

And then there was a desperate phone call from Keyhole.

'Darling, I'm expecting again! Can you believe it! And I thought we'd done with nappies for ever! Meg, I just cannot bear it!'

Meg made the usual sounds and thought that in this age of easy contraception it surely could not be an accident.

Miranda said, 'I've done everything I can to get rid of it and Peter won't hear of an abortion!'

'Miranda – for goodness' sake! It's not the end of the world. You've said how good Katie is with Seb. It will be the same with the new baby.'

'Meg, I feel so rotten. Can't you come down and be with me? Please?'

'Darling, I have got a job, you know.'

'You can work down here. Meg, I just cannot stand this place in the winter. Couldn't you come for Katie's birthday at least?'

'Well, I suppose—'

'It wouldn't be worth you going back till after the New Year then, Sis. We could go for walks. And you can see the new Christmas lights . . . please, Meg.'

'I'll see.'

By 1975 parking spaces were limited in Keyhole during the summer months. Twelve cars could wedge themselves along the West Pier, but the East was on two levels and was always full of nets and big wooden crates and old-fashioned lobster pots. Maybe a decrepit, rusting van would draw on to it occasionally and load up with fish, but even an undersealed 'R' registration job hesitated to venture along its uneven length. Its driver would say dismissively 'suspension', and reverse into the congested yard of the Coastguards Inn before taking the road out of the place while his passengers crossed 'Keyhole' off their tourist list and settled back for a swift run to Lamorna.

For most of the winter, the problem did not arise. The piers were empty; the bus, trundling its way from Penzance, could negotiate the hill and hairpin bends without too much difficulty. Keyhole belonged to itself again. Except in December.

On December the tenth, the Keyhole Christmas lights were switched on and tourists came from miles around to view them. They'd been featured in the children's television programme *Blue Peter* and they were worth the long walk from the new cliff-top car park. People trooped down the dark lane, waving torches about helplessly and telling each other it was well worth the effort. Which, of course, it was. What with the fake yachts outlined in red and green in the harbour, Nessie's curving back emerging from the wavelets in an arc of purple, and the neon Christmas trees lining each of the piers, Keyhole was a sight to behold. 'Like a fairy grotto for adults,' Meg murmured as she and Miranda scrambled along the shingle below the Coastguards Inn and climbed on to the West Pier.

Miranda, who now knew all the disadvantages of being three hundred miles from London on the very toe of the country, heaved herself alongside a large silver Volvo, grunting with the effort, and said simply, 'Yes.'

Meg grinned into the darkness and took her sister's arm. 'Come on. I'll get the tea for the kids and you can put your feet up in the studio and watch the lights in comfort.'

Miranda, incapable of more than monosyllables, said, 'Nice.'

They struggled past knots of people blocking the road

and gazing wide-eyed around them. There was a traffic jam at the entry and exit to the village, so that meant a solid line of cars all along the harbour. Miranda had to walk sideways to get her abdomen through safely; Meg gave up her arm and tried to forge a way ahead. The glorious smell of sea and shore was drowned by exhaust fumes. Someone said, 'Oh look! What's that up there – red and white?' Someone else giggled and answered, 'It's a pair of breasts!' And Miranda turned and snapped, 'It's Christmas puddings! There's a whole line of them if you look properly!'

Meg reached back and pulled Miranda to a gap on the rails. They leaned for a moment, breathing.

Meg said, 'Idiot. Why do you bother?'

Miranda said gloomily, 'Trouble is, I might have thought that was funny at one time myself. A pair of breasts indeed! You can see what the cretin meant, can't you?'

Meg said, 'I suppose you hate all of us. Invading your privacy and making vulgar remarks.'

'*You* don't make vulgar remarks. And even if you did I'd never hate you. And you wouldn't know how to invade anyone if you tried!'

'Oh, Sis. Cheer up. Christmas is a-coming and all that.'

Miranda said gloomily, 'That was practically a vulgar remark – watch it!' She hugged Meg's arm to her side. 'Anyway, I don't think those people were vulgar. I think we're vulgar. Gilding the lily. That sort of thing. They're merely drawing attention to it.'

'It's pretty and it's Christmassy and Alex and Katie and Sebastian love it. And what's good enough for them—'

Meg's determinedly cheerful effort was interrupted by Miranda pointing like a dog into the black depths of the harbour. She then lifted her voice above the babble of other voices, idling engines, sea-sounds. 'Is that you down there, Alex? If you get your jeans wet again, I'll kill you!'

There was a scuffle below and a clatter of pebbles, then silence. Meg, also pointing now, said, 'It can't be him. He was going to play dominoes with Katie and Sebastian.'

'Like hell he was going to play dominoes! As soon as our backs were turned he'd be off! He's like his father – no sense of responsibility whatsoever!'

Meg said gently, 'Darling, Peter is not irresponsible. He has to be faithful to – to—'

'Go on, say it! To his art! To his bloody art! While I'm responsible – not to – for – the cooking, cleaning, washing, drying, ironing, Alex, Katie, Seb, and now this new one!'

'Miranda, you mustn't get so excited!' Meg dropped her voice in the vain hope that Miranda would do the same. People, all in holiday mood, were glancing at them with amusement.

'Sorry. Sorry, darling. You'll be wanting to leave us if I go on like this!' She sighed. 'It's just that after Seb was born I said no more. And I joined the am-dram group and began to feel like a human being again. Five glorious years of freedom. Then I forget the pill just once and I'm pregnant yet again!'

Meg seemed to remember Peter wanted four children. She said, 'Come on. I'll cook the supper tonight. And you can have a tray of tea upstairs and send the children down to me.'

'You're an angel and I don't deserve you. This baby is making me feel so *irritable*!' Miranda peered down again. 'In a way, I hope it *is* Alex getting his jeans wet. I feel like thumping someone!'

Meg laughed, hoping it was a joke. Miranda often spoke about her husband and children as if they were her mortal enemies; it was just her way. But certainly

Alex – Meg's very special godson as well as nephew – had borne the brunt of his mother's irritation lately. Meg smiled even as she thought of him. If things had been just a little different he could have been her son, and she loved him slightly more than the other two because of that, perhaps. And because he was so much Peter's. His dark hair and eyes and his craziness . . . especially his craziness . . . She began to make plans for waylaying him in the kitchen with a dry pair of jeans. But there were no such things in the Snow household.

She said, 'Oh look, Miranda! Up on the hill! Is that a turkey just being illuminated?'

Miranda glanced up. Her enormous cascade of red hair spilled out of the hood of her duffle coat and she shovelled it back inside irritably.

'It's a bunch of holly for God's sake! Honestly, Meg. You must get glasses.'

Meg said nothing. She had glasses but Miranda had told her when she arrived that she was looking staid, so she had not taken them out of her suitcase.

The two women trudged past the town hall and turned left into Fish Street. Meg felt a shock of surprise each time she saw the cottage, and it happened again as they drew level with the stone steps to the front door. Peter had completed the renovations in record time so that it was warm and comfortable for the arrival of the precipitate baby, but she had never got used to the dormer windows in the roof and the enlarged cellar. It was exactly as she had planned, even to the Aga. That had hurt her when she had visited them for the first time to see her nephew; then she told herself it was a compliment. When she returned for the births of Katie and Sebastian she had suggested other refinements, and had discovered them in situ the next time she visited. Peter never spoke frankly to her as he had done on the day of the wedding, but sometimes she felt he was desperately trying to tell her something.

Miranda crouched to go through the low cellar door and Meg followed swiftly to shut out the cold and wet. Immediately they were embraced by the warmth from the Aga. There was a dim light filtering down the stairs from above. While Miranda fumbled for the switch, Meg could imagine the cellar to be as she had seen it first, a big cave of granite bedecked with old baths, nets, cobwebs. The light sprang out and she saw the reality which she was largely responsible for; when she had arrived a week before the whole house had been in chaos. Now there were strings of onions clothing one of the sturdy granite pillars, a new rug before the Aga, the stone-flagged floor was scrubbed clean of its year-old dirt and freshly ironed clothes hung over the airer. And just beneath the airer Alex's nine-year-old figure was outlined, hopping out of saturated jeans, reaching up for pyjama bottoms.

Miranda let out a shout of anger and leapt forward with flailing hands; he ran; Miranda ran. There were poundings up the stairs and through the living room above. Peter's voice resounded from the top storey, asking a question in which the adjective 'bloody' yelled several times was the only word Meg could hear.

She picked up the kettle with resignation, filled it at the tap and stuck it on the Aga. She knew exactly what would happen: Peter would intervene before Alex's thrashing could be accomplished; there would be a three-way row during which Alex would be dismissed to his room; then a two-way row between Peter and Miranda; then Peter would sit Miranda down and rub her neck and probably they would make love. Meg had never actually witnessed their many reconciliations, but Miranda made sideways references that could mean only one thing.

Katie and Sebastian appeared as soon as the shouting

ceased. Both of them looked sheepish, as if the whole thing might have been their fault. Katie, flame-haired and wilful, dragged five-year-old Sebastian to the table and sat him down with great force.

'Just stay there while I help Aunt Meg to get the tea,' she ordered as if he might protest. Sebastian rarely protested about anything; he sat peaceably, cuddling an old blanket with one hand, tracing the knotholes in the pine table with the other. Katie collected five plates from the dresser and banged them around the table.

'Alex has been sent to his room,' she explained over her shoulder to Meg.

'Yes, I thought so. And I am taking Mummy's and Daddy's upstairs. So just the three of us, darling.'

Katie rolled her eyes, fetched a tray and put two of the plates on it.

'All right, both of you?' Meg put a hand on Katie's head, willing tranquillity into the tense little body.

'No.' Katie was nothing if not direct. 'Alex will say it's all my fault.'

'Why on earth would he say that?'

'Because he always does.'

Sebastian removed the blanket from beneath his nose and said tentatively, 'It was a bit our fault, Katie.' He smiled at his aunt. 'We wanted to make houses with the dominoes and he wanted to teach us proper. And when we wouldn't listen he said bugger the pair of you and went off to play with Zach.'

'Sebastian!' Katie looked goggle-eyed from her brother to Meg.

Meg made two pots of tea, one in the earthenware family-sized one, another in a silver one that boasted matching milk jug and sugar basin.

'We'll make the tray look nice, shall we, Katie?'

'Can I take it up?' Sebastian asked propitiatingly.

'No. You'll drop it,' said Katie. Then, realizing her aunt was a broken reed in the discipline department, she added, 'And you should never ever ever swear, Seb. God could come and punish you, you know.'

'He'll lose the use of his legs if you never let him do anything,' Meg commented. 'Let him take it.'

Katie simmered while Sebastian laboriously struggled upstairs with the tray. She waited till the door shut behind him then she took issue with her aunt.

'You shouldn't let him swear. An' you only let him take up the tray 'cos you don't want to see Miranda and Peter snogging!'

The swearing had not shocked Meg; Katie's accusation did. She said weakly, 'I wish you wouldn't call them Miranda and Peter!'

Katie said, 'That's how they were christened, you know!' And Meg could hear Miranda's voice.

'Anyway, Seb wasn't swearing. He was reporting what Alex said.' Meg poured tea. 'You're as cross as two sticks, Katie. Relax and have a scone for goodness' sake.'

Katie sat down and sighed deeply. 'Oh, Aunt Meg, I just hate it when Alex is sent to his room. It'll get worse when the new baby is born, you know. Couldn't you stay for longer this time?'

Meg sat down too and surveyed this small replica of herself and Miranda. She said slowly, 'Katie. You are seven years old.'

Katie was surprised. 'I know,' she agreed.

'You shouldn't be worrying about – about – ' Meg waved her hands helplessly and said – 'relationships!'

Katie looked irritated. 'I'm not worried about any ships!' She slowed her voice to deal with her aunt's obtuseness. 'I'm worried about my brother!'

Meg choked on a laugh and gathered her niece to her. She rocked her back and forth. 'I love you,' she said.

'But you know what I *mean*, don't you? You love Alex almost as much as I love him!'

'Yes. I do.' Meg put the small girl back in her chair and began to butter a scone for her. 'I might not be able to stay too long at a time, Katie. But I will come more often. How's that?'

Katie took a moody bite of scone. 'Better 'n nuffin',' she said, spraying crumbs uncaringly. She caught Meg's eye and, in an instant of communication, acknowledged her own bad behaviour and its one-off indulgence. She grinned, revealing her new second teeth coated in unpleasant-looking paste, and Meg burst out laughing and shook her head.

'You are so like your *mother*!' she said.

And was not reassured when Katie wailed, 'Oh no! I want to be like you!'

After their tea she put the two children to bed and pretended not to notice when Alex emerged from his room and sat by her to hear the nightly reading. He was as silent as the grave until she paused to turn a page, then he spoke.

'Are you cooking supper, Aunt Meg?'

'Yes.'

'Will she let me stay for it?'

Meg looked up from the book, opened her eyes wide at him, then went back to the house on the prairie.

'If she doesn't will you bring me something in bed?'

Katie exploded. 'Stop intrupting, Alex! Seb can't hear a word with you going on and on!'

Alex looked at the other bed where Sebastian was already fast asleep, his blanket apparently stuffed up his left nostril. Katie said crossly, 'Tell her the news. Then she'll let you stay up for supper.' She pulled the bedclothes up to her chin. ''S not fair. Just because you're two years older than me—'

'Your turn will come, Katie. And you're not interested in food anyway.' Meg tilted the book so that Katie could see the picture and read on. And Alex, primed by his devious little sister, crept away. Meg found him ten minutes later peeling potatoes at the sink.

Miranda chose to ignore his presence at the supper table until he unwisely asked if anyone wanted the remaining loin chop on the meat dish.

'If it was the last food in the universe and you were starving, I would not let you have that chop!'

She was half-joking; whatever had taken place between her and Peter during their teatime had put her in a much better mood. Alex sensed this and grinned amiably at her.

'I heard some news tonight, Ma.'

'Will you kindly *not* call me Ma!' Miranda rolled her eyes at Peter. 'My name is Miranda.'

Alex could not bring himself to be so familiar. 'It's a shortening of Miranda,' he offered. 'And the news is that Prospect Villa has got a tenant at long last!'

Meg smiled to herself as she dished up a Malvern pudding. Katie would have made that story last so much longer; Alex was practically without guile. She wondered how he would survive in this household.

Miranda said, 'That dump? I don't believe it!'

Peter looked across the table, then away. 'You went to see it ten years ago, didn't you, Meg?'

Meg sat down, startled. Of course. Prospect Villa. Where Peter had lurked, then followed her right down to Fish Cottage.

She said as naturally as possible, 'Surely it's been lived in since then?'

Miranda looked at her sharply. 'I thought you were interested in the Old Shop?'

'I was. But Prospect Villa was one of the places . . .'

'Zach says it's haunted.' Alex gnawed the chop bone hungrily. 'You can see a light in it sometimes.'

Meg and Peter spoke almost in unison. 'It's the reflection from the Land's End lighthouse.'

Miranda took a spoonful of cinnamon apple and breathed through her mouth. 'Hot,' she apologized. Then, 'Is that the reason the house has stayed empty, d'you suppose?'

Alex knew when his mother was intrigued. He over-expanded. 'Someone was murdered in it hundreds of years ago and bloodcurdling screams—'

His father said quickly, 'It was built in the 1930s, Alex. It's been empty because it's damp.'

'Is that why you turned it down, Meg?' Miranda was still looking at her sister.

'Yes.'

'On Peter's advice?'

Meg looked up and met Miranda's very direct gaze. After the terrible scenes ten years previously, when Miranda had discovered she was pregnant and had told Meg everything, they had never discussed the frightful climax of their twinship. It had happened and they got on with it as best they could; both Meg and Peter had accepted that. Meg had assumed Miranda had also accepted it.

'I don't think so.' She made a conscious effort to be honest. 'No. Definitely not. I hated the place.' She grinned at Alex. 'I don't believe in ghosts, but it certainly had an unpleasant atmosphere.'

Miranda ate her pudding, apparently satisfied. Alex finished with his chop and accepted his pudding appreciatively.

'Zach says it's been taken by a man who has escaped from Dartmoor,' he mentioned, almost casually. Even he did not believe that.

He was surprised when his mother became interested again.

'A man? On his own? My God. The females of Keele will be agog at this. Who will clean and cook for him?'

Alex shrugged and said nothing, his mouth being full.

Miranda answered herself. 'Janis, I suppose. Now that her mother's dead, she must have plenty of spare time.'

Peter tried to turn the conversation. 'She's full-time at the Coastguards, you know.'

'She doesn't go in for the lunchtime opening,' Miranda said definitely. 'So she's got all day. She's the only one who could take it on. I was going to suggest we went round to see poor old Arthur tonight anyway. She'll be able to fill us in.' She glanced belatedly at Meg. 'You're all right to baby-sit, Sis?'

'Of course. Give Arthur my love.'

'My God, I shan't get a chance. He's always on about you. Talk about favouritism!' But she laughed. Then added, 'You should go and see the poor old thing, Meg. He's in a bad way.'

Meg did not point out that she was too busy to do much visiting. She nodded and said, 'Yes. He is almost crippled now.' Then she pushed the dish towards Alex. 'D'you want to scrape out, Alex?'

Alex looked apprehensively at his mother, but for once she did not tell him how greedy he was. Gratefully he took the dish and began on the delicious burnt bits of custard along the edge.

The lounge bar at the Coastguards had not changed since Arthur had served Meg's coffee there and brought her newspapers. The red flock paper was now claret-coloured and the granite fireplace was blackened beyond the help of soap and water, but it was also still warm and cosy and most of the trippers had disappeared, leaving it to the locals. Peter found two stools at the bar and reached into his smock for his sketching block. Phil Nolan and Billy Majors turned to him automatically. He was one of the reserve lifeboat men with them, and could be included instantly in reminiscences of rescues and drills. They had long ago accepted that he was unable to talk properly without a pad and a soft-lead pencil in his hands. Peter nodded, laughed, captured their faces beneath peaked caps, wreathed in tobacco smoke. Miranda perched next to him, turning sideways to accommodate the new baby, one elbow on the bar as she leaned towards the barmaid.

'The usual please, Janis. And whatever you fancy, of course. Oh, and Bill and Philip I suppose.' Miranda glanced at the older men without pleasure. She was willing to bet they had never been inside a theatre in their whole lives.

Janis put ice in a glass, a measure of gin, a slice of lemon. 'Heard about Prospect Villa, have you?' she asked.

Janis had been one of the stalwarts of the amateur dramatic group and would be more so now that her mother no longer took up her time. Miranda decided to be nice to her.

'No?'

'Bloke's took it. On a year's lease. Course he don't know nothing about the happenings up there.'

'Is he on his own?'

''S far as I know. No woman would want to live in Prospect House now, would they?'

'It's very damp, I understand.'

'Damp? It's pouring with water! And what between that and the lights and the sounds . . . Gawdelpus, I wouldn't go there if you paid me!'

Miranda was disappointed. 'I should have thought

you'd have been glad to do for him, Janis. Time must hang heavily for you. And you could ask the top rate.'

'I certainly could. He won't get no-one else.' Janis looked across the counter as she pushed beer glasses towards the men. 'You know the place is haunted?'

'Well. The children like to tell stories—'

'Lights was first seen up there ten years ago. Ten years almost to the day, matter of fact.'

Miranda frowned. Ten years ago last month, Meg had still been looking for a house down here and had gone to see Prospect Villa. And she had become . . . alert . . . when Alex mentioned the place.

She echoed what Meg and Peter had said then. 'It was the reflection from the lighthouse.'

Janis shrugged. 'Coulda been. 'Cept that Lannah headland cuts across the beam.'

Miranda said, '*Does* it now?'

'Then there's the ticking.'

'Ticking? Mattress ticking?'

Janis was impatient. 'N-o-o! Ticking like a clock!'

'Well. Obviously it hasn't worried this new tenant. I expect he enjoys it. He's probably a poet. Lonely. A bit like you, Janis. You ought to take pity on him.'

'He might be mental.'

'And he might be rich too. Learn to rely on you. Leave you all his money!'

Miranda nudged Peter to pay for the drinks and watched her words take effect. Janis was probably nearly fifty, but she nourished an idea of romance that flourished in spite of receiving no encouragement at all.

She put change on the counter and leaned towards Miranda.

'Bit like *Rebecca*, innit? I wonder if he looks like Laurence Olivier?'

Miranda lifted her glass. 'Only one way to find out,' she said.

Arthur came into the lounge and sat heavily on the sofa. Miranda left her seeds to germinate and moved almost as heavily towards him. She always made a point of talking to Arthur, as if, by listening to his eulogies on the subject of Meg, she could somehow make amends for what had happened ten years before. One day he might forgive her, then perhaps she could forgive herself.

But tonight Arthur seemed to have left condemnation upstairs.

'I'm glad to see you, Mrs Snow.' He took a breath with difficulty; what with arthritis and bronchitis he ought to be dead. 'See that magazine programme after the news, did you?'

'No.' Miranda settled her bulk next to his and prepared to be bored. Her relief that the Suez Canal had been reopened was very limited.

He was outraged. 'You mean, Miss Patch hasn't seen herself?'

'Seen herself? What d'you mean?'

'She was on tonight.' He looked over his shoulder as one of the kitchen staff went through. 'Sibyl – wasn't Miss Patch on the box tonight?'

Sibyl paused momentarily, smiling. 'She were that. Though I thought it was you at first, Mrs Snow. Don't know your sister. Thought it was you in glasses.'

'Meg doesn't wear glasses,' Miranda put in.

'Oh, it was Miss Patch right enough.' Sibyl grinned. 'Your hair do mark you out. An' 'ers is fluffier than yours if you don't mind me saying.'

Miranda did mind; her hair had always been thicker than Meg's. But she passed that by and turned to Arthur for further information. Peter had put away his sketch block and was behind her. Odd how he had picked up the conversation when so often he was in a world of his own.

Arthur took the floor with aplomb.

'They were talking about book illustrators. Whether pictures sell children's books. You know the kind of thing. There was that bloke who does the funny ones – wotisname – all scribbles and scrawls—'

'Charles Kovacks,' Peter put in.

'That's the chap. He did all the talking. And he mentioned Jill Forsythe – I've heard Miss Patch talk about her – and then, would you believe it, up comes a photograph of Miss Patch herself at her drawing board and he said she was a good example of the Rossetti school – a sprite he did call her. And I reckon that suits her, don't you, Mrs Snow? A sprite?'

Miranda did not reply; she was amazed. Meg hardly ever talked about her work and when she did she was modest to the point of denigrating it.

Peter said, 'Why on earth didn't someone let her know? We could have watched it together. What a crying shame!'

Miranda said truthfully, 'She wouldn't have wanted to have seen it, Peter.'

'No, but we would!'

Miranda was not so certain. Hadn't it been she who was going to be famous? Meg hadn't wanted fame. And anyway what was a still photograph on a television magazine programme? Certainly not fame.

Arthur proceeded to describe that part of the programme in detail; Miranda was certain he must be making most of it up. It had lasted no longer than two minutes; there was no way Charles Kovacks could have gone on about Meg as reported by Arthur. But he convinced Peter.

'This is just what Meg needs!' he said as they walked back along the mist-drenched harbour and up the suddenly enormously steep steps of Sunday Street.

Miranda scoffed at that sincerely. 'Meg doesn't need any kind of adulation! She gets on with her work and that's that.'

But Peter was adamant. 'Her opinion of herself as an artist is much too low. I remember when she came down for Katie's birth and told us that she had enough work from McEvoy's to keep her going, she was almost ashamed. She said something about coming to terms with the reality of her small talent—'

'Well, naturally, to you—'

'Meg knows my failings as well as I know them myself,' he came back sharply.

'She admires your work – my God, she thinks it should take precedence over our marriage!'

'What the hell are you talking about now, Miranda?'

'She told me today your first responsibility was to your work! As if you were some poverty-ridden genius!'

He was silent while they stood at the top of the steps for a moment until Miranda's breathing returned to normal. The tiny village was bathed in one of its typical sea frets; Miranda knew Peter still found it beautiful and was disappointed because she did not share his feeling. She knew that in many ways she was a disappointment to him.

She put a protective hand beneath her abdomen and said resentfully, 'Well, we're not poor, Peter! And you really are famous – in the proper art world! And we bury ourselves down here where the kids can't get a decent education and I'm dying of boredom—'

'Darling, I'm sorry.' His contrition was instant as always, so that she knew he felt guilty about their mode of life. 'I know it's not your cup of tea. I don't agree about the kids – it's a wonderful place for children – but I can see that for you it's the back of beyond.' He put one arm around her shoulders and smoothed her smock with the other. His hand was warm and comforting; he never seemed to feel the cold and damp. 'Listen, just wait till this new baby is old enough to be left and we'll have a winter in London. How does that sound? I'll rent a studio near the Heath somewhere and you can do the theatres and shop and—'

She wasn't going to be so easily won round this time. 'Each time I'm pregnant you say that. But Seb was almost five when I fell for this last one and we still hadn't managed to find a suitable studio! And then when it looked as if we'd got something, we're having yet another baby!'

'Sweetheart – please don't get cross again. I told you before we were married that we'd have four children—'

She suddenly lost her temper and pushed him away furiously. 'You did *not* tell me anything of the sort! It's another of those little gems you told Meg, I expect! No wonder she didn't want you! And now you can't remember what you said to who!' She sobbed at her own bad grammar and turned to march up the road towards their back gate. 'Sometimes I almost hate you, Peter! You trapped me in the first place just because I was carried away by—'

He caught her up at the gate and pinned her against it almost frantically. She tried to move her face away from his but he was everywhere, kissing her, talking into her ear, holding her head, fingers in her hair, winning her as he always did by the sheer force of his own ardour.

'Listen – honey – baby – sweetheart – listen to me. You know it was meant from the word go – you and me – when you saw me on the harbour – when we coasted down into that bloody water for the second time – when we couldn't keep our hands off each other. All right, we have our quarrels, but then . . . oh, Miranda . . . we're right. You know we're right together—'

She let herself be kissed. She returned the kiss. Through the thickness of their clothes they did the things that they always did. And at last he picked her up, baby and all, kicked open the gate and staggered down the steps into the yard, where he put her down. Meg looked up, startled, as they crashed through the fish cellar and took the stairs one by one, gasping their laughter, making the old banisters creak as they lurched from side to side. She looked away and just for a moment, Miranda felt guilt flood through her. And then she thought of the single man in Prospect Villa and wondered if he might be the answer. There had never been another man in Meg's life since she and Peter got married. And that would be the answer; for Meg herself and, more especially, for Peter.

She watched him when they reached their bedroom and he tore tremblingly at his clothes. Very occasionally it crossed her mind that Peter's intense outbursts of passion were caused by guilt. Just as hers were.

And then she forgot everything for almost half an hour. And when she was capable of coherent thought again, she remembered that they had not told Meg about the television programme.

Peter kissed her drowsily and murmured, 'We should go downstairs and behave like civilized people.'

It was comforting to realize that he too had forgotten that Meg had appeared on the all-important 'box' that night.

Miranda kissed him back. 'Do we have to, darling? Let's just go to sleep.'

'Mmm. OK.'

And then of course she felt guilty about that too – as if she'd seduced Peter away from Meg all over again!

She was angry with herself; she was getting paranoid about nothing at all. She thought again of the unknown man in Prospect Villa. That was the answer. That, most definitely, was the answer.

She fell asleep.

Ten

Miranda was almost entirely happy that Meg stayed on
after Christmas. She felt like the side of a house with still
three months to go; Keele was incredibly boring at all
times, but especially so in winter; finally, the kids got
on her nerves.

Meg's presence eased all that. She was effortless
company and she adored the kids and played with
them for hours. And of course she did all the housework; Miranda hated housework.

But there were snags. For one thing, without much
to occupy her, Miranda found herself competing with
Seb, Katie and Alex for Meg's attention. She was forced
to join in their games: Snakes and Ladders and Snap
were about all Seb could manage and if there were two
games Miranda hated more than any others, they were
Snakes and Ladders and Snap.

For another thing, her ambivalent feelings about Meg
became much stronger after the television programme
which had mentioned her work. There was still the awful
guilt about filching Peter from under her nose all those
years ago. But to counteract the guilt was a definite sensation of her own nose being put out of joint. And Peter
kept talking about it: what the publicity would mean,
how Meg simply must consider herself an important
artist, et cetera, et cetera. Miranda somehow became an
outsider; Peter and Meg were artists. She was pregnant.

She tried to put this right by spending time with him

in the studio. But on Boxing Day he left the house at eight o'clock and did not return until the teatime dark. He explained, without apology, that he'd walked to St Ives and back over the moors. And after that he took to locking his studio door.

'I'm working on something rather special.' Again, no explanation or apology, indeed he sounded excited about it all. She tried sulking when they got to bed and found it had no effect; she tried to be seductive, but petulance ruined that and she usually ended up lying with her back to him. The really infuriating thing was, Peter did not appear to notice.

Miranda told herself that her general malaise was down to the pregnancy. Meg was wonderful – as ever – and Peter had always been obsessive where his work was concerned; he would have long fallow periods when he took Alex out in their leaky dinghy or spent most of the day with the crew of the lifeboat, then he would begin painting like a dervish.

But the evenings were difficult and that was a fact and nothing to do with her present paranoia. By the time the supper things were away and the children in bed it was nearly always nine o'clock and they invariably went upstairs to watch the television news, which Miranda hated. She could do nothing about anything, and it merely upset her that the death toll in Northern Ireland was over a thousand since 1969 and that the president of Bangladesh had been assassinated with all his family.

When the news came through about the new oil rigs off the Scottish coast she enthused madly in the hope of avoiding a discussion about the other dooms and glooms.

'Just think! Self-sufficient in oil by 1980! Won't that be absolutely wonderful? We'll be able to run the car for nothing!'

Peter said, 'I have a feeling it won't be like that.'

Miranda gave a sigh like a small explosion. 'Oh, honestly! Let's really wallow. We might all be dead by 1980 anyway! That will be fun, won't it?' She leaned across and turned down the volume on some news about an Anglo-French plane called Concorde. 'Was that Alex? If he's woken Seb I'll—'

Meg stood up immediately as Miranda knew she would.

'I'll go and see.'

Miranda did not readjust the volume control. She reached across to Peter's chair and took his hand – with some difficulty.

'Let's go to bed, darling.'

He looked at her without enthusiasm.

'Honey, it's only just gone nine! We can't leave Meg here on her own yet.'

'She won't mind. And I'm awfully tired. Really, Peter. I mean it. I'm not trying to seduce you.'

He did not laugh.

She tried to keep the petulance out of her voice. 'I'm entitled to feel tired, darling. The baby is due on the ninth of March!'

She made to withdraw her hand; unexpectedly he gripped it tightly and said in a low voice, 'It's me, isn't it? I'm coming between the two of you.'

She was completely taken aback; all right, she had seen the three of them as a triangle, but she and Peter were on the base line; Meg way up on the topmost point. Untouchable.

He stood up, then suddenly kissed her fingers hard and released her hand.

'Darling, I'm going upstairs to finish off some stuff. Have an hour with Meg. Please. I hate to think of you two drifting apart.'

'What on earth are you talking about? We go for walks every day! We spend an hour after breakfast chatting – we could never drift apart, Peter!'

But he was at the door, blowing her another kiss, sliding off to his precious work again. Triangle indeed; there was yet another rival. She had forgotten his painting.

Meg appeared at the door with Alex in tow.

'He had a dream, Miranda. May he come and sit with us for a while?' She looked around for Peter; she had of course banked on Peter's acquiescence. That could have been annoying but Miranda was genuinely tired and could not be bothered to expostulate.

'Switch off for me, there's a dear, Alex.' She sighed dramatically. 'There was a play on the other channel. Caroline Decker had a bit part. Too late now.'

'Was that the woman whose husband financed the Arbitrary?'

'I think he did once. She left him again. She was an actress first and a wife much later.' Miranda put her hand on her tummy. No such choice for her. She hadn't wanted this child and she still didn't want it, but whatever, she would always have to be a mother first and actress second. She was trapped.

Meg said, 'I didn't realize you were still in touch with any of them.'

'Christmas cards, that's all. The Markhams sent one and mentioned that Caro had a part in a costume drama.'

Alex said comfortingly, 'You'll be famous one day, Ma.'

'Don't call me Ma for God's sake!'

He went on quickly, 'Have you seen the man from Prospect Villa yet?'

'No.'

Miranda was not cheered by this obvious turn in the conversation. She had seen Janis just before Christmas and learned that the tenant of the 'damp dump', as Janis called it, intended to look after himself.

Alex went on eagerly, 'Well, Zach says he really has been to prison. We – Zach – went up there to offer to do the garden and the man would not open the door. He shouted through the letter box to go away.'

Miranda said, 'Alex, I have expressly forbidden you to pester anyone for money!'

'I didn't . . .' Alex caught his mother's eye and swallowed. 'I was just with Zach. I didn't say a word. I just wanted to see him so I could tell you about him. That's all.'

'And you didn't see him.'

'No.'

'So what makes you think Zach is right about his prison bit?'

'Well. Zach's mum says the vicar keeps calling.'

Miranda did not immediately pooh-pooh this doubtful evidence. Keele shared their Anglican priest with several other parishes, and one call on a new arrival was as much as he could manage.

She said, after due consideration, 'Doesn't mean a thing. He could be after help with the painting of the chancel ceiling.'

Alex acknowledged the truth of this with a judicious nod. The Prospect man had again provided a topic of conversation with his mother which made him well worth his salt. Unexpectedly Meg then joined in.

'Billy Majors told me yesterday that the poor man is practically a recluse. He goes into Penzance once a week for food and stuff and stays indoors for the rest of the time.'

Miranda opened her eyes at her sister. 'How on earth does Billy Majors know that?'

Meg shrugged. 'He's been up to sell him fish. And was

told that he got all his needs on Thursdays in town and preferred to be left strictly alone.'

Miranda almost said, 'How interesting!' but swallowed the words. The whole matchmaking idea suddenly seemed less unrealistic. Meg was no recluse but she was such a terribly private person she was next door to being one. And if the Prospect man was a recluse because he was nursing a broken heart or something, Meg might be just the one to comfort him. Miranda knew she would have to play the whole thing very carefully, very carefully indeed.

She said, 'Poor man.' And then she made a great fuss about standing up and holding out a restraining hand to her sister. 'No. Let me go, Sis. I need to move around a bit otherwise I shall cramp. I'll make a jug of cocoa and Alex can take some up to Peter. Stay put. Both of you. I insist.'

Their apprehension was an indication of how little she did these days; it was an unintentional reproach. She went very slowly downstairs, almost wishing she had the courage to let herself fall and perhaps be done with this baby and turn their reproaches on themselves. But a deeper instinct made her move slowly and deliberately to the saucepan above the Aga, to the fridge for milk and the dresser for mugs. At the beginning of her pregnancy she had done her usual things to be rid of such a burden; hot baths and gin, long walks and rock scrambles had been the order of the day. But when it hung grimly on to its foetal life, she looked at Seb who was her favourite and told herself she would love it, eventually.

She re-entered the sitting room with the tray balanced on the shelf of her abdomen and announced resignedly, 'I've just seen your shoes, Alex! We'll have to go into Penzance tomorrow and get you kitted out for school. In fact we might as well all go, then if there's anything in the sales for Katie and Seb we can get it.'

Alex smiled sleepily. This was the kind of thing that only happened when Aunt Meg was around. Proper family shopping expeditions like other kids had. Probably tea at a Wimpy bar and singing in the car coming home. He said happily, 'I do like it when we're all together.' Meg and Miranda exchanged glances and smiled, united by Miranda's family as well as their twinship. And, Miranda noticed with secret amusement, no-one realized the full significance of their trip to Penzance. Tomorrow was Thursday. When the Prospect man bought his weekly provisions.

Halfway up Market Jew Street she pleaded total exhaustion and went to wait for them in the Wimpy bar. She did not share Alex's passion for burgers, but the place was pristine clean and had an enormous window looking on to the street. Stationed there she could keep an eye on the shoppers on both sides of the road.

A man on his own was looking in the window of the record shop on the raised pavement opposite. She watched him with some interest. He wore brogues with jeans instead of the usual wellingtons, so he wasn't local. His parka was huge, with a hood fit for the North Pole. No, he certainly wasn't local. After a while he went inside the shop. She watched avidly. He emerged with a woman in a fur coat. His arm was possessively across her shoulders and he held her shopping bag and a square polythene carrier of records. Miranda wrinkled her nose exasperatedly. She had been so certain he was the Prospect man.

Meg appeared outside holding Sebastian's hand; Alex and Katie followed behind. Miranda's exasperation grew; how come they behaved like normal children when they were with other people, and like animals when they were with her? They trooped in and Meg ordered tea and cakes.

'You shouldn't,' Miranda said. 'They'll want another tea when we get home.'

'It's a treat,' Meg explained. They showed off their new shoes. They all had new shoes. Another of Aunt Meg's treats. The shoes had extra laces in different colours.

'I'll tie yours for you, Seb,' Katie promised. 'We'll change them each week.'

Meg rolled her eyes expressively at her sister and Miranda was prompted to say, 'I've just been having a game. Does anyone want to play?'

Alex turned to her instantly. 'Yes please!'

Katie said, 'What is it, first?'

'It's Spot the Prospect man.' Miranda grinned at them conspiratorially. 'It just occurred to me that he is probably in Penzance at this moment, buying his groceries for the week. And the place is almost empty so . . .'

'But we don't know what he looks like,' Sebastian objected, practically.

'Ex . . . actly!' Miranda kissed the soft orange curls. 'So we have to guess. He's not going to look like a Cornishman. But probably he won't look like a tourist either. He's terribly shy so he might have his head down—'

'And he'll be carrying lots of shopping bags,' Katie put in.

'And a gun,' Alex giggled foolishly.

'Don't be absurd, Alex,' Miranda said curtly.

'How do we know if we've won the game or not?' Katie asked.

Miranda was nonplussed. She had planned to arrange some encounter with a likely suspect and force a mutual introduction, but she could not tell the children that.

Meg said, 'Well, next week when school starts, Keele

will be empty and he's absolutely bound to come down into the village. So we shall know who won then.'

Miranda flashed her a grateful smile and pointed to a likely candidate.

'Why?' Katie asked.

'Elementary, my dear Katie. No camera so he's not a tourist. No coat either so he's got a car handy. Right age. On his own.'

Sebastian hoisted himself on to his mother's shortened lap. 'I want the green laces,' he said to her confidentially. 'Green is my best colour.'

Miranda said, 'Then you shall have the green laces, my precious. Or whatever colour you would like.'

'He can't, Ma! They're mine!' Alex held his shoe box to him.

Meg said, 'We'll have to get another pair each. You can choose which colour.'

'You spoil them, Meg!' But Miranda had seen someone who was certain to be the Prospect man.

'He's dishy too,' she enlarged after pointing him out. 'I actually saw him in my mind as a redhead. But dark hair can be very nice.'

'Dad's hair is brown.'

'Yes.'

'He's with that lady,' Alex said. And he was. And it was most unfair that his mother seemed to blame him.

Miranda needed things from the chemist and lingered there while Meg took the children to choose their shoe-laces. She picked up a henna rinse and some nail varnish and was looking at the face packs when a male voice on the other side of a display said, 'It won't kill the spiders, will it?'

The assistant hesitated. 'It doesn't say on the can, sir.'

Miranda adjusted the mirror above the lipsticks. She was still unable to see him.

He said, 'No. But if it slaughters flies and moths, one would assume—'

'We have a separate can for spiders, sir.' Another voice, smoother, assured, took over. 'This one is for flying insects. If you need—'

'No. I don't want to get rid of spiders. I like them.' The voice dropped and Miranda moved close to the intervening display. 'I'm afraid . . . previous tenants must have had cats . . . not very clean . . . I really need . . .'

'I understand completely, sir. Keele is full of cats. They come where the fish is, of course. Though they hate the sea.'

'I'm amazed they stayed in my house then. It's running with water.'

'Damp is it, sir?'

'You could say that.'

The voice had a hard flat quality which Miranda thought she might have heard before. But one thing was certain: this at last was the Prospect man. She put down the hair rinse and nail varnish and waited until the till clanged shut, then she swept around the display, head down, looking into her purse. Naturally enough, she cannoned straight into the man as he made to leave the shop.

'Oh!' She doubled over her pregnancy bump without conscious effort; the many shopping bags he was carrying had hit there first. But her feeling of triumph was intact; she had run down her quarry, thrown in her hook, now all she had to do was to tow him gently towards Meg.

'My God!' The voice was unapologetic. 'Where are you going, woman!'

She looked up, preparing to roast him roundly for

his lack of consideration, and was immediately turned to stone, mouth open in amazement. And she watched him adopt the same expression.

It was John Meredith. The man of some importance in Cheltenham. The man who had wanted to pay for a cold night with her, back in the snows of 1963. A man from another time and another life.

And even as she opened her mouth to exclaim and perhaps laugh at the ridiculous child she had been then, she was caught by that mesmeric stare. Like an echo, she remembered the charge of electricity followed by the weakness; the hardness of his nature subduing the tempestuousness of hers.

She remembered that it had been like playing with cold fire. Dangerous; but oh, so very exciting.

Meg knew she had got to get away. She had never stayed in Fish Cottage for so long before but Miranda seemed particularly helpless with this pregnancy, the children so sweetly dependent on her. It was hard to make the break. But that Peter should try to break down the careful barrier they had built between them . . . that was unbearable. She would have to go.

It started the morning after the television programme; he had been far more excited than she was about all that. And he had used it as a means of trying to regain their old . . . friendship.

She attempted to water down his enthusiasm.

'Kovacks did mention the programme. It was recorded some time ago.'

'You didn't tell us.'

'No. Well, it didn't seem important. You know how I earn my living.'

He rolled his eyes. 'Honestly, Meg! As if that's all it is – a living! You should be proud.'

'Proud? I hadn't thought . . . I'm not a creative artist like you. That's all I meant.'

He produced a book cover from behind his back. 'This is the illustration that was featured last night, apparently. This is what I would call creative.'

It was her design for the cover of *The Old Apple Man*. A stylistic orchard shed apples everywhere and they formed the shape of a face.

She smiled. 'I didn't know there was a copy of that book in the house.'

'We bought it for Alex. He's terribly proud of you.'

She filled the kettle and put it on the Aga. 'Well, I am his only aunt.'

The conversation embarrassed her; she was thankful when the children came bounding down the stairs for their breakfast.

But it was on the afternoon of Boxing Day that she felt the first flutter of panic. Everyone got up very late, the children pretending hangovers. Seb sat at the table, unable to sniff his blanket because of an incipient cold. He began to cry.

Miranda gathered him to her. 'Darling, please. Mummy loves you to distraction but that noise is going right through her poor old head. What is it?'

He did not know. Katie explained tersely. 'Christmas is a year away.'

He shook his head. 'It's not that. When the baby comes I won't be the baby any more. I don't want a new baby!'

'Oh, I know!' Miranda clutched him and seemed on the point of breaking down herself.

Meg said, 'You'll be like Katie. You'll look after the baby and you'll enjoy it.'

Katie nodded, but Seb was past easy comfort. 'Where's

Daddy?' he asked, suddenly in need of both parents.

'He's in the studio, darling. And the door will be locked. Go and knock.'

Miranda knew Peter's studio was sacrosanct, but her head was throbbing.

It was when Seb came down in floods again that they knew Peter wasn't in the house.

'The door isn't locked and the studio is empty!'

Meg took over. Miranda went back to bed, Katie and Alex went for a walk and Sebastian dragged his blanket upstairs to 'wait for Daddy'.

Meg took drinks upstairs at midday and found him huddled under one of the dormers. She had not been up here since that day ten years ago when Peter had been so suddenly and unaccountably angry with her. It was unrecognizable. The roof had been lined and the skylights replaced with dormers. The easel held a square of hardboard covered with a sheet. Other work in progress stood around the walls: a half-finished portrait of Billy Majors, some sketches of the lifeboat, the *King Solomon*.

'I think I'll come downstairs now, Aunt Meg.' Seb finished his cocoa and stood up. As he made for the stairs, his blanket brushed the edge of the easel and beneath the sheet she saw a flash of orange paint.

'Right. Off we go then, Seb. Let's make a bed for you in the sitting room and watch some television, shall we?'

He went ahead of her down the stairs and she turned back and lifted the sheet. It was her hair, like threads of light surrounding a small secret face. He had found her portrait. Was he going to rework it? Paint over it? There was no way of knowing. She followed Sebastian, trying to tell herself it meant nothing. But it did not help when Peter arrived home at teatime and told them he had walked to St Ives.

* * *

So after they had been to Penzance to buy new shoes for the children, she broached the subject of her departure. She and Miranda took their coffee to the sitting room, while Alex and Peter washed up the supper dishes. Miranda had been very quiet since they got home, and Meg was worried she might have caught Seb's cold. Cold or no cold, she simply had to go back to Kilburn.

'Sis, are you all right?' she began tentatively as Miranda settled herself with a groan in one of the armchairs.

'Of course I'm all right!' Miranda looked across the hearth almost angrily. 'Why on earth wouldn't I be? It's this damned chair! The trouble with you, Meg, is you assume that pregnancy means ill-health! Quite the contrary! I feel fine!'

Meg thought wryly of all the fetching and carrying she had done over the past month.

'You're unusually quiet,' she said pacifically.

Miranda was obviously on the warpath. 'That's another thing! I have to be the extrovert in this family! I have to be piggy-in-the-middle between you and Peter! It's ten years since that ghastly mix-up and you both act as if you're frightened to look at each other! It's ridiculous, Meg!'

Meg was appalled. 'Darling, I really don't want to talk like this. As you say, it's ten years ago and best forgotten.'

'But you won't forget it, will you?'

'Miranda. If you're really feeling OK, I think I should go home.' Meg was determined not to be deflected from her original intention. 'That was why I was asking whether you were all right. Nothing to do with Peter. Nothing to do with . . . any of that—'

'Go home?' Miranda looked stunned. 'Go home? You can't go home now, Meg! Not now!'

'Come on, Sis. Be sensible. Katie's birthday . . . Christmas . . . New Year . . . they've all come and gone. I shall have been here five weeks. I've got a job, you know. My own house.'

'That dump in Kilburn! That might be your house. This is your *home*!' Suddenly Miranda was crying. 'You know it is, Meg! It was your home before it was mine – you belong here – with Peter and me and the kids—'

Meg was horrified all over again. She slipped out of her chair and on to her knees to hold the red head to her shoulder.

'Darling, what on earth's got into you? What's this all about? Really?'

Miranda let Meg take her weight and sobbed helplessly.

'I want you to be here. Just be here. Please. Please, Meg . . .'

Meg patted and murmured and stared into the flames over Miranda's head. The old connection between them had long gone and she had no way of knowing what was disturbing her sister, but she knew something was.

At last she drew away and looked into Miranda's eyes.

'What's up?' she asked bluntly.

Miranda shook her head and her hair flew around like an aureole.

'Nothing specific. It's just . . . I don't think I can face Keele on my own for much longer, Meg. Does that sound awful?'

'Frankly, yes. And you're not alone.'

'No. I'm not, am I? If I were alone I suppose I could leave.'

'Listen. Sis. It's a bad time. Mid-winter . . . being pregnant . . .'

'Don't say any more! I know you're going to say you're going anyway.'

'Miranda, I have to go back.'

'Will you stay another week? Just one more week?'

'Why? The children begin school on Monday. You'll be able to rest all day—'

'Just one more bloody week, for God's sake! Surely it's not too much to ask?'

Meg frowned. The heat from the fire had turned Miranda's pale skin to fiery red. She looked almost bloated. In spite of her denials, was there something wrong?

Meg said slowly, 'Next Thursday. Till next Thursday.'

Miranda flung her arms around Meg's suddenly reluctant shoulders.

'Oh, darling! Thank you! I need you so much! I love you so much! You'll never know . . . I want you to stay here for ever! You could work down here—'

'Till next Thursday, Miranda. You have to promise that you'll accept that.'

'I promise. I promise. And you promise that you'll stay.

'Well . . . I know you will because you said so.' She drew back, but the orange-gold hair was tangled in Meg's and though they both laughed as they unknotted it, Meg saw it as symbolic. And rather frightening.

Eleven

Miranda could feel herself getting into what Aunt Maggie many moons ago had called 'a state'. She wanted to pretend John Meredith wasn't there. Then she wanted to pretend that she didn't care whether he was there or not. When he had piloted her outside into the winter twilight of Market Jew Street, there had been no electrical current from his hand to her arm. And when he had said, 'My God, this is fate! Come back with me to the house,' she had shaken her head dumbly. When he'd said, 'Don't be absurd, you know you have to,' she had almost gabbled Meg's name like a lucky charm. 'Meg is waiting for me in the car. Meg. My sister.' Because Meg was her good side.

'Tomorrow morning then.'

'I can't. The children . . . I've got three children.'

'And another on the way.' In the lamplight she had seen him smile again and thought it was like a tiger's smile. He put his hand on her abdomen and even through her coat she felt it. She had talked of her sister and her children. Not her husband. So he smiled.

But then he became deadly serious.

'I shall be in Lannah Cove at low tide on Saturday morning. That's the little beach next to the harbour. You can walk around the headland.'

She said, 'Alex is playing football in the afternoon.'

As if he knew them all intimately, he said, 'Good. Then Meg can look after him.' She'd gone on staring. And then she'd turned and left.

The one landmark in the midst of her 'state' was Meg. When Meg talked of leaving it nearly drove her mad. If Meg left her with Meredith she was lost. Peter . . . well, Peter had never really been hers in the first place, had he? She'd never admitted it to herself before, but it had always been obvious had she cared to face up to it. And . . . Meredith had been the first.

So she decided to go to Lannah Cove to tell him that her sister was staying with her and there was no way he could get to her while Meg was there. She forced herself to smile into the mirror as she did her hair. She really was making a big drama out of this. He was a man from her past – all right, the first man – but all she was doing was satisfying a very natural curiosity. She wanted to know if he really had been in prison as Alex reckoned. She wanted to know if he'd been married. Got children. If he really and honestly was still attracted to her now that she was practically middle-aged and pregnant. Very pregnant.

The lump was terribly obvious. Meg had given her a velvet jacket for Christmas, rather like a smoker's jacket, flared from the shoulders with patch pockets and gold braided cuffs. The lump pushed gently at its front and she stuck her hands in her pockets and thrust it forward. She had never hated being pregnant quite so much before. Especially did she hate it now. She was definitely no longer Ophelia.

Meg was already cooking breakfast. How on earth was she going to cope domestically when Meg went back to London? Was there a way of ensuring that she did not ever go back to London?

'Sis! You're up early! I was going to bring you a cup of tea.'

Miranda shrugged. 'Peter went up to the studio while it was still dark. I thought I'd go for a walk.'

'Darling, wait till I've done this. I'll come with you. Alex will see to the others.'

Miranda hesitated. Was that the answer – to take Meg with her?

'Not this time, Sis. I think I'd like to be on my own. It's low tide so I can go across the sands.' She opened the door and looked out. It was not an inviting prospect; grey as usual with the damned mist shrouding the jetties.

Meg followed her. 'Oh. Lovely morning. Pastel.'

Miranda crouched and went outside. 'Jolly dark pastel,' she commented. But at least no-one would see her cross the harbour and go around the headland.

It was hard work negotiating the slippery steps and picking her way between pools and pebbles. Keyhole was such a dump; what the hell was Meredith doing down here? And what was she doing down here? She was an actress, and here she was as far from a stage as it was possible to be. She had a sudden flash of a daydream. Meg and Peter, together at last, looking after the children for her. Herself, backed by Meredith – who might well have become some theatrical impresario since she'd known him – on a West End stage.

The dream squelched away as she went ankle-deep into a pool. She stood still and cursed aloud, 'Damn and blast this awful place!' From six yards into the mist ahead of her, a hard voice said, 'Hear, hear!' And she laughed and ran forward as if she were greeting a friend. It was just as natural for him to gather her up and clear the little streamlet that always flowed between the jetties with one of his long-legged strides. Not so natural to put her down with a thud and devour her with a kiss.

As she submitted to that kiss, so she was lost. It was submitting to his obsession. She knew obsessions were not natural but that she could provoke such an intensity of feeling in a man had to be flattering. Her husband might love her because she was Meg's twin, but this man had never seen Meg. Silently – she remembered that silent concentration now – he kept up the frantic kissing while he pulled at her clothing. She could not have resisted successfully had she tried, so she did not try. The electrical current was suddenly switched on for her, and the brief coupling against the streaming, limpet-crusted wall of the west jetty hardly long enough to satisfy either of them.

She gasped and wept as he left her.

'Oh God – oh God – what is happening to me?'

As before, he ignored her while he saw to his own clothing. Then he said, 'Cover yourself up. It's cold. Come back to the house with me.'

She wept in earnest. 'I can't. Oh, my back – my new jacket will be ruined!'

'Don't come the injured party! You knew what was going to happen.'

'I didn't! I wanted to talk to you – see you again – you – you raped me!'

He laughed, putting a hand on the wall and bowing his head to it. Then he straightened. 'Christ. Those limpets are sharp, you're right. Come on up to the house. It's a damp tomb but the bed is OK.'

'I hate you. I'd forgotten how you . . . used me . . .' She was tugging frantically at her knickers. She had trodden them into the wet sand and they were horrible.

He grabbed her suddenly. 'Listen. I've never forgotten you. And you've never forgotten me. Don't fight it.'

He held her so hard she could scarcely breathe. But the current was on and her legs would not have supported her if she had not clung to him in return.

She whimpered, 'I'm pregnant. How can you feel the same when I'm pregnant? You fell for Ophelia—'

'I wouldn't have believed it possible either. But I fell for you. Whether you're young, old, pregnant or not.'

He propped her against the limpets again, stood back and stared at her with his hard gaze. Then he said slowly, 'If you won't come to the house now, come tonight. I'll expect you tonight.'

He moved back another pace. The mist seemed to blot him up. After a few seconds of staring at where he had been, she called, 'Meredith?' And when there was no answer she shouted loudly, 'I can't come! I can't do it!'

Disembodied, full of that cruel amusement, his voice came back. 'Bring that sister of yours! Maybe I'll prefer her!'

Miranda bowed over her pregnancy lump. Meg. Meg was her only hope of sanity and safety.

Meg and Katie were making a pork and apple casserole.

'We'll put in some soy sauce,' Meg said, trying not to watch Katie wield a knife among the apples. 'That will give it a sweet and sour ambience.'

She used a heavy French accent and Katie laughed delightedly.

'Can I pour in the soupy stuff?'

'The stock. No. It will hiss and bubble like a cauldron. You·can make a spell instead.'

Katie was intoning 'Abracadabra,' when Peter appeared at the top of the stairs. She ran to him. 'We're having sweet and sour pork for lunch, Peter! And we're having it early cos we're going to watch Alex play football at Gulval!'

He hoisted her up and sat down at the table.

'Great.' He beamed at Katie, kissed her head, said something about her 'crazy hair' and turned the beam on Meg. 'I thought there might be some coffee going. Where is everyone?'

Meg saw him hazily through the steam from the pan, but his happiness with the moment was transparent enough. She swallowed and kept the wooden spoon turning.

'Miranda went for a walk on the beach. While the tide was out. She wanted to be by herself.'

Katie said, 'Alex is training.'

'And Seb is still in bed. I went in and blew his nose for him and hopefully he'll manage a nap till the next blockage!' Peter continued to beam as he added, 'It's not like Miranda to want to be alone.'

Katie snuggled into her father's arm; she wanted nothing to spoil this mid-morning bliss.

'Miranda is never alone,' she said in her actress voice. 'The baby is always with her.'

Peter put his head back and laughed, and after a moment Meg joined in.

They drank coffee and ceremoniously tipped the contents of the pan into a large casserole which went into a side oven.

Peter said, 'Katie, I want to ask your Aunt Meg a great big favour. And I don't know how to go about it.'

Katie grinned. 'Tell me and I'll ask her,' she offered largely.

Meg took the coffee cups to the sink and fetched a tablecloth from the dresser. She wondered how anyone could be so happy yet so full of dread all at the same time. She loved it at Fish Cottage, yet she could not wait to leave.

Peter intoned sonorously, 'Katie child. Will you ask your aunt if she will do me the honour to sit for me?'

Katie turned to Meg.

'Aunt Meg,' she mimicked her father's voice exactly. 'I wonder if you would do Peter . . .' she fumbled for words then swept on grandly, 'the honour – yes, the honour – to sit for him?' She picked up the tablecloth which had somehow fallen out of Meg's hands and presented it with a bow. 'In other words,' she resumed in her normal voice, 'can he paint you?' She turned

235

back to her father. 'That wasn't much of a favour! Everyone sits for you without knowing they're doing it!' She laughed. 'Hey, if it's nearly time to eat, I'll go and see if Seb is coming down.' She pushed her hair behind her ears and added seriously, 'He still needs so much help with his dressing, you know.'

And she was gone up the stairs.

Meg shook out the cloth and waved it helplessly. Peter caught one end and between them they spread it over the table.

Peter said, 'I've been working towards this ever since you arrived, Meg! I know I've made my reputation – what reputation I have – with my Stanhope Forbes stuff – but I still do portraits, you know. In my spare time. D'you remember I liked to do people sort of emerging from somewhere?'

Meg said woodenly, 'Mrs Pascoe.'

'Mrs Pascoe? God, yes. My old landlady at Newlyn! You remember her!'

'Yes.'

Surely he must realize this was dangerous ground?

But his excitement was taking him past all the warning signs. He said, 'I gave her that painting. She was coming out of a frying pan!' He laughed delightedly. 'I'm doing one of Billy Majors wreathed in tobacco smoke. Arthur Bowering would like it for the Coastguards.'

She fetched cutlery and began to lay the table. It was one of those automatic tasks that was suddenly very difficult.

He leaned back in the old Windsor chair and clasped his hands behind his head.

'That night – just before Christmas – when Arthur told us about your television programme . . . I was annoyed with you for hiding your light under a bushel. For your complete lack of – of – self-esteem. I put your painting on the easel and looked at it and couldn't find any answers – just like before.' He was no longer smiling. His dark eyes were looking back, narrowed, focused as if he was peering through a tunnel. He went on, 'Then on Boxing Day I walked to St Ives. I did the things we did before. I swam. My God, it was icy. But of course I'm ten years older now.' He puffed a laugh. 'I couldn't see any of the Scaife work – the galleries were closed, of course. But I walked back over the hump and looked. And looked. And I began to realize that the key to that painting *is* its mystery. You are emerging from that mystery – just a hint of you – like Billy emerges from the smoke. Like Mrs Pascoe from the frying pan.'

She put the cruet in the centre of the table and knocked the pepper pot from its holder. She was trembling. She sat down and put her hands on her lap.

He registered her silence after a heart-stopping minute, came out of his tunnel and looked at her.

He said quietly, 'Probably I'll never know you, Meg. But I know just enough now to be able to finish that painting.'

She said, 'Please, Peter. Miranda—'

'This is nothing to do with Miranda, Meg. This twin thing . . . you are separate people, different as chalk and cheese. If I paint Miranda, I haven't painted you.'

'I wasn't suggesting—'

'Meg. I am asking you to sit for me. That is all.'

'Yes.' She did not meet his dark gaze. 'I'm sorry, Peter. Probably you don't realize . . . Miranda would not like it.'

'Miranda can lump something just for once.'

She smiled slightly at the tablecloth. 'Yes. But I cannot lump it for her.' She looked up at him and down again. 'I could never hurt Miranda, Peter.'

'For God's sake!' He was suddenly furious. 'You are encouraging her to be petty and unreasonable!'

She stood up. Obviously neither Alex nor Miranda were going to rescue her from this situation.

She said very steadily, 'Miranda knows more than she realizes. She knows how I feel. About you.' She walked to the stairs. 'We'll say no more about this, Peter. I have promised to stay till next Thursday, then I shall go.'

He did not turn to watch her go upstairs. He stayed rigidly still in the high-backed wooden chair and stared at the upset cruet. And after a long moment he reached across and replaced the pepper pot.

The football pitch at Gulval was high above Penzance with a wonderful view of St Michael's Mount between one set of goal posts. There was no definite horizon line and the castle seemed to be hanging in the grey sky like a mirage. Meg concentrated on it so that she would not have to watch Peter marshalling his little flock out of the car. Suddenly they had become all the things she could never have. And it was her own fault.

Miranda stayed in the car, her face dead white in the frame of the windscreen. Surprisingly she did not insist that Sebastian should stay with her, and he ran off with Katie and Alex towards the tumbledown shed at the entrance, referred to grandly as 'the clubhouse'. Peter ambled after them and joined other fathers who would doubtless have to help with bootlaces.

Meg opened the car door and sat sideways on the back seat.

'Darling. Are you sure you're up to this? You're not yourself, are you?'

Miranda tried to be flippant. 'No. I'm me and some-one else!' She patted her tummy and laughed. 'Actually,

I'm feeling bad because I've committed you and me to afternoon tea. And I forgot we were coming up here.'

'Is that all?' Meg laughed too and reached over the seat to pat her sister's shoulder. 'Why on earth didn't you say before? We could have phoned from the cottage and put it off!'

'Well, I was hoping we could do both.' Miranda made a face at the pitch, still muddy from last week's game. 'This isn't my idea of heaven exactly. And as long as Peter's around to yell and cheer . . .' Miranda put up a gloved hand and held Meg's fingers to her shoulder. 'Please come with me, Meg. It . . . it's rather important.'

Meg looked at the pitch too. Katie and Sebastian were squelching between the far goal posts; Peter had disappeared inside the clubhouse. They would be all right; it was a chance to distance herself from Peter.

'Of course I'll come with you. If you think we can be back to take them home—'

'Easily.' Miranda was eager now to be off. 'Can you go and tell Peter what's happening? No, don't bother him. Tell Katie.'

That suited Meg. By the time she had got across the field and back, Miranda had reversed the car on to the road. It was as if she knew how anxious Meg was to get away from Peter's vicinity.

Even so, she drove much too fast. The lanes twisted across the spine of land in a series of blind corners and Miranda took each one without changing down.

Meg stuck it for as long as she could, then said, 'Darling, if we meet a tractor we've had it. What's the hurry?'

Miranda slowed obligingly. 'No hurry. Not really. I wasn't thinking.'

Meg looked sideways; the small face was still pale and set. She said slowly and carefully, 'Miranda. I know it's none of my business. But . . . have you and Peter had a row?'

'A row?' Miranda flashed a surprised look into the mirror. 'We're not . . . but no, we haven't had a row.'

'You're not what?'

'We haven't made love for ages. Not since before Christmas. That night we went to the Coastguards actually.' Miranda laughed. 'Satisfied?'

Meg's face was hot but she was determined not to back down this time. 'That is just over two weeks ago, Miranda! And you are very pregnant!'

'True. Too true.' Miranda sighed suddenly. 'You see, it's our main way of communicating, Sis. You probably communicate more deeply with Peter than I do!'

Meg said nothing to that. There seemed nothing to say.

Miranda turned left on to a road signposted Lannah Cove. 'I mean, you both paint. So you've got that in common. And you can stand and look at things for ages.' She laughed. 'I just get bored.'

'Oh, Miranda.' Meg felt a pang of pure distress.

Miranda reached for another laugh. 'I shouldn't have given up the stage, Meg. That's my trouble.'

'You didn't have much choice really, did you?'

'I could have got rid of Alex.'

'Oh my God.' Meg was horrified. 'You mustn't talk like that, darling. And anyway there was Peter. You loved Peter and he loved you.'

'What the hell is love, Meg? You loved Peter too and he loved you. Peter and I were – are – superb together in bed. Is that love?'

'Yes, of course it is. An aspect of it. Miranda, why are you talking like this? We've never said these things before – what are you trying to tell me?'

'I'm trying to tell you that the only true love for me is the love I have for you. That is love. Pure love.'

'Well, of course. But one love does not exclude another.'

'Don't get deep on me, Meg. I know only one thing at the moment, and that is that I want you near me. For always.'

Meg felt she was walking a ridge with an abyss either side of her.

'Sis – I know – I miss you terribly too. But I told you the other evening – I cannot live with you and Peter—'

'Because you love him too?'

The question was a bolt from the blue for both of them. Meg heard Miranda's indrawn breath and knew that until that moment she had not faced the possibility of Meg still loving Peter.

She said swiftly, 'For goodness' sake, Sis—'

But Miranda let her get no further. She wailed helplessly, 'Meg! I knew of course – I felt your love for him and the pain when you couldn't give yourself to him! I felt it back at Miss Pugh's that night . . . and yet I imagined it was now non-existent!' She held on to the wheel as if it were a lifebelt, they skidded to a stop very near the ditch. 'Oh, Meg, what have I done – all these years—'

'Be quiet, Sis!' Meg heard her own voice, stern, almost cold. 'My feelings have got nothing to do with this. Nothing at all. You have no need to worry on that account—'

'I've known! All the time! And I wouldn't acknowledge it!' The floodgates of truth were opened and would not be shut. Miranda put her head down on the wheel and wept.

Meg held her and made noises and wondered what to do.

Miranda said, 'That's why you want to leave. Obviously. Obvious except to me, of course.' She banged her head against her gloved knuckles. 'Stupid, thick me!'

Meg said, 'Miranda, stop this. You're acting. Stop it.'

Blessedly there was a pause in the hysterical outburst, then, incredibly, Miranda snuffled a laugh.

'Oh God. Am I? I don't know any more. Oh God.' She sniffed hard and peered round at her sister. 'Meg, I mean this – I love you more than anyone in the world – more than my children. Certainly more than Peter. And that's real. True. Genuine.'

Meg too managed a grin. 'Don't protest too much!' she warned.

'Oh, Meg.' Her eyes filled again. 'All those years when I was so self-sufficient! Well, I thought I was desperately in love with Brett St Clare of course, but when I discovered . . . you saved me from that.'

'Miranda – I knew nothing about it until a long time afterwards.'

'No, but it was when I was still lacerated from that, that your feelings broke through mine. And I knew then where my true love lay.'

Meg took a breath. 'Darling, we shouldn't be talking like this. What good will it do? I am going home on Thursday, you know. And that is that.'

Miranda sat up slowly and leaned back, easing her neck.

She said, 'I met the Prospect man on Thursday in Penzance, Meg. And again this morning. I think I'm in love with him.'

Meg stared at her in total disbelief. 'Miranda! Please! Is this some kind of an act?'

Miranda kept her gaze directed doggedly through the windscreen. 'I knew him before. It's an amazing coincidence, Meg. Like fate. I think I've been in love with him all the time.'

'You're mad!'

'Maybe. Quite possibly. But mad or not, you *are* my only hope, Meg. I do love you better than anyone else.

Better than this man. That's why I've . . . brought you here this afternoon.'

'You mean – it's him we're going to see?' Meg was so appalled she hardly knew what to do. 'Reverse the car, Miranda! We're going back!'

'No.' Miranda's voice was strange. As if she were in some kind of trance.

Meg said firmly, 'Listen. If you won't come with me, I am getting out of this car. I refuse to come with you on some ghastly assignation—'

'You are my only hope, Meg. If you leave me now, I shall go to him. That is absolutely certain.'

'You're ill. Miranda – darling – please—'

Suddenly Miranda turned and seemed her old impatient self.

'For goodness' sake, Meg! All I'm asking is for you to come and meet someone with me. I need to know what you think. Is that too much to ask?'

Meg stared, knowing this sudden reasonableness was false but not quite able to put her finger on its flaw.

'The circumstances – what you have just told me – that's what makes it too much to ask!'

Miranda shrugged. 'It's really up to you.'

There was a short silence in the car. Meg put one hand on the door and with the other gathered her bag and gloves into a bunch. Then she sat back again.

After waiting another half-minute, Miranda started up the engine and turned the car into the narrow track to Prospect Villa. She parked and turned to her sister.

'He wants to meet you. I think he must have had something awful happen to him since I knew him. He's come down here to escape something, I'm sure.' She smiled fleetingly. 'He won't have a spider killed in the house!'

'He's expecting us?'

243

'He asked me to bring you. This afternoon.'

Meg said, 'Remember we have to be back at Gulval in another hour.'

'Of course,' Miranda said, and opened her door.

The house had not changed in ten years. It still had the gaunt, haunted look that had so put Meg off before. And its new tenant did nothing to reassure her. He opened the door for them, looked at Miranda with a smile that was triumphant, then past her at Meg and said, 'Ah. The twin. How very interesting.' And promptly turned and disappeared into the room on one side of the hall, leaving them to follow if they wished.

Miranda went ahead and Meg closed the front door with some difficulty. The wood had swelled with the damp and did not fit the frame. She looked down the hall and could see bubbles in the paper. It was colder indoors than out. She glanced at her watch. Five past three. They must leave at ten to four at the very latest.

The sitting room was probably the lightest room in the house. Nineteen-thirties bay windows pushed out of two of the walls and there was a superlative view of Keele harbour from the front one. Already the Christmas lights were starting to twinkle. Meg looked at that to avoid looking at the tall, thin, predatory man standing much too close to Miranda.

Miranda's eyes were enormous. She said, 'Meg – this is—'

He leaned forward from the waist and took Meg's unwilling hand in both of his. 'John Stonehouse,' he said, the smile wide and without humour.

'John Stonehouse?' She wondered if he was making a joke. John Stonehouse was the Member of Parliament who had disappeared recently.

'No connection, dear lady.'

She withdrew her hand and put it in her pocket as if laying claim to it. Was it her imagination or was he trying to take possession of Miranda and herself? He made no attempt to fetch tea, but crowded them into the window and pointed out various landmarks still identifiable in the twilight. Meg hated this proximity. Miranda sat on a chair, looking round and up at him now and then with a kind of intimacy that made her feel sick.

'Lannah Cove is just down there.' He leaned right over again to point into total darkness. 'It's the only swimming beach apparently.'

Miranda made small interested sounds and Meg said sharply, 'We were brought up in Keele. We swam off that beach when we were only three years old.'

'You never told me that, Miranda!'

He looked down at her with a kind of teasing reproach and she laughed as if it were funny.

'It did not come up. But you must have guessed we have lived here for some time.'

'No. I imagined an artist of Peter Snow's calibre would be based in London.'

Meg said, 'Peter would loathe London. So would the children.'

'Yes. Quite. Ideal for children down here, I suppose. And it's probably an artist's paradise too. But I know how you feel about it, Ophelia.' Again they both laughed, sharing a special joke.

Meg said sharply, 'We should be going. Alex would like us to be there in case he scores a goal. And there's sure to be tea in the clubhouse.' She could hear herself rattling words like machine-gun fire into a silence that was taut with awareness. She moved to the fireplace where a fire smouldered sulkily. 'It's very cold in here, Mr Stonehouse. I remember looking at the house back in 1965 and thinking that it would probably be damp.'

He turned from Miranda at last.

'It is more than damp! The kitchen walls literally run with water at times! And there are fleas!' He looked at her very directly as he spoke. She had always associated eye contact with frankness; there was nothing frank about this man. His stare challenged her to look right at him and be absorbed by him in some way. She raised her eyebrows and said, 'Oh dear, I am sorry. In that case we had better leave. It's really no place for my sister.'

Miranda did not move. 'I expect the last tenant kept cats. Hasn't the spray helped, John?'

'Yes. I believe I'm rid of them. But the fact remains that the house was practically unfit for habitation.'

'It's too bad.' Miranda looked at Meg. 'Isn't it, Sis?'

Meg drew on her gloves. 'Was the agent's name Allen?' she asked laconically.

'It was. You know him?'

'Of old.'

Miranda acted as if some great discovery had been made.

'He was the man who messed you about over Fish Cottage, wasn't he? And he's still around? John – isn't that another coincidence?'

John Stonehouse bared his teeth again. 'Makes us practically blood kin!'

They both seemed to find this amusing. Meg made for the door.

'We really do have to go, Miranda.'

Miranda stood up at last. 'Well, thank you, John. I'm glad you've met my sister.'

'So am I.' Meg was struggling with the door and did not look round. She heard Miranda gasp a little laugh and did not wish to see why.

She settled herself in the driver's seat and held out her hand for the keys. Miranda seemed to take an age to make her farewells, come down the path and open the car door.

Mr Stonehouse called, 'See you tonight, Ophelia.'

Miranda did not reply. She got into the car, bumping herself everywhere. They had to reverse down the track and Meg needed all her concentration, but Miranda knew she was fuming and said soothingly, 'Take it steadily. We've got loads of time. We were only there half an hour.'

Meg manoeuvred on to the road. 'Half an hour too long!' she said. 'Miranda, what are you thinking of! He's . . . horrible!'

Miranda lost her temper quite suddenly. 'You made no effort whatever, Meg! You looked down your nose like some supercilious llama! And when you told him how cold his house was – well, that was just plain bad manners!'

'Rubbish! It's not his house anyway.' She waited while they rounded the next bend, then said, 'Exactly what is going on, Miranda?'

'Nothing is going on, as you put it! I met him when we went shopping on Thursday afternoon. He was buying flea powder in the chemist's. We recognized each other, of course. The . . . the feeling . . . is still there. He's a charming man!'

'Charming? That is the last word I should use to describe Mr Stonehouse!'

'Dynamic, then.'

'Miranda, don't be ridiculous. He's a cold fish.'

'Analytical, yes. He can see through people. He reminds me of Svengali.'

'My God! And do you see yourself as Trilby?'

'I don't know.' She sounded sulky now.

'Miranda, Svengali was a sinister hypnotist, for God's sake!'

'He brought Trilby to life. Perhaps you need someone to bring you to life, Meg! Then you'd understand. If you – right in the beginning – if you hadn't been so cold towards Peter, none of this would have happened!'

Meg spoke crisply. 'Miranda, you are behaving like a schoolgirl. I find the whole subject distasteful. We'll drop it.'

Miranda seemed to accept this and there was another long silence while Meg struggled with the car. Then they took the last of the bends and approached the magnificent view of St Michael's Mount. Lights were everywhere, outlining the Mount, twinkling all over Penzance. The two teams were being dragooned into shaking hands. Alex detached himself from the crowd and came towards them. He was covered in mud, his white strip unrecognizable.

'We won, Ma! Three two! Zach scored in the last five minutes else it would 'a bin a dror!' He approached the open car door. 'Ma, what's up? You're crying? Is it the baby coming too soon?'

'No, of course not.' Miranda hugged him suddenly, possessively, as if she might not see him again. 'I'm just so pleased you won.'

'Ma, you'll get muddy!' Alex pulled away and ran off to join Zach. Katie took his place.

'It's tea in the clubhouse, Miranda,' she said, her face long with disapproval. 'You only just got back in time.'

'Sorry, Katie.' Miranda was blithe again. Her mood changes were mercurial. She got out of the car and took Meg's arm. They plodded across the mud. Peter waved and herded Sebastian into the brightness of the clubhouse. Katie galloped ahead to join Alex and Zach. The fragrance of hot tea wafted towards them.

'I suppose you think this is marvellous?' Miranda said pleasantly. 'Family life. A cameo thereof. You don't know what it's like to be not quite a part of it.'

Meg said, 'Are we back to Mr Stonehouse again?'

'And me,' Miranda replied shortly.

She paused in the door. It was chaos inside and everyone seemed to be laughing. She looked back.

'He wants me to go there tonight,' she said with a frankness that was brutal. 'If it weren't for this – ' she touched her abdomen – 'I'd be able to send you in my place. It would be history repeating itself, wouldn't it?'

She went into the cacophony of the tumbledown clubhouse. Meg stared after her, aghast. She thought she knew her sister; and then something like this happened. And she wondered if she knew her at all.

Twelve

In spite of their absence, the football match was an enormous success for the rest of the family. Miranda went straight into the kitchen of the clubhouse to help with the teas, something she would normally have left to Meg. She emerged at intervals carrying heavy trays, laughing with the other women, toasting Alex in lemonade, her hair flying, her eyes glinting emerald lights, the life and soul of the party. Alex grinned mightily, so proud of her he seemed about to explode. Zach's mother was fat, fair and forty and until now he had thought she was the ideal maternity symbol.

Peter managed to find Meg, a snuffling Sebastian on her lap, behind the pile of clothes in the corner.

'What's happened to Miranda?' he asked humorously. 'Was your afternoon tea laced with rum or something?'

She met his eyes fleetingly. In the embarrassment – horror – of the afternoon she had temporarily forgotten that Peter now knew how she felt about him. Remembering what she had said increased the sense of near-nightmare.

She ignored his question and said, 'Sebastian has a temperature. I think we should get him home as soon as possible.'

Peter leaned down and slid his hand across his son's forehead. Sebastian seemed to be in a fitful sleep.

'He looked OK during the match. Katie and him . . . they were shouting fit to burst.'

Katie appeared with a glass of lemonade.

'This is for Seb,' she said in her usual authoritative way. 'He's been thirsty all afternoon and they – ' she jerked her head at the mothers of the other team – 'they wouldn't let him have a drink.'

Peter knelt down and held the glass to Sebastian's mouth. The little boy opened his eyes and gulped thirstily.

'Is it over?' he asked, emerging with bubbles still popping on his upper lip. 'Can we go home now?'

Katie said, 'Alex won't want to leave till everyone else. Perhaps Zach's mum and dad will bring him home. Shall I ask them, Peter?'

'No.' Peter lifted Seb from Meg's lap and stood up with him. 'We'll take him home and come back for the others.' He looked down. 'Katie, will you tell Miranda what is happening after we've gone? She's so happy, I don't want to spoil it all for her.'

Meg could have told him otherwise. She actually opened her mouth to say that she would take over from Miranda and let her go home with her husband and small son. Then she did not. Suddenly being with Peter was by far the lesser of the two evils. Suddenly, horribly, she could not bear to be with her sister.

Peter sat in the back of the car with Sebastian held beneath his overcoat. Meg drove carefully down to Penzance and then out to Keele through Newlyn. Already the moon was up, a full moon bathing everything in a pale blue light. Sebastian emerged from the nest of his father's coat and peered at it; he was looking more normal.

'It's not a man. Not really, is it?' he asked apprehensively as the moon appeared to swing from the side window to the rear.

Peter laughed. 'No. It's another planet, like us. It's our special planet. Called a satellite. Can you say that word? Satellite.'

Sebastian repeated parrot-fashion, 'Saturlite.'

Peter laughed and after a moment Meg joined in. Sebastian said, 'I want Mummy.'

'I'll fetch her as soon as we've got you to bed,' Peter reassured him. 'Look at the shadows of the hills and valleys on the moon. Just before you were born a man landed on the moon, so we know quite a lot about it.'

Sebastian said stubbornly, 'I want Mummy.'

Meg changed down to take the hill into Keyhole. They rounded the bulk of the Coastguards Inn and the Christmas lights twinkled at them.

'Oh, look.' She smiled into the mirror. 'They've switched on early. Specially for you, darling.'

Sebastian laughed and reached out to the ribbon on Meg's ponytail. He pulled and her hair flew out over her winter coat. He stroked it fondly. 'Oh, Mummy, you are funny,' he said.

Incredibly Peter laughed too. 'She is, isn't she?' he said.

It increased Meg's nightmare feeling to screaming point. But she drove the car along Fish Street with even greater care and said, 'We can park outside for ten minutes. Just while we get you inside. Then Daddy will have to leave to pick up Mummy and Katie and Alex, won't he?'

Sebastian laughed again, sleepily this time, and cuddled back inside Peter's coat while Meg fitted the key into the low door of the fish cellar and went ahead to switch on lights and put the kettle on the Aga. And not even those everyday actions could banish the feeling of complete unreality.

She was telling Sebastian a story when she heard the door open and the others erupt into the kitchen. Sebastian, almost asleep, smiled and said, 'Isn't it nice when every-one is happy?'

'Yes, darling,' Meg said steadily.

'Go on with the story. About the moon babies.'

Meg racked her brain for inspiration. Sebastian had not wanted *The Little House on the Prairie*; he had wanted a moon story. She said, 'Tomorrow I will draw them for you, Seb. Two clouds and two moon babies.'

'Just like you and Aunt Meg?' Sebastian murmured sleepily.

Meg felt tears in her eyes. In this suddenly strange and reversed world, she wished so much that Sebastian were hers, really hers.

She whispered, 'Yes, darling. Like Aunt Meg and Mummy.'

Miranda was not with Katie and Alex. Before she could make any enquiries, Peter said quickly, 'Miranda went off with someone else. She'll doubtless turn up any minute now.'

Alex was wound up to breaking point.

'You'll have to be Ma tonight, Aunt Meg! There's no diff!' He ran halfway up the stairs and hung upside down over the banisters. 'This has been the best day of my life!' he announced. 'I think I'll be a proper footballer and earn tons of money—'

'I'll sort them out, Meg,' Peter said, chivvying Katie ahead of him to the stairs. They could be heard laughing and chattering in the hall and then up to the bedroom landing. Peter's voice said humorously, 'Pack it in, you two!' A door opened and closed. There was comparative silence.

Meg hardly knew what to do. She flapped the cloth over the table then folded it again. She could not share a tête-à-tête supper with Peter. She made more tea and drank some so hot it burned her palate. Why didn't Miranda come? Where was she? Why had she wanted Meg to stay on until next week? Was it to protect her from herself?

Meg went to her handbag, found aspirins and took three. She had never felt quite like this before. Even during the terrible first years of Miranda's marriage to Peter, Meg had never felt angry with her. None of it had been Miranda's fault. If anything, Meg herself was to blame for not admitting her love for Peter; for refusing to let it take her over; for being stupid and scared.

Peter was saying goodnight from above and coming downstairs. It was very early for Alex and Katie to settle down for the night; Meg glanced at her watch. Not quite eight o'clock. She was conscious of her heart beating very steadily, with great emphasis. She rubbed her palms together and held them towards the Aga. How long before she could plead tiredness and go to bed?

He ran down the last flight into the kitchen and stopped in mock amazement at the sight of her standing there doing nothing.

'No supper? No cocoa?'

He had been light-hearted like this in the car. And at a time which – surely it was obvious – was deadly serious. Or was she over-reacting? Why had the word 'deadly' sprung to mind? She had hated Miranda's 'John Stonehouse', but he was no killer.

'I've made tea. D'you want some?'

'Rather. Haven't you planned any supper?'

'I thought . . . there was food at the clubhouse. Perhaps Miranda will want something later.'

'You've eaten nothing.' He leaned across her for the teapot and she closed her eyes suddenly.

'I'm not hungry. I thought the children—'

'They were tired. They agreed – in the car – to go

straight upstairs. If they'd been around when Miranda came in, there might have been . . . arguments.'

'Why?'

'She'd gone off with the chap from Prospect Villa. Or so Alex said. He was so proud of her. Then she did that. He might have said something silly.'

Her heart thumped. She was silent.

He poured his tea and took it to the table. After a while he said, 'I know something is going on, Meg. Can you explain?'

'No!' The word was over-loud, like a protest.

'All right. I'll ask her when she gets home.'

She swallowed. 'I think I'll have an early night too—'

'Don't leave me, Meg. Not again.' He looked round and she turned too. They stared for a moment, then dropped their gazes simultaneously. He said lamely, 'Nothing to be done, Meg. But stay till she comes back. Please.'

She knew she should go. Just go.

'All right,' she said in a low voice.

'Thanks.' He tossed back the rest of his tea and became buoyant again. 'Seb woke up and said you were going to draw some moonbeams. Let's go to it!'

He was full of enthusiasm, rushing around fetching paper and a new packet of soft lead pencils. Meg began to feel sick and wondered if it was the aspirin.

'A frieze, do you think? A big comic strip? How do you see moon babies exactly?' He was laughing, doodling an enormous face with fat cheeks.

Meg forced herself to concentrate. 'Let's . . . let the moon blow out feathers. Each feather a moon baby.'

'Hey, Meg!' He was full of an admiration which could not possibly be sincere. 'I can see why you're featured on telly!'

'I wasn't featured. Not like that.' Now she wanted to cry. Instead she leaned over and began one of her

255

painstaking drawings, full of minute detail. Peter swooped instant sketches of moon faces in various stages of shocked surprise.

'You could do a book yourself, Meg. Why don't you?'

She did not bother to reply. He went on, apparently unable to stop.

'Working together like this makes everything . . . all right. Doesn't it, Meg? Like it was ten years ago.'

She drew in a breath and straightened convulsively.

'Don't go!' He dropped his pencil and took her by the wrist. 'You're embarrassed! I understand that. So am I. But let us be honest, Meg. You feel something for me now, don't you? Wasn't that what you were saying?' He shook her arm impatiently. 'Meg, I still love you. Tell me – please tell me – how you feel.'

She pulled free but did not move away, and he took that as a reply and kissed her. It was a strange kiss. His hands did not touch her; he leaned across the distance between them and laid his lips on hers. It was a kiss full of tenderness. She closed her eyes and let it happen. When it was over he stared at her and awareness built up between them. She leaned to him and returned the kiss like a salutation. Then she turned away.

'Good night, Peter,' she said and made for the stairs.

He said, 'Wait! You can't just walk away now!'

She held the banisters and looked at him. 'Now is the time I can walk away. And we both know that I must. Miranda will be home soon.'

'Meg. It's past eleven o'clock. Let's stop playing games. Miranda has gone.'

In spite of what she knew she was shocked to the core.

'Of course she's not *gone*! Not in the way you mean! For goodness' sake, Peter! She's pregnant – there are the children – you—'

He said steadily, 'More than us, there's you. She's left you, Meg. And that means she's gone.'

The truth of that was suddenly obvious and even more appalling.

She shook her head, stammering. 'Listen. She's not herself – the baby – and she knew this man a long time ago! She's acting a part. Can't you see that? She's Trilby and he's Svengali. I know . . . I realize it's hard to . . . but she'll be back!'

'I don't want her to come back! I knew, the moment she entered that clubhouse this afternoon, that she was going to someone else. Meg . . . we've never been able to let our passion mature into anything lasting. It's like striking a match, Meg. It flares, then it goes out. She had so obviously struck a match with someone else. And I was free. It was wonderful.' He laughed, actually laughed. 'When I went back for them and Alex said she'd gone off with the Prospect man, I felt . . . marvellous. I was coming home to you, Meg. We've always been friends, Meg. But now, at last, we can be more than friends.'

'Peter – stop—'

They both knew the protest was meaningless because she did not move from the support of the newel post.

'We can't stop. Not now. Not again. Miranda has given us this opportunity, my love. Until we've struck *our* match, we'll never be proper beings. Whole. Can't you see that?'

She could not see anything; understand anything. In spite of the anger she had felt earlier towards Miranda, she knew she could not betray her sister.

And then it happened. Just as it had happened before in the hostel room at Higher Compton. It was the same man. The same cruel man as before. And, as before, the pain without the passion went through her body again and again so that she cried out and sank into a crouching position, clutching the banisters, pushing her head into them, fighting off the terror of what was happening to Miranda.

'My God – what is it – Meg – my darling—'

Peter was with her, his arms around her holding her together. His strength was all she had left; again and again the pain ripped at her torso. She gasped, 'Like a tiger – like claws – Peter – what is happening?'

'Something – I don't know – I'll get the doctor – can you hang on—'

'No!' Her hands left the banister at last and she clung to him frantically. 'No. You mustn't go! This is . . . the . . . last . . . straw!' She took a shuddering breath, screwed her eyes tightly shut and willed the pain away. It began to ebb. She waited. As it left her, she sobbed.

'Meg, is it easier? Can you talk?'

She lay limply against him, tears unstoppable. When he made to move towards the telephone, she hung on to him.

At last she said, 'You're right. We owe no more allegiance, Peter. She is with him now. It is . . . unspeakable.'

'Oh God . . . 'He realized suddenly what had happened and his arms tightened around her.

'Don't think of it, my darling. She promised. And she has broken her promise. For a whim. Just a whim.'

She lifted her tear-drenched face. 'Yes. I love you, Peter. I knew that as soon as you and Miranda made love. Ten years ago. But I'd been too scared – I thought friendship was separate from love.' She kissed him, small frantic kisses over his face. 'And then . . . even then, I could have done something about it. But I thought Miranda . . . and the baby . . . I'm sorry, Peter. So sorry.'

He lifted his face to her kisses as if to the sun.

'It's all right now, my Meg. Everything will be all right now.'

At three o'clock when they were still awake, still in a no-man's land of self-absorption, a car whined into Sunday Street and stopped, its engine running. They heard a sound at the cellar door. Then the car drove away.

Peter's head was on Meg's shoulder. He lifted his mouth to her ear. 'He's delivered a note. From Miranda. My God—'

He stopped abruptly as there was a curious scraping sound from below. They both became rigid. Meg felt her ears sing in an effort to hear the first footfall on the stair.

Peter whispered, 'Darling, we must tell her. Now.'

She hissed back, 'We can't tell her, Peter! For God's sake . . . it's three in the morning!'

'She'll come upstairs in a moment – d'you want us to be caught here like a couple of—'

'Don't say any more!'

They were silent, somehow untangled and separate after so long as an entity. Silence was everywhere, thick, cold, impenetrable.

Meg sat up and swung her legs to the carpet.

'She's not coming up. She guesses. Of course. It's probably what she intended all along. We're like her puppets. I can't bear it—'

Peter hugged her from behind.

'Listen. Meg. Just listen to me. We're no puppets. We go downstairs and tell her we're in love. All right – I know she will need support until after . . . but then—'

She was silent. His forehead against her spine was already so familiar, so dear, so much part of her, that it was impossible to imagine life without him.

At last she whispered, 'I can't face her. I still . . .

I don't like her any more. But perhaps I love her. I simply do not want to see her.'

'Darling. Then she's got her way. Hasn't she? She is forcing us to act the way she wishes. Making this into – what – a one-night stand? Bringing it down to the level of her escapade. Is that what you want?'

She shook her head violently. And after another long pause she turned and took his head in her arms.

'All right. We'll go down. And try to talk to her.'

They clung together for another moment, then she disengaged herself and leaned down to feel for her slippers. He did the same. And only then did they switch on the light. The awful thing was, even when her eyes became accustomed to it, Meg could not look at Peter. And she was almost certain he could not look at her.

There were no other lights on in the house; nothing reflecting up from the kitchen. Peter went ahead, running down the stairs to the landing, then pausing at the head of the cellar steps until Meg reached him.

'Miranda?'

Her voice came very calmly from the chair by the Aga.

'Yes, I'm here. I'll stay put if you don't mind. Go back to bed. I'll still be here in the morning.'

Peter hesitated for a moment; Meg could sense his indecision. And as if to prove to him that he had been right all along, she reached beyond his shoulder and snapped on the kitchen light.

Miranda was revealed below them, sitting in the carver chair by the Aga, huddled in her old maternity coat with a scarf over her red hair and her hands deep beneath the swell of her abdomen. At first they saw only her grey-white face, twisted in a grimace. And then they saw the swollen and blackened eye, and then the blood staining her stockings, her shoes, oozing insidiously on to the flagstones.

'Oh Christ—' Peter leapt the last few stairs and was on his knees in front of her. 'What happened? Oh God—'

Meg was at the telephone, dialling 999. Through her own calm voice giving the address, asking for an ambulance, she could hear Miranda.

'I think it's called just deserts, darling.' She gave a funny gasping laugh. 'If only you'd have waited till the morning. They would have been the final just deserts.'

'Miranda – you fool – why didn't you yell out?'

'Because I asked for it. Surely you realize that? Where's Meg?'

'I'm here. Get your legs on to this chair.' Meg pulled out another chair and went for the tablecloth. But it was for reassurance only; there was nothing to be done until the ambulance men brought blood and took her to hospital.

'Don't leave me, Meg. Will you?'

'Of course not.' It was rather like picking up a weight which she had only just laid down. Her muscles ached.

Miranda gave another gasping laugh. 'You were right, Meg. I shouldn't have gone. I thought . . . told myself . . . it would put everything right. But I was just . . . you know . . . playing with fire.' She drew in a whistling breath and closed her eyes. Meg took her hand and rubbed it between her own. It was a dead cold weight.

She said, 'We'll go to the nursing home, darling. There's a theatre there – everything you will need. People you know. Don't worry.'

'I'm not worried. I deserve to die.'

'Don't talk like that, Miranda!'

'I knew he was mad all the time really. Brett told me. But I thought he felt . . . something for me. I thought he was Svengali and I was Trilby . . .' She sobbed suddenly. 'He thought he was Caligula. I tried to run. He caught me . . . he caught me . . .' her words ended in a whimper.

Peter said strongly, 'I'll kill him! I'll come with you to the hospital – I'll be with you – I won't let you die—'

'Stay with the children, Peter.' Miranda was suddenly urgent. 'And don't let them out of your sight. Alex was right. Meredith had been in prison. For this kind of thing. Keep the children indoors all the time.'

'Oh my God—'

'And don't talk about killing, Peter. I knew what he was like. There was a time before – when I was with the Arbitrary – I – I knew him then.'

'I know. Don't talk.'

The ambulance men came in at a run. They set up a drip immediately; one of them looked at Peter.

'Who has done this to her?' he asked, striving to keep accusation out of his voice.

Miranda lifted her head, eyes wide and clear. 'It was my own fault. But the man . . . I think he is dangerous. His name is John Meredith.'

'We must inform the police.'

Her voice was suddenly a thread. 'Everyone will know. And then the children . . .'

'It is a police matter, my dear.' They trundled Miranda outside and slid the stretcher on to its runners. Peter said, 'Put it out of your mind, my darling. Just get better.'

Then the doors were closed on him and they began the journey into Penzance.

There was an operation the next morning, and afterwards Miranda lay like a dead thing connected to tubes and monitoring machines. She had had a complete hysterectomy and a repair. Meg stayed with her, sleeping on an armchair close to the bed, willing her to live. And on the last day of January, when Katie brought in some snowdrops and the first of the daffodils from the Scillies arrived in baskets, Miranda seemed to make a conscious decision to do just that.

She smiled at Katie and asked her to put the snowdrops right under her nose.

'I can smell the summer,' she murmured.

Katie waited for no more. 'You're better! I'm going to tell the others!' And she ran out of the ward.

Sebastian was contentedly happy, but Alex was unable to control his tears.

'I thought . . . I thought you might die,' he sobbed, while Miranda stroked his hair and made soothing noises.

'So did I,' Miranda admitted with her old brutal honesty.

Katie patted his arm. 'Aunt Meg would have stayed with us then,' she comforted.

Meg's gaze met Miranda's and they both smiled as if they knew everything there was to know.

Alex said, 'Oh, I know. But we need both of them, don't we?'

And Meg said, 'Yes. That's true.'

John Meredith, or John Stonehouse, disappeared from Keele. The police mounted a search. A month later in the high spring tides, his body was washed up in Cadgwith Cove.

Arthur Bowering, who had announced that there was not a man in Keele who would allow such a monster to stand trial, was the first to assume loudly that it was suicide.

'What else was there for him to do?' he asked rhetorically in the lounge of the Coastguards. 'After what happened to Mrs Snow, he knew his life wasn't worth a shilling!'

There was a silence and before it could become awkward, Billy Majors said, 'Gawdelpus but you're behind the times, Arthur! We bin decimalized for four year now and there en't no such things as shillings any more!'

Arthur accepted the change in the conversation and shouted raucously, 'Five pee, then! That suit you better?'

Billy, notorious these days for his weak bladder, headed for the Gents amid gales of laughter.

Meg heard the news with considerable relief. Miranda was coming home the very next day and she had twice said, almost casually, 'I wish they could find that man before I come back to Keele.'

Peter wanted to move the family to London. Somewhere within easy reach of Kilburn.

'A completely new start,' he said enthusiastically, holding Miranda's hand between his as he always did when they visited.

Strangely, she was no longer keen.

'Let's stay at home. Please, Peter. I don't want to leave Fish Cottage.'

'Whatever you say, my darling.'

They had all been changed by that night. Miranda seemed to take some of Meg's characteristics to herself; she confided to Meg that she never wanted to leave Keele again. And Meg was different too; she and Peter did not sleep together again but she was no longer afraid to be near him. During those first terrible days when he wept, she held him to her and comforted him. She was amazingly strong; sometimes she wondered at herself.

Before Miranda came home she told Peter what she intended to do.

'It was a wonderful time, Peter. I don't regret it. I don't want you to regret it. That's why it mustn't happen again, and that's why I am going back to London quite soon – as soon as Miranda is fit to cope.'

'How can you do that? How can we sweep everything under the carpet as if it never happened?' He still became distraught very easily; she turned on him with some of Miranda's old impatience.

'What else is there to do? Ruin everybody's lives? Our own included? Because we should never be happy at the expense of them! You're not thinking straight, Peter, and you must!' She was ironing at the kitchen table and she glanced at the clock. 'The children will be home from school in five minutes. Why don't you take them with you to visit Miranda? I want to get everything up together here so that I can spend some time with her tomorrow. And you must work again. Let everything be as it was, Peter. It's the only way.'

'I can't live without you, Meg!'

She was scornful. 'Of course you can! Just as I can live without you! And you have Miranda too, who is at least half of me!' She grinned, trying to get a return smile from him. 'Listen, Peter. We're both artists. We'd never see eye to eye – remember how affronted I was by Gerald Scaife's stuff? It wouldn't work.'

'But Miranda isn't happy down here.'

'Miranda has changed. Miranda knows now that she needs you and the children and her home. Things will be different now.'

He was silent until he saw her looking at the clock again. Then he grinned. 'You've changed too. You're bossy now!' She laughed and he went on, 'And you called yourself an artist. I'm glad about that, Meg. Just remember it – you are an artist!'

She spread one of Alex's school shirts and thought about it. Then she nodded.

'Yes. Of course I am.'

She left ten days later after the inquest on John Meredith.

Miranda clung to her and begged her to stay for always. But Meg was adamant.

'I shall be back, of course. But I must go home and do some work, Miranda.'

'You won't be back. There'll be no more babies. You won't be back until next Christmas. If then.'

Meg knew that Miranda was right. It was very doubtful that she would spend next Christmas here. She lied brightly. 'I shall be down in the summer. We'll swim together again. The tadpoles. D'you remember?'

Miranda said sadly, 'How could I forget?'

Meg hugged her suddenly. 'Darling, try to be happy. For my sake. I love you and I love Peter and I love your children. I want you to be happy so much. If you're not, I don't think I can be either.'

Miranda looked at her. 'Will you settle for contentment? I really am content down here.'

Meg laughed. 'Oh yes. I can settle for that. It's far more permanent than the other kind!'

And so, in the end, it wasn't too terrible to leave Keele. She drove to the top road and saw Prospect Villa in her mirror and tried not to think too deeply about all that had happened.

She stopped in Plymouth to see Mr Bracknell. He had retired in 1970, but she could trust no-one else.

'Of course I will see to drawing up a will for you, my dear child. But you should get to know Mr Passmore. After all, I won't always be here.'

'I can't imagine life without you, Mr Bracknell.' She smiled at him and he blinked because in spite of the orange hair and blue eyes, she had something of her Aunt Maggie about her.

She gave an expurgated account of the ghastly happenings in Keele, and then was silent while he waited for her instructions.

At last she told him quite briefly why she wished to make a will.

'I'm having a baby, Mr Bracknell. And as I am his or her sole parent, I need to tie everything up legally. Just in case . . . at the birth . . . you understand.'

He had difficulty with his breathing for a moment. Miranda . . . well, that had not surprised him. But Meg. Meg was so like Maggie.

And then, looking into her clear blue eyes, he understood. This should have happened a long time ago. It was simply . . . delayed.

He said, 'There will be no problem, Meg. Leave it all with me and I will send it to you for signature in about two days' time.'

Unexpectedly she leaned forward and kissed his cheek. And that was something she would never have done before.

He smiled. 'Am I the first to congratulate you?'

He saw her swallow. 'Yes.'

'What an honour. I am so happy for you, my dear. And your aunt would be too.'

She raised her eyebrows. 'Yes. Yes, she would, wouldn't she? I hadn't thought of that. Thank you, Mr Bracknell.'

And as she left to continue her journey to London, she was smiling. She was still smiling when the train steamed out of the station. She saw her own reflection in the window and straightened her face quickly. What on earth was there to laugh about? But it did have its funny side. First Miranda. And now herself.

Thirteen

Meg slept soundly that first night. She had become adept at postponing any serious thinking and when she arrived in Kilburn she had concentrated on unloading the car, finding the vacuum flask of milk from the Keyhole dairy and making herself a cup of cocoa. Then she had switched on the electric blanket to air the bed, stuck the aerial into the television to watch the news and tried to feel something significant about Chou En-lai dying. And then she had gone to bed.

The next day was Saturday. She looked at her watch on her bedside table and noted it was eight-thirty. If she was still at Keele she would be halfway through getting the various breakfasts by now. Miranda had been persuaded to have porridge during the past week; the children liked odd things such as French toast and griddle cakes. She wondered how they would manage, what they would eat. And then she deliberately switched out of Keele and into Kilburn.

Her head ached slightly when she stood up and the faint nausea which had been with her for the past ten days swam from diaphragm into throat. She swallowed, tied her dressing gown unnecessarily tightly and went downstairs, leaning hard on the spiralling banister to slow herself down. Everything looked so small, almost mean, in the tiny front living room. And it was bitterly cold. She had forgotten to switch the heating on last night. She thought about going back upstairs to remedy that and couldn't face the climb without a cup of tea so went on through to the verandah. At least the pale February sun filled this room. She stared around it. Plenty of room for a pram. But she'd have to install some kind of washing machine.

She lit the gas and filled the kettle, then warmed her hands over the lid while the water boiled. Tea. And aspirin. She needed both.

Afterwards, feeling much better, she went back into the living room and looked around her.

'You've got to be a haven,' she said aloud to the little house. 'You've been a place for me to sleep and work. Now you've got to be something else. All right, you can't hope to feel like Fish Cottage, but you'll have to give a bit more than you're giving now.'

A terrible wave of nostalgia for Keele and Fish Cottage swept through her and was gone, briskly evicted by this new common sense.

'Perhaps this is Mother Nature,' she mused, going to the window and looking down the road. 'Her way of protecting this new life.' She touched her abdomen and watched a car turn into the road. 'Damn!' she continued without pause. 'Kovacks.'

She considered pretending she wasn't back, then realized her car was visible down the side road where she always parked it. And anyway, she had to get into the routine of work. If he had something special for her, that was all to the good.

She adjusted her dressing gown again and unlocked the front door. He got out of his car with difficulty, one elephantine foot first, then the bulk of his enormous body. He grunted audibly and reached back inside the car for his briefcase – the same one he had brought with him ten years ago. Probably the same overcoat too. She felt an unexpected pang of affection. He really was a friend. Rather like a slightly younger edition of Mr Bracknell.

'You managed to tear yourself away from the good life, then?' he asked sourly as he stumped up the short front path. 'When I said to you last bloody November to take as long as you liked, I didn't really mean the whole bloody winter!'

She closed the door after him.

'It's very nice to see you too, Charles,' she said demurely. 'Let me take your coat.'

'Not yet. It's freezing in here.'

'I forgot to switch on the heating. Light the gas fire while I make some coffee.'

He did so with much huffing and puffing. She could hear him pushing the two armchairs close to the heater, and when she brought in the coffee he was standing so close to it she could smell his ancient overcoat scorching.

He said, 'It's still not warm enough here. You'll catch your death!'

'I told you. I forgot to switch on the heating.'

'You mean it still isn't on? Christ, woman, why not?'

'The panel thing is upstairs and I couldn't be bothered to go up again.'

He stared at her in amazement, then took the tray from her and placed it on the hearth rug.

'Go upstairs. Now. Switch on the heating. Get dressed. Tie up your hair or something.'

'Let's have some coffee first.'

'Now. You look wanton. I've got my reputation to consider.'

She had forgotten that he could make her laugh. She pulled herself back up the spiral staircase and made for the bathroom. When she came down he was in the kitchen reheating the coffee and there were croissants on a plate next to the cups.

'I got them from that little place by the station. You've had no breakfast. Get stuck in.'

'How did you know I was home?' She spoke through a mouthful of flaky pastry; she had not realized how hungry she was.

'Because I telephoned your sister. I was getting worried. I thought you would ring me after the telly programme.'

'I didn't see it actually.'

'You didn't *see* it? God, woman, I gave you a special mention and a decent still photograph and you didn't take the trouble—'

'I didn't know it was on. And I wasn't keen on the idea anyway, I told you that.'

'Stop being so bloody selfish! It was for the firm, not you!'

'Peter was pleased about it. He thought it would give me a bit of self-esteem.'

'Did it?'

'Yes. Other things happened too. Yes, I feel like a professional artist now.'

That silenced him. He finished his coffee and stared at her disconcertingly. She could be no more than six weeks pregnant but she had put on the sloppiest sweater she could find and she pulled it down self-consciously now.

He said slowly, 'You've changed. Really changed. Your brother-in-law told me that you'd been working very hard, looking after all of them since your sister lost the baby.'

She smiled fleetingly and reached for the last croissant. 'Yes. You could say that. But I loved it.'

'Yes. I can imagine that. You missed your forte somewhere along the line, Meg. You like looking after people, don't you?'

Her smile widened. He could not know how close to the truth he had come.

271

She said, 'These croissants are delicious. Thank you so much, Charles.'

'That's another thing. I've never seen you eat like this. There were four croissants there. Two each. You notice I've not had one!'

She burst out laughing, broke the end off the last one and passed it over.

'Sorry, Charles. Better for you though.'

'Why is everybody worried about my weight? I'm not!'

'Well, that's all right then.'

He pretended to choke with surprise. 'There's another change! You've been the one to nag me in the past! Spouting words you don't understand – like cholesterol and cirrhosis! Come on, what's been happening to you?'

She had not intended to tell a soul for ages yet, but of course Charles would have to know eventually, so why not now.

She said quietly, 'I'm pregnant. Might that be it?'

He was stunned. He'd been surprised before, but this was different; he held himself still, unwilling to reveal any reaction at all.

She smiled, 'It's all right, Charles. Really. I am absolutely fine. It's just that . . . I shall probably have to go away for a while later on and I'd like you to know why.'

He let out his breath slowly, but all he said was, 'Christ Almighty.'

She said, 'Have some more coffee. And there's brandy in the cupboard if you need it.'

He got up immediately and fetched the brandy, dousing his coffee with it liberally.

She said, 'Actually, it's your drinking that worries me, Charles. And I know exactly what cirrhosis means. And cholesterol.'

He said, 'Oh God.' And then, 'Are you going to tell me any more?'

'D'you want to know?'

'I'm not sure. I know you've always had a thing about Peter Snow—'

'How did you know that?' She was startled out of her calm.

'Oh, lots of things. I know you pretty well, Meg. Ten years, isn't it? Man and boy.'

She stared at him, then nodded. 'Right. Well, you know everything then.'

He returned her look and asked, 'Does he know?'

'Nobody knows except my solicitor and you.'

'Your solicitor?'

'I stopped in Plymouth to change my will.'

'Christ Almighty,' he said again, this time with more emphasis. 'You really have changed. But . . . I can see why.' He drew a deep breath and sat back, nursing his coffee between his ham-hands. 'Well. I don't know what to say. I'm thankful you're all right. There was a piece in the press while you were away. Some lunatic rapist washed up on a beach in Cornwall. Just for a ghastly moment, it crossed my mind—'

'He raped my sister.'

He stared again. 'My God. It's been quite a couple of months, hasn't it?'

'Yes. You could say that.'

There was a curiously companionable silence in the little room. Then a train went by and rocked them both.

She said, 'Only one snag about this baby. I don't want Peter or Miranda to know about it.'

'Ah. That could be tricky.'

'Yes. She will want to visit me. And she will want me to visit her.'

'How are you going to get round that one?'

273

'I don't know yet. I might have to go right away somewhere. Would you be willing to send me stuff?'

'Of course.'

She smiled. 'Then that's solved already.'

'Temporarily. But surely you need something long-term? This is for the rest of your life.'

'"Sufficient unto the day . . ."' she quoted piously at him.

'Bollocks. Same as saying don't cross your bridges till you come to them. What if there's no bridge? Handy to have a canoe hidden under the trees somewhere.'

She laughed again. 'Oh, I'm glad to see you, Charles. And . . . grateful . . . that you're not shocked. You know, it's practically incest.'

He did not deny it. 'And you of all people. In spite of the red hair you're so . . . so . . . balanced!'

'I'm a Libran. It doesn't mean a thing. So is Miranda and she could never be described as balanced.'

He said acutely, 'You balance each other, of course. You should have married brothers and lived next door to each other. Miranda could have gone off and done her theatrical bit while you minded house.'

'Sounds exciting.'

His three chins quivered with amusement. 'There you go again. The old Meg would have thoroughly enjoyed that life. This new Meg is not so sure.'

She stood up and dusted crumbs from her baggy jumper. Then she went to the window and stared again at the very suburban view.

'I've developed a knack for postponing serious thought, Charles. But I know that somewhere just outside this magic periphery there are going to be lots of difficulties, embarrassments, maybe even hardships. I should be scared at what kind of world I'm bringing this baby into. How I'm going to support it—' She held a hand up as he

274

started to interrupt her. 'It's all right, I'm not scared. And I'm not worried about that periphery, either. Because . . . oh, Charles, I know this is crazy, but you see I've always loved Peter Snow. And now I'm having his baby.' She turned and her pale face glowed with colour. 'Charles, I've never been so excited about anything before! When Miranda used to fizz about being in a play, I felt . . . excluded. Even when we were kids I was never that worked up about opening our Christmas stockings. But this . . . oh my God, Charles, I could explode with excitement!'

He stared at her for a long second, then levered himself out of his chair with the usual difficulty and opened his arms wide. It was obviously the right thing to do. She ran to him and hugged him, laughing like a child. And he swung her gently from side to side and noted objectively that the orange hair had escaped from its rubber band and was flying in his face.

Charles wanted to take her out to lunch, but she knew he normally visited his mother at weekends and as Mrs Kovacks was now in a nursing home in the country, Meg thanked him and sent him on his way quite soon. That was something else new; usually Charles called the tune about arrivals and departures. Well, he had decided to arrive, but she had quite definitely fixed the time of his departure. She smiled at the thought while she changed again into something very respectable and went out for provisions. Charles's role had always been – obviously – her boss. Certainly they had shared lunches and dinners, but only so that they could discuss work in hand. She knew he looked on her as his protégée, but was determined not to presume on that. From talks with Mrs Kovacks she gathered that Charles had lost most of his old friends in the Russian invasion of '56, and was very cautious about getting close to anyone.

She stacked a trolley high in the local supermarket, amused to find herself reaching for exotic items like pickled peaches and Gentlemen's Relish. When she emerged into the car park the bitter cold enveloped her insidiously; it had been so much milder in Keyhole. She loaded her boot, relocked the car and walked briskly into Kilburn High Street again. She went into a travel agency. Her reflection in the plate-glass window smiled back at her; she straightened her mouth. She seemed to be always smiling lately and probably looked completely gaga.

The girl labelled conspicuously 'Teresa' obviously thought so.

'There are so many isolated islands in the world, madam. Can you narrow down the area slightly?'

'Well . . . it has to be warm. But not too hot – not equatorial or anything. And it must be fairly inaccessible too. I don't want visitors.'

'You intend to reside there . . . wherever . . . for some time?'

'If I like it. But at first I would go for a holiday. People do have holidays in the sun in the winter, don't they?'

'Oh yes. Certainly, madam. But they usually know where they wish to go.'

'Yes. I'm sorry. Perhaps some leaflet things?'

'We have brochures – ' Teresa emphasized the word as she produced glossy magazines from a shelf – 'on the Bahamas. Bermuda. The Canary Islands. Madeira. The West Indies—'

'I don't want all of these.' Meg began to feel slightly flustered. 'Maybe . . . yes, that one. Greece . . . well, all right. But not the West Indies. They are much too far away.'

'You did stipulate inaccessibility.' Teresa was pleased with her words and took the sting out of them with a smile.

Meg beamed back. 'Oh, Teresa, I'm sorry. Isn't it silly – but I won't know where I want to go until I see it!'

Teresa was won by the smile but flummoxed by the words.

'Ah,' she said noncommittally.

Meg gathered up the brochures and promised to be back next week. Again she spotted her reflection grinning madly and straightened her face.

The only trouble with this strange new happiness was that she found it very difficult to settle to any work – or indeed anything. When she got home she found an assignment pushed through her letter box. She opened the enormous envelope, stared at the galley proofs which she must read before planning her illustrations and shoved the lot back into the envelope again.

'Later,' she said to the house.

She made herself a high tea, put the gas fire on full blast and sat with a tray in front of the television. When the telephone rang she was amazed to find it completely dark.

It was Miranda.

'Meg. Are you all right?'

'Of course.' Meg stretched the cord as far as it would go to draw curtains and switch on lights. 'I was going to ring when the cheaper rate came in.'

'It's Saturday. Cheap all day. And anyway it's eight o'clock!'

'Oh, Miranda, I'm sorry. How are you, darling?'

'We're all fine. But I was so worried, Meg. You didn't ring last night so I thought you might have stopped off somewhere. Then I waited till I was certain you would have got there and rang and rang—'

'Late morning, early afternoon?'

'I don't know. For ages anyway. Where have you been?'

'Shopping. I didn't have a thing in the house. Only that milk I brought back from you. Miranda, I'm really sorry.'

'Oh, never mind all that. I don't want you to feel you have to be worrying about us all the time anyway. But it was so unlike you.'

'I know. I do feel different somehow. Maybe something positive has come out of the whole awful business, Miranda.'

'Yes. When we talked about it before, I thought you were just saying that to be . . . you know, reassuring. But now you're not here, I think you're right.'

'You mean, you feel the same?'

'Well, I'm not sure, Sis. But I'm different. I know that. I thought at first it was still shock – that I'd been beaten into the ground somehow. Subdued. Defeated.'

Meg waited. Miranda's voice was different too; hesitant, lighter. And she searched for words in a way the old impetuous Miranda never did.

'I thought I'd go to pieces when you left, Meg. But I haven't.' She laughed. 'D'you know, I got up at seven this morning and cooked a proper breakfast for everyone. I thought I was doing it for your sake. But then . . . Meg, I enjoyed it. When we sat down together, I felt good. Not really happy. But sort of . . . contented.'

Meg felt her eyes fill suddenly with tears. 'Oh, Sis.'

'Yes. It doesn't sound like me, does it? I'm wondering if some of you . . . if we're kind of . . . borrowing from each other.'

Meg hung on to the phone, wishing so much she could tell Miranda about the baby. Then Miranda said, 'I'm on my own here, darling, so I can say something that I wasn't up to saying before. It's . . . we had to get something out of our systems, didn't we? That awful business back in '65 . . . it had to be – what's the word – expiated?'

Meg repeated quietly, 'Yes. Expiated.'

'And now. It's over. Isn't it? Over and done with. And we can be twins again. Nothing between us.'

Meg leaned against the underside of the spiral staircase and closed her eyes. 'Yes,' she said meaninglessly.

Miranda said, 'Oh, Sis. When can you come down again? Will you come for Easter? Please?'

'I'll try.' Meg recognized her own selfishness and did not care. This was how Miranda must have felt when she was in the Arbitrary Group and fending off Meg's invitations to come to Plymouth. 'Someone at work wants me to spend a holiday in Greece somewhere. Don't know where. But I'll be back by Easter. Of course.'

'Meg! How wonderful! Who is it?'

'At the office? No-one you know. Anyway, I don't know whether I'll go.'

'You must! It would do you good, darling. You need a proper break after Christmas down here!' Miranda managed a laugh, then said, 'Alex has just come in from the football club party and wants a word. Look after yourself, Meg. Please.'

'You too . . . Alex, what party is this? You didn't mention a thing about it while I was with you.'

'I wasn't going to go. It was a Valentine's social. But Katie wanted to go and Ma said she could if I took her. And she's not a bad little kid really, is she?'

'She's not bad at all.'

'Aunt Meg, when are you coming back?'

She said, 'As soon as I can. I've got a lot of work to catch up on, Alex. Will you do something for me?'

'Yeh.'

'Look after your mother and Katie.'

'What about Dad and Seb?'

'Your mother and Katie will look after them.'

He laughed appreciatively. 'What about me?'

'Ah. There has to be someone in charge.'

He liked that. 'Can I tell them you say I'm in charge?'

'Only if the need arises.'

He laughed again. 'OK. 'Bye, Aunt Meg.'

''Bye, Alex.'

She replaced the receiver carefully and went back to the fire. She looked at the fat envelope on the hearth rug. Tomorrow she would begin work. She'd got to earn for two now; she must begin work.

But she did not. Instead she leafed through the brochures over a good solid breakfast, then got dressed and went to church. When she arrived back, Charles's car was parked outside though there was no sign of him in it. She had bought chops for Sunday and Monday and she put them all in the oven, surrounded by vegetables, and picked mint from her window box. When he knocked on the door the sherry was on a tray by the fire and she had just made an apple pie.

'I came to take you out to lunch,' he protested half-heartedly, inhaling like one of the Bisto kids.

'Give me twenty minutes over the hot stove and this will be ready,' she promised. 'Meanwhile, unless you'd prefer your newspaper, look at these leaflets. Choose somewhere you think would suit me.'

He looked pointedly at the full envelope on the floor and took the proffered brochures without a word. When she came to announce the meal was ready he was halfway down the sherry bottle.

'Well?' She settled him at the kitchen table and took hot plates from the oven. 'I couldn't see a thing that took my fancy.'

He removed the cover from a vegetable dish and helped himself to potatoes. 'Real mint? And why the Greek Islands?'

'Need not be the Greek Islands.'

'There are dozens of them, of course. The Ionian side as well as the Aegean. You could fly to Athens and investigate most of them from there.'

'I could, couldn't I?'

He ate appreciatively and had a second helping. And then some apple pie. Then he said, 'I thought you might have had a look at the galleys I sent round.'

'I was going to. And then . . . I think I might have slept because when Miranda telephoned it was dark.'

He was silent, watching her as she cleared the table and made coffee. He was used to her economical movements and noted that she went twice to the fridge for milk and forgot coffee spoons on the tray.

He said, 'If I take you for a run to the country this afternoon, will you spend an hour tonight reading and thinking?'

'Of course.'

'Good.' He stood up and carried the tray into the sitting room. And after the coffee was gone he washed up neatly and would not let her help.

'Why all this pampering?' she asked, hovering uncertainly in the kitchen doorway.

'You know why.' He hung tea towels over the stove.

She sighed exasperatedly. 'Good lord, Charles. I'm about six weeks, that's all!'

He raised his eyebrows. 'What's that got to do with it? I want those illustrations by midweek.'

She looked even more uncertain. 'Oh,' she said.

He nodded. 'Quite. You've changed in that way too. The old Meg would have had those galleys on one corner of the table and a sketching block in front of her.'

She said, 'Could you tell me the story, Charles? It's just . . . it seems such hard work.'

'Are you telling me that McEvoy are buying boring stories now?'

'No. Of course not. But . . .'

He wrapped his scarf twice around his neck and began the arduous task of getting into his coat.

'It's about a family of squirrels who live in a walnut tree and can't crack the hard walnut shells.'

She said, 'Oh, don't go on. They have to find a magic nutcracker and the wise old owl takes them on a long search.'

He snapped, 'As a matter of fact, it's a silver hammer. And it's hidden beneath the old oak tree.'

'There you are then.' She passed him his gloves. 'I can already see Mr Squirrel. Mrs Squirrel will wear an apron, naturally. And all the little—'

'Squirrel Smiths actually.'

'You're joking!'

He sighed. 'Get your coat on. Have you forgotten I'm taking you for a drive?'

She had, and was ashamed to admit it. She wished he would go away and let her curl up with the brochures again, but actually she did feel much more alert after Charles had driven into Hertfordshire and they had had tea somewhere near St Albans. He dropped her again outside the house and watched her unlock the door. And then suddenly he wound down the window and poked out his head awkwardly.

'Listen. Meg. Don't bother with those damned drawings tonight. I was kidding.'

She looked back at him with another pang of affection. It was when he said things like that that she knew he had not been kidding at all.

But it was cold in the verandah and the passing trains – fewer on a Sunday, as a rule – seemed to rattle the glass more than usual. She tried working on the floor in front of the gas fire, but crouching down made her feel sick.

On Monday she tried again. She could not get the feel of the story; usually she felt an instant partnership with her authors and could let their words make pictures in her mind without any conscious effort. This particular squirrel family left her completely uninspired. She was delighted when the telephone rang and hoped it would be Miranda.

It was Jill Forsythe. Jill's husband had left her two years ago and she still worked from home amid a family of very demanding children.

'Kovacks tells me you're thinking of moving somewhere warmer!' she began without preamble. 'Meg, I'm devastated!'

Meg felt fairly devastated too. 'He didn't waste much time spreading the news,' she remarked.

'Well, I went into the office after lunch and asked after you – as I always do – and he more or less told me not to disturb you as you were trying to get something done before you departed!'

Meg smiled, relieved that Charles had not spread all the news and that he was casting himself in the role of her protector. Jill's visits were always family affairs – she had to take her three children with her wherever she went – and they could be fairly disruptive.

'It's sticky going,' she admitted. 'I'm going to stop for some lunch now—'

'Lunch? My God, it's teatime! I'm just about to hack a loaf to pieces for the brood!'

The glass roof let in every last vestige of daylight and Meg had not realized the time. Not that it mattered.

She said, 'You remind me so much of my sister. Or at least, how she used to be.'

'Oh, Meg, I'm sorry. How did it go? *That*'s where I thought you'd bury yourself – down in that smelly little hole.'

'Don't be horrid about Keele, Jill, please. It really hurts.'

'Meg!' Jill was surprised; Meg was too. She had not realized how much Keele was in her blood. Jill went on, 'I'm sorry, love. You obviously had a wonderful time and hated coming home.'

Meg nearly told her that her only home was in Keele, but that could not possibly be true. She said instead, 'Well, in many ways it was wonderful. But my sister was very ill, so I was quite busy.'

Jill made sympathetic sounds, then turned from the phone and shouted something angrily. 'Sorry, Meg. Kids fighting. I swear I'll kill them one day.'

Meg smiled again; Jill really was like Miranda used to be.

She went on, 'Listen, is it the one about the squirrels and the silver hammer?'

'It is.'

'Kovacks said you were the only one who could make something magical out of it. It's because you idealize kids, Meg. You think they've got these wonderful imaginations whereas in reality—' She squawked again at one of her children and Meg burst out laughing.

'Honestly, Jill, if you were a man you'd be sexist! I've had three children to look after for the past two months!'

'Yes, well, never mind that. There's a line somewhere in that book about a squirrel being special because of his tail. And I can see you making wonderful things out of the tails. You know, fans, sweeping brooms, blankets . . . bit like Dumbo and his ears. What do you think?'

Meg thought. Then said slowly, 'Jill, you're an angel. I've done a day's uninspired work and you've switched on the light for me.'

'Oh well.' Jill sounded smug. 'Any time, you know. In

between being sexist. And harassed. And anything else you can think of—'

'Shut up, Jill. I'll be taking these in on Thursday. Shall we meet for coffee?'

'Lovely. And don't go off to warmer climes without letting me know!'

Meg did not wait to say goodbye. She replaced the receiver and went back to the kitchen table.

On Thursday she had the flat feeling that usually followed a spate of work. She had not glanced at her brochures again, and had gone outside only to hang out some laundry.

Charles nodded, well satisfied.

'Good. I know the story is trite, but these will lift it into the Beatrix Potter class and the author's got a well-known name too, so it will be a very commercial package.'

'Credit to Jill. She rang me on Monday and told me what to do.'

He looked glum. 'Liar. But, yes, co-operation is everything in our trade. We know that.'

'Yes.' She smiled at him, remembering how much he had helped her right at the beginning.

'Thought any more about an island?' he asked, making the idea sound ridiculous.

'No.' She went to the window. The office, just off Edgware Road, looked down on a nursery school and an Asian woman was waving to her child through the railings. Her gaily coloured sari, peeping out of a very English coat, was incongruous on this grey February day. Meg said slowly, 'If it weren't for this baby I could go back and forth to Keele just as Miranda wants me to.'

'Miranda . . . yes. How would your brother-in-law feel about that?'

She glanced at him. He had always referred to Peter by name, and she wondered if he was attempting to drive home the sheer impossibility of everything by calling him her brother-in-law. She could read nothing from Charles's typical Buddha-like expression and shook her head slowly. 'I don't know. I feel so sorry for him. He loves us both. I should have had the baby aborted. If ever he finds out . . . it would drive him mad, I think.'

'Then no more talk of going back and forth to Keele because he would find out, abortion or no abortion, and he is too good an artist to be expendable.'

She came back to the desk. 'Sorry, Charles. I wasn't serious. But, yes, you're right. The sooner I get myself installed somewhere far away, the better.'

'Right. I was just checking. I might have heard of somewhere. D'you want lunch?'

'I'm meeting Jill here.'

'Enough said. I'll be round tonight. It won't be in your brochures, but read up about the Dodecanese.'

She was startled. 'Really? Aren't they Turkish?'

'No. Greek. And there's one – not on many maps – on lease – about hundred years – to a shipowner who was in love with my mother back in the twenties.'

She spurted a laugh. 'Are you serious?'

'Absolutely. And I think I hear Jill. Or the offspring.' He stood up and shuffled the galleys into order. 'Get them out as soon as you can. And promise me you won't bring yours up to be a hooligan.'

Jill entered like a surf-rider on the crest of a wave, and enveloped Meg in a hug.

'It's OK. They're going to my mother's. And half-term only lasts a week anyway.' She slapped hands away from Charles's desk. 'It's something to do with orange squash – I read about it the other day. Makes them hyperactive. They can't help it.'

The three boys gathered around Charles.

'Mr Kovacks, could we use the enlarger?' The youngest was the spokesman. 'Douglas has done this super drawing and if we can make it bigger we can print notelets and sell them for a lot of money.'

Charles was demoralized. 'Last time I let you loose on it you broke it,' he whinnied. 'Jill – take them away—'

Jill snapped, 'You can't use any of the equipment. And you're not to sell things unless it's for charity. How many times . . .'

Meg had heard this before. Miranda had said something similar to Alex. She met Charles's eyes and looked away in case he could read her renewed longing for Keele. The thought of an island in the Dodecanese suddenly frightened her.

But the lunch with Jill was fun. And the feeling of achievement from her work was good too. She went back to Kilburn and sat by the fire without a guilty conscience, and the next thing she knew, Charles was knocking on the door.

He looked at her, waved her back into the chair and went straight through into the kitchen. She sank back without protest – which was not like her – and smiled gratefully when he appeared with tea.

'I don't like this,' he said, stirring the pot fiercely. 'I don't like it at all.'

'You need not have done it. I'd have got myself together.'

'You should go to the doctor, Meg. You know very well what I'm talking about. You are constantly tired. You are vague. You are unmotivated—'

'That's just not fair!' She sat bolt upright. 'I've been working all hours on that damned manuscript! Naturally I am tired. And I'm just home after a traumatic fourteen

287

weeks when my family were nearly torn apart – quite literally—'

'Sorry. Sorry. Sorry.' He held up placating hands. 'But even taking into account all that, I don't think you are well.'

'Rubbish. I am pregnant.'

He stirred a mug of tea and handed it to her. 'I know it's too much sugar but perhaps you're lacking it. Drink up.'

She sipped and made a face.

He said, 'Did you read up about the Dodecanese?'

'No.'

'Right.' He reached into his case and brought out a rolled map and spread it on the floor. Grunting, he reached inside his jacket for a pen and used it to point to a scrap of green and yellow in a densely blue sea. 'That's it. Androulis built three houses there – holiday homes for his family. My mother went to one of them several times before the war. She used to tell me about it. It sounded idyllic.'

'I—' she felt a hollow in her stomach. 'Now that an actual island is being mentioned, I'm not sure any more, Charles. It's so far away.'

'From what?'

'Home, of course.'

'Or Peter Snow?'

'Not even Peter.' She looked at him through the steam from her tea. 'More Miranda.'

He sat back and replaced his pen slowly before he spoke. Then he said, 'You told me once you could tune in to your sister.'

'Yes. Sometimes very . . . strongly.'

'Then cultivate that. Or . . . ruin her life. And her family.'

She put her mug on to the tray; the tea slopped over the rim.

He said, 'Sorry, Meg. But that's how it is. You know that – you told me how it was yourself. Now you're trying to forget it, you're trying to pretend there are other solutions.'

'Maybe there are. This is 1976, Charles. People live together – Peter and Miranda are Bohemian enough, heaven knows. You should see the state of the house every time I arrive—'

'Stop talking sentimentally, my dear. Even if they are unconventional, you are not. You could not live in a *ménage à trois*. And what about your sister's children? They attend local schools. Children can be cruel. How do you picture this Bohemian set-up? You as housewife and skivvy? Tending the lamp of Peter's talent? What place is there for Miranda then?'

She turned her head. 'Charles, stop it. I know you're right, of course.'

He leaned down with difficulty, picked up her tea again and handed it to her. 'Listen. Go out to Androulis' island. Look at it. Have a holiday – quite short if you're worried. And ask yourself if it's the sort of place where – *a*, you could raise a child. And *b*, write a book.'

'A book? Me?'

'Yes. You.' He shifted in his chair; for him it was practically a bounce. 'Meg, I've been going to suggest it for some time now. You have a natural talent for seeing a story from a child's eye view. You're an artist first, so draw pictures. Anything you feel like drawing. And then . . . write your story. Meg, you can do it. And you need to do it. You need a progression in your life. For the past ten years you have been doing the same thing. It's time for a change. That change has been forced on you by this baby. Make the most of it, my girl!'

She swallowed some tea; it went the wrong way and she

coughed desperately. He passed her a pristine handkerchief and waited.

She said, 'I'm not sure, Charles.'

He said, 'The island is called Artemia. The legend is that the moon goddess rested there on her way to Arcadia.' He paused as Meg gave an involuntary exclamation. 'Yes. Quite. Artemis is the protector when it comes to childbirth.'

She said, 'It wasn't that. I didn't know that actually. But I did some drawings for Sebastian when I was at Keele. Peter and I . . . it was the night of . . . it was a story about moonbeams.'

'There you are then. The whole bloody thing is preordained!'

She looked at him, her eyes still wide.

He said impatiently, 'Well? Isn't that what you want? To be shown the way? It couldn't be clearer, surely?'

She said, 'It's so . . . precipitate. It's frightening.'

'Well, at the risk of frightening you off completely, there's one more thing.' He began the business of getting himself out of the chair. Once up, he made for the window. No-one had drawn the curtains but it was quite dark. He peered sideways at the nearest street light as if he was expecting another visitor. Then he grunted disagreeably and said, 'The sooner you're out of here the better. But of course your sister will have to know where you are. She might decide to come for a holiday. Anything.'

Meg turned in her chair to look at the breadth of his back. She said, 'That *is* a bridge I can cross later, Charles. And as for rushing off this instant, there's no need. Perhaps in a month or two—'

He shot her an angry look. 'And meanwhile you'll be sleeping most of the time, will you?' He sighed deeply and ran his finger along the ledge of the sash. 'Meg, get over to Artemia and start writing your moon story.

You know very well you're not interested in illustrating other people's stuff any more.'

She tried to laugh. 'I must admit the squirrels were hard work.'

'Quite. And you need a complete change. Sorry, my dear, but you are looking pretty dreadful.' He ignored her second attempt at a laugh and ploughed on in a determined way. 'There is one more thing, Meg. I think it might solve the whole problem in one fell swoop. Business arrangement, of course. Purely a business arrangement.'

He stopped and coughed deliberately, then took a breath. 'We could get married.' He held up his hand as if to silence her. 'All right. You're still very young and I'm over forty. And not a fit forty either. But that could be an advantage in a business arrangement. The child would have my name. All right, your sister might guess something, but it would only be a guess. You wouldn't have to see too much of them but if they visited . . . well, what I'm saying is you can tell one big lie instead of a lot of little ones!'

She was speechless. She wanted to remind Charles of his mother in the nursing home in Essex; of his business in the Edgware Road. She could say not a word.

He waited for a while, then said, 'You must know I was married before. I was twenty and she was eighteen. She was killed in the Uprising, but it would have died anyway. We were too young. Too foolish.' He drew a deep breath. 'Obviously you would still go to Artemia. I realize it would be unworkable to stay here. I'd visit you just often enough to make the whole arrangement seem credible. I would suggest you flew home for the actual birth. Otherwise you need not see me at all if you did not wish it.'

Still she did not speak and after another wait he hunched his shoulder irritably.

'I see. I've embarrassed you past speech, have I? Well,

Meg. Think about it carefully. Don't mention it again if it's thumbs down. But please go to Artemia. Look at it. Imagine working there. Please.'

He turned and picked up his briefcase. And left.

Some time later she looked at the map still spread on the floor. Just right of it was an envelope bearing a typewritten name and address. 'Miss Amy Smithers, Artemia, Dodecanese.' And in Charles's handwriting – 'Scribble her a note, tell her when you're arriving. She'll organize everything.'

It sounded so simple. An English name – the same name as Meg's own mother. Meg folded the envelope carefully and put it on the mantelpiece. And then she picked up the map and stared at the blobs of green and yellow in the Aegean Sea. And thought about Sebastian and his moonbeams.

Fourteen

It seemed to take forever to get a passport and book a flight to Athens. Meg felt as if she were now running from everyone. If only Charles had not been so obviously sensitive about the whole thing, she would have gone somewhere else; not even told him her destination. Except that if she wanted work sent out to her . . . but then hadn't he said that she should write her own book? Did that mean he would no longer supply her with work? She was in a curious, muddled frame of mind; not quite certain any more why she had to go to an island owned by a Greek shipowner in the middle of the Aegean. But she certainly could not rest in Kilburn any more. And she could not go where she wanted to go, which was Keyhole. Artemia seemed the only alternative.

Charles kept away from Kilburn but the post brought a fat cheque and a note saying simply, 'Whatever you decide to do, the very best of luck.' She folded the note and put it with a wad of photographs in her handbag. And she did sums much as she had done them back at the Coastguards so many years before. And discovered, as she had then, that she could probably manage quite well wherever she lived.

But there must be something deep in her subconscious that wanted to go to Artemia. She wrote to 'Miss Amy Smithers' and asked a pageful of questions. A reply came very promptly indeed. Besides Amy there were apparently two families living on the island. Both of them sent their men to join the sponge fishermen from Kalymnos every year, and presumably lived from the sale of their catches. Supplies came from Skyros or were flown out from Volos. They were probably expensive, but the fishermen's families would not be able to afford them, so it was obviously possible to live from the sea. There was a garden surrounding the villa and it had been cultivated before the war. Presumably Meg could cultivate it again. She packed beans, peas, cabbage seed, in fact every kind of vegetable seed she could buy.

The decisions, the tasks . . . they all seemed endless. She talked to Jill who offered to supervise letting the Kilburn house, but she still had to put it in the hands of reputable agents and they had to take an inventory and measure the rooms. Getting a passport photograph and buying drachmas seemed almost insurmountable obstacles.

Miranda rang nearly every other day and was beginning to pester about Easter.

'Darling, I might not be able to make it.' It was one more step in the path of deceit she was on where the Snows were concerned. She spun a story about a trip to Athens to meet one of the authors. 'It's a wonderful opportunity, Miranda. I must have mentioned it before.'

'You said something about going abroad. Oh, Meg, I'm so disappointed.'

'So am I. Needless to say.'

'As soon as you get back—'

'Hang on, Sis! I am a working girl, you know!'

Miranda was silent then said quietly, 'Are you trying to cut loose, Meg?'

Meg wondered how much Miranda knew through the telepathic link between them. She took a deep breath. 'Listen. That's a ridiculous idea. But . . . darling, there is someone here who is – who has – asked me to marry him.' That at any rate was the truth. She waited until Miranda's exclamations died, then went on, 'Well. As you know I cannot be in love with him. But I need to get away.'

'Come here, Meg. Please.'

'That is not the answer.' After all, Miranda understood how she felt about Peter. 'Sorry, Sis. Perhaps I do have to cut loose. For a time.'

Miranda said slowly, 'Like you did before. Even Plymouth was too close, wasn't it? You had to go to London.'

'Sis, that is all in the past. And anyway, it's just not true. I came to London to work.'

'It was when I hurt you. When Peter hurt you.'

'Sis, please! Stop raking over old ashes!'

'Is that how it is this time, Meg? Have we hurt you again?'

It was an inversion of the truth; she had hurt them and they did not know it. They must not know it.

She said solemnly, 'We went through that terrible time at Christmas . . . together, darling.'

Miranda said with some of her old fierceness, 'Sometimes I wish we'd never split up after the Uncle Cedric business! If we'd made enough fuss they'd have kept us together! And then I'd have never seen the Arbitrary and we could have bought a house and grown old like a couple of peas in a pod!'

Meg laughed; it was a truly ludicrous idea, especially coming from Miranda. Then she said anxiously, 'You're all right, aren't you? You sounded so content before.'

'I am. I am. It's as if I'm seeing Keele through your eyes, darling. A little paradise on earth. But there has to be something missing otherwise I'd think I really was dead! And the missing bit is you!'

'I'll keep in touch. Promise.'

'I know. It's just that . . . sometimes I think we'll never be properly together, Meg. And that . . . worries me.'

'When I said I'd keep in touch, I meant that. We're more together than people who live next door to each other!'

'Yes. Of course we are.' Miranda spoke bracingly now and went on to recount some of the escapades the children had got up to during the half-term.

'Thank God Meredith finished himself off that night, Meg. I couldn't have let them play so freely if he'd been still alive.' She drew an audible breath. 'I found out last week, Meg. The baby was a girl. She was formed and everything. She was a girl.'

Meg squeezed her eyes tight shut. 'Oh, Miranda.'

Miranda said, 'It's OK. It was a nightmare and I'm properly awake. Don't worry. But . . . I just wanted you to know.'

'You've still got Katie.'

'Yes. And she's such a darling lately. In fact they all are. It was a nightmare for them too and it must be such a relief to wake from it.'

'Exactly.'

She replaced the receiver carefully. There was no turning back now. She had to put a lot of miles between herself and Fish Cottage.

She was never to forget her first glimpse of the Islands. Almost laconically the pilot announced, 'there are over a thousand uninhabited islands in the seas around Greece, some owned by the very rich as havens from their busy lives. 'Rhodes is the largest of the Dodecanese. There are also the Cyclades and the Sporades.' He spoke parrot-fashion with a definite American twang, but it did not matter. The subject matter was there for them to see.

He went on to talk about the tourist attractions of Mykonos, and then they were circling Athens airport and the routine of seat belts was under way. Meg swallowed against the pressure in her ears but continued to look back at the translucent sea, suddenly and inexplicably excited. She and Miranda had taken Alex to the Scillies in a helicopter for his fifth birthday treat, and she recalled now the magical effect of an island-studded sea. Charles had known exactly what he was doing.

The taxi drivers were fiercely competitive, invading the exit lounge, standing by passengers who were waiting for their luggage and practically snatching cases from them. Meg succumbed to the biggest smile she had ever seen in her life and surrendered her case and hand luggage with pleasure. After Heathrow, Athens was very warm. Teresa at the agency had warned her that it could rain 'cats and dogs' at this time of year in Greece, so she had worn her raincoat. She followed the cab driver into a very ordinary arterial road and shrugged out of the coat immediately.

'Is thunder soon,' he told her, stowing her luggage in the enormous boot of an American car. 'You need English Burberry.'

She smiled at such random vocabulary and showed him the address of her hotel. He leapt into the car and drove off like a maniac, but then she had expected that. She held on to the back of his seat and tried to register impressions. Disappointingly, most of the suburban buildings seemed to be constructed of concrete but the colours were many. White predominated, sea-green and bright blue were also favourites. She was amazed at how modern and close-packed everything was. Her hotel was in Syntagma Square and was horribly modern. But she had decided on a night in Athens before flying on to Volos and then taking a boat to Artemia. Teresa had simply booked her into the one used by the agency.

Her driver swung her luggage into the foyer and help descended immediately; perhaps a modern hotel was not such a bad thing. He pressed a card into her hand before leaving; it was incomprehensible, but there was a telephone number. 'Andreas,' he told her emphatically. 'Me, Andreas. Demand Andreas!' She returned his beaming smile and let herself be checked in and taken up to a typical hotel room, high enough to see over the huddle of flat-roofed buildings towards what must be the Acropolis and Parthenon. She unpacked eagerly and looked at her map from all angles. She had until tomorrow afternoon to discover Athens! She took the map to the window and tried to identify buildings and streets. And then, suddenly almost drunk with all the new impressions, she sat on the bed and stared at the room itself. Her peculiar lethargy that was so bound up with unwillingness to make any move had gone. She said aloud, 'My God. I'm free. For the first time since I met Peter Snow, I am free!' She closed her eyes and thought of Miranda. She could picture her clearly: as she had been, vibrant, almost dominated by her wild orange-coloured hair; and as she was now, very pale, thin, all eyes and nose, her hair somehow subdued and flattened.

But though the mind pictures were so clear, there was nothing more. There was no . . . connection.

She opened her eyes and looked around the room again. The furniture was white with gilt fittings and very fancy. For a brief instant there was a pang for her functional, pared-down arrangement at Kilburn, and then for the stripped pine of Fish Cottage. Then that too was gone.

She spoke to the twin wardrobes guarding the cheval mirror between them. 'Perhaps . . . I mean, I'm having Peter's baby. Is that enough? Is that why they've all become . . . unreal?'

The furniture gave her no answer. And anyway it didn't matter. She grinned at her reflection in that ridiculous mirror and headed for the bathroom. She would soak in a bath, dig out a thin jersey-knit frock that fell from a high princess waistline, and go down to dinner. And then she would ask someone to ring the number on Andreas' card, and tomorrow she would splash out on a conducted tour of Athens.

She did all those things and found Andreas an excellent guide. Also very understanding.

'All this, too much. But later, you think it round straight.'

Meg, staring at the evzones in their national costumes as they changed guard outside the Parliament Building, knew exactly what her guide meant.

She said, 'The Parthenon would have been sufficient . . . but you're right. And I might not have time again to see Athens.'

'You buy sponge?' A sponge seller walked past the cab hung with bunches of sponges that bounced and moved as if having a life of their own.

'I'd rather an ice cream.'

Andreas was out of the cab in an instant, a line of traffic honking furiously behind him. He returned with a dish of multi-coloured ice cream and a silver spoon.

'But . . . the traffic – no time to return these!' Meg looked wildly out at the man wheeling an ice-cream cart.

'I give back next time around,' Andreas said largely and drove off at high speed towards the Royal Palace and yet more evzones. Meg found herself laughing and eating her ice cream and wishing very much Andreas could come with her to Artemia.

A surprise awaited her at the airport. She had booked an air ticket with Olympic Airways to fly to Volos and then take one of the island steamers from there. But Andreas – still with her at three o'clock in the afternoon – conducted her proudly to a small heliport.

'Your ticket is OK for the air taxis, madame. And I am friend of Theopholis who is flying the Alouette here. He take you to your door in Artemia. No problem.'

It was a favourite phrase of every Greek who knew a little English. 'No problem,' pronounced Theopholis, discovered asleep in the tiny bubble which had to take everything. He went into a torrent of Greek as he stowed her case and several pieces of hand luggage. Andreas answered him and translated briefly to Meg.

'We talk of family, madame. His wife is having baby.'

'Oh,' Meg beamed again, certain that fate was with her and everything was wonderfully, beautifully predestined.

She almost changed her mind as the tiny craft rose from the ground with an unexpected jerk and whirled around in midair before setting off in a long curve over Piraeus. In less than two minutes, Andreas and his red taxi had disappeared and they were zooming over the beaches around Athens and heading over the sea. In spite of her seat belt she held on almost frantically to the edge of the door; there had been no sensation of movement in the enormous plane which brought her here yesterday; the world had drifted past the window and the plane had been a still centre. This was quite different. The random, hectic speed was terrifying. And they were so close to the sea! She could practically see the fish beneath its surface; she could certainly see the facial expressions of fishermen and tourists as they looked up at the annoying invasion of sound and space.

The flight took just over half an hour, and she still had not got used to the frightful clatter when the helicopter hovered over an island that looked like a jewelled leg of lamb thrown into the sea all anyhow and apparently moving gently with the waves. The colours were stunning: green, gold and purple. Theopholis grinned at her and put his thumb down; they began to descend towards the thick end of the island where a flag could be seen fluttering spasmodically from a white mast. Meg clutched the door even harder and tried to narrow her distended eyes. Beyond the flagpole there were several small houses, flat-topped, very white. She hoped that none of them was Charles's.

They settled on a square of flattened grass and the engines faded. The little helicopter creaked slightly as it relaxed on to its skids and then a kind of ear-splitting silence settled around it as the rotors drifted to a halt. Theopholis leaned across her and released her door and she let go of it and sat back tremblingly. He leapt out of his side and hurried round to help her down. Her legs were like jelly; she held his arm for a moment until she could stand properly. Andreas' driving had been hair-raising enough, but this was a completely new experience.

By the time her luggage was out of the bubble and stacked around her, a woman had emerged from the cluster of buildings. She was dressed in traditional black with a headscarf pulled tight beneath her chin. She looked about eighty years old.

Theopholis burst into a babble of Greek and waved his hands first at the woman, then at Meg. The woman approached and smiled toothlessly.

'Meta Taxos,' Theopholis made brief introduction. 'Madame . . .' he consulted her ticket. 'Madame Patch. From England.'

The old woman grinned and nodded and spoke impatiently to Theopholis. She already knew about Meg.

Theopholis said, 'You are too early. Miss Smithers is meeting the steamer at sunset.'

Meg nodded. 'Yes. Well, I thought . . .'

'No problem. Meta Taxos lend you donkey.'

Meg was certain that a donkey was not part of her predestiny.

'I've no idea where the villa is,' she protested. 'And there is the luggage.'

There was more conversation in Greek and Theopholis' smile returned.

'No problem. Donkey knows the way to Miss Smithers's villa. You will manage OK. Yes?'

Mrs Taxos was already turning away, presumably to round up the donkey. Meg wanted to hang on to Theopholis until she returned but he was already ducking beneath the dejected rotor blades.

'My wife having baby,' he explained as he clambered aboard.

'Oh. I didn't realize she was actually . . .' Meg retreated hastily as the blades began to rotate. Her hair lifted and her dress fluttered in time with the flag. And then the Alouette was spinning like a top and curving off over the Aegean.

She waited by her luggage feeling helpless, wondering if Meta Taxos would appear again. She wished heartily that she had followed the schedule worked out so carefully by Teresa back in Kilburn. Presumably if she'd arrived on the steamer at sunset Miss Smithers would have met her and driven her to the villa, and things would have proceeded in the same well-ordered fashion as before. Now she wondered if she would still be standing here when the boat arrived. If this was where the boat arrived.

She looked around her uncertainly. The huddle of houses was actually three separate dwellings arranged triangularly around a well. The land appeared to drop towards the sea on one side of the triangle and to lift to a wooded escarpment on the other. She walked a few paces towards the trees and looked around again. The sea glinted milkily beneath her. Was there a harbour down there? She marched on and was soon climbing steeply. She could see beyond the houses now. There was a bite out of the top of the leg of lamb. A wooden jetty ran from one side of the bite and two boats lifted and sank lazily from it.

She began to walk towards what was obviously the harbour; she would just have to sit there and wait for the evening boat. There must have been a misunderstanding between Theopholis and the old lady. Anyway she was much too ancient to be rounding up donkeys for an able-bodied young woman. There was absolutely no need to feel bereft or deserted; everything was fine.

She rounded a wall that was sprouting wild flowers like a Cornish hedge, and came face to face with a goat. And an untethered goat at that. They stared at each other, then he – or she – lifted a shaggy head and made a sound like a lost soul in torment. He or she had a full set of large yellow teeth. Meg retreated behind the wall. An angry voice shouted something behind her. She looked round. A hundred yards away, standing stolidly by her abandoned luggage, was a donkey. Another one, led by Mrs Taxos, was approaching the first. It was Mrs Taxos who had shouted.

Meg hurried across the short grass.

'I'm sorry – I thought you'd gone—' She was panting and obviously apologetic. Mrs Taxos went into a mumbling grumble interspersed with sudden shouts and nods towards the wall and the goat. Then, with an unmistakable mime – legs planted wide, gestures with hooked fingers – she indicated that the goat was about to give birth.

Meg almost laughed. Greece seemed to be populated with fertile females. It was certainly the right place for her.

She watched – helpless again – as Mrs Taxos loaded luggage in two panniers on one of the donkeys. She strapped and tied everything with care – not for luggage but for donkey – and indicated the unburdened animal.

Meg smiled propitiatingly. 'I've not ridden a donkey since I was about six years old,' she began.

Mrs Taxos mumbled crossly again and opened one gnarled hand on the donkey's back. Meg approached cautiously and stroked it. Dust rose from her fingers. There was no saddle. Mrs Taxos spoke sharply and Meg scrambled all anyhow on to the warm fur back and gripped the springy mane.

The next moment Mrs Taxos gave a mighty yell and slapped the donkey's rump and they went into motion.

Meg held on hard. She dared not look round to see if the old woman was following with the luggage, all her concentration was needed to stay on the sun-hot animal rolling around beneath her. She gripped hard with her knees and tried to roll with the tiny plodding hooves. If she fell off would she be trampled? Would she lose the baby? She felt a sudden terrible pang. She must not lose Peter's baby.

It took almost five minutes of terror before she realized she could almost touch the ground with her feet either side of her steed, so there was no question of falling beneath the ridiculous little hooves. She remembered paintings, one especially of Don Quixote astride a mule. Pelvis forward, legs hanging slightly to the rear, eyes most definitely up and looking around, never fixed on the ears of the mule. She tried it; immediately she relaxed, her hands opened on the mane and she seemed to roll with the movements of her obviously good-tempered animal.

'Are we going to be all right?' she asked, still apprehensive. There was no reply. She risked glancing behind. The other donkey was a few yards to the rear, her case on one of its flanks, hand luggage on the other. Mrs Taxos had hooked her sun-hat over his ears and he looked like one of the stuffed animals the tourists brought back from Spain.

But he was quite unattended. Mrs Taxos was doubtless back in her flat-roofed cottage cooking up moussaka. Or fish stew. Meg's laughter was not only for the sun-hatted donkey, it was for her own situation. It was all so crazy. She was used to her well-ordered life being turned upside down every time she went down to Keyhole, but not like this. Never like this. There was something so . . . so . . . happy about being here. Sitting astride a donkey. Her luggage on another. She said aloud to the donkeys, as she had said to the furniture last night, 'I am free!'

The track hugged the coast for perhaps a mile and then turned on to what must be the thinner end of the leg of lamb and began to climb towards the trees. The coast seemed to be entirely rock on this side, but as the donkeys plodded higher she could see what looked like a replica of Lannah Cove on the southern tip of the island. She wondered if it was accessible and scanned the trees for signs of a coombe. There were no obvious breaks in the foliage going towards the sea, but further to the north a windmill appeared as the donkeys turned landward. Below it was a cleared plateau of very green grass and from the trees at the edge of the plateau arose a thread of smoke.

For a moment she thought it might be a brush fire and she straightened her back in an effort to see any glow in the dense growth, but the spiral continued so thinly it could only be coming from a bonfire. A garden bonfire? It sounded too suburban for Artemia. And then the donkey pushed his way through a tangle of shoulder-high fern, and the plateau became fully visible. The smoke came from a chimney. The chimney belonged to a house which might once have been rather like the flat-roofed houses down by the harbour, but was now covered in vines and creepers of all description, recognizable only by its glinting windows and the solitary chimney.

Unexpectedly the donkey stopped as if allowing her a

moment to gaze, but actually in response to a loud 'halloo there!'

Meg stared again as a figure emerged from the organic house and started down the path towards them. If she had not known that Amy Smithers was the only person on this side of the island, she would have assumed this was a man. The ancient grey flannels and shirt, the battered panama, the lined face . . . there was nothing feminine there at all. But the smile and the veined, liver-marked hand which was extended long before Meg could possibly clasp it, were unexpectedly feminine and beautiful. Meg slid off the donkey and took the hand, her own smile an automatic response. She had not known what she had expected in Miss Amy Smithers, but it had not been this elderly, eccentric figure. Maybe a writer, maybe another artist. Not someone whom Uncle Cedric would have described disapprovingly as having 'gone native'.

'My dear girl, you're much too early! I saw the whirly bird and wondered . . . should have come down straight-away but thought I'd better get a fire going and some food moved in.'

'Miss Smithers – so nice to meet you – ' the donkey was gently pushing them both up the path towards the plateau – 'changed plans suddenly and – I'm so sorry—'

'No need for apologies, child! You're here. Safe, sound and in one piece. Trust Meta's donkeys. Better than homo sapiens any day of the week! Look, call me Amy. And you signed yourself Meg rather than Margaret—'

'Oh yes. Call me Meg.' They were on the plateau. The grass appeared to have been expertly mown. The donkeys tucked in. Meg said shyly, 'My mother's name was Amy.'

'Well, I'm old enough to be your grandmother!' Amy Smithers's laugh was a hoarse bark, and as if in reply the donkeys brayed with a suddenness that shocked both women then convulsed them with giggles. Meg registered that Amy Smithers could giggle; it was something of a relief.

'I say, it's so pretty!'

Meg looked around, her face wide with pleasure. The plateau was a far cry from the workaday cottages by the harbour. For one thing the views were superb; the length of the coast she had just crossed could be seen, though no sign of the small sandy cove.

'The prevailing winds come from Asia, so we've got our backs to them.' Amy unbuckled the girth that seemed to hold the luggage in place on the donkey, and hoisted a bag on to her shoulder. 'I'm further along in the trees – we need not see each other if we don't want to but in case of emergencies we've got foghorns.'

'Foghorns?' Meg picked up her case, bemused with impressions.

'Old Androulis put them in for both of us back in '36.' Amy went to an opening in the vines next to one of the glinting windows; it proved to be a door. 'Eva and me.' She turned and flashed a smile at Meg; her teeth were large and yellow like the donkeys'. 'We didn't get on too well in those days so he had to build us separate houses. When he wasn't here he thought we might fall ill or something, so he installed the foghorns. The Taxos families can hear them right down by the jetty.'

'I . . . didn't know . . . Charles hasn't told me . . . much.'

Meg humped the case into near-darkness. She blinked hard. The ground floor seemed to be one big room. Somehow, peculiarly, she recognized it.

Amy put her bag on a table in the middle of the stone-flagged floor. She said briskly, 'Nothing much to tell. I knew Androulis before Eva. Crewed for him on his yacht. The Kovacks joined us one year. She was stunning.

Eventually he installed us here and I've been here ever since. Eva got out at the beginning of the war. I've seen her since. We're good friends now. That's it.'

'Oh.' It was quite possible to imagine Mrs Kovacks as a *femme fatale*, discarded husband and all; but Amy Smithers was a different kettle of fish. Meg felt a bubble of anticipation somewhere beneath her diaphragm. She would have time to find out about Amy Smithers, and that was an exciting thought.

Amy grinned again. 'Yes. A bit much to swallow in one gulp, I imagine. Kovacks should have warned you. Anyway, not to worry, first things first. Let me show you around. Then I'm going to leave you in peace till eight o'clock when I shall collect you and take you to my villa for supper. In the meantime, start making a list of stores you'll need and I haven't got. I live pretty frugally myself, so I'm sure to have missed out on something. But Spiros Taxos will be going to Kalymnos tomorrow and can bring back most of the basics.'

She strode to the back of the cottage and indicated a door. 'Bathroom. Septic tank arrangement. Tell you about that later.' She moved past a shallow sink served by a small hand pump and opened the door of an enormous refrigerator. 'Milk and cheese – goat's of course – eggs. I made you a loaf. There's a sack of flour in the store room – tea – salt – sugar.' She pointed to a wood-burning stove. 'That's for when the generator breaks down. Doesn't often happen but it usually goes when you're in the middle of baking. I lit it because it gets very cold once the sun goes down.'

'The generator works from the windmill?'

'Yes. The first thing Eva had installed was this Westinghouse!' Amy laughed. 'I had electric light just about everywhere. Eva said she preferred candles and ice with her drinks! That sums up the two of us.'

Meg spread her hands. 'I don't know what to say. You've done so much. Thank you – thank you very much indeed. You must let me know how much I owe you.'

'No trouble, dear girl. Money doesn't enter into it. Kovacks tells me you're going to spend time here until just before the birth of your baby and you want to write a children's book. Any friend of his is welcome anyway, but someone who is going to work *and* produce a baby is very welcome!' Amy made for the door again. 'I'll send the donkeys on their way and be over for you in a couple of hours. D'you like asparagus?'

'Yes!'

'Good. I grow my own and it's early this year.'

Meg stood in the doorway and watched her push the donkeys off the short grass of the plateau and on to the path. She crossed the plateau herself with the easy lope of a woman half her age and disappeared into the trees. Meg thought of Eva Kovacks in the nursing home in Essex and knew who had the best life.

She went back into the house. She had not noticed Amy filling and plugging in an electric kettle, but it was singing efficiently next to the cooker. She rummaged around and found a teapot and a mug. The goat's milk did not smell good, but she used it anyway.

'My first cup of tea on Artemia,' she said aloud and knew she sounded the image of Miranda. That made her laugh. She cradled the mug in her hands and looked around the living area. Amy – or someone – had cleaned the little windows, all six of them. And had scrubbed the stone floor and the steps leading to the bedrooms. And someone must have mowed that grass outside too. She drank and smiled. How clever of Charles to simplify the whole thing to its basics. She was having a baby and she was going to write a book.

She finished the tea and went upstairs to look at

the sleeping arrangements. Two bedrooms, each with a double bed and a vast chest of drawers. She flicked back white counterpanes and discovered crisp linen, stiff with starch, huge pillows, not very soft.

Downstairs again she investigated the stove, then unpacked her luggage and put aside things that had to be taken upstairs. She took her sponge bag into the bathroom, expecting something primitive, and paused, surprised yet again. The bath had claw feet, the lavatory looked like a carver chair, there was a dressing table with an enormous mirror and a gilt stool.

'Very art deco,' she murmured, dumping the small sponge bag and some towels and retreating.

She had unpacked, used the bath and put on fresh clothes by the time Amy Smithers returned. And, surprisingly, it was good to have some company and to be closing her own front door again and knowing she would be coming back to it quite soon.

Amy led her through the trees to the base of the windmill.

'Let you have a good look around before it's completely dark,' she grunted, clambering on to its concrete base. 'Come up here, Meg. This is the other side of the island. The Turkish side.'

It was quite different; already dark because the sun was setting on the west side. The trees dropped precipitously to narrow sandy beaches on a scalloped shoreline.

'Is that the cove I could see as I came up the path?' Meg asked, pointing to the right.

'That's our cove. Mutton Cove, Androulis called it. I swim there most days. Do you swim, Meg?'

'My sister and I were called the tadpole twins when we were small. I still swim when I visit her in Cornwall.'

'You're a twin? That means you are a magical person. The gods smile on twins. Especially in Greece.' She clambered back down to the ground. 'I'll take you to Mutton Cove tomorrow, then you'll be able to swim whenever you feel like it.' She held out a hand for Meg. 'Come now, I want you to see my garden.'

They went on through the trees for perhaps a quarter of a mile. Then there was another clearing and an enormous arched entry. Beyond the arch the short grass was dotted with apple trees like an English orchard, and among the trees were stone sculptures of all shapes and sizes, some taller than the trees, others quite small. Beyond the stone-and-tree orchard was a replica of the cottage on the other side of the plateau.

Meg stared. 'You're a sculptress,' she said.

Amy was delighted. 'People usually ask me what they are – some even think they're indigenous – they never dream I've done them. How did you know?'

'You called it "my garden". It's a sculpture garden. I've seen one like it. But very small. This is – this is staggering!'

Meg went to a tall megalith standing benevolently by a very old gnarled tree. 'You've gone one further, haven't you? They're abstract, but each one relates to the trees.'

'My God! I'm getting through to someone! No wonder Kovacks thinks you're special!'

Meg hardly heard her; she was entranced. It was like walking into one of the children's books she had illustrated. She said wonderingly, 'It's *The Old Apple Man*. Only much better. If only I'd seen this before I did the drawings—'

Amy's smile was beatific.

'It's getting too dark to see them properly. Come tomorrow and you can explore them properly. There's one you can get inside – like a child inside its mother's womb! You'll like that one.'

Meg allowed herself to be taken into the house. Amy

flicked switches and her enormous kitchen sprang into life. The same sink, table, cooker . . . but there similarities ended. Half of Amy's cottage was also her studio and huge chunks of stone took up the space under the windows.

'Sorry about the mess. I'm going to get a shed place built at the side one of these days. This is only work in progress. I store my stone outside.'

'It's good to see it in here – part of your life.' Meg was still wide-eyed, a child in Aladdin's cave.

'Trouble is, bloody stone dust gets into everything. I'm not sure if it's good for one to eat it!' Amy poured wine into very delicate glasses and handed one to Meg. 'Come on, let's drink a toast before supper. To your health and happiness—'

Meg shook her head. 'Not tonight. I've only just come into this particular picture.' She smiled and lifted her glass, inspired. 'Let's drink to Artemia. And Artemis. She'll look after us.'

'Oh, wise child!' Amy drank deeply, then pulled out one of the solid chairs beneath the table. 'Sit you down. I have to look at the snappers, then we'll munch our asparagus rolls and you can tell me about Eva.' She looked at Meg, her smile gone. 'I don't think I shall see Eva again. You can fill that gap for me.'

So Meg did, and the evening flew by. And by the end of it she knew that she would have to plant most of her seeds in the next few days; that she could have a share in Amy's goats and it was they who 'mowed' the grass of the plateau, that Meta Taxos was not old at all and had cleaned the cottage and would do so again if necessary, and that 'snappers' were delicately pink fish, delicious in a sauce made from goat's cheese and local olives.

It was as she went back into Eva Kovacks's kitchen that she recognized her sense of *déjà vu* for what it was. The kitchens, designed perhaps by the mysterious Androulis of long ago, were replicas of the fish cellar in Keyhole. And with the realization, Miranda's presence was with her. It was a tranquil connection, quite unlike anything that had ever happened before. Meg could not believe it at first and searched that part of her mind for signs of distress or pain. There were none. Miranda was content. Just as she, Meg, was content.

She got ready for bed. The stove would have to go out; she had not yet found the wood-store which Amy said contained green wood necessary to keep it smouldering overnight. The door was locked with a wooden beam but the outside shutters were pinioned open with the vines and ivy, and anyway without them would doubtless fall off. There were no curtains to the small windows; the moonlight was brighter than her candle and she blew out the steady flame long before she climbed between the stiff sheets. She punched the overstuffed pillow into submission and lay flat on her back, hands on abdomen. All the anxieties of the past few months had gone, beginning to dissolve as the Boeing came in to land. That glimpse into Miranda's contented mind was all she needed to complete a sense of utter peace.

She closed her eyes and knew she would sleep.

Fifteen

Miranda sifted the warm sand of Lannah Cove through her fingers and tried not to flinch when Alex shook his wet hair over her bare shoulders.

He said loudly, 'Ma, is Dad asleep?'

Miranda rolled her eyes. 'He was.' She squinted against the sun. Alex was starting to grow, he would be ten in a few weeks. In two or three years he was going to look exactly as Peter had at fourteen when she had first met him.

Peter did not budge though she knew he was awake.

She smiled. 'Can *I* help you?'

'Well, it would be nice if you came in the sea. But . . .' He gave her the sideways glance that she was used to now. He had avoided looking directly at her since 'the accident' as her affair with John Meredith was euphemistically called.

'But what?' There was still a trace of the old antipathy between them. She told herself she wanted him to face it . . . say exactly what he meant.

'Well, I don't suppose you want to, do you?'

That was true enough. The thought of the icy water on her hot skin was torture.

She said, 'You've got Katie for company. And that little horror Zach was around. Have you drowned them both?'

He grinned unwillingly. 'No, but it would be more fun if Dad would come too.'

'I thought it was me you were asking.'

'Well, yes. If Dad is asleep. And you didn't mind.'

Peter opened one eye. 'Your mother is supposed to be resting. I'll be with you in ten minutes.'

Alex's face lit up. 'OK, Dad! I'll just go and drown Zach!'

He dashed off with another sideways look at his mother, but Miranda did not acknowledge the joke. It was so obvious that Alex saw her as second best.

Peter propped himself on one elbow. 'No peace for the wicked.' He grinned at her then said, 'All right, darling?'

'Of course.' She forced a smile. 'Honestly, Peter, you don't have to be forever anxious about me. Not now. I'm all right. I'm really all right.'

'I know.' He put his hand over hers and she stopped sifting sand for just a moment. 'You're wonderful, my love. Coping with all of us, always so calm and collected.'

'Not the old Miranda at all, in other words?' She smiled again but there was sadness in her voice. She was only too well aware that the craziness had gone from her and though that was a good thing, still the craziness had been part of her and sometimes she missed it.

'We're both different, Miranda.' He felt her fingers dig for more sand and tightened his grip. 'Perhaps it's just old age?' He leaned over and kissed her nose. 'Neither of us would want to shimmy down a rope into the harbour any more, would we?'

'No . . . this one doesn't even want to get into the sea today – and it's surely the hottest day of the year.'

He made a face. 'This one isn't that keen either. Haven't been in at all this year.'

She was surprised. 'Haven't you? I thought you went with the children on Saturday afternoons.'

'I take them. I don't get in.'

She met his eyes for a brief instant then looked away.

315

Peter had changed just as she had. But she had salvaged something from the wreck of last Christmas: the loss of her crazy streak had been replaced by a quietness of mind she had never known before. Peter had achieved nothing. She was not certain how much he had lost; he had not painted anything significant since then. Now it seemed that he no longer loved swimming. Perhaps when he had lost Meg, he had lost everything. She gave a sudden, frightened sob and he gathered her up and held her tightly.

'It's all right. Don't think about it, my love. It's all right.'

She spoke into his neck. 'It's not that. I'm sorry, Peter. Sorry. If there was something I could do to make it better—'

'Just get well. That's all.'

She knew that her frailty must manacle him and she wanted so much to set him free.

She said suddenly, 'Peter, we'll both get in. Now. We'll go swimming with the children. Together.'

He was doubtful. 'Are you strong enough?'

'I'm doing practically everything else now. Of course I'm strong enough.' She sat up and began to pin up her hair. She said, 'Meg goes swimming every day, you know. Usually before breakfast.'

'Yes. But the Aegean is a darned sight warmer than the Atlantic! And Meg is as strong as a horse.'

Alex pounded up the beach, water hanging from each eyelash.

'You're *both* coming in? Great! Super!' He remembered something heard in his infancy. 'The tadpole and the shark!'

Miranda ran into the shallows and dived into the first wave. That way no-one would know that the salt water on her face came from sudden tears.

Meg was indeed happy. A pattern had been established from the first morning in Artemia and it suited her very well. It would not have mattered had there been no pattern at all, she could have lazed her days away contentedly enough on her own, but the pattern gave her a sense of purpose, achievement and fulfilment – in that order.

By July the weather was so hot that any manual work had to be completed by midday. She and Amy gave up their early-morning swim in favour of a precious two hours' work in their separate gardens. Spiro Taxos had cleared the undergrowth and weeds in Eva Kovacks's old vegetable patch, and already Meg had beans twining up trees everywhere and had picked her first peas. The winter greens were too advanced but in any case would have to be harvested by Amy. Meg knew that she would be gone by then, and although she said she would be back with the baby as soon as possible, she could not be sure about that.

After the gardening, she spent the rest of the morning painting. Her book, simple enough, depended for its charm on the pale watercolours she liked best, and the villa with its aura of the 1920s seemed to encourage the detailed drawings, now so out of fashion. There were no bold outlines, no stark and simple figures. The chief character, 'Daughter of the Moon, Nokomis', trailed clouds of stardust as she drifted across each page. Behind each star was a moonbeam, some mischievous, some sad; all of them worth looking for and recognizing. It was probably coincidence that Amy was taken with spherical shapes at this time. She insisted that the structure of enormous stone footballs, which she was starting in her English orchard, represented fertility and was a propitiation to Artemis.

'In other words, those shapes are moons,' Meg teased.

'Not at all. I modelled them on the shape of your abdomen when you strode out of the sea last month. It was the first time I'd really recognized your pregnancy. I liked its roundness.'

Meg looked at the older woman with mock sternness. 'You can get away with that kind of remark in 1976, Miss Smithers. But you must have shocked the world back in the twenties.'

Amy smiled smugly.

They invariably took a late lunch to Mutton Cove and slept and swam the afternoon away. It was here that, fragmentally, they spoke to each other of their experiences and discovered common ground.

'I think I was always jealous of Eva.'

'But you became friends, you said?'

'Eva was always my friend. She loved everyone. Eventually . . . because I knew that I loved her . . . I *permitted* her to love me.'

Meg thought of Peter and of how she had eventually permitted him to love her. She said nothing.

Amy sat up and rubbed her gnarled legs slowly. 'It is so difficult for some people to accept friendship. They feel they have nothing to give in return – *their* friendship doesn't count, it seems a worthless gift to them.'

Meg nodded. 'I suppose we . . . those kind of people . . . have no real sense of their own value. No self-esteem.'

'That's it. I thought Androulis kept me around because I crewed better than any man. It wasn't that at all.' She barked one of her hoarse laughs. 'The bloody man loved me! He loved both of us. Eva and me. And when I accepted that, then I could love Eva.'

Meg nodded. She understood that completely. She began, haltingly, to tell Amy about Miranda. And Peter. And afterwards Amy said, 'And since this baby, you're free of this peculiar bond you have with your sister?'

'I think so.'

'And that is why you're so happy?'

'I'm not sure. This whole . . . holiday . . . is such a hiatus. It seems to be the reality I've been looking for all my life. But when I go back . . . will it be a dream?'

'No. Because I'm here. Holding the fort for you. I live my dream. Therefore so can you.'

'Perhaps. Anyway I'll have done my book. And left Peter and Miranda free. And I've made a garden.'

Amy said, 'And a friend.'

Meg said warmly, 'Oh yes! That's the most important thing of all!'

That evening they walked down to meet the steamer and borrowed the Taxos donkeys to carry back their supplies. Meg had been taken with an idea for another book, and in between stopping to admire the breathtaking views and encourage the donkeys she discussed it with Amy.

'It would mean I'd have to draw every sculpture you've done in the orchard,' she said, breathless not only with excitement for a new project, but because she had doubled her size since arriving on the island and the upward path seemed twice as steep. 'I'd call it *The Stone Garden* and all the shapes would have names . . . do you think it sounds too twee and awful for words?'

'Not if you do it. You have a touch of acerbity that takes all the preciousness out of your stuff. Some of those moonbeams were nasty little chaps.'

Meg exploded with laughter.

'I'd show you every drawing and the text, of course.'

Amy said thoughtfully, 'You won't finish it before baby-day. Therefore you'd *have* to come back.'

'I would, wouldn't I? I think it would be for older children. I want the – the – beings – to have existed in the stone always. And you release them when you start chiselling. How does that sound?'

'A bit frightening.'

'Exactly.'

'Well, it won't be twee, will it?'

'No . . . this hill is definitely steeper than when I arrived.'

'I agree. Back in 1929 it was just a rise.'

They laughed again and said no more until they arrived at the plateau and unloaded. Amy slapped the donkeys back to the path and they watched silently as the grey shapes plodded home through the dusk.

Then Amy said, 'I'll collect my stuff tomorrow. Too tired now.' She took three steps across the nibbled grass and turned. 'I had another letter from Kovacks this morning.'

'Is he all right?'

It was the one thing Meg had not confided: Charles's proposal. She wished he had never made it. In effect it meant that Amy had letters from Charles and she did not.

'Sounds fine. Suggests you fly home as soon as possible.'

'He's making too much fuss. I don't want to sit around endlessly.'

'Yes. Especially as your friend . . . Jill something is it? . . . has tenants in your house. You'd have to stay at an hotel.'

'Yuk.'

'Exactly.'

It was almost dark; Amy was a silhouette against the darker grass of the plateau. Her voice was disembodied.

'Perhaps you should know something. Eva might not tell him, you see. Then, if anything happened to me, he wouldn't know. Yes, I don't think I'm betraying a confidence. Someone else – someone outside the family, should know.'

'Amy, come on inside. I'll light the Tilley lamp and we can have—'

'No. Must get back.' A slight pause, then, 'You see, Eva's husband left her when she had her fling with Androulis. Natural enough, I suppose. They weren't in love. It had been an arranged marriage. Happened straight after finishing school in Vienna. Ridiculous really. That's why Androulis set her up here. And me with her. Sort of companion.'

Meg was silent, staring at Amy's shape. She had heard this before. A triangle. Androulis, Amy and Eva. Like Peter, Miranda and Meg.

'The baby was born here. In the villa. Eva still had a position to keep up back in Budapest. Her family . . . they knew, of course . . . but they could not have accepted Androulis' child publicly.'

'So . . . Charles is Charles Androulis? Not Kovacks at all?'

'Nobody knew. Just Androulis, Eva and me. I have no idea how Eva squared it with her husband, but she did. Charles was brought up . . . conventionally.'

Meg wondered what she was supposed to say. It was all so long ago, so unimportant.

She made an effort. 'Does it matter now?'

'It could do. Legally. Anyway, I've told you. Just remember it if . . . it is necessary to do so.'

'I . . . all right.'

Amy was practically invisible, her voice disembodied.

'I haven't seen much of him for a long time. Nor Eva. But . . . he has sent you. And that is the best thing he has ever done for me.'

And she was gone.

It was a wonderful summer for the whole of Europe, and Cornwall was packed with holiday-makers all chortling that their friends had struggled to Spain or the Algarve and were getting no more sunshine than Penzance, Newquay or Falmouth. It was difficult to get in and out of Keele with the narrow roads blocked by cars nearly all day, just as they had been for the Christmas lights.

The Snows became heartily sick of fighting their way to the tiny village shops or finding a place on the beach, so at long last Peter took his family to London. It was not only a question of trying to escape the summer crowds. It seemed as if he needed to break away from the place he loved best in order to see it properly and begin painting it again. And he thought the change would do Miranda good; she assured him she was all right. She simply was not Miranda any more.

So they stayed in an hotel in Hampstead and did the sights and enjoyed some of the fruits of his undoubted success. Three of his paintings were chosen for the summer exhibition at the Academy; two were in the Tate already in a collection of work by the Newlyn school. He smiled at the one of Mrs Pascoe emerging from the steam of her frying pan; he still liked it, though Meg had been right, he owed a lot to Frans Hals.

He said to Miranda, 'This winter I'd like to resurrect a painting of Meg I started years ago. Would you mind?'

'Of course not.' She smiled at him. 'I'm glad you can tell me.'

He thought about that, then nodded. 'Yes. So am I. I've hidden it for so long and I worked a little on it before Christmas. Then stopped.'

'And you couldn't tell me then. Now you can. Why is that?'

'Because . . .' He frowned. He could do so much with his paint brush, but words eluded him. 'Because . . . the bit of Meg I couldn't find, I've found in you.'

'My madness.' Her smile became lopsided. 'That's gone now, Peter. Probably for ever.'

'It doesn't matter. And it wasn't madness, darling. It was passion. You had a passionate nature.'

'And has that gone?' she asked.

'No.' He held her very gently. He was so gentle with her now. 'No. It's deepened. It's tender.' He kissed her and she knew he was near tears. 'Miranda. Darling. I wish . . . there are things I still cannot tell you. And now that seems . . . awful.'

She held his head and kissed him. 'I think I know. But even if I don't, it doesn't matter, Peter. I was a fool. Mad. Not passionate, just mad. Somehow we've weathered that.' She looked closely into his eyes. 'What happened then, does not matter. Must not matter. We came through it. I . . . sort of . . . committed suicide. And yet I'm here. And you're here.'

'Yes.' He nodded violently, wanting to be convinced. 'Yes. That is all that matters.'

But it was as if they both knew there was more to come.

It was Alex's last year in the Penzance junior school and he would be sitting the eleven plus immediately after Christmas. He had hopes of getting a place at a very good school in Truro and he did not wish to miss a single day of the autumn term. Accordingly, they had planned to stay until the new school term began. But amazingly Miranda, who had lived out of a suitcase for so long, did not thrive in London. By mid-August she was so white and lethargic, Peter suggested they should go home.

'Yippee!' commented Katie.

Alex said, 'I thought you wanted to hang on until the exhibition opens, Dad?'

'I'd like to see it. Perhaps Miranda and I can have a

couple of days up here when the weather is cooler.'

'Who will look after us?' asked Sebastian apprehensively.

'Janis won't mind staying a few days, will she, darling?'

Miranda shook her head, privately thinking that once she was home she would stay home. Peter would be better off without her tagging along anyway.

So it was that when the call came from Gladys Pugh in early September, she and the children were back in Fish Cottage.

'I don't expect you remember me, Miranda? Gladys Pugh. Ollie's auntie in Exeter, you know.'

'Oh, how could I forget you!' Miranda felt a rush of tears and real affection. 'You were like a mother to me! Your house was a home to me.'

'I was always fond of you too, Miranda. I've kept your perch in the kitchen all these years. D'you remember your perch?'

'How could I forget?'

Miranda swallowed a knot of nostalgia for those foolish, carefree days. Even her devotion to Brett St Clare had been . . . fulfilling at first. And now she realized that Olwen had been protective too, never the *femme fatale* she had imagined.

'I've still got your name in my book, too. One of these days I shall be pointing it out to newcomers and saying – you might be as famous as Miss Patch one of these days!'

'Oh, Gladys!' The tears spilled over now. Miranda knew one thing for sure. She would never be a famous actress.

'There now – don't get downhearted. I heard as how you'd got a nice husband and regular little family. Your time on the boards will come after they're growed up. You'll see.'

'Oh, that doesn't matter now. It's just . . . you know, remembering the stupid girl I was!'

Miss Pugh's voice grew warm. 'You weren't stupid, Miranda Patch. You were full of fire . . . oh, maybe you were cunning with it too! You thought you had to be cunning to get what you wanted, didn't you? Nothing to be ashamed of there. You never hurt no-one . . .' Her voice became uncertain and Miranda wondered if she knew something about Meg. Or Peter. Then she went on, 'It's just that . . . poor Mr St Clare was never quite the same after you left.' She added hastily, 'Not that that was your fault, child. He is what he is and that's that. Nothing to do with you.'

Miranda said, 'Yes it was. I hurt him, Gladys. I wanted to hurt him, and I did. But . . .' she sighed. 'I didn't think it would last. He had all of you. I felt much more hurt myself . . . and alone too.'

'Oh, he's been all right. Don't get me wrong. Just sort of . . . regretful. But that happens to us all as we get older.'

'Yes.' Miranda nodded at the receiver.

'But . . . well, he hasn't been well. And now . . . I might as well come out with it, my child. He's got cancer. No pain—' she said as Miranda drew in her breath audibly – 'he's under sedation. In the old front bedroom – you remember that too – where you used to practise your lines.'

'He's in bed? All the time?'

Gladys's voice became sombre. 'I reckon about another week or so. But he's been rambling on about you, Miranda. And I thought if he could talk to you—'

'You want me to come and see him?'

'He's written a lot of stuff down on paper. But I think he would be happier in his mind if he could talk to you. And the drugs are so powerful that in a day or two I reckon he'll be past talking properly.'

'Oh, Gladys!'

'There now, don't cry. He's quite reconciled to it all. But I think it would be wonderful for him if he knew you had . . . forgiven him.'

Miranda could not stop the tears. Somehow she managed to get across that she would be in Exeter tomorrow morning as soon as she could make arrangements. She put the phone down and collapsed into the nearest chair in the cellar. Suddenly she was quite desperate to see Brett. There was no question of her forgiving *him*; but if he could forgive her, then it was just possible she might be able to forgive herself. She experienced a sense of predestiny, just as Meg had felt when she went to Artemia. She should have contacted Brett years ago and obtained some kind of blessing from him. And then she smiled wryly. How could she have done that until after John Meredith? Until then she had not even known she needed a blessing. From anyone; never mind Brett St Clare.

She rang Arthur Bowering and he said he would send Janis up as soon as she arrived that evening. She met Sebastian from the tiny village school and told him what had happened. By the time Alex and Katie arrived from Penzance, he was reconciled to the thought of being in Janis's care.

'Katie will look after me anyway,' he said, standing very close to his red-haired sister.

'We'll look after each other, Ma, never fear,' Alex said, remembering his promise to Aunt Meg not so long ago.

Miranda hugged him, something she rarely did. 'I know you will. Get to bed at a decent time and I'll creep in and say goodnight about midnight.'

'Don't close the curtains, Miranda,' Katie requested.

'Seb and I like to make sure our moonbeams can get in through the window.'

'Aunt Meg's story still?'

'And Peter's,' Katie said in her matter-of-fact way. 'They ought to get together and make a proper book about moonbeams.'

Miranda said, 'Perhaps they will one day.'

Meg pumped some water into the shallow stone sink and rinsed her face and hands before settling at the table to do some work. *Nokomis, Daughter of the Moon* was finished and ready to take to London at the end of the month, and she was starting on *The Stone Garden*. Ideas came into her head almost too quickly. That afternoon she had made sketches of two intersecting sculptures in Amy's orchard and suddenly she saw them as twins. Herself and Miranda? Gemini figures? She waited with a soft lead pencil poised over virgin paper; she knew with complete confidence that it would become obvious at any moment. There was no hurry, no frantic searching for possibilities. She was conscious of herself at the big table in the cavernous living room of the cottage, cocooned by the darkness as her baby was cocooned in her womb. She had a place in the scheme of things; she had significance, even importance. Quite suddenly there was a sense of taking responsibility for her own and her baby's future. Things had happened to her almost involuntarily for most of her life; decisions had been few and far between. Now the reins were being passed to her. She looked through one of her uncurtained windows at the indigo velvet sky and felt a tremor run through her. Was it fear or excited anticipation? Anyway, what could she do about anything? She could write her books and try to make a secure home for her baby. Otherwise, like everyone else, she was in the hands of the gods. Especially Artemis.

She smiled at that thought and wrote 'Gemma and Minnie' at the top of the paper, then put her pencil down and half rose at the thud of footsteps on the plateau outside. There was a knock and she opened the door to Amy. She smiled sudden relief.

'It didn't sound like you. Did you forget something this afternoon?'

'No. I found something actually. When I got home for supper.'

As usual they had spent a long afternoon in Mutton Cove. Meg was very big now and she had postponed the long haul back to the plateau until the early twilight.

'Sit down, Amy. You look shattered. Is it "The Devil's Advocate"?'

Amy had recently started chiselling some marble specially ordered from the mainland. It was hard work and she was unhappy with it, yet the stone had been so expensive she felt bound to continue. She had named the three-foot-high shape emerging from the marble 'The Devil's Advocate'.

She shook her head and sat down at the table, breathing heavily. Meg subsided too; she realized that Amy had been running. Amy never ran.

'It's Kovacks,' she said bluntly now. She glanced up; her thin face reminded Meg forcibly of a horse's. 'He came over on the afternoon boat. He'd flaked out on my bed. I found him about an hour ago.'

'Charles? Charles is here? Actually here?'

'That's what I said.'

'But . . . why?'

'He had some news.'

Meg bit her lip; she had really meant why had he gone to Amy's cottage and not here to his mother's.

Amy looked down again. Her long beaky nose seemed to quiver. 'Eva's dead,' she said. 'I didn't think it would

328

matter quite as much as it does. I feel . . . bereft.'

Meg dragged her chair close and put her arms around the older woman. Amazingly Amy laid her head on Meg's shoulder and her hands on the thickened waist. She hung on tightly; Meg could feel tremors running through the ancient skinny body. She thought, shocked: Amy is crying.

She said in a low voice, 'You *are* bereft. She was your friend.'

'I should have gone to see her, Meg. I knew she was in that bloody nursing home. I could have brought her back here. Let her die in the sunshine.'

Meg smoothed the thin hair. 'She wouldn't have left Charles.'

'No. I know. But I should have gone to see her. Two damfool stupid women. That's us.'

'Two wonderful women.'

'Oh, Meg.' There was a silence and the tremors eased off. 'Oh, Meg. You're such a comfort. I don't deserve you.'

'The boot's on the other foot entirely. But don't let's start that. Would you like a cup of tea?'

'Yes. No. Have you got some brandy?'

'In the medicine box. Hang on.'

Amy disengaged herself and Meg got up to fetch the brandy. She said, 'How is Charles?'

'I don't know. He disappeared. That's why I came here. I thought he might have—'

'No, he didn't.'

'He said he had to go back tomorrow. But he had to tell me in person.'

'Does he want you to go back with him? To the funeral?'

'I don't know. He looked haggard.'

'That doesn't sound like Charles. How does such an enormous man look haggard?'

She tried to smile as she gave Amy the brandy. But Amy did not smile back. She took the glass in both hands and sipped.

'Was he enormous? He was tall and slim the last time I saw him. But that was twenty years ago. He's a big man. I wouldn't have said enormous. And his face is thin. And grey.'

'Poor Charles.'

Amy finished the brandy and put the glass on the table. 'Eva was the last of his family. And you know how that feels, Meg.'

Meg shook her head. 'I've got Miranda.'

'I was thinking of you and Miranda as one . . . unit. You were quite alone in the world by the time you were fifteen.' She levered herself up by the table edge. 'I must get back. If Charles has gone for a walk he mustn't find the house empty on his return.'

Meg said with difficulty, 'What about . . . will you bring him to see me? Tomorrow.'

Amy looked up. 'Won't you come across as usual? We could walk down to the harbour with him.'

Meg hesitated only an instant. 'Yes, of course,' she said.

She saw Amy on her way across the plateau and went back to the table. But Gemma and Minnie seemed foolish now and after a few minutes she blew out the lamps and climbed the stone stairs. Eva Kovacks was gone. This was her cottage and she would not see it again. Meg stared out at the moon as she always did and wondered whether her childhood dreams of an afterlife were true and in some other place Eva was greeting the mysterious Androulis again. Or if her life-force had returned here where she had been so happy. Perhaps in the very stones of the island which Amy carved so assiduously.

Meg got into bed, suddenly tired to the point of exhaustion. She wished very much that Charles had come to see her this evening. They had been such friends. Such very good friends. Almost as companionable as she and Peter Snow had been all those years ago when they had rambled along the spine of Cornwall.

She got up early and worked unproductively for an hour on *The Stone Garden*, then decided to walk down to Mutton Cove for a swim. It was a glorious September morning; her thoughts, constantly with Eva and Androulis, moved sideways to Charles and how it might affect him to know the identity of his real father. And then, for some reason, she thought of Miranda and the shadowy figure of Terence Patch. Why had Terence never really materialized for them?

She stood at the top of the steep path leading down to the cove and tried to recall a memory of her father. Any memory. With a sense of near-panic she found she could not. And neither Aunt Maggie nor Uncle Cedric nor even Amy had enlarged on him. There were no apocryphal stories to pass on to her own child.

'Your grandfather was an actor with his own company. He had a brother and a sister and they lived in Plymouth.'

She started down the path, going slowly and carefully. At least she could talk about Terence to her child; she would have to be very careful what she said about Peter. A hopelessness swept through her so unexpectedly she gasped as if in pain and grabbed at a tree root to prevent herself falling.

But when she arrived on the fine white sand of the cove the question was still there, unanswered and unanswerable. She had swept it away for the last six months, lived in a fool's paradise. But the problem was there and with Eva's death and Charles's arrival, it could no longer be tucked in a cupboard. It was a mess . . . she had created a ghastly mess. Just as Eva had borne a fatherless Charles, so she must do the same for her child. At least Eva had been able to put up a pretence for the past forty-odd years; a social protection for Charles. There would be no such protection for the baby waiting now to be born.

She swam slowly out into the sea, waiting for the ghastly ennui to pass. It was as she turned to swim back that she felt the sudden grip of a pain across her back. It was something that had happened before; she had turned awkwardly. And almost at once she saw Charles halfway down the donkey path watching her, and she forgot her back in her concern for him, her pleasure at seeing him, her determination not to let any embarrassment grow between them because of his silly quixotic proposal.

She waved and he waved back and came slowly on down to the sand. Even as she swam back she could see how changed he was. It was almost six months since she had seen him; she doubted very much whether he could have managed the steep donkey path then. He had lost a great deal of weight and it made him look taller than ever. He had shaved off his beard too. He looked years younger.

It made her shy with him when she wanted to re-create the old natural banter they had had.

'Hello, Charles.'

She stopped half a dozen yards off and pushed her wet hair behind her ears and draped her arms protectively across her undisguised bump. She was ridiculously pleased to see him. Her awful sense of hopelessness disappeared.

'Hello, Meg.'

He moved casually to the jut of rock where she had left a towel and held it for her. She turned her back and let him put it across her shoulders, then took the ends and held them loosely in front of her.

'You look very well, Charles.'

'So do you.'

'I feel well.' She looked at him. 'Charles, I'm so very sorry about Eva.'

'Thank you.' He spoke formally. 'She liked you. She liked the thought of you and Amy being here together. She kept saying it was history repeating itself.'

'I . . . yes.'

'Has Amy told you about the two of them and their admirer?'

'She has mentioned it.'

'I was actually born here.'

'So Amy said.'

'There was some kind of rift with my father and we were here for a long time. Five or six years. I remember it well.'

'You had two mothers.' She smiled at him and he frowned suddenly and looked away.

'No father though.' He began to walk back up the beach. 'Amy was better than any father. Taught me to fish. Make a fire. Keep chickens.'

'Yes.'

They plodded to the base of the donkey path. Her back was aching badly now and she viewed the steep climb with some dismay.

He said, 'I'm leaving on the noon boat. I want you to come with me.'

'But Jill has still got tenants in my house.'

'I've booked you into a quiet nursing home in Maida Vale.'

It was a good excuse to pause and look round at him in surprise. 'Rather high-handed of you, Charles!'

'Sorry.'

He did not sound a bit sorry and she almost smiled because she had forgotten how Charles bulldozed his way through life.

She said teasingly, 'I thought you said Maida Vale was your idea of hell?'

He did not laugh. 'Be sensible, Meg, please.'

She plodded slowly on for another twelve steps, then paused and held her side.

She said, 'If my letters are postmarked from London, Miranda will be up to see me. They were up doing the galleries last month. She is so much better, nothing would keep her away.'

He snorted with sudden annoyance. 'Listen. Meg. If you're worried I might repeat my stupid proposal, you can forget it. I won't come anywhere near Maida Vale!'

She began to walk again and tried to whip up an answering annoyance.

'For goodness' sake, Charles, can't we forget that you suggested a marriage of convenience! I have vetoed other business arrangements you have cooked up – nothing new about that! I simply do not wish to be incarcerated in a nursing home earlier than is strictly necessary!'

His voice changed, he sounded forlorn. 'I thought you liked Maida Vale!'

They were at the top. She laughed with relief. 'I do. I adore it. It's you who can't stand it!' She looked round at him and smiled properly. 'Thank you, Charles. You are very kind.'

'Then come back with Amy and me today.'

'Amy too?'

'She is coming to my mother's funeral.'

Meg had to admit to herself that that made everything look very different.

'Well, perhaps . . . yes, of course I'll come. To the funeral too, of course. I hadn't thought . . .' She looked at him, suddenly doubtful. 'You won't mind me coming to the funeral, Charles?'

He looked away. 'I won't mind,' he said gruffly.

He came into the cottage with her while she packed. She could hear him prowling around the kitchen and when she went down he was looking through her manuscripts.

She smiled. 'I've finished *Nokomis* and started *The Stone Garden*.'

'Nokomis?'

'Daughter of the moon. The book you told me to write.'

He was thrilled. 'Why didn't you tell me?'

'You didn't write to me. I felt I couldn't write to you.'

'But that's work! That's different!'

'Not to me it isn't.'

'Oh . . . Meg!'

And thankfully he laughed.

She said, 'I'm almost ready.' She went round closing shutters and putting plugs in the sink and bath against spiders. Then she went back up the stone steps to check the bedrooms while Charles carried her case and bag outside.

She called to him from the upstairs window. He looked up, dazzled by the sun.

'Meg? What's happened?'

She said slowly, not sure whether she was happy or frightened, 'I'm not coming with you after all, Charles. I think . . . the waters have just broken and the backache and things . . . I think they're contractions.'

He was startled. 'The baby's not due till next month!'

'I don't think it knows that.'

She could not bandy words any longer. She turned and went to the bed and the very next moment was seized by what felt like a giant hand squeezing her lower torso. She heard Charles's feet on the steps and then he was holding her, almost drawing her away from the pain, talking to her in a language she could not understand, calling her his darling, telling her it would be all right.

And it was all right, but the pain came again and then again, and perhaps it wasn't all right. Charles detached himself from her and was not back when the next pain pressed and ground her into the bed. She tried to call him but he could not have heard her because the air was filled with the terrible blare of a foghorn. She thought incoherently, 'He's summoning Artemis. It will be all right now.'

The tall house in Exeter looked smaller and smarter, but twelve years ago it had been a haven and now it was just a big old house.

Miss Pugh was so delighted to see her that Miranda could guess at the frightful strain of nursing Brett.

'Come into the kitchen, my dear. That's where we always had our chats, wasn't it?' The burly figure, so like a fully-rigged galleon, sailed ahead of Miranda to the long kitchen, and drew out a stool. 'Well? Will you sit here?'

'Of course. Where else?'

Miranda sat and smiled up at Miss Pugh. 'You haven't changed.'

'No more have you.' The weathered face creased still more. 'Who are we kidding? I'm nearly bald and you're thinner than you were at sixteen.'

Miranda ducked her head. She knew it wasn't only her figure that had changed.

Miss Pugh said quickly, 'Just right for character parts now, my dear. You looked too young before.'

'A lot has happened just recently—'

'Aye. Three children. You must be run off your feet.'

'No, not really. But I had a miscarriage at Christmas. That's why I'm thin.'

'Ah . . . child . . .'

'It's all right. Really. I'm alive and well.' She swallowed. 'How's Brett?'

Miss Pugh lifted her tired shoulders. 'As you might expect. The Group are in Bristol at the Royal. Ollie pops up most days. He worries about them.'

'The Royal? That's a good booking.'

'Aye. It's a going concern at last, you'll be surprised to hear. Since your Mr Bracknell put some money up, they seem to have turned the corner.'

'Mr Bracknell?'

'He put Mr St Clare on a proper footing all those years ago. Made him into a company with shares and suchlike. Told him to take on regular pupils and charge decent fees. Well . . . you know Mr St Clare. Any mother could trust her daughter with him.'

Miranda watched the rough hands as they laid out cups and saucers. Poor old Bracknell. In love with Aunt Maggie and trying to mop up the messes her niece seemed to leave around.

'What about Oliver Freres?' she forced herself to ask.

'He's in charge. Mr St Clare asked him to take over last month when things got bad.'

'I see.' Miranda did not know what she had hoped for. A renunciation of Oliver and a declaration of true love for Miranda herself? She almost smiled at the naivety.

Miss Pugh said, 'I thought at first he just wanted to say goodbye to you, m'dear. You being the child of Terry Patch and his special protégée or whatever the word is . . .' She smiled in self-deprecation, then went on, 'But it's a bit more than that, I reckon. He's chewed the fat with Mr Freres and Ollie and been trying to write things down . . . I don't know what it's all about.'

337

Miranda sipped at her cup of bright orange tea. 'I'll go upstairs as soon as I've had this.' She smiled her old wide smile. 'Oh, it's as if the past twelve years never happened – no-one has made tea like you since then!'

Miss Pugh smiled, well pleased.

The stairs were recently carpeted and the paintwork had changed from antique brown to pristine white. Miranda trod carefully, fully aware that they were probably Gladys's pride and joy. She put her head into the room she and Jennifer had shared and saw that its present occupants were as messy as she had been, and then she tapped on the door at the end of the landing as she had done so often in the past, and opened it slowly and with dread.

At first she thought Brett was asleep. In spite of the warm weather he was huddled beneath Miss Pugh's best eiderdown, his back towards her, the famous leonine head so like Tyrone Power's, suddenly skull-like on a bank of pillows. But he wasn't asleep; a thread of a voice said, 'Has she come yet?' and an arm appeared from the eiderdown in a preliminary effort to move the body to face her.

She hurried around the bed. 'I'm here, Brett. Don't move!'

She caught at the hand and held it between both of hers. It was skeletal. She had thought of so many ways of greeting Brett; now all she could do was to crouch on her knees by his bed and hold her face level with his while tears poured from her eyes. All she could say was, 'Oh, Brett!'

He managed a smile. He was still beautiful, flaking skin stretched over wide finely-etched bones.

He spoke in the same rather strange thin voice. 'Now then, Patch. Show you're an actress. Stop crying.'

She put her forehead down to his fingers. 'I can't. Brett, I'm so sorry. So very sorry.'

She meant that she was sorry he was here, like this, ill and dying. But he said, 'Ah . . . don't be sorry, Patch. You loved me, then you wanted to hurt me. It's perfectly natural. You have always been natural.' His fingers moved against her hair as if he were blessing her. 'I'm very glad . . . very glad to see you.'

She looked up, amazed at how he had cut through everything to the heart of their break-up.

She said simply, 'I still love you, Brett.'

'I'm glad. Glad you know it, too.' He smiled again, he did not want to talk about it; emotions, past pain, they were unimportant to him now. She saw that and lowered her head again to touch his fingers with her lips.

He said, 'It's all written down but it's better that you should know from me.' He tried to summon another smile. 'My last will and testament, that is. Old Bracknell really is old now. He would have explained it to you, but maybe he'll die before I do – who knows? Besides . . . you were such a naughty girl where he was concerned. You would never listen to him.'

She said nothing, forced her mouth to stay still, let her eyes dry hotly.

'You will be the new owner of the Arbitrary, Miranda.' He closed his eyes to stop her protests and his fingers twitched in hers. 'Don't say anything. I've talked to Oliver and he doesn't want it, but he'll be your manager if you like. I know you can't go on the road yet – young family and so on – but after Bracknell hands over I want someone to hold the purse strings who has a – a – part of the Group in – in—'

'I know what you mean, Brett. Oh my God. Oh, Brett, I'm not strong enough.'

'You're Terry's daughter. You'll be a link between the

339

Wessex and the Arbitrary. If you like you can change the name back to the Wessex—'

'Never!'

'Good. So you'll do it.'

'Brett—'

'I'm not asking you – you have no choice in the matter.' He gave her another painful smile. 'Do you think you could support my head and give me a few sips of that glucose muck? My mouth is drying up after all that talking.'

It was not easy. Miranda had always declared herself 'hopeless' in a sick room and had left such things to Peter or Meg. Eventually by sitting on the bed she could very gently hoist Brett's head on to her shoulder and leave a hand free to hold the glass to his lips. It was an intimacy she found repugnant at first. As the bedclothes were disturbed a sweetish smell rose from them which could have easily been from the flower petals Miss Pugh kept in her airing cupboard, yet could also have been the insidious stench of illness. She tried to stopper her nostrils against it and control any signs of shuddering. And then as Brett's teeth clinked uncomfortably on the edge of the drinking glass, something strange happened. An enormous sense of peace flooded the room, or perhaps it was generated in Miranda herself. She kept her eyes on what she was doing, but her smile became less fixed and she felt her shoulder relax beneath the weight of Brett's head and her arm enclose him more comfortably.

He sipped twice more then averted his face.

'Enough,' he breathed, exhausted by the effort. She replaced the glass, lowered him carefully on to his pillows and slipped back to her knees.

'Do you want me to go?' she asked.

His eyes were closed. He murmured, 'No. Please stay.'

She put the palm of her hand on his cheek and left it

there. 'I'll stay for as long as you want me, Brett.'

He smiled slightly. 'You've changed.'

'I'm older and wiser, my dear.'

He did not reply and she thought he might be asleep. She looked into his face and tried to see in the pared-down features a remnant of the young boy who had loved her father. Perhaps now she would be able to tell Meg about it; she wanted no secrets between them any more.

Miss Pugh crept in with more orange tea and a plate of buttered teacakes, and Brett stirred and opened weary eyes.

'Can Miranda feed you a bun, my lovely?' Miss Pugh leaned over him. 'Just the tiniest bit. Make a change from your Complan.'

'Not now. Later perhaps.' He produced his smile for them both. 'If she can stay.'

'I can stay,' Miranda said steadily. She was deeply thankful that she could say that sincerely, that she could leave her hand cupping his face, that she could return his smile and eat her bun naturally. The repugnance was gone.

The evening sun slanted through the window and still she was there. He wanted her to talk about the Arbitrary and how she would run it, so she forced her mind to accept that it was a *fait accompli* and that she had to make plans.

'There's all the paperwork.' She tried to keep panic out of her low voice. 'The bookings. The takings. Expenditure.'

He murmured, 'I've kept careful records for the past five years. Agencies come to us now. Old Bracknell will tell you . . .'

'And the pupils?'

'Keep an eye on them. Let them stay with you when they're resting.'

'Sounds . . . possible. I won't let you down, Brett.'

'I know.'

But as she talked meaninglessly to him about a season of Wilde interspersed with Restoration plays, she wondered how on earth she would cope. Sebastian was only six. If Alex got into Truro College he would need constant support. And Peter . . . what would Peter think?

Brett seemed to read her thoughts. 'It won't be easy, Miranda.'

'I've always liked a challenge,' she smiled reassuringly.

'If you can't . . . don't worry. Don't feel guilty. You'll find someone . . . Oliver will help you . . . don't feel . . .'

It seemed he was asleep.

She rang Janis to tell her she would not be home till the next day.

'How are they?'

'Good as gold. Billy Majors is going to take the two of 'em into Penzance tomorrow morning. And I can walk young Sebastian up to school myself.'

'They're expecting me back tonight. I promised I'd slip in to see them and Katie will stay awake.'

'Mr Snow should be back before midnight. He telephoned you just after you'd gone and I told him what had happened. Gave him your phone number too. Didn't he ring?'

'No.'

'Running for his own train I expect. He said he'd be back tonight any rate.'

'Oh . . . good.'

He telephoned her the next morning to tell her that everything was fine at home and she was to stay as long as she needed. But by that time Brett had slipped into a coma and Oliver was sitting by his bedside and she had decided to leave Exeter until she was really needed.

It was on the train returning home that it happened.

Just as it had happened back in 1965. One minute she was staring at the view of Dawlish Warren with Exmouth in the distance, thinking of Brett and the Arbitrary and what on earth was going to happen; the next she was crouched forward over her knees and pain gripped her with a malignancy she could not have imagined. It had not been like this at Christmas when she lost the baby; it certainly had not been the same at the births of Alex, Katie and Sebastian. Yet she knew the pain was a birth pang. And as it held her helpless within its grasp, so the being of Meg washed her from head to toe and took it away.

Gasping, she stayed where she was, holding her knees, trying to disguise her obvious distress from the eyes of other passengers. The train drew in between the high walls of Teignmouth station and in the hurly-burly of exits and entrances she got a grip on herself and sat up slowly with closed eyes.

Someone paused by her. 'Are you all right, dear?'

She opened her eyes on an elderly lady with a concerned face.

'Yes. Indigestion.' She smiled somehow and the woman passed on down the aisle. She was all right. The pain had gone. But she still knew exactly what had happened; it had not been indigestion; it had not been her pain.

She stared bleakly and unseeingly at the passing view. Meg had just given birth to a baby. It all made sense now. Meg and Peter. Last January. She had given them carte blanche . . . to get each other out of their systems . . . just as she was getting all her repressions out of her system with John Meredith. And just as her peculiar, rebellious, wilful escapade had gone wrong . . . so had theirs.

So many things now added up. Meg's determination

not to see her; her red herring about the mysterious proposal of marriage. Meg was giving Peter what Miranda had lost on that terrible January night, another baby. Hadn't he said he wanted four children?

She pressed her forehead against the grubby window of the coach and closed her eyes.

Sixteen

Meg wanted to call the baby Amy Charles.

'I couldn't have done it without you two,' she said
very soberly a week after the birth, sitting out on the
plateau with the tiny human bundle in a basket by her
side. 'I was going to call her Amy anyway – unless it
had been a boy – ' she giggled weakly. 'And I thought
about Eva for a second name. And then I knew that
Eva would like it to be Charles.'

'Bloody stupid name for a girl,' Charles commented,
making a conscious effort not to look at the way the
baby was lifting her minuscule fist to the deep blue
sky.

'Not at all.' Amy was definite. 'Sounds like a family
name. You'd prefer it straight like that than bastardized
into Charlotte, wouldn't you?'

'Only you could see the feminine version of Charles
as a bastard,' Meg said. She glanced at Charles and
they both laughed. And then she began again, 'Seriously.
You were both absolutely—'

'Please. Not another repeat performance of the Mutual
Admiration Society.' Amy rolled her eyes heavenward.
'OK. We're marvellous. You're marvellous. But the most
marvellous of all is that little creature there. In spite of
the three of us, there she is, thriving, shaking her fist at
Artemis – who incidentally probably masterminded the
whole thing—'

'Determined to oversee another baby on her island,'

Charles echoed. He gave up pretending not to be interested in the baby and leaned over her cot. 'Listen, kid. You and me got something in common. OK?'

Little Amy shouted gladly. And again they all laughed.

Meg said wonderingly, 'I don't think I've ever been so happy before. It's still a horrible mess, but it doesn't seem to matter any more.'

Charles rolled on to his back. 'I hate to break it up, ladies, but I'll have to go back and look after things in London.' He squinted against the sun. 'No question of you coming now, Amy. We can't both leave these two girls.'

Meg did not protest as she might have done a week ago. Amy said, 'Darling boy. I have to tell you I was dreading leaving Artemia. Perhaps Amy knew that and arrived a month early for my sake.'

'And will the two of you – sorry, three of you – be all right? I'll be gone about a week.'

'If there is anything to worry about at all, Spiro will radio for a doctor.'

He had to be content with that. Meg's twenty-four-hour labour had shaken him to the core. He had told them afterwards, 'I've never been so frightened before. Not even when I went into Buda to get my mother out practically under the Russian tank tracks. I had a gun and I could have shot our way out. There was nothing to be done for this baby. You and she had to do it by yourselves, Meg.'

But Meg had shaken her head decisively and started what Amy senior now called the Mutual Admiration Society.

He was gone exactly one week. And he had been with them only one week before that. Yet they both missed him as if he had been a fixture on the island for years.

'He's so reassuring,' Amy mourned. 'Even when he failed to fix the generator last week, it didn't seem such a catastrophe.'

Amy was sleeping at Eva's cottage now. The foghorn had brought her very quickly when Meg's labour had started so fiercely. It had also brought Meta Taxos with two donkeys loaded with the two-way radio, blankets, a sterilizer and the handwoven baby basket. And in response to Charles's frantic calls, the doctor from Mykonos had arrived two hours later and administered an injection which had helped with the pain. But when he left assuring everyone that all was well and nothing would happen for a very long time, it had been Charles and Amy who sustained her through that night and into the morning. And it was Amy who had sutured the umbilical cord, while Charles held the slippery baby and then, so gently, cleaned it with olive oil and put it into Meg's arms.

Meg loved having Amy close at hand, yet she knew she had to stand on her own feet some time and she felt guilty at taking the older woman from her precious sculpture.

'But we managed before Charles arrived. And we can do so again.' She tried to sound very brisk. 'You might as well get back to "The Devil's Advocate", Amy, and let Little Amy and me start coping properly.'

'You'll have to throw me out first,' Amy said laconically. 'Anyway I can't face that bloody marble. It won't yield up its secrets without a struggle and I can't be struggling just yet.'

'You're tired out!'

'I admit it. So are you. And if we share and share alike we can both get some rest.'

'You're so stubborn!'

'It's not that. I couldn't live through another blast on that foghorn!'

And – as usual – the discussion ended in laughter.

They walked down to meet Charles off the boat and escort him back to the plateau. Little Amy's basket swung from one side of the donkey, Charles's case the other. They could not believe he had been in London only that morning, and plied him with questions.

'Very hot. Crowded, but not as crowded as usual. I contacted the agents and told them you would be needing the house. The lease is not up until just before Christmas but it is possible the tenant has found somewhere else.'

'Oh.' Meg looked at him blankly, nearly asking him why she needed the house.

He went on, 'Your book is wonderful. Jill's seen it and there was a meeting yesterday so I could show it around. I've got a concrete offer, but we can discuss a contract suitable to you.'

Meg said, 'Oh,' again. It seemed an age since she had reinvented Nokomis and drawn all those moonbeams.

Amy prompted him. 'And the funeral?'

'As well as . . . possible. She knew a prayer – it was a bit of English she learned as a child. "Now I lay me down to rest." I felt . . .' He was silent for a moment then cleared his throat and said strongly, 'I felt she was at rest.'

Amy said, 'Naturally. Eva was a relaxed person in life.'

He took her hand and pumped it. 'Are you threatening us with your afterlife, Amy?'

She did not smile. 'I can't imagine being at rest. I shall have to go on chiselling stone wherever I am.'

Meg took her other hand. 'Then you will be happy.'

'Of course.' Amy swung their hands like a child and so they climbed the last few feet to the plateau and stood there while the donkey cropped the grass and Little Amy made some of her weird and wonderful sounds that Amy senior called her 'moon songs'.

'Now you're here, I can go back home.' Amy turned

immediately. 'I need to be with the goats. The yield has not been too good with me just popping in to milk them twice a day. They need conversation.'

Charles restrained her physically with a hand on one shoulder. 'Hang on there, woman! I'll see to your smelly goats and you can stay with Meg. But first let's have a cup of tea. I've got something to tell you.'

'They are not smelly!' Amy protested vigorously as she was propelled into the kitchen. 'And if you're thinking of the proprieties, you must be mad! It's obvious to me what ought to be happening here! And it should be obvious to you too!'

Meg caught just half of that as she unstrapped the baby basket and carried it indoors. She guessed the rest from Charles's expression.

She said quickly, 'I'm going upstairs to feed Amy.' She looked at Amy senior. 'Let's have dinner together. Please, Amy.'

The older woman sighed and nodded. 'And we'll have to change my name. This is getting complicated.'

Meg paused halfway up the stairs. 'Would you mind . . . if we called you Grandma?'

She had to wait so long for a reply she thought Amy had taken offence. Then in a hoarse voice, her friend said, 'Not at all. And . . . thank you.'

Charles's news seemed to puzzle the new grandmother a great deal.

'You're certain about this, Kovacks?' she asked.

He nodded emphatically. 'Maman had a solicitor she trusted. Another refugee from the Russians. Hungarian, Czechoslovakian, he speaks most European languages including Greek!' Charles smiled around the table. 'Maman left her share of Artemia to you, Amy. It's all neatly and legally tied up.'

349

Meg's face split into a grin of delight. 'I didn't realize you had half of it anyway . . . Grandma! How marvellous!'

But Amy continued to frown. 'It's just that . . . when Androulis died it was an unholy muddle. Everything went to his daughter Kristina. And there were three or four other islands as well so she wasn't interested in developing this one. She came to see me and said I could stay here for my lifetime – and the same would apply to Eva.'

Charles shrugged. 'She made a mistake. Artemia was left to you and Maman jointly. No strings attached whatsoever.'

Amy was finally convinced. She raised her glass. 'To Eva Kovacks.' She looked at Charles. 'Not for the gift of the island – though that is absolutely marvellous. But for a family.' She touched his shoulder almost shyly. 'She wouldn't mind, would she, Kovacks? I've got no son and you've got no mother. How about it?'

Charles could do no more than nod.

Amy went on, 'Indirectly because of Eva, I've got Meg and Little Amy. And now I've got you. That's worth a toast, wouldn't you say?'

They both hugged her impulsively. Meg said, 'I've never been so happy!' And Amy rolled her eyes and groaned, 'Here we go. The Mutual Admiration Society are sitting for the fortieth time in two weeks—'

And unexpectedly Charles cut across, 'Shut up, Granny. She's right. It has to be voiced often.'

Amy spluttered something about manners and the younger generation, and Meg said, 'To propitiate Artemis. That's why it has to be voiced, Grandma. As an offering to our very own goddess.'

Amy stayed in Eva's cottage and Charles went to hers. But she made no bones about ridiculing the situation. Two days later when they were in their favourite place on the plateau with the whole of Artemia's west coast spread below them, she got down to the subject in earnest.

'I've said it before and I'll say it again. You two must be blind. If you got hitched, Meg's problems would be gone. Nonexistent. You could come and go between London and Artemia. Meg's sister could come here for holidays. Bring her brood—'

Charles said, 'Meg is still in love with Peter Snow. Obviously she has told you the circumstances of Little Amy's . . .' He cleared his throat and resumed, 'And, being Meg, she will always love the father of her baby.'

It sounded portentous and Amy snorted derisively.

'Who is talking about love, for God's sake!' She leaned forward, checked the baby, and leaned back again. 'And what is love, anyway! So much talked about it! So much done in its name – evil, terrible things!' She pulled her old hat over her eyes irritably. 'I was in love with Androulis and all it did was ruin my friendship with Eva!'

Meg said with difficulty, 'You see, Amy, I feel it would be a bit of a . . . cheat. For Charles.'

'I'm talking about friendship!' snapped Amy. 'You wouldn't cheat him on that, would you?'

'I wonder . . . can friendship exist between men and women?' Meg felt extremely embarrassed. She had never talked to Charles about her relationship with Peter. But it had started in much the same way.

Charles said strongly, 'Amy, listen. Meg and I have already discussed a marriage of convenience and decided against it. Now please let it drop.'

'No!' Amy lifted her hat and glared at him. 'Because I'm not talking about a marriage of convenience! I admit it would be extremely convenient, but don't let that get in the way of the true nature of such a marriage. Friendship. Companionship. Mutual support.' She slapped at his upraised hand. 'Don't wave me down, young man! I know what I'm talking about! I know all there is to know about loneliness! Why do you think I chisel away at my stone half my days?' She levered herself up from her old-fashioned deck chair with some difficulty and pulled her hat back down. 'I could knock your heads together! And meanwhile I'm going to go and talk to my goats and chickens. They've got more sense than the two of you put together!'

And she left.

Charles and Meg stared after her, unwilling to look at each other and begin talking again. Then Little Amy woke and shook her fist at the sky and sang a moon song. And Charles laughed.

'She's trying to tell us something.' He looked into her basket. 'How small and insignificant we are in the scheme of things? How little our strivings really matter?'

Meg watched him as he smiled down at the baby he had helped to deliver. She never knew why she – quite suddenly – saw the sense of Amy's diatribe. Perhaps because she realized now that the advantages of a marriage would not be all on her side. Charles was alone in the world with a legacy from the past that must weigh more heavily than hers.

Whatever the reason – and she gave up reasoning quite quickly – she said, 'Charles, is your offer still open? Shall we get married after all? We are such friends and Amy . . . Amy needs a father.'

For a moment, as his large head came up from the basket, he looked heartbreakingly raw and vulnerable. But all he said was, 'You would trust me to be a good father?'

'To the ends of the earth,' she said simply.

He looked down at Amy, three weeks old, already such a personality to them all. And then, very gently, he lifted her out and held her in his large hands. For a long moment he sat there, smiling at the child who seemed to be singing her song for him. Then, without glancing up, he said, 'I'm honoured to accept your proposal, Meg. Thank you.'

Meg laughed and said, 'My pleasure!' and it seemed to be settled. They did not shake hands or exchange a glance. Eventually he said, 'You know, Amy isn't shaking her fist at all. She's taking something out of the sky. Catching something.' He held her a little way from him. 'See? She's being showered with gifts.'

And Meg, at last certain of her destiny, nodded gently.

They were married in Athens four weeks later, in a civil ceremony pleasing to them both. Amy held her granddaughter. Meg had telephoned the taxi number she still had and found Andreas and his taxi, and what was more, he brought Theopholis, his wife and their new son. Meta Taxos stayed on Artemia and made a proper Greek wedding supper; it was an occasion to remember. Amy said it was all her doing and they were both happy to let her take the credit. She had certainly pointed out in no uncertain terms that there were advantages for them both. In the light of Meta's cooking fire that evening, they constantly exchanged smiles. And if Meg had had secret fears that friendship might include a great deal more than she was willing to give, she was reassured that same night when Charles automatically took the bedroom next to her and Amy.

Miranda did not know how to order her frantic thoughts. For the rest of that journey home she thought she might be going mad. She experienced the same disorientation she had suffered when she lost her baby at the beginning of the year: a sense of disintegration, of grasping hopelessly at pieces of events and trying to fit them into a pattern.

The train drew in at Plymouth and she got up, all ready to dash up to Mr Bracknell's and tell him what had happened and ask what there was she could do. And then she sat down again. She could not betray her link with Meg like that. What she knew was Meg's secret and private thing, and if Miranda were not her twin she would never have known it. Besides, what on earth could an old buffer like Bracknell do? She bit her lip and banished that thought as quickly as the others. She should know better than to scoff at Bracknell. There was very much more to him than met the eye.

The stretch from Plymouth to Penzance seemed interminable. Liskeard, Lostwithiel and Bodmin . . . hadn't Amy made up a rhyme incorporating those place names? 'Liskeard, Lostwithiel and Bodmin, Three names on a list down at Admin . . .' She remembered no more but the jingle stayed in her head and increased her sense of incipient madness. She had to think what to do. She had to find an answer so that Meg and Peter could be together and bring up their child. But there were other children too: Alex, Katie and Sebastian. At the thought of Sebastian her eyes filled with tears. He had not wanted the new baby and now he would always be the baby of the family. Except that he now had a tiny half-brother or -sister. She was back on the treadmill . . . Liskeard, Lostwithiel and Bodmin . . .

Peter was there at Penzance. She hung out of the window as the train wheezed to a halt and saw him beyond the barrier, his shirt, stiff with paint, sticking out like a maternity smock from his body. She wanted to fling herself at him and hold him to her with all her strength, but she no longer had the right to do that.

He held her anyway and rubbed his beard against her cheek affectionately.

'It's good to see you! I should have come home before

– you've had all this sadness . . . are you all right?'

'Of course. I was always tough, Peter. What was the exhibition like?'

'Good. But never mind that now. What about this Brett Sinclair?'

He shepherded her outside and into the car. She breathed deeply. This was all she wanted: Peter and the children, home.

'He's not good. Oliver Freres is with him now. I've told you about Oliver.'

'Yes. Poor devils.'

'Yes. I didn't always think so.'

Peter ground the gears as usual and drove out on to the Promenade.

'Why did he want to see you? Old times' sake?'

'Yes. And he wants me to take on the Arbitrary.'

Peter risked a startled sideways glance. 'The theatre group? Darling. How marvellous. It's what you've always wanted, isn't it? You told me that when you first had your legacy you intended to put it into that.'

She remembered that time as if it were a dream. 'I did, didn't I?'

She'd got what she wanted all those years ago. And she'd lost what she wanted now. There was a kind of justice in that.

She told him about Brett and Miss Pugh and her perch, by which time they were drawing up at the back entrance of the cottage in Sunday Street.

'Are the children . . . all right?'

She had been afraid to ask; if justice only gave something when it took something else away, her children were at risk.

'Of course. Wouldn't I have told you straightaway if they hadn't been?' He kissed her fondly on the nose.

She said, 'I'm not sure.' And as she clambered out of

the car she murmured like a charm, 'Liskeard, Lostwithiel and Bodmin.'

'What's that, darling?'

'Nothing.'

'You're exhausted. And no wonder. Janis has gone – I'll make some tea and we'll take it into the sitting room and look at the view. We're both home again now.'

She continued to do nothing. Whatever she did she would hurt her children, so she did nothing. The Michaelmas summer turned into a chilly autumn. News came from Gladys Pugh that Brett St Clare had died in his sleep. Peter took Miranda to the funeral; he was amazed at the crowd of people who came to pay their last respects to this man who had obviously had such an effect on Miranda.

'To be honest, I did not realize he was so ... respected,' he confided as they stood around on the stage of the theatre where Brett had wanted them to foregather after the service.

'There are not many of these little repertory groups left.' Miranda looked around her nervously. What an enormous load Brett had placed so fairly and squarely in her lap.

Mr Bracknell, eighty if he was a day, came up to her and shook her hand.

'Nice to see you, child. I'd like to go through some paperwork with you before too long. Unless you decide to opt out – and Mr Sinclair was emphatic that you must always feel able to do that – you ought to know just what the position is, financially.'

Unexpectedly Peter said, 'Don't worry about that, sir. Miranda can afford to keep the Group afloat. I'd like to help too.'

Miranda and Mr Bracknell both looked at him in surprise. He grinned.

'The theatre is in Miranda's blood. I know she's tied now, but in another year or two she will be able to tour with them.'

He took her arm and squeezed it gently but imperatively. 'It's what you've always wanted, darling, don't look so bewildered.'

She nearly said, 'It's not what you've always wanted!' But perhaps it was now? He was loving and kind, just as he'd always been, but he never expected anything of her. As if she were an invalid; or even crippled. He did not really think she could cope with the Arbitrary. He thought it might be a hobby to take her mind off the real things of life. Like Meg and him.

She thought suddenly and fiercely: that is what I'll do! Exactly what he wants me to do! I'll take on the Arbitrary and as soon as I can I'll tour with them. Actor-manager. Like Brett. Like my father. And eventually . . . that will leave the way clear for Meg.

She smiled and returned his arm-hug. 'You know me better than I know myself, darling.' She turned to Mr Bracknell, smile in place. 'I'll be in Plymouth tomorrow. May I call on you in the office?' She waited for his nod and continued, 'And now I'd like to talk to Oliver and the rest of the cast. D'you think you could round them up for me? We'll go into the big dressing-room.'

She fooled them all, even old Bracknell. They looked up at her as she stood on a chair, as if they were drowning and she were a lifejacket.

'Olwen . . . Marjorie . . . Miss Pugh . . . Oliver . . . you know what Brett's wishes were. And why he wanted me to take on the Arbitrary. The rest of you have never heard of me.' There was a murmur of dissent. Brett had paved her way. She forced a smile. 'Well anyway, I was with the Group twelve – fifteen – years ago.' Everyone nodded. 'I just want you to know that I was as surprised as you must have been when Brett asked me to take on the company. I wondered if I could do it. I have a young family who must come first. But now . . . I am determined I'll look after the Arbitrary for Brett. I can do the bookings and handle the money, leaving Oliver and Olwen free for production and casting. Everything will go on just the same as before. We'll have fairly regular meetings and I'll come to the first night of each production. We know we can never find another Brett, but for his sake we can work as hard as before. Are you all happy to stay on for the bookings we have already made?'

There were vigorous nods from everyone. Olwen said, 'We need someone who can raise the cash, Miranda, and we know you can do that.'

Miranda looked at her sharply but Olwen was wide-eyed, very near tears. She must be almost forty now; her whole life was the Arbitrary. Miranda could only guess at the strain they had all been under while Brett was so ill.

Afterwards Olwen and Oliver Freres stood close by her and introduced the new members of the group.

'Zoe. She trained under Brett.'

Oliver said, 'Most of our young students leave quite soon – they often get parts in television. But Zoe stuck with us.'

Zoe said fervently, 'I'm glad to stay on, Mrs Snow. Brett told us a great deal about you. He said you were a natural.'

Oliver nodded. 'Perhaps, later on, you can do a role now and then, Miranda?'

She looked at him. He was so obviously what Uncle Cedric would have called 'an old queen'. She felt a pang of compassion and was thankful for it.

'That will depend on my husband and family, of course.' Peter started to say something but she went on, 'Meanwhile I can take any of you when you're not working. Hear lines. That sort of thing.'

Eventually they got away and she was surprised by Peter's congratulatory attitude.

'Darling, you were just right. Not pushy, but entirely supportive.'

'Was I?' She looked sideways at him. He drove their nice new car as if it were a bus, leaning over the wheel to restrain it. She wished suddenly she had come alone.

He said, 'It's the first time I've really been able to imagine your life with the Group. I knew it was an enormously important period, but I think I imagined it was also a fallow five years.'

'Like Meg's?'

She felt his hesitation and touched his arm reassuringly. 'I wasn't saying anything special then, Peter. We're twins and it was natural for you to imagine I was merely waiting for life to start. Like Meg was. Training myself . . . that sort of thing.'

'I suppose . . . yes, I suppose I did think that.'

'And now?'

'Now I see it wasn't like that.' He grinned without humour, his eyes still boring into the road ahead. 'Miranda, I'm sorry. I've trivialized your acting, haven't I?'

She said very honestly, 'It was fairly . . . trivial, actually.'

But he would have none of that. 'No! No, it wasn't trivial. And it's not trivial now! Listen, darling. You must be free to . . . what do they call it? . . . do your own thing! I mean it, Miranda! You've inherited this theatre group – it's more than the Arbitrary, isn't it? It's like the one your parents ran! It's almost as if you're a bridge—'

She forced a laugh. 'Hang on there, please, Peter! I might have theatre in my blood, but first and foremost I'm a mother!' She hesitated, wondering whether to mention that she was also a wife before she was an actress. Then decided against it. She went on, 'No way am I going off to leave Sebastian and Katie in Janis's tender care!'

'No . . .' He filtered grindingly into the nearside lane, ready to turn for Plymouth and Mr Bracknell. 'No. What about boarding school?'

'Not on your life!'

'OK.'

They were silent, negotiating the myriad roundabouts and traffic lights of modern Plymouth. When they pulled up outside the solicitors, he sat back with evident relief and said in the most matter-of-fact voice Miranda had ever heard, 'What about if Meg came and saw to things now and then? After all she can do her work anywhere.'

Miranda made a big thing of reaching into the back for her handbag. There was pain across her chest, she had to concentrate on taking a breath. But her voice sounded very normal when she eventually spoke.

'That's an idea. I could trust . . . everything . . . to Meg.'

Peter got out and slammed his door hard.

'We'll see how it goes,' he said.

At Christmas an enormous carton arrived from Meg. She had done her shopping in Athens and the presents were unusual and exciting. There was a special cake for everyone, apparently made of dates, figs and raisins glued together with ouzo. There were crackers and biscuits and exotic tree decorations. Peter had a set of camel-hair paint brushes and a matching smock and beret that made him look, as Katie said, 'like a real painter!' Alex had a tiny electric train set made in Japan; Sebastian, a model farm; Katie, a dress of tussore silk, many-layered, exquisite. Miranda had a Greek peasant dress, including cap and ribbons to twist into her hair.

'She's spent the earth,' Peter said, stupefied.

Miranda waved the accompanying letter. 'She's married her boss!' she shrieked. 'Meg is married! And I didn't know – unless . . .' She paused and stared intently at Peter. 'There was a moment, last autumn, in the train . . . I thought it was something else. Perhaps . . . anyway, she's married!'

Everyone was amazed and agog at the same time. The children wanted to know every detail, especially how rich he was. Peter was silent, staring back at Miranda, unbelieving, knowing something was wrong somewhere.

Miranda swallowed. 'Hush, hush! I'll read the letter. He must be fairly well-off – doesn't he own most of McEvoys? His name is Charles Kovacks. He was on the television . . . that time. D'you remember, Peter?'

Peter spoke at last. 'Read the letter,' he suggested.

Miranda held the flimsy sheet of paper at arm's length. She remembered that Meg had to wear glasses now and knew that she should too.

' "My darlings," ' she began, and then cleared her throat convulsively. She wanted so much to see Meg. ' "I do so hope the parcels will make you laugh and give you a Christmas thrill. I had such fun choosing them. We had a day in Athens – Amy Smithers came with us to help and we laughed nearly all the time. Did you hear us?" ' She looked up at them. 'She's as crazy as ever, isn't she?' Sebastian and Katie nodded and, in unison, put their thumbs in their mouths. Alex was staring at the letter eagerly; Peter was looking at his hands. Miranda went on, ' "Anyway, all of you, a very happy Christmas. I shall be thinking of you." ' She had to clear her throat again. She began in a lower register in an effort to make the incredible news acceptable. ' "I have something rather special to tell you. I should have written ages ago, but everything here drifts by like a dream. I was married, darlings, last October, to Charles Kovacks and we have stayed on here ever since. As you know he is my boss and he has been a good friend for a long time. Do you remember, Sis, I told you someone had asked me to marry them? Well, it was Charles and eventually I did!"'

Alex said cautiously, 'I've seen his name somewhere. Inside the cover of *The Apple Man* or somewhere.'

Peter said, 'He's an illustrator himself. I think he started off as a cartoonist. He's famous.'

Katie took her thumb out of her mouth long enough to say, 'I wish she'd told us. I could have been her bridesmaid.'

Miranda went on reading. ' "I have written two books for children, one is called *Nokomis, Daughter of the Moon* and the other is called *The Stone Garden*. I seem to have a great deal of money, so don't worry about the cost of the presents – which I know you will!"' Miranda paused and glanced up. No-one said a word. ' "I expect we shall come home in January and my address will then be 25 Sussex Gardens which is a very nice flat near Hyde Park. I will be down to see you all as soon as we are settled. Look after yourselves. Love to everyone. Meg."'

There was a silence. Even Sebastian knew that Aunt Meg was putting them off.

Peter said heavily, 'Well. There goes the idea of Meg looking after things here, my love.'

Alex said sharply, 'Why? Are you going away, Ma? What about my exams?'

Sebastian whimpered, 'You're not really going away, Mummy? Are you? Are you?'

Miranda shook her head. 'No.'

Katie removed her thumb again and put on her wise expression. 'You want to go and act again, don't you, Miranda?'

'No,' Miranda said.

362

Peter folded his new smock carefully. 'Your mother will go back to the stage one day, darling. When you're older.'

Sebastian immediately started to ask how old was older. Katie put her head on one side. 'Perhaps Aunt Meg's new husband would come down with her to look after us?' she suggested.

Peter folded the smock to a foot square and pressed it hard between his flat palms. He seemed relieved when Alex said emphatically, 'We don't want him down here! Aunt Meg is ours!'

Miranda stood up and went to put on the kettle. 'Don't talk like that, Alex,' she said automatically. She did not know what to think about this Charles Kovacks. In one way it took things out of her hands. And if in fact she had been wrong about the baby there was no need for her to be conscience-stricken any longer. But it hurt that Peter was jealous. Because, yes, Peter was jealous.

Winter came slowly to Artemia. On Christmas Day the four of them went down to Mutton Cove and Charles dabbled Little Amy's feet in the water. She sang a quick falsetto note and jack-knifed her legs precipitously.

'Like an undercarriage pulling up,' Charles commented.

'My God, she's only three months old,' protested Amy. 'Stop him, Meg!'

Meg laughed. 'She'll tell him. She's got him in the palm of her hand.'

'We'll take her to that heated pool Jill talks about,' Charles said, striding out of the shallows and wrapping Little Amy's feet in a blanket. 'We can teach her to swim before she walks.' He laughed at Amy's horror. 'It's all the thing now, Granny. You can come and watch if you like.'

'You know very well I'm not coming home with you,'

Amy said snappishly. 'And I really don't know why you're going either! It's much better for Little Amy out here. And the business seems to be running itself very nicely, Kovacks.'

'Well, that's where you're wrong, actually, Mrs Know-All.' Charles draped his free arm around the skinny shoulders and Little Amy grabbed for someone's nose. Both Charles and Amy suffered in the scrabble. Charles continued, with streaming eyes, 'The business is marking time and businesses cannot go on marking time indefinitely. I want to be there to get *The Stone Garden* on its way. Little Amy needs to be in a house with a dampcourse and some decent heating. She's going to have to be immunized against all sorts of things. And Meg wants to see her sister.'

Meg took the baby into her arms and they started back up the path.

'Please come with us, Granny. We shall miss you so much. I can't quite imagine life without you actually.'

'Well, that's one good reason for me not to come, Meg.' Amy dropped her impatient tone and spoke very soberly. 'You will have to spend a lot of time in England in the future – Little Amy's schooling and so on. So you need to imagine life without me. Because I'm not moving from Artemia.'

They reached the top of the cliff and stood looking down on the cove while they regained their breath.

Meg said, 'I suppose you're right about school.' She shifted the baby from one hip to the other. 'I did so want to bring her up here.'

'She can spend summers here. And all school holidays,' Amy said.

Charles said, 'You're evading the issue, Granny. There's nothing on earth to stop you coming and going with us. Becoming a permanent part of the set-up. We would not then need to imagine life without you.'

But Amy was not to be drawn into another argument. She said very seriously, 'Kovacks, I have lived on Artemia since 1930. The Germans did not move me. If I leave this island I shall die. It's as simple as that.'

They were both shocked into silence. Then they tried to hug her at the same time and Little Amy had a field day with their adjacent noses. Laughing, apparently crying too, they drew apart and surveyed each other.

Charles said, 'All right. No more nagging. We shall be back – you know that.'

Amy nodded.

Meg had been to Charles's flat when Eva had been in charge and she was rather dismayed at the way it had run down. In Eva's day there had been a housekeeper and a daily help; the housekeeper had left when Eva went into the nursing home and Magda, the daily help – aggressively Hungarian – did the cooking and let everything else go. Obviously Eva's things were still everywhere; wardrobes of outdated clothes, racks of Cuban-heeled shoes, a collection of fans – several autographed by famous people – a dressing table cluttered with make-up. Charles's first editions, his Tenniel drawings and Lear illustrations, were in piles on the floor of the enormous living room. For years now he had used the place as a pied-à-terre rather than a home and it showed.

Meg worked hard to change things and felt she was fighting a lone battle. Charles, so capable in Artemia, seemed like a fish out of water in his own flat. He would rather play with Little Amy, bath her and put her to bed, than make decisions about how best to arrange Eva's fans, the china and glass, his own books.

'There are those display cabinets,' Meg said, looking at the tall glass-fronted monstrosities lined up like soldiers at the back of the room. 'But . . . they're a bit daunting . . .'

'You choose something, Meg,' he said largely. 'It doesn't bother me. Honestly.'

'But . . . I can't make that kind of decision on my own,' she protested. 'It's your home, Charles – it was your mother's.'

'And now it's yours.' He shook his head impatiently. 'If you don't like all this rubbish, chuck it out! Start again your way. I loved the sparseness of your Kilburn place. Do it like that.'

She stared at him, amazed. 'Charles. Kilburn was tiny. Two armchairs, some bookcases and a television. That's all there was in that little sitting room. Look at the size of this kitchen. The living room is like a baronial hall. And there are three enormous bedrooms and two bathrooms!'

'So?' He crossed one leg over the other and tucked Amy into the resultant niche. 'What is this stuff? Strained carrots. Yummy.' He made an ecstatic face at Amy and she gurgled appreciatively.

'Charles, we've got that posh feeding-chair you insisted on buying!'

'She likes it better on my knee.'

'What about your trousers?'

'They don't mind.' He grinned up at her. 'Stop fussing. Fix the place up how you like. Have you phoned Jill?'

'No.'

'Why not?'

'Because we arrived two days ago and we haven't finished unpacking. Because I'm trying to communicate with Magda – who incidentally hates me.'

Charles said quietly, 'And because you don't know how to explain Amy.'

'Well . . .'

'Meg. For Amy's sake, you have to go through with

what we said. Hopefully no questions will be asked. You simply say that when you became pregnant you went to Artemia where I followed you and insisted on us being married. If you put it like that you won't have to lie. Except by default.'

'I feel . . . all the time I shall feel I am cheating you, Charles.'

But he would not discuss that either. He grinned. 'Then in order to make it up to me, you decide what happens to all the muddles. And let me feed Amy the way I like to do it!'

And as usual she laughed and let the subject drop.

He was determined she should have no time to think too much. He rang her to say he had made an appointment with his mother's doctor for Amy to have a check-up. He met her in the surgery and introduced Dr Heine almost ceremoniously.

'My wife, Herr Doktor.' He smiled at Meg reassuringly. 'Dr Heine had to run from the Nazis as we had to run from the Russians. He has always looked after us.' He smoothed Amy's cap of gloriously nondescript brown hair. 'And this is our daughter. Amy Charles.'

'Charmed. And charming.'

Meg had never met a doctor like this one before. There was coffee in small demitasses and a plate of petits fours. Health, or the lack of it, was never mentioned.

Afterwards Charles was suddenly contrite.

'Meg. Did you mind having old Heine foisted on you like that? All the émigrés stick together, you see. He would have been so terribly hurt if we'd gone elsewhere.'

'It's Amy who matters. And I told you before, I trust you with her completely. If you think Heine is a good doctor—'

'I do. He is the best. You barely noticed – Amy did

not – he was checking her all the time. Ears, sight. When he held her up he was testing her limbs. And when he cuddled her he was listening to her heart and lungs.'

'Then . . . foist away!'

He was as protective of Magda, unfortunately. Meg insisted she needed her only once a week and wished she could do without her entirely. Not only did Magda speak very bad English, she was a complete snob. She told Meg immediately that Mr Kovacks was married 'in the beginning' to an aristocrat of 'ancient lineage'. The fact that Amy had obviously been conceived out of wedlock appeared to her to be a cunning trick on Meg's part to inveigle Charles into marriage. She was not mollified to discover that Meg and Charles occupied separate bedrooms.

'In Hungary, this would not happen,' she muttered on her first visit, holding two corners of a clean undersheet while Meg held the others. 'No man would permit himself to be called a cuckold!'

Meg felt this was grossly unfair, especially in view of Eva's escapade with Androulis.

She made hospital corners on her side of the sheet as Aunt Maggie had taught her, and noted Magda's surprised eyebrows with satisfaction.

'Of course,' the voice droned on, still disapprovingly, 'no Kovacks makes up the beds. Nor does cooking. Nor looks after babies.'

Meg scooped up Amy expertly and went to the door. 'I think you are quite wrong, Magda,' she said. 'Eva Kovacks brought Charles up on a deserted island in the Aegean Sea!' She swept into the kitchen mentally offering apologies to Amy, who had probably done all the work in those far-off days. She mixed cereal with one hand and sat down to feed her baby, wishing to goodness Charles did not have such feudal ideas about his old retainers.

Charles got round the problem by bringing home a book for her to illustrate.

'It's a Marcus Traddles,' he said as if that explained everything.

Marcus Traddles had written *The Old Apple Man*, and after its success had insisted on Meg illustrating his subsequent books.

'Charles, just at the moment, there's rather a lot to do.'

'I know, Meg. But you'll cope.'

'I was hoping to go shopping for a cabinet this week.'

'But that won't take you long. An hour or two.'

'Charles, you must be joking! It takes an hour or two to wrap Amy up sufficiently to take her out!'

'Meg, you mustn't take her out in this cold weather. She's not used to it.'

'OK. I'll leave her here on her own, shall I?'

'Magda will look after her! Don't worry, I'll ask her. She'll do anything for me.'

'Probably. But she won't do this. Sorry, Charles. I am not leaving Amy with Magda.'

It was snowing the next day, but she dressed Amy in two vests, a flannelette dress, woollen leggings, a matinée coat and a sort of sleeping bag with arms, and kept the pram hood right up. The baby seemed to delight in the snow as she had delighted in the blue skies of Artemia. She pulled off her mittens and tried to catch the larger flakes in her bare hands. Meg trudged to Marble Arch and down Oxford Street and replaced the mittens six times. After three hours of shopping Amy was cold and frustrated and wept unhappily and hungrily all the way home.

Charles burst in before Meg had settled her. He looked fitter than she'd ever seen him; skin glowing with health and dark eyes alight.

'They're tobogganing on the Heath!' he announced. 'Let's take Amy and have a go!'

'It'll be dark in an hour!' Meg was horrified at the thought of going out again in the cold.

'It doesn't matter. Why is she crying? Let me have her. Hello, Little Amy – what is it?'

Suddenly she was too tired to tell him that she had ignored his advice and taken Amy out shopping. Her objections to Magda seemed unbearably petty. She let him cradle Amy and soothe her against his shoulder, and suddenly, inexplicably, she wanted to weep.

'Come on. The pair of you could do with a treat. I've bought a splendid sledge – it's down in the car—'

He bundled them up and drove them to the Heath. And it was fun. Like the Muscovite Russia of her imagination. Lanterns and bells and sleighs making wonderful slithering sounds on the packed snow.

But that night she woke up shivering and switched on her electric blanket, then fell asleep. When next she woke she was in a lather of perspiration and Amy was crying. She switched off the blanket hastily but before she could get out of bed, Charles appeared in the doorway.

'What is it?'

He flicked on the light and saw instantly that they were both ill. He was full of remorse.

'Oh my God! Why didn't you tell me you felt ill? And Amy – I should have known she wasn't crying for nothing. She never cries for nothing!'

He did not know what to do first. She sat on the edge of the bed nursing Amy while he fetched some fruit juice.

'Put it in a bottle, Charles,' she called weakly. 'It might soothe her to suck.'

He brought the bottle and wonderful hot tea. Then he

took Amy while Meg sipped her tea and swallowed some aspirin.

'What should I do without you?' she asked weakly.

'You would not have caught this cold for one thing,' Charles said.

'It wasn't tonight. I didn't want to tell you. I took her out shopping. We were ages. And we got chilled to the bone.'

'Why didn't you want to tell me? You were scared?'

'Not scared. I feel . . . sometimes . . . so inadequate.'

He stared at her, his eyes very dark.

Then he said, 'Do not ever say that again, Meg.'

And that was that.

Magda came in every day for a week. Meg lived for the Thursday when she always visited Eva's ancient housekeeper.

'I not go this week,' Magda said.

'Of course you will go. Mr Kovacks would be distressed if he thought we were changing your plans.'

Meg tried a smile, but the hawk-like face did not lift in return.

'Mr Kovacks not go to office?'

'I hope he will.' Meg longed to get her partial independence back. They had been in England six weeks and she was still disorientated.

But Charles agreed with Magda.

'I'll stay home.'

'You will not. And Magda must only come once a week from now on. I simply cannot cope unless I have some space!'

'How about if I telephone Jill and ask her to pop round?'

'Charles, I am quite capable of phoning Jill myself.'

'I'd like old Heine to take another look at both of you.'

'We had *colds*, Charles.'

He simmered into silence.

After Magda's departure, she walked around the flat, carrying Amy on her hip, already composing a long letter to Amy in which she would make all this terribly funny. She went into Charles's room: it was spotless, so was her own. The bath gleamed, all Eva's crystal glass sparkled from the sombre old cabinets in the living room; everything was clean in the study yet nothing had been disturbed.

Meg put Amy down for her nap and looked without much interest at the Marcus Traddles book. And then she sat down and read it properly. Then she drew her sketchbook towards her and began to draw. An enormous pumpkin appeared on the pristine paper. It was covered in portholes, each porthole containing a character from the book. She roughed them in quickly. On top of the pumpkin she placed a squat figure in a coachman's caped cloak and top hat. At first he looked rather like a potato, but suddenly she knew that this was no bland vegetable. She reached for her glasses and began a separate sketch. A peculiar face began to emerge from the paper, cunning yet ingratiating. She stared at it then said aloud, 'The Devil's Advocate!'

When Charles came home it was snowing and she took his coat carefully and hung it over the bath.

'For Magda's sake,' she explained. 'She has hoovered everything.'

'You're getting on better?' Charles asked hopefully.

'Well . . . maybe.' She said honestly, 'I'm prejudiced, I think. We had Hungarian refugees back in Plymouth, you know. I've never told you. I blamed them for Aunt Maggie's illness.'

'Oh . . . Meg.'

'Ridiculous, I know.'

'How did you bear me?'

'You were often insufferable.' She laughed.

'And I am still. I know it.'

'No . . . how can you think that?' She took him into the study and told him about the Devil's Advocate. He was thrilled by this evidence of her complete recovery.

'It's terrific.' He looked through the sketches and said suddenly, 'Meg, it will be all right, won't it?'

'Of course. But . . .' She laughed again. 'I shall be glad to get back to Artemia. It's so much easier there.'

'Yes. I know. But . . . I wish—'

'What?'

'You are always so . . . retiring, Meg. I think Artemia is another escape place. I'm not putting it well . . .'

She looked at the broad back bent over the desk. What did he want of her? A hostess at literary parties? Or more?

She said quietly, 'You have known me for a long time, Charles. I don't think I can change now.'

He said, as someone else had said a long time ago, 'There is so much of you hidden away. It was there for Amy to see in Artemia. Now . . .'

She was almost relieved to hear the baby's cries announcing that her nap was well and truly over.

And then came a knock at the door.

He said, 'I will fetch Amy. You answer the door.' He looked at her straightly. 'It might be Jill.'

'Oh no!' She was suddenly angry. 'Honestly, Charles!'

He waited for no more. She could have smiled at his precipitate departure if she had not been so annoyed.

The bell rang again and she opened the door unceremoniously. Her hair was loose and flying all over the place; her hands covered in coloured chalks. That would not bother Jill.

But it was not Jill who was standing there.

It was Miranda.

Seventeen

Miranda had decided against a letter or phone call. She had spent two long months in a state of terrible indecision, busying herself frantically in an effort not to think, mentally exhausted all the same.

The previous Saturday she had taken Zoe and Katie to see the Minack theatre and while Zoe was posturing on a rock and Katie was running up and down the natural amphitheatre, she had looked out across the wintry sea and seriously considered diving in and just swimming and swimming until she could surrender herself to it as Meredith must have done. She was immediately shocked by her own thoughts and turned irritably on Zoe.

'Let's do a sound check. Run up to the top with Katie, will you?'

'I'd like to do a Hamlet soliloquy, Mrs Snow—'

'I daresay. Off you go.'

She waited, watching the two of them as they clambered the last few feet. Katie got on quite well with Zoe. Alex and Sebastian saw her as a threat. And Zoe saw herself as Hamlet, did she? Miranda smiled slightly and thought about the pale tortured character as played by Brett St Clare on the lines of Laurence Olivier. Hamlet was no conventional hero as Zoe doubtless saw him; he must have had a streak of sadism in him to put Ophelia through it until she drowned herself. A touch of Meredith?

She cleared her mind and let someone else's misery

replace her own. Hamlet . . . a selfish man, drowning in his own uncertainty.

She walked two paces forward and stared up at Zoe and Katie. And then she spoke very quietly.

' "O! that this too too solid flesh would melt, Thaw, and resolve itself into a dew . . ." '

She paused and half-turned away to say with tight anger, ' "Or that the Everlasting had not fix'd His canon 'gainst self-slaughter." '

She went on with the speech without obvious passion, keeping her voice low. At the end she looked up. Zoe began to clap ecstatically and after a moment's hesitation, Katie joined in.

'I could hear every word, Mrs Snow!' Zoe called down. 'Even with a full house, it would be perfectly audible!'

Miranda nodded thoughtfully. 'The only thing we cannot cope with is a wind. We don't need a wind. That's what whips sound right away.' She walked up to meet them. 'I'll see what gaps they've got in their bookings and we'll talk about it at the next casting meeting.'

Zoe was suddenly shy. 'I can see why Brett said you were a natural. I can't believe you haven't worked for over ten years.'

Katie said staunchly, 'Miranda is in the Newlyn Players. She used to do all the female leads before . . .' she glanced at her mother. 'And I was in the panto one year, wasn't I, Miranda?'

'Yes, Katie.'

'I just love the way the children call you Miranda. So bohemian,' Zoe gushed.

'Only Katie does that.' Miranda put a hand on the crinkly orange hair so like her own. 'And that's probably because she is going to be an actress one day.'

Unexpectedly Katie's face reddened, she grabbed her mother's hand and pulled it down to her lips.

Zoe couldn't get over it. 'Three generations! Like the Redgraves!' She stood by the car, looking over the breathtaking views. 'And in this place too! It's amazing.' She turned to Miranda as Katie scrambled into the back seat. 'You know, you should get back on the boards as soon as possible, Mrs Snow. You really came alive just now.'

Miranda got into the driver's seat and started up. It was strange that someone like Zoe should be able to put a finger on her pulse. Of course she should go back to work. There was no part for her down here except as a half-hearted mother. Certainly not as a wife. The scenes she had so carefully stage-managed in the past when Peter had swept her into his arms and carried her to bed were no longer possible. She was sterile and . . . damaged. But out there, with the Arbitrary, were a dozen parts for her to play. A thousand.

She caught Katie's gaze in the mirror. Zoe was rabbiting on about something and Katie very slowly closed one eye. She was nine years old but she would understand. And if only Meg . . . Alex and Sebastian were better off with Meg. And so would Peter be . . .

She had to see Meg.

For the first five minutes their pleasure in seeing each other superseded everything else. Miranda had been unimpressed by the outside of the flat, anxious only to get out of the intense cold of London. She had travelled all day in an inadequately heated train, delayed twice by frozen points. She had nowhere to stay in London and had to go on to Swindon the next day for a meeting with the rest of the players. When there was no car visible on the gravelled frontage of 25 Sussex Gardens, she had bitterly regretted her decision to arrive unannounced. Meg and her new husband had obviously gone away somewhere and she was going to be stranded without a bed for the night.

And then the door opened and there stood Meg, unaltered in the fifteen months since she had seen her last.

'Oh . . . *Meg*!' was the best she could manage.

It was enough. Meg engulfed her in an embrace which whirled them both round in the high Victorian lobby.

'Miranda – darling – I can't believe it!'

They were laughing, almost crying, hanging on to each other, their hair mingling and half-smothering them. They came to a halt by a gargantuan jardinière containing what looked like a pineapple tree, and rocked gently from side to side.

Miranda said, 'Oh, Meg . . . Meg . . . why have you stayed away so long . . . fifteen months . . . the most we've ever been apart.'

'I know, I know. But I needed . . . I told you, I had to . . .'

'I know.'

More sobbing laughter, more convulsive hugs. Then at last a slight relaxing and drawing apart.

Meg said, smiling, 'Where are the kids? And Peter?'

'Home. Keele.' Miranda's smile was slightly strained. 'They don't even know I'm here!'

'Darling! Why? What—'

'Nothing awful. I'm meeting the Arbitrary lot – I told you all about that in my last letter – we meet up every month and this month it's at Swindon and I thought if I came a day early I might see you.' Her smile shook at the corners of her mouth. 'I began to think if someone didn't break through we'd never see each other again!'

'Rubbish! Rubbish! Rubbish!' Meg's arms embraced her again, but not before Miranda had seen the sudden glance towards the closed door behind them. And then Meg said urgently, close to her ear, 'I have to tell you something, Sis. Explain—'

Before she could say any more the door opened and a very large man stood there holding a baby. Miranda knew it was Charles Kovacks, of course; and she knew the baby was not his. And in that blinding moment it was as if she saw them all, even this stranger, her sister's husband, as terribly wounded. And she was the cause of the wounding.

She hung on to Meg for a split second longer, emptying her mind as she had done at the Minack, letting someone else fill her being.

Then she said, 'My God! Meg! You didn't say anything about a baby!' And she held Meg at arm's length, smiling delightedly, looking from her to the man and child, praying that no-one would say anything that would precipitate them all into chaos.

But Meg and her Charles had evidently rehearsed this before. Meg's smile was strained; Charles, on the other hand, was word perfect.

'It's Miranda. Good lord, I knew you were like peas in a pod, but this is ridiculous!' He held out a ham-like hand as unlike an artist's hand as she could imagine. She took it and drew herself up to his face and pecked him.

'And you're Charles Kovacks. You got all our cards of congratulation but we've wanted to meet you and couldn't understand . . .' She let a hint of roguishness creep into her voice. 'Now I understand why!'

He put his hand on her shoulder. 'Come on in. Meet Amy properly. Have dinner. You can stay the night?'

Miranda let herself be piloted into an enormous room that looked more like a museum than anything else. She was settled into a chair the size of a small sofa and the baby was placed on her lap.

Just for a moment she did not know what to do. She did

not dare let herself acknowledge that this tiny girl-child, named for her grandmother, was Peter's. Peter should have had another daughter . . . Miranda had destroyed Peter's daughter . . . Meg had given it back. Those thoughts were for later. Now she put her hand on the tiny back and looked into hazy eyes that would soon be brown, and said, 'She is beautiful. I can see both of you in this little face.' The child smiled beatifically and made a high cooing sound.

'That's her moon song.' Meg spoke for the first time since Amy's arrival. 'I was writing the moonbeam story while I was expecting her and a lot of it seems to have rubbed off.'

Charles said, 'It also means she is hungry. Shall I take her into the kitchen and give her some tea, Meg? While you and Miranda catch up on the news?'

Miranda handed the baby over and stood up. 'We'll all go into the kitchen.' She risked a smile at Meg. 'I'd love a cup of tea, darling.'

If she hoped that the kitchen would be less awesome than the living room, she was disappointed. It was more like a laboratory than a kitchen; so white it hurt the eyes. The dining area at right angles to it was polished rosewood but it was still terribly stiff. The worst bit was watching Charles Kovacks settle the baby he knew wasn't his in the crook of his knee with obvious expertise, then begin to feed her. Miranda found herself hating it; he had no right . . . no right to Meg and no right to the baby.

Meg seemed to be feeling her way into her role. She poured tea and said apologetically, 'You can see now why I went away. Artemia half belonged to Charles's mother, Eva, and it was a paradise. Really. You would love it.'

'I doubt it. I've had enough of quiet backwaters, Meg. I want to get back to work.'

'Well . . . that's good.' Meg looked doubtful as she

passed a bone china cup and saucer. 'The children would love the island though. Perhaps . . . perhaps they could come out with us at Easter, Sis?'

'You're going back there?'

'Yes. As often as we can until Amy starts school. And then the holidays.'

'I see.' Miranda sipped. 'But you don't need to run away any more, Meg. I mean . . .'

Charles appeared to be concentrating very hard on the next spoonful of strained apple.

Meg said, 'It's not running away, darling. Amy was born there. And her grandmother lives there!' She laughed at Miranda's expression and started on a saga about Amy Smithers whose name had cropped up often in Meg's few letters home. It sounded as if the old girl had gone completely native and was probably gaga by now.

Meg said, 'She's terribly talented. Listen, I'll let you have an advance copy of *The Stone Garden* – let Katie read it to Sebastian and if they're keen they can come with us at Easter. How's that?' Belatedly she turned to her husband. 'Will that be all right, Charles?'

Miranda was resentful of her sister having to ask permission of a stranger, but the smile she turned on him was still bright.

'Thank you, Charles. I'm not sure what the reaction will be. My children are nothing if not unpredictable. But the invitation is very kind. Especially as you don't know them!'

He looked up and his dark, European eyes were unfathomable. 'You are all Meg's family,' he said.

She recognized her cue and began to talk about the children. Katie's burgeoning theatrical ambitions, Alex's chances of a scholarship to Truro, Sebastian's sweetness. Meg finished her tea and began to get dinner. There was a casserole – 'one of Magda's,' Meg explained mysteriously

– and vegetables, and a fruit salad, and some strange-looking cheeses. Miranda found it all delicious but oddly foreign. She wondered fearfully what Meg had bartered for her respectable married status. Certainly she appeared to have handed over her daughter: Charles bathed her and put her to bed and could be heard singing a kind of descant to one of Amy's 'moon songs'.

Miranda watched Meg put things in the dishwasher and ventured a near-protest. 'I would have seen to the baby for you, Meg. I wish you'd told me you'd been so low.'

But Meg said tranquilly, 'Charles loves to do it. He's hopeless around the house, but he'll do anything for Amy.'

Miranda hated that too. Meg should be keeping a little space between Charles and Peter's baby. This overwhelming relationship was unnatural.

She said suddenly, 'Actually, darling, if you mean it about Easter, I know darn well the kids would adore to come with you. And it would mean I could set up something at the Minack. A kind of pageant. You know, as it's Jubilee year.'

Meg was just as suddenly excited. 'Sis, I'd love it. Next to having you over there it would be . . . splendid.'

'Then take it as settled,' Miranda said quickly before Charles could reappear.

She went to bed early. She was very tired for one thing, but she could not bear to see Charles . . . she couldn't think of the word . . . appropriating was too strong. He did not exactly appropriate Meg. But he was so damned caring. Putting a shawl over her knees, fetching her coffee . . . it was all very well, but he had no right to her. Meg belonged to Miranda. And – to – Peter.

Miranda gasped as the thought formed in her head. She was jealous. Not only for her own sake, but for Peter's.

She put her hands over her ears and turned into the pillow. And as she forced herself to begin planning a Jubilee festival to be held at the Minack theatre, she fell asleep.

Amy was there to meet them from the steamer. She stood, decrepit in her old flannel trousers and panama hat, next to Mrs Taxos clothed head to toe in morbid black, while Spiro and one of his many sons caught the mooring rope and whipped it around the squat capstan on the jetty. The Snows alighted nimbly and Alex held out his arms for Little Amy and held her, while Meg superintended the unloading of their few cases.

Katie said, 'I'm Katie Snow. Meg says we can call you Grandma. Do you mind?'

Amy said, 'I like it. And it saves a lot of confusion with Little Amy.' She shook Katie's hand solemnly then turned to the boys. 'Let me guess. Sebastian. Alex. And Little Amy Kovacks.' She looked at the boat with narrowed eyes. 'I can see Meg. Where is Charles?'

Alex grinned. 'He said he'll come later. He put me in charge.'

'I see.' Amy blinked, then smiled. 'And you're doing quite a job. How was the flight?'

Sebastian said, 'It was cold in London. Then it was hot in Athens.' He breathed deeply and looked around him. 'It's just right here.' He took Amy's gnarled hand. 'Have you missed us?' he asked with obvious affection.

Amy, quite unused to his ways, looked surprised. 'How could I miss you when I don't know you?' she asked honestly.

Sebastian was not to be deflected. 'Now you know us, did you miss us?' he insisted.

Amy did not fail to note that Katie's gaze was on her. She answered, 'Obviously.' Katie smiled so she knew it was the correct answer.

They loaded the donkeys and Meta gave them watered wine to drink.

'It's foul,' Katie said.

'Smile when you say things like that, Katie,' Alex advised. 'I think Spiro belongs to the Mafia.'

'That's Italy, you idiot!' She turned to Amy. 'Peter has seen *The Godfather* twice and has told us all about it.'

'I think Alex is teasing you. But it would do no harm to smile.'

Amy let Meg hug her and hotly denied that she was thinner than ever. 'Why didn't you insist on Charles coming with you?' she asked.

Meg joked, 'Charles resists insistence!' Then she said, 'And don't change the subject!'

But Amy, falling behind the last donkey, smiling at the boundless energy and enthusiasm of the children, knew who had changed the subject.

It was a halcyon four weeks. There were crises: the generator broke down and everything in the fridge melted disgustingly. Spiro came up and showed Alex how to deal with the ancient belt mechanism which ran from the windmill to the generator's drive. They communicated with odd words and many gestures and the next day Spiro's youngest son, Constantine, joined Alex for a swim in Mutton Cove.

'He must have thought I invited him,' Alex said, surprised but pleased. 'He's a terrific diver. He's going to go for sponges this season with his father.'

'How do you know?' Meg asked, puzzled.

'Well . . . he gets it across somehow,' was all Alex could say.

The worst emergency was when Sebastian fell down the cliff path one early morning and lay unconscious on the beach below. Alex pounded across the plateau for

Amy who blew her foghorn for the Taxos clan. There were no broken bones and Sebastian would have gone swimming had he been allowed. Meta would not permit him to put a foot to the ground. Between them all they got him back to Eva's cottage where he drove them mad during his enforced rest until Katie said furiously, 'Well, go out then! See if I care! If you drop down dead it will be your own fault!' Sebastian did not drop down dead.

But, for Meg, worse than the many little catastrophes was Amy's subtle withdrawal from their lives. She got on extremely well with the children and never minded if they were around while she was working; she joined them once a day for a swim; she doted and gloated over Little Amy's sudden progress. But she no longer cooked while Meg cleaned; she was not there on the plateau in her old deck chair during Amy's afternoon nap; she asked questions Meg could not answer. 'What is Kovacks working on at the moment?' 'Have you been to the theatre?' 'What do you think of Eva's book choice?'

Meg had to admit that life was not easy in London.

'It's been . . . uphill work. Magda is a terrific worker but she has to be told all the time. And I'm no good at that. The place was so . . . I don't know . . . uncared for . . . when we arrived. Eva's stuff, Charles's stuff—'

'Kovacks has trained himself not to put down roots, perhaps?' Amy sounded tentative yet stern, a paradox only she could manage. 'Whipped away from Artemia to live with his grandparents. A "suitable" marriage, I don't doubt – heaven knows what kind of homes they got together between them – he was unbearable during that period of his life. Then Hungary drowned beneath the Russians . . . and a foothold in London with his mother. Probably Eva got things fairly decent and then off she went to that nursing home.'

Meg wanted to say childishly, 'Well, it's not my fault!' but Amy could not possibly be blaming her.

So she said instead, 'He puts all his – energy – into Little Amy. As soon as he comes in he picks her up. Probably he sees her as . . . providing roots? Anyway, he doesn't talk about work much. Brings stuff home for me to do – sort of therapy, I think. We were just getting into a bit of a routine with that when Miranda turned up.'

'Ah,' was all Amy said.

'It was marvellous to see her again.' Meg spoke almost defensively though she did not know why. 'Little Amy and I had had bad colds—'

'Haven't you been out together at all?' Amy persisted.

'Yes of course. We took Amy to meet Dr Heine and to get her injections. And we went tobogganning one snowy night.'

'You and Kovacks. By yourselves.'

'Amy – you know it's not like that!'

'Friends tend to go out together.'

'Don't be sarcastic! It's not that easy – not like over here. Baby-sitters are hard to find.'

'What about this Magda? She thinks of herself as an old family retainer by the sound of it.'

'I wouldn't leave Little Amy with Magda!'

'Why not?'

'She doesn't approve of me, Amy! She thinks I inveigled Charles into marriage! I'm just a peasant in her eyes!'

'But she believes that Little Amy is a Kovacks. She could be trusted with her. You *should* trust her, Meg. You would win her over like that.'

'Amy – I don't want to "win her over"! I'm not used to having people in the house – I don't like it!' Meg felt beleaguered and could not understand why. Amy was on her side; her best friend; her surrogate mother.

Amy was silent for some time. She checked on Little

Amy asleep in her basket, leaned back in her chair and closed her eyes.

'Children all right?' she asked, settling down for a nap.

'Hopefully. I'm on pins when they're exploring but that's half the fun of the island. I can't stop them.'

'No. Certainly not. They learned to be careful after Sebastian's fall.'

'Yes.'

Meg tried to relax too. She looked sideways at the face beneath the panama hat and chided herself silently. What had she expected of Amy after all? The same kind of commitment she'd had when Little Amy was born? Only this time for three extra children as well? If she was about the same age as Eva, she must be nearly eighty.

Amy spoke quietly. 'Why didn't you bring Kovacks with you this time? It would have been much easier all round.'

'He had a lot to do.'

'But you don't know what it was because you don't talk about work.'

Meg could have wept with frustration.

'Amy. He didn't want to come for four weeks, that's all! He might join us later.'

'No he won't.'

'How can you *say* that?'

'Because I know him and his damned Hungarian pride. He's not going to push himself between you and your family.'

'It's not like that—'

'Why didn't Miranda come with you?'

'For goodness' sake! I've told you – the children have told you – she's putting on some sort of Jubilee pageant!'

'Quite.'

Meg waited, simmering. Amy's eyes remained closed.

Meg said at last, 'Well? What did you mean – "quite"?'

Amy opened her eyes and stood up. 'Nothing particular. Miranda is a very clever girl. She knows about Little Amy. She thinks you belong with Peter.'

'I – *what*?'

Amy looked into the basket again.

'I have to get back to the goats.'

'Amy – wait. Don't be cross with me – I can't bear it!'

'I'm not cross with you. And I'm not cross with Miranda because what she is doing must be hurting her a great deal. But I'm furious with Kovacks for letting her sacrifice herself and him for what . . . nothing! A dream. Worthless.'

She looked round at Meg and smiled. 'I could easily be cross with you, Meg. And then I look at you and the crossness goes away.' She folded up her chair carefully. 'Did I tell you that after your letter arrived I got out "The Devil's Advocate" again? He's emerging at last.'

'Good.'

Meg wondered what else she could say. And whether Amy was right about Miranda knowing everything. No. Definitely Amy was wrong in that. Not even Miranda was that good an actress!

Miranda had such a wonderful time at the Minack she forgot to worry about Peter or Meg or Amy or anything. It was practically an improvised performance. She assembled the Group at Fish Cottage and invited the Newlyn Players over, and together they hammered out a pageant, taking in the royal wedding, the Coronation, the four royal children, the death of Churchill, some hilarious mimicry of Harold Wilson and James Callaghan and a wonderful mock-up of an Apollo space rocket. Miranda called on the local children for singing and dancing and longed for Katie to be among them. However, Katie could not be in two places at once, and she was better off with Meg.

Miranda knew from their letters that they were all getting on well. Her three were very possessive and proud of Little Amy; that was the most important thing to come out of this holiday. If they were all eventually to live together, they must love Amy first as one of their own. Not that Miranda had made any plans for the future; it seemed to her that things would evolve naturally. She must establish the children with Meg; and she must establish herself with the Arbitrary. During that Easter she managed both.

Peter stayed at home for the first week of planning, script-making and rehearsals. He painted some props for them and went into Penzance to buy yards of curtain lining for costumes. Gladys Pugh and Marjorie Markham borrowed sewing machines and worked like Trojans on Coronation robes. Nylon net was tacked into loose gowns for the children to represent the 'sky over Britain'. The natural backdrop of the Atlantic Ocean would provide all that was necessary to evoke 'our sea-girt isle'. It was this last phrase that was too much for Peter; he went up to London the next day and put up at an hotel.

The only trouble with that was he had nowhere to paint; and too much time to think.

Ever since Meg's letter had arrived announcing her marriage to her boss, he had nursed a secret pain. She had been his; the awfulness of Miranda and John Meredith had come between them, but she had been his. And quite suddenly, she was not.

Peter had long trained himself out of introspection. Back in 1965, when he had fallen in love with Meg and married Miranda, he had made a conscious effort not to think. Just to be. To cope with Miranda's elemental nature; and then to make sure Alex was all right. And Katie. And Sebastian.

It had been wonderful to see Meg now and then; somehow because of Meg, Miranda became more desirable, and he had been happiest when they were all together under one roof. Miranda, Meg, and the three children. He had done his best work when Meg was there. And that long winter, he had produced the stuff that had gone into the Tate and the Royal Academy. And then . . . Meg had come to him.

He had thought it would never happen; that Miranda would always have to give the love and Meg the inspiration. But she had come to him of her own free will. She had stopped him going after Miranda; she had been his. And even though his life had caved in afterwards, even then – and ever since – the inspiration had stayed with him. He was driven by what had happened, but he knew he was producing his best work. In a curious way he was happier with Miranda now that 'all passion was spent'. And when she inherited the Arbitrary and he could see some sort of independent and positive future for her, he began to think he might be able to justify what had happened at Prospect Villa that dark winter's day over a year ago.

Until that letter.

And then Miranda had gone to see Meg and discovered the baby. At first he had some wild idea that it was his child, but Miranda had said they'd come home to have the birth in England, which meant it must have been conceived in February or March of last year. Meg had gone from Keyhole straight into the waiting arms of Charles Kovacks.

He forced the thought of that out of his mind and tried to concentrate on his work. He had to have a studio. He was obsessed with the need to work, convinced that if he had a studio he could finish the portrait of Miranda/ Meg and even come to terms with the idea of being in love with an amalgam of two women.

He telephoned McEvoys after two days of trying to work in his hotel room. It was midday and he hoped that Charles Kovacks would be at lunch. When a girl's voice answered he stated his business without preamble.

'I'm enquiring about a house owned by Mrs Kovacks. I understand it is being let out for short periods and I wondered if it was free at the moment.' He stared down at the bedroom carpet and saw that he had dropped some paint on it.

The girl said, 'Oh yes, sir. Mr Charles Kovacks is dealing with that in his wife's absence. I'll put you through.'

Peter started to say it did not matter, but she had gone. The next minute a deep voice came on the line. Peter tightened his hold on the receiver. This was Meg's husband, the father of her child.

Kovacks said, 'My secretary tells me you are enquiring about my wife's house. It is in fact empty for three weeks between lets. Would you like to see it?'

Peter hesitated, almost replacing the telephone. Then he let his breath go with self-exasperation.

'Kovacks? We haven't met. I'm Peter Snow, Meg's brother-in-law.'

There was the briefest of pauses then Kovacks's voice came over strongly. 'Is everything all right? Meg wrote last week – everything was fine then.'

'Yes. Sorry. Didn't mean to worry you.' Miranda had warned him that the man was possessive of Meg. 'It's just that I've got out of Miranda's way while this play-thing is all happening and I need somewhere to work. It occurred to me that Meg's house would be just right. I've seen it twice, but it struck me as an excellent studio.'

'Ah. Sorry. Of course.' A sound of throat-clearing. 'Yes. It's all glass at the back. Noisy though.'

'I remember.' Peter had a crazy impulse to say I knew Meg long before you did, but realized he was being ridiculous.

'Well . . . I certainly don't need references and things from you. Would you like to meet me there? Or call here for the keys?'

'I'll call. This afternoon?'

'I have a meeting this afternoon.'

'Could you leave them with your secretary?' It sounded brusque. Peter laughed apologetically. 'It's just that – if I don't get somewhere soon I'll go mad!'

'Of course. What about . . . you know where the heating switch . . . ?'

'Yes. I know it well.' Peter hadn't the faintest idea where the heating switch was, but he certainly did not want Charles Kovacks showing him round Meg's house. Peter imagined Kovacks as his book jackets portrayed him, enormous, ancient, out of condition, waiting patiently for something to happen to force Meg into his arms.

'Then, well, that's OK then.' This Kovacks sounded uncertain. He did some more throat-clearing and said, 'If I can do anything – help in any way – you'll ring me?'

'Thank you.' That was fine. In other words if he didn't ring, there would be no more contact. Yes, that was fine.

Peter bundled his clothes into a case all anyhow, and scrubbed at the carpet with a handful of tissues. This idea was heaven-sent; the fact that the house was empty was preordained. He was going to work where Meg worked, sleep where she slept. He was trembling with eagerness as he paid his bill and hailed a taxi.

Charles left the keys of the Kilburn house with his

secretary as arranged, and stationed himself in a store room on one of the many half-landings leading to the office. The door of the store room had a kind of porthole at eye height. Feeling stupid yet stubborn, Charles kept watch there and had three seconds in which to view Peter Snow going upstairs and another three seconds to watch him going down.

Then Charles sat on a carton and looked at the dusty floor between his size eleven shoes. Meg had described Peter once as 'a proper artist' and Charles could see why. The long bearded face, tapering fingers could have belonged to anyone; it was the intensity of Snow's persona that proclaimed him to be dedicated to something. In the six seconds of observation Charles could feel the man almost burning up with his efforts to reach a certain goal. And Charles was enough of a 'proper artist' himself to recognize that drive.

There was another factor in the equation. Charles squeezed his eyes shut as if to blot it out of existence. But it was still there. Little Amy with her nondescript mouse-brown hair and her almost-brown eyes was so obviously Peter Snow's child.

Charles put his head in his hands. He knew he did not stand a chance.

For the rest of that Easter holiday Peter worked like a man possessed. He completed his original portrait of Meg/ Miranda. And at last satisfied that he had captured the essence of the twins, he went on to capture the composite in other poses. Swimming in Lannah Cove – he labelled that one 'The Tadpole' – standing at the range in the fish cellar hanging clothes over the airing rack, looking wistfully out of the window at the view of Keele . . . six paintings in all were completed by the end of his stay in London. He was exhausted.

He telephoned Miranda.

'Darling, I've been working like a maniac – forgot to keep in touch. Forgive me?'

'Peter, don't be an idiot. I'm the same. Exactly the same. Listen, how are you?'

'Fine. I've worked something out of my system, I think. What about you?'

Miranda laughed. 'I've worked something into my system! Darling, it's been wonderful. I feel so . . . alive!'

He said, 'Thank God. You sound wonderful.' But it had worked the other way for him; he felt dead. 'What about the kids?'

'Meg is bringing them home this weekend. Ready for school on Monday.'

'You mean – she's bringing them to London?'

'No. Keele, darling! She's going to bring them back here.'

'No need. I can meet her flight and take them off her hands.'

'Well, actually, she said she would stay. Just for a few days. I didn't know you'd be home and I asked her if she'd take over while . . . something's come up, Peter. The Arbitrary has a booking at Plymouth. They're doing *Dream* at the Playhouse. Ollie suggested I try for Cobweb. Peter – it's a fantastic chance to get my hand in. I couldn't say no. It would please Brett so much—'

'Darling, Brett is dead!' But Peter couldn't help laughing. It was marvellous to hear Miranda like her old self. It was like a weight lifting from his shoulders. If she could be happy and independent, it would mean he could . . . do something for himself perhaps. Talk to Meg?

'Not to the Arbitrary he's not!' She too was laughing, knowing he was pleased. 'Darling, it's incredible that Ollie should suggest it! She was always somehow against me. It means . . . it means she has more than accepted me. She actually *wants* me!'

'My God, of course she wants you – you're Miranda Patch!' He thought of something. 'Darling, can I come and see it? I'd like to paint you as Cobweb.'

'Oh, Peter . . .' Her voice became soft, full of nostalgic longing. 'Oh, darling, it was good between us, wasn't it?'

He hung on to the phone and tightened his facial muscles against tears. 'Yes, my love. It will be again, you know.'

'Perhaps. But not with me, Peter.'

'Rubbish, Miranda. Don't talk like that.' He swallowed. 'Anyway, darling, you can cancel Meg. I'll be home tomorrow.'

'I can't cancel her, Peter. She's already left Artemia. But she'll need your help down here so don't delay.'

He was still, staring out of the window at the view of parked cars. He felt Miranda's stillness too. She wanted him to talk to Meg. She was leaving the way clear. Just as she'd done before.

She said, 'You will come down, won't you?'

He breathed carefully. 'Darling, as you said, Charles Kovacks is a very European sort of a husband.'

There was a pause. Then she spoke emphatically.

'Peter. Believe me when I tell you – Meg's marriage was for convenience only.'

He forced a laugh. 'I'm not sure this Kovacks knows that. I haven't told you. I took Meg's house for two weeks. I didn't meet him – he left the keys with his secretary. But he sounded . . . possessive.'

Her voice was amused. 'Oh, I know. I spotted that too. But when you see Meg, you'll see instantly what I mean.'

'Miranda . . . I'm not sure . . .'

She was blithe, unconcerned. 'Well, see how it goes, darling. But don't worry about the almighty Kovacks!'

He replaced the receiver slowly and stayed exactly where he was for at least ten minutes.

Meg would be in Fish Cottage probably some time later today. Fish Cottage. Where she belonged. And he could go down there, quite legitimately, and be with her.

He sat on the bottom step of the spiral staircase and let himself think of her properly.

Eighteen

The journey to Artemia had been difficult, but the excitement of arriving in Athens and the boat trip to the island had been so wonderful for the children that Meg had taken it all in her stride. Going home was different. For one thing Amy was still holding back from her in some strange way; it was almost as if she blamed Meg for Charles's non-appearance. She certainly did not like the idea of Meg going back to Cornwall to look after Miranda's family.

'It's so selfish!' she fumed when Meg told her about Miranda's 'big chance'. 'It's you who needs looking after! You had your first child barely seven months ago – you were pulled down by that really bad cold—'

'And a long recuperation in this miniature paradise.' Meg smiled reassuringly. 'Granny, please don't worry. I'm so used to the routine at Fish Cottage – it's a second home to me.'

'I don't like it,' Amy said flatly.

'Charles doesn't mind,' Meg offered. 'He replied by return and told me to go ahead.'

'Well, he would, wouldn't he?' Amy commented scornfully. 'And how are you going to manage at Heathrow, for God's sake! Four children, all the luggage, Amy to be fed—' She narrowed her eyes suddenly. 'Is Peter Snow meeting you? Is that what Miranda has in mind?'

She had gone too far this time. Meg folded the letter

and put it with the passports in her bag. 'He's away on a painting trip,' she said briefly.

So the sadness of parting was not alleviated by the old flow of affection between them. The children did not want to leave either. Alex was going back to dreaded exam results, time was running out for Sebastian at his cosy infants' school. It was left to Katie to say, 'Look, we shall be coming here in the summer – Aunt Meg says so. And that's only three months away. And three months is only twelve weeks—'

'More than that. Thirty-one days in May and July,' Alex said gloomily.

'All right. Thirteen weeks.'

Sebastian looked apprehensive. 'Thirteen is unlucky,' he put in.

Spiro loaded them aboard his boat at four in the morning so that they could catch a plane from Volos at eight. Even with a quick change at Athens they would not reach Heathrow until past two, then they had to get a taxi to Reading to pick up the afternoon train to Penzance. Amy was right, it was going to be a long and difficult trip.

Meg watched Amy's scrawny figure in its outlandish clothes until her eyes watered with the effort of focusing. She wished so much there had not been that slight acrimony between them. Perhaps Amy wished it too, because it looked as if she might stay on the jetty all morning.

Once in the air, they all gave way to depression. The sheer hard work of boarding and strapping themselves in and handing Amy around like a parcel to keep her happy, stopped the children from actually weeping, but as the plane rose and they saw the islands beneath them, Katie and Sebastian caved in helplessly and Alex sat very still biting his bottom lip.

The arrival at Heathrow was just as bad. It was raining

and their cases seemed to take ages to appear on the conveyor belt. Amy began to protest at the top of her voice and Meg's heart was in her boots when suddenly, out of the blue, Charles was there. Moreover he had a trolley with him and loaded the luggage expertly even as she was exclaiming and trying to introduce the children and control Amy, who recognized him instantly and was singing a very high-pitched note of excitement.

'Charles – this is marvellous – how on earth did you know we'd be here? Alex – Katie – Sebastian – this is Charles Kovacks.'

Katie was immediately infected with Meg's relief. She held out her hand and Charles left the luggage temporarily to shake it. 'Hello.' Katie gave her special actress smile. 'You were supposed to come to Artemia and Granny was very disappointed. Shall we call you Uncle Charles?'

'Why not?' Charles shook hands all round with great seriousness. 'Let's make tracks. I've got the car really close.'

Alex was won over by the car. 'It's a BMW,' he said, awe-struck. 'Are you going to take us to the station?'

Charles closed the boot robustly and climbed into the driver's seat. 'I'm going to take you home,' he said. 'Your Aunt Meg wrote and told me she was going to look after you for a few days and as I couldn't get to Artemia to see you I thought I might come to Keyhole. What do you think?'

There was a chorus of approval from the three children.

'What about work?' Meg asked, wide-eyed.

'Organized.' He looked at her quickly and she thought he might be going to ask if she minded. She was glad he did not; she simply did not know. She could not imagine Charles at Keyhole.

Alex said, 'By the way, it's called Keele.'

Charles knew that but he said, 'Really? How interesting.'

Sebastian chipped in. 'If you say Keyhole, Keyhole, Keyhole, Keyhole—'

'Shut up, Seb,' Katie advised.

'No, but if you do, it starts sounding like Keele,' Sebastian explained.

Charles tried it. They joined in. Amy sang happily. Meg laughed. She had not known whether to hope for Charles's appearance on the island or not. It could not be the same as before when it had been just the two Amys and herself. She wondered whether their marriage had signalled the end of their friendship. But this was better still. The children on their home ground, hosting their new uncle.

They stopped at Exeter and had a cooked meal and Amy had some of her canned soup and a bottle to settle her. By the time they were driving along the coast road through Newlyn, the other three children were also asleep.

Charles said in a low voice, 'Is it very much further?'

'Two or three miles. Shall I drive into the village?'

'Not unless you want to.'

'I don't. Amy might wake if I move.'

'How is she?'

'Fine. She recognized Granny.'

Charles murmured an appreciative laugh. There was silence in the car for a while, then Meg asked, 'How did you know which flight to meet?'

'Amy. She wrote to tell me off for not coming over and said if I wasn't at Heathrow to meet you, she would not speak to me again.'

'Typical Amy. She was born aggressive.' She hesitated, then said, 'I can't tell you how glad I am that you can stay. The children are so good, but . . . there will be a lot to do.'

He said carefully, 'Will Miranda mind?'

And Meg said with equal care, 'Of course not. Why should she?' Before he could feel a need to reply she went on, 'Left here. Then right along the harbour.'

Charles drew a breath. 'My God, it's beautiful. As beautiful as Artemia in its way. No wonder you . . .'

He did not finish the sentence and Meg never asked him about it. They were too busy negotiating the narrow road from Fish Street into Sunday Street.

Peter took the keys of the Kilburn house to Charles's office the next day. He hardly knew what he was doing any more; his actions were those of an automaton. Clean house, pack, take keys back, catch train to Penzance, taxi to Keyhole. At the end of the journey – and he could visualize that quite clearly – Meg would be waiting for him, knowing he would come to her somehow. He would tell her everything. Everything. He had no idea whether Miranda guessed at his secret – he could not put it into words for her in case he reawakened the nightmare of Meredith. But he could pour it all out to Meg. The thought of being able to talk, to explain, to be understood and therefore forgiven, was like the promise of life again. For over a year now he had lived either for Miranda or for his painting. He wanted, quite desperately, to be able to live for himself again.

It was a relief to learn that Kovacks was out of town. Those were his secretary's words, 'out of town'. Peter hated him for being out of town when Meg was back home, but delighted too. There could not be much between him and Meg after all. He ran back down the two flights of stairs and got a taxi immediately, which was another good omen.

All the way from Paddington to Penzance, he let himself think of Meg. He knew that Miranda was doing the *Dream* in Plymouth to leave the way open for himself and Meg. He wondered if it would be possible to keep Meg with them from now on. How would it affect Alex and Katie and Seb? He shivered and blocked that thought quickly. He would let his mind go no further than meeting her and talking to her and being with her again.

The taxi was in the station yard at Penzance. It was six o'clock, a chilly April evening. He had been in London only three weeks, yet everything looked different. Clean, sea-washed. The taxi cruised past his old studio in Newlyn and he thought how he and Meg could visit Mrs Pascoe. And with that thought came another, insidious, ridiculous, yet so tempting. He could pass Meg off as Miranda. No-one would ever know. Except Miranda, Meg and himself. Not even the children.

The driver said, 'Up here is it, sir?'

'Yes. Right, along the harbour, right again into Fish Street, straight up into Sunday Street and left there.'

The taxi revved furiously up the narrow connecting street and stopped in a cloud of exhaust outside Fish Cottage. He noticed his hand was shaking slightly as he paid the man off and dragged his case inside the gate. And then he was fitting his key into the door of the cellar and breathing in the smell of clothes drying over the range.

Because of the clothes he knew that they were back and in residence, but he also knew immediately that the house was empty. It was a terrible disappointment; he had keyed himself up for the meeting which was supposed to happen now. He pushed his case and painting gear far enough inside to close the door and stood uncertainly, trying to remember what day it was; what could be happening. It was Tuesday and the kids started back to school the next day. So, at seven o'clock at night, they should be there. Had Meg taken them for a picnic . . . or a walk?

He picked up his stuff again and went upstairs, dumped it in the hall and continued into the sitting room which went from the front to the back of the house. From here he could see across to the Coastguards, already full of lights and customers. He stared down at the little harbour but could see no sign of Katie's flying hair, Alex's tall figure. And then from the back came the sound of a car negotiating the ramp from Fish Street. He hurried down the room and looked out on Sunday Street. A BMW was drawing up outside the gate. Its doors flew open. A man emerged; Peter recognized Kovacks with a shock. He was no longer burly and enormous, no longer old. He went around to the other side of the car, and reached inside. Meg's arms appeared, holding a baby. He took the baby and stood there, smiling at it, nodding his head. Katie and Sebastian crowded around him, obviously demanding the child. Alex held the door right back and Meg emerged. The six of them stood, arguing and laughing, and faintly through the window Peter could hear the child cooing loudly and joyously. And then Kovacks held her aloft so that she could look down on them all and Peter could see her face for the first time.

He drew back sharply and pressed himself against the wall to control the shaking which had now spread through his body. He closed his eyes, breathing deeply, almost panting for air. The shock of knowing he was about to faint seemed to pull him together for a moment. The back gate clicked and he could hear Alex saying loudly, 'We've had burglars! The door is unlocked!'

Meg's voice, 'That's me. I was last out. Sorry, Alex.'

Muffled thumping began as everyone piled into the fish cellar and the door closed on them.

Swiftly Peter crossed the room and slid on to the landing. Everyone was talking at once downstairs. He heard the tap running into the kettle, Charles's voice singing, 'Dance for your daddy my little lady', Katie saying, 'It's laddie actually Uncle Charles, but lady is very good.' Throughout it all the child's voice, cooing, gurgling.

He opened the front door inch by inch, bent and picked up his two bags. Then he was down the steps and in Fish Street, moving away from the tiny cellar windows, running down to the harbour and up the road towards Newlyn. There were bus stops along here at intervals, but he had to keep moving otherwise he thought he might go mad. He walked fast, then ran a few steps. His bags dragged at his arms and he began to sweat profusely. A car drew up and a male voice said, 'Missed the bus? I can give you a lift into Penzance.'

He got into a car containing three fishermen. They smelled atrocious. He asked if they would drop him at Newlyn, and he geared himself to return pleasantries and make small talk. They dropped him outside Mrs Pascoe's and the front door was open as usual.

She appeared from the kitchen. 'Oh, it's you, Mr Snow. Cases and all, eh?'

Her face was almost exactly like Hals's gypsy girl. He said, 'Can you put me up for the night, Mrs P? Please?'

'You can have the attic.' She looked at him. 'Had a row with yer missus, have you?'

'Yes. Something like that.'

'Go on then. I'll bring you up a nice cup of tea soon as it's brewed.'

And when she appeared twenty minutes later he was sitting in his coat, staring at the unfelted slates of the roof, and tears were running down his face.

Miranda was cautiously pleased to see him.

'I didn't think you'd . . . have you been to Keele?'

'Yes. They didn't need me – Meg's new husband is there

giving a hand, so it seemed like a good chance to see you as Cobweb.'

'Well. Lovely.' She looked almost her old self; even her hair was springier. She pulled a piece forward and tickled her nose with it just as she used to do. 'I bet the children were pleased to see you,' she said, her eyes watching him.

'They didn't.' He pulled a face. 'Matter of fact, darling, when I saw . . . Charles Kovacks there, I didn't declare myself. It will take some time to get used to the thought of Meg married.'

'Yes. I know. But you'd already met him.'

'No. I talked to him on the phone. He wasn't there when I picked up the keys to Meg's house. Nor when I returned them.'

'Oh. Well, he's pleasant enough.' She shrugged. 'It's a marriage of convenience, that's all.'

Neither of them had sat down since he arrived. He now moved to the window and looked out. The digs were near the Barbican and he could see a narrow street a long way down. He said, 'Yes. So I gathered.'

Miranda flipped her hair back and then put her hands behind her. 'Listen, Peter. I have to go soon. Will you come with me? The performance starts at seven-thirty.'

'No. I'll get something to eat first.'

'When did you eat last?'

'Yesterday? No. I can't remember.'

'Oh my God. I thought you seemed a bit other-worldly. Listen, the landlady won't give you anything. Turn left when you go out and there's a pub called the Cranberry. They do pasties in there.'

'All right. Good luck, Miranda. And . . . thanks.'

She went to the window and held up her face. He kissed her lips very gently. And then she left.

It was such a small part, but she had the only decent singing voice and she sang the spell as if she were protecting Peter as well as Titania. She looked like a cobweb with her hair floating about her face and the wispy muslin lifting in the heat of the footlights. She wanted her performance to be an offering and a solution to Peter. She tried to show him that she could be independent now.

He did not come backstage. The cast knew him but no-one had seen him. Miranda did not wait for the others. She took a cab back to the digs and flew up to the room at the top. There was a note on the table.

'Darling, I found the car keys on the mantelpiece and asked the dragon landlady where you'd put it. I'm going to drive somewhere. Don't know where. I need something new. I'll leave a message at Gladys Pugh's. Peter.'

She sat down slowly and put her head in her hands.

But in fact Peter drove back to Newlyn, stabled the car behind Mrs Pascoe's and took up residence in his old studio. Every morning he watched Charles Kovacks drive his children into Penzance and every night he watched him drive them home again. In between, he took his paints on to the moors and began to paint the standing stones and dolmens and the gaunt engine houses of old tin mines. He did not dare go into a pub in case Meg found out he was near at hand. He phoned Gladys and asked her to tell Miranda not to go home until he gave her the all-clear. And he waited.

Meg had looked out Sebastian's old playpen and Little Amy was able to draw herself up on its bars and crow with delight at her own achievement. The children would sit around the big old table and pass her scraps of food as if she were a puppy.

'Have some of my toast, Amy-Maimie.' Sebastian did not enjoy crusts and Amy did. She mumbled on it, dribbling happily, while Katie mashed her egg-yolk and prepared to spoon it into her.

Charles said, 'That baby will be twice its size by the time we go home.'

Sebastian showed his usual apprehension. 'You're not going home for ages yet, are you?'

'Not till Mummy and Daddy come back,' Charles said.

Katie squatted by the playpen and held out her spoon. 'We don't call Miranda and Peter Mummy and Daddy,' she explained. 'Alex and Seb call them Ma and Pa. Or just Dad.'

Alex defended himself. 'Ma is short for Miranda and Pa—'

Meg intervened. 'We'll stay till they get back,' she promised.

She watched as they got ready. Sebastian had settled into his new school with surprising ease; there was something reassuring in seeing him tug on his cap expertly. Alex had had no results as yet and was a bit more nervous each day, but hid it well. Katie was calm to the point of being blasé. None of them showed the slightest sign of missing their parents; Meg did not know whether to be pleased or sorry about this.

After Charles had taken them off, she cleared up the cellar and took Amy upstairs with her to make beds and dust. She held her to the window to wave to Charles when he came back. Amy sang lustily and banged the glass with her flattened palm. It was good to see him laughing up at her. It was good that he was so at home down here. It was as good as being in Artemia.

She went back downstairs and Charles played with Amy while they had coffee. He put her down and then worked at the kitchen table, chatting desultorily while Meg prepared their evening meal. Then after an early lunch they took Amy for a walk in Sebastian's old pram. It bounced over the cobbles so that Amy's moon song was disrupted by apparent hiccoughs; Charles laughed down at her and she laughed back.

Meg said impulsively, 'I'm so *glad* you like it here, Charles! Amy too!'

He negotiated the steep alley on to the harbour. 'Yes. Well, it's more of a home than the flat has ever been.' He glanced at her. 'Meg, listen. If you'll come back, we'll sell up and move. Somewhere more homely. And I'll pension Magda off. She must be nearly seventy anyway.'

She was shocked. 'Of course I'm coming back – you didn't imagine this was a permanent arrangement, did you?'

'I don't know.' His expression was wry. 'This place . . . it's where your heart is, Meg. I have to acknowledge that – it would be foolish not to. Anyway, having seen it, I can understand how you feel.'

'Charles! For goodness' sake! That's all in the past! We agreed—'

'Hang on. We'll always be friends, whatever happens. Don't say any more. But remember that.'

She had to run a step to keep up with him. 'I'm going to say more! Of course I'm coming home! And of course we're not going to move! And of course you mustn't pension off Magda! You haven't given the flat – Magda – me – half a chance yet! Everything was against us when we got back from Artemia. But we're acclimatized now and . . .' She was panting for breath. 'Just you wait and see! And could we go slower, please!'

He laughed. 'Sorry.' He stopped and turned the pram so that Amy could see the sea. 'D'you realize that a year ago I couldn't have walked up this hill?'

'I do. Do *you* realize I haven't mentioned words like cirrhosis and cholesterol since you arrived in Artemia last summer?'

He said, 'When you left England I went on a keep-fit routine.' He laughed. 'I had to be fit to survive it!'

'Oh, Charles.'

'Maman suggested it. I told her I'd hoped we could be married and she pointed out – in no uncertain way – that a girl would have to be blind to want to marry me!'

'I don't believe you!'

'It's true. Maman could be as frank as Amy Smithers. I hate to think of the rows they must have had in the old days.'

'Yet they became friends.'

'The best.' He moved off again and said casually, 'Because they could be frank. And honest. Even if it hurt. Like us.'

'Us? Have you got something unpleasant to say to me, Charles?' She laughed quickly.

'No. But I want you to be honest about the flat. And Magda.' He smiled as Amy bounced hopefully. 'Look, she's asking to be taken back over the cobbles!' He joggled the pram. 'I *will* be honest, Meg – I know you love it down here with the children. I'm worried you'll want to stay.'

'There's no place for me here. You know that.'

'Yes but . . . do you want to stay?'

'Well . . . don't you? We're doing well, I thought. I mean – as well as when we were in Artemia. And we haven't got Granny to – to – tell us how to behave!'

He laughed at that. They came to the cobbles again and Amy crowed her delight. He said, 'I'd better go for the children. It's three-thirty.' They made for Fish Street. He said, 'It's marvellous down here, Meg. But there isn't really a place for me. And my work is in London. I can't stay indefinitely.'

She touched his arm. 'Neither can I,' she said.

But he knew that Miranda did not see it that way. Miranda was clever. And devious. And closer to Meg than anyone. He wondered what plan she had. The next day he knew.

Alex was crazy with joy that night. His place at Truro College was assured and Zach was going with him. The next morning the post brought a list of school uniform and games equipment. It was very impressive.

'Ma will have to come home to get me this stuff!' he declared with a touch of aggression.

'Or Peter.' Katie checked the list with her mother-of-pearl fingernail. 'Peter would be better really. He knows about things like rugby kits.'

Charles got up and fetched a tissue for Amy's chin. Miranda certainly was clever. And devious. Charles knew now that when he left Keele, Peter would arrive. As if Katie had spoken the words, he saw that if he hadn't met Meg at Heathrow, Peter would be here now.

He said, 'It's still school today, old man. Better get yourself ready.'

'Can't I stay at home and celebrate?' Alex asked. 'If Pa was here he'd let me stay off school today.'

'I don't think so.' Charles smiled amiably enough, but the three children went upstairs immediately for their outdoor clothes. Alex said loudly, 'They prob'ly don't have public schools in Hungary.'

And Katie came back, 'Peter wouldn't let you stay home anyway, Alex. You get in the way of his painting!'

Charles slipped outside to get the car out. He wondered where Peter Snow was at this moment. And whether Miranda was monitoring his presence. And how. He waited in the car for the children to appear. It was just as before, when he had sat in the stationery room of the office. He did not stand a chance.

He left the next day. He would have gone anyway because he had a phone call from Traddles about the colours of Meg's illustrations. As he remembered them, the colours had been exactly right. He did not mention anything to Meg. Just that he must leave before lunch and Billy Majors had promised to pick up the children that afternoon.

He tried desperately – hopelessly – to avoid the inevitable. 'You'll be up to your eyes at the weekend, Meg. Why don't you ring Miss Pugh's place and insist on Miranda coming home?'

'We'll see.' She patted his arm reassuringly. 'Don't worry about us, Charles, please. Sort out this muddle – whatever it is – and come back as soon as you can.'

He stared around the big kitchen and wondered if she knew that Peter Snow was waiting for him to leave. He said, 'Do you mean that? Do you want me to come back here?'

She was so genuinely surprised he knew his momentary suspicion was completely unfounded.

He went on quickly without waiting for her reply, 'D'you know, this kitchen reminds me of the one at Artemia.'

She smiled, pleased. 'I remember thinking that. Eva's kitchen.'

'Yes.' He picked up his case. That was why she had been so happy in Artemia. It had reminded her always of Keele and Fish Cottage. She was the faithful kind.

He said, 'Don't come out. There's an awful wind. Amy might catch cold.' He gave her a kind of avuncular hug and made for the door. 'Listen, Meg –' He frowned, trying to word things very carefully indeed. 'If anything ever happens . . . I mean, if you want something else . . . in the future . . . please remember that our marriage was just for convenience. Don't let it stand in your way.'

She stared at him, more uncertain than before.

'Amy said that it was a marriage of friendship.'

'My dear Meg . . .' He swallowed hard. 'We can be friends without being married.' He opened the door and pushed his case ahead of him. 'Just remember what I've said. Don't ever feel tied to me. Or guilty. Or responsible.' He forced a laugh. 'Be happy.' He closed the door firmly behind him.

Peter watched him drive beneath the attic window; noted his London suit and the luggage on the back seat. He closed his eyes and regulated his breathing. Then he stood up too quickly and knocked his head on one of the eaves, just as he'd done so many years before. It seemed like an omen. Perhaps it was the same beam. He rubbed at the incipient bump and went downstairs more slowly, taking his pain to Meg like a child in need of absolution.

She picked Amy up from her playpen and sat with her on her lap, feeling like one of the small sailing boats in the bay, out of wind, sails flapping helplessly. The suspicion that Charles had had enough of domesticity, of looking after someone else's family, quickly became a conviction. She was appalled at the way she had taken for granted his support and loyalty. He was no saint; he had been married before, he owed Meg no allegiance, she had thought she could give him something – fill a gap in his life. All she had done was take.

She put her face into the angle of Amy's neck and shoulder and gave a quiet groan. How on earth could she have been so content in Artemia and especially down here? The mess was still there; it hadn't gone away. No-one could really solve anything.

Amy gurgled and reached round as usual for a nose. She found it and gurgled more. With streaming eyes, Meg too laughed and stood up to take her daughter upstairs for her morning nap. The day stretched ahead interminably; she told herself she had heaps to do – she could clean the salt off the front windows – but with Charles's departure all motivation had gone. She stayed with Amy until the minuscule thumb went into the puckered mouth, then she pulled up the side of the cot and wandered around the house like a lost soul. She was making herself peel vegetables at the sink when Peter arrived. There was a tap at the yard door, it opened, and there, incredibly, he was.

She stood, a carrot in one hand, knife in the other, mouth open with shock. It was almost eighteen months since she had seen him last and he had changed anyway in that time; the last few weeks had changed him still more. He was gaunt, his beard tangled and obviously unwashed, his hair in rats' tails on his shoulders.

She exclaimed, 'Peter!' And then, dropping knife and carrot, automatically drying her hands on her apron, she said, 'My dear. You're ill.'

He had not known what to say, but with her usual empathy she had slipped beneath any front he might have put up. He shook his head violently.

'I'm not ill. I'm sick. The only thing I can do is paint. It's like that dot game you told me about. I have to keep painting to find a pattern. An answer. Some way I can . . . live properly again.'

'Oh, my dear,' she said again, terribly distressed. She pulled a chair to the Aga. 'Come. Sit here. Let me . . .' She manoeuvred him out of the stiff donkey jacket and piloted him to the chair. He was shivering uncontrollably.

The jacket was heavy with water. Had it been raining?

He leaned towards the warmth gratefully.

'I had to see you, Meg. You're the only one . . . I have to talk to you. Will you listen to me?'

'Of course. Have you been sleeping outside?'

'No. At Mrs Pascoe's. Where I could watch Kovacks take the children to school and bring them home. I saw him leave this morning.'

'Oh my God. There's some soup . . . I'll heat it.'

'He's nothing to do with it, Meg. He's an outsider. Even Miranda . . . Miranda understood that. She knows I have to see you.'

Meg closed her eyes momentarily and pulled at the damper. The Aga roared satisfyingly. She found the basin of soup in the fridge and transferred it to a saucepan.

She said, 'Your jacket. It's saturated.'

'I was painting at Gulval. Two days ago. It poured.'

'And it's still wet. Mrs Pascoe would have—'

'I won't let her come upstairs. She brings food sometimes. I ate it at first but I can't bear it now.'

'She should have sent for a doctor.'

'No. She's on my side.'

She poured soup and held a cup towards him. 'We all are, Peter,' she said quietly. 'Now, drink this. Then you can talk.'

He sipped, slowly at first then faster until he was slurping hungrily. She bent down and removed his shoes. The smell was choking. She fetched a bowl of warm water and lifted one foot in at a time, sock and all. By the time he had finished the soup she was able to peel the socks off in strips like skin.

He said, 'Meg. I'm sorry. I've let myself go. I'm sorry.'

'There has to be a reason for this, Peter.'

'Yes. Actually—' He sounded calm, almost formal. 'Actually, I think I might be going mad.'

'Perhaps.' She forced her voice to be just as objective. 'Probably overwork. You've had to see to things here for a long time, then you went off by yourself to paint—'

'Meg, I've done some good stuff. Really good stuff. It's all right when I'm painting. I took your house – did Kovacks tell you?'

'No.' She felt a little shock that Charles had kept something so important from her.

'I thought, this is where she has worked, this is where she has lived and breathed and—'

'Why did you leave here? Was there a row with Miranda? Is Miranda all right?'

He gave a tired laugh. 'Always Miranda. She is always your first concern, Meg.' He shook his head, then held it between his hands. 'I had a bump this morning. On the roof. D'you remember when I did it before? I thought you might sympathize. But you didn't then. And you're not now.'

'You had enough sympathy for yourself.' She forced her voice to be hard. 'Why did you leave here, Peter?'

He sighed. 'All right. Miranda. Miranda. Miranda.'

'Yes?'

'At first she was so frail. D'you remember? She needed me. For the first time in our marriage she needed me, Meg. That's how I lived then. By putting everything into looking after Miranda. And she began to get well. She loved Keele and the cottage and my work – and most of all, me!' He rubbed the palms of his hands on his knees fiercely. 'It was all right then, Meg. I did it for her and she was needing me and it was worth it.'

He paused and she poured more water into the basin. He stared at the top of her head and then closed his eyes tightly.

She said quietly, 'Go on.'

'Then . . . Brett St Clare died and left her the bloody

414

drama group. Whatever they call themselves. And she did not need me any more. And I couldn't stop her living again, could I? But I couldn't . . . justify . . . myself any more. To myself. Oh God . . . I couldn't tell her what I'd done. And I couldn't live with what I'd done. So I went to your house and I worked. And gradually I knew I had to tell you.'

'Tell me what, Peter?'

He opened his eyes and looked at her quite blankly. He was still rubbing the palms of his hands on his knees and she covered one of them and stilled it.

He said, 'The strange thing was, Miranda wanted me to see you too. She arranged it. Did you realize how cleverly she arranged it? She thought it would happen before this. She didn't reckon on Kovacks coming down here with you. But . . . well, it's happened now.' He flung himself back in the chair and closed his eyes again. 'When I saw the baby, I knew why she'd arranged it. She knew it was my child. And she wanted me to know. She wanted to bow out. To leave the cottage to you and me and the baby.'

She clenched her hand over his quite suddenly. Then she straightened her back and went to the rack for a warm towel.

'How ridiculous,' she said calmly. 'Typical of Miranda. Dramatizing everything.'

He sat up and looked at her incredulously. She met his eye and smiled slightly.

'No. I'm not denying that Little Amy is your child, Peter. Obviously Miranda realized it – she really is a very good actress. And she wanted you to realize it. But there's no way on this earth that we can live together and bring up the four children together. I don't want to. You don't want to. It's as simple as that.'

He flinched slightly as if she had struck him.

'Then . . . what can we do?'

'I will go back to London with Amy. And you will stay here and look after your family, Peter. And after a while Miranda will rejoin you. And we will learn to live with the muddle that we created. And not inflict it on the children.'

The pupils of his eyes were fully dilated; she noted that. He whispered, 'You said that there is no way on this earth that we can live together. I had already thought of that, Meg. While I was painting on Gulval. No way on this earth. But maybe there is a life after death which we could share.'

'Stop it, Peter!' She threw the towel at him. 'That way most definitely leads to madness! Now dry your feet and go and have a bath and put on clean clothes.'

He obeyed her like an admonished child. She had to control her shocked horror as he shambled up the stairs; he had lost so much weight; his boyishness had gone for good.

Ashamed of her motives, she listened for the bathroom door and immediately it clicked she ran upstairs and fetched Amy. The child was still asleep and remained so as Meg laid her on the floor of the playpen. She could not believe that Peter would harm her, and yet . . . he seemed in the middle of a full nervous breakdown.

She laid the table scrappily and put out bread and cheese and pickles. Amy woke up and was surprised to find herself out of her cot. She wept a little until Meg took her on to her knee and gave her her lunch, and then she sang one of her soprano moon songs and was still singing when Peter reappeared.

He was subdued to the point of being withdrawn. He barely looked at Amy and she seemed to sense his malaise and stopped her song to bury her head in her mother's shoulder.

Meg said, 'You'd better eat something, Peter. I usually take the baby for a walk until the other children get back from school. I'll stay out late today so that you can see them alone.'

'No!' He looked up, apparently terrified. 'I can't see them, Meg! Look at me! It wouldn't do!'

She did not deny this. 'Then what are you going to do?'

'I thought . . .' He leaned forward suddenly and Amy whimpered and clutched her mother. 'Darling, don't leave me – please don't leave me! Not now!'

'Peter, I don't know what you want me to say or do – ' Amy was beginning to gasp little cries of fear. Meg stood up and jogged her. 'This is your home. And I cannot leave it until tomorrow now. Why can't you—'

'Because unless we stay here together – properly together – I cannot go on living! Don't you see that, Meg? I have to be with you now. And you have to be with me. It's the only way!'

'Peter. We have already said all these things. There is no way—'

'But there is! Miranda did it before! You can do it! No-one can tell the difference between you!'

Amy wailed and Meg said, appalled, 'What are you suggesting?'

'Tell the kids we've come back together, Meg. Please. I'm not very well so you've put me to bed. You can tell them about the play – I think it's *The Tempest* – or *Midsummer Night's Dream* – or something! Pretend you're Miranda, my darling. Stay with me. No-one will ever know! Miranda will agree to it – it's true justice after all!'

He was gabbling and Amy was screaming. Meg took her to the window and showed her the tubs of dwarf tulips that came up every year. Gradually the child calmed down and pointed with her tiny finger, hiccoughing on her last few sobs.

Meg said, 'You really are mad, Peter. What you are suggesting is completely insane. And if you're talking of justice, think back thirteen years very carefully.' She looked over her shoulder. 'Peter, when will you realize . . . in spite of everything that has happened, it is Miranda you love.'

'But Miranda doesn't love me! And you do!' He crumpled over his plate of bread and cheese. 'You do love me, don't you, Meg?'

'I don't know.' She remembered something Amy had said. 'Perhaps I don't even know what love is. That . . . night . . . when we were together . . . was that love? Or was it anger with Miranda for throwing away something so precious? If I hadn't loved you then, Peter, you would have gone for her – rescued her—'

'But if you don't love me – if Miranda doesn't love me – then I did it for nothing!'

She came slowly to the table and sat down opposite him. 'What did you do, Peter?'

He made an impatient gesture. 'I killed John Meredith! That's what I did. I hit him. I kept hitting him. And when he lay still I dragged him down those steps to Lannah. And I held him under the water for nearly half an hour! I thought Miranda was dying in the hospital. She had you – she wanted you. And that left me to deal with . . . so I did.'

Meg stared at him, understanding at last. And Amy, as if she too understood, gave a scream and turned frantically away from her father.

Nineteen

Billy Majors parked his old station wagon in the Coastguards yard and walked the children back along the harbour and into the house. They were less ebullient today.

Billy watched them making a fuss of Amy and said in an aside to Meg, 'Reckon young Alex feels he's driven your 'usband back to London, missis. Could hear him talking to yon maid about it. Regretful he were.'

'No need.' Meg was amazed at the way she could smile so easily. 'Charles had to go back – business.'

'Thought so. These three – they're not cheeky kids. Seem well settled with the two of you looking after them.' He grinned. 'When 'e comes back down, bring him along to the Coastguards. Arthur 'ud like to meet him.'

Meg nodded. 'Perhaps I will, Billy. But Mr Snow came home today, so probably I shall be back in London myself soon.'

Katie overheard that and came leaping around them. 'Where's Daddy gone? Has he taken the boat out? When did he come home?'

Alex pounced. '*Daddy?* Did likkle-pickle Katie call him Daddy, then?'

Katie rounded on him with her satchel and there was a free-for-all. Sebastian said hopefully, 'Is Mummy back too?'

'Not yet. I phoned Miss Pugh and she is going to ask Mummy to ring us as soon as she can.'

Sebastian ran to the playpen. 'Mummy's coming home, Amy! You'll like Mummy. She's zackly the same as Aunt Meg, so you're bound to like her really, aren't you?'

Meg looked at the stairs which had proved practically insurmountable for Peter two hours ago. Was that the trouble with him too? Could he see no difference between his wife and his sister-in-law?

She explained how ill he was and they crept like mice into the big double bedroom overlooking the harbour. He seemed to be sleeping and they peered at him in turn and then started to withdraw. He held out a hand then, and when Katie took it between both of hers he drew her close and moved his face as if for a kiss. She gave it to him and looked up startled.

'Daddy's crying!' she announced fearfully.

It was the second time she had called Peter Daddy and this time Alex did not tease her.

Meg tried to reassure them. 'He's very weak. That's all it is. Let him see how pleased you are that he's home.'

Alex took the pleading paint-stained hand and stood close to the bed. 'Good you're back, Pa,' he said gruffly. 'Get better soon. Want you to help me buy my gear for the College.'

Sebastian knelt close to Alex and leaned over to put his forehead against Peter's. 'Everything is fine now, Daddy,' he said confidently. 'You're back in Keele. Keele makes everyone better. Remember how it made Mummy better?'

Meg said, 'Let him sleep now, children. You can come and see him again after tea.'

They trailed out with her, relieved to be going down to such normality as tea and Amy playing in her pen.

Meg talked to them matter-of-factly.

'Daddy has been overworking.' She smiled as she poured chips into the pan which was all she'd had time

for during that eventful and awful day. 'He's terribly
pleased with what he's done. I think . . .' She shook
the chip basket vigorously. 'I really do think, my loves,
that your father is one of the greats. You take him
for granted because you live with him and his painting is part of your daily lives. That's good. How it
should be.' She opened the side oven, removed a casserole dish, tipped the chips into it and started on some
more. She felt very flushed. 'You – we – haven't realized
perhaps that his work has been changing – developing
– into something very special.' She laughed and shook
the chip basket again. 'Perhaps I'm prejudiced. Anyway.
When people produce something from deep inside themselves . . . their souls, maybe . . . then they're sort of
drained. Can you understand that?'

Alex said, 'Of course. It stands to reason.' He got up
and fetched a bottle of tomato sauce from the cupboard.
'If you pour out your ideas and thoughts, then your brain
empties.'

Sebastian nodded. Katie said thoughtfully, 'It's different when you act. You have to empty yourself first and
then fill up.'

Meg looked round at them with surprise. They were all
nodding like old men. But after all they were the children
of talented parents.

She brought the casserole to the table. The nodding
stopped and a very normal childish cheer went up.

'Chips! We haven't had chips for yonks!'

Incredibly, after all that had happened, with Peter lying
ill and shattered upstairs, she laughed.

Katie hugged her arm affectionately.

'Aren't we all lucky, Aunt Meg?'

'Are we?'

Sebastian said, 'The only thing is we can't be in one
place at the same time, can we? Granny will never leave

Artemia, so we ought to go out there all together. Ma and Pa and you and Uncle Charles and Little Amy and . . . us.'

Katie said definitely, 'That won't happen.'

Alex helped himself liberally from the casserole. 'Doesn't matter. 'Cos Ma and Meg are linked anyway.' He looked down at Amy. 'Can she have a chip, Aunt Meg? She's holding out her hand for one.'

Meg said, 'Actually she's catching moonbeams. And I think she's too young for chips.'

Miranda did not phone. When the children were in bed Meg rang Miss Pugh again. Miss Pugh had not heard from Miranda either. She had rung the stage door at Weymouth where the Arbitrary had taken their production of *Dream*. She had left an urgent message and had assumed that Miranda would have been in touch by now.

'It's . . . her husband is very ill. He refuses to see a doctor. I'm not quite sure . . . what to do.'

'Feed him up, Mrs Kovacks. Miranda was never much good in the kitchen and the few times I've met the lad he seemed much too thin to me. I reckon he's in good hands with you.'

'Yes but—'

'She'll ring after tonight's performance I'll be bound. And if she comes through to me I'll tell her what you've said.'

Meg had to be content with that. She had been looking forward to going to bed early herself. She sat for a long moment in front of the phone, staring at the granite walls. If only she was able to ring Amy! She longed to hear the sensible, impatient voice, telling her exactly what to do. Wearily she got up and went to the table, intending to write to her. But a sound from upstairs had her hurrying up to check on Little Amy who appeared to be singing in her sleep. Meg had moved the cot and herself into what had been the old kitchen on the end of the dining room, now supposedly a study. For some reason she did not want to be on the same floor as Peter. However, she went on upstairs again and looked in on everyone. The children were all asleep in abandoned attitudes. Peter apparently had not moved. His knees were drawn up almost to his chest, his hands crossed in a foetal position. She leaned close to listen for his breathing. It was shallow but otherwise normal. She squashed a moment of terror that he might die during the night.

She went back down and placed writing paper and envelopes on the kitchen table. And then she went to the telephone and dialled the Sussex Gardens number. She pulled the chair to the phone and sat down, weak with relief at the thought of talking to Charles. She hadn't wanted to burden him with this nightmare, but the decision made, she could only feel thankfulness.

The clicking eventually stopped and the phone started to ring in the flat. And continued to ring. She began to count; when she reached thirty, she replaced the receiver very slowly and carefully.

Suddenly she was trapped. She could not leave Keele – she could not leave Fish Cottage – until someone came. And she could not tell Janis or Billy Majors or even dear old Arthur Bowering what was happening. For a moment a surge of panic overwhelmed her. And then, forcing herself to be calm, she began to write.

Miranda did not phone and the number of the Sussex Gardens flat continued to ring emptily.

Meg worked hard to make the impossible situation seem normal and on occasions, especially at mealtimes, she almost convinced herself. At the weekend she suggested to Peter that he was well enough to move from bedroom to living-room sofa where he could at least share the television viewing with the children. He moved his head weakly in negation.

She said, 'Peter, you're getting up to go to the bathroom. It would mean one flight of stairs only.'

'No point,' he said in the toneless voice he had adopted after the terrible histrionics of his 'confession'.

She said crisply, 'Of course there's a point. You have to begin to integrate into the household some time. And it would mean one less flight of stairs for me to climb with your meals!'

He flinched slightly. 'I don't want any meals, Meg.'

'You have to eat. You have to get well, Peter.'

'Why? All I want is to be with you and if I get well you will go away.'

'I'm not going until Miranda gets back.'

'She won't come back, Meg. She doesn't need me any more. And she is an actress.'

'And you are an artist.' She pushed him forward and dealt with his pillows, forcing him into a near-upright position. In spite of himself he was looking better. And whatever he said about not wanting meals, he was eating them by himself now. That first twenty-four hours she had had to spoonfeed him.

He got up that evening and sat with them watching a games show on the television. Unfortunately his effect on Amy was catastrophic; she yelled lustily at the sight of him and refused to be comforted by anyone except Meg. It was a good reason for leaving them alone in the big sitting room and making a long hour of Amy's bath and supper routine.

On Sunday evening, realizing they would be relatively alone once more the next day, Meg tried to ring Charles again. Again without success. She dialled Gladys Pugh's number and drew a blank there too. Gladys could have been at church; Charles most certainly was not.

So their strange domestic arrangement limped into its second week. Billy collected the children and after Meg had put Amy down for her morning nap, Peter appeared and prowled around the kitchen as if he were constantly searching for something. Meg felt her own nerves stretch to breaking point. She thought she had put his 'confession' out of her mind, but Amy's evident fear of her natural father brought it back. She went out for their walk earlier each day and did not return until she saw Billy's old car manoeuvring along the harbour. She became angry with Miranda; furious with Charles. The situation was ludicrous, yet potentially catastrophic.

On Friday morning she said casually to the children, 'I thought of taking Amy up to Plymouth tomorrow. If I can arrange it, will you make sure your father eats his meals and takes care of himself.'

Sebastian asked quickly, 'Are you coming back?'

And before she could summon the will to lie to him, Katie said, ''Course she will, idiot! She's only going to see Miranda in her play.'

Alex scoffed at that. 'Ma's in Weymouth – you're about four weeks behind!' He grinned at his aunt, supremely confident now that his exam result was through. 'We'll keep an eye on Pa. Never fear, Alex the Great is here!'

Sometimes she was amazed that the three of them, so sentient at times, could be so obtuse at others. When Billy came for them she arranged a lift to Penzance station for the next morning. Then she stood by the door, Amy in her arms, waving to them, feeling that at last things were improving.

Peter was appalled.

'Meg. Please. You can't leave me – not again!'

'Well, we certainly cannot go on as we are!' She felt a

distinct irritation with him; she was tired to the bone. She had always believed that Peter was a genius – never more so than now – but she also knew from her art history that geniuses were impossible to live with.

He said, 'Sit down. Let's talk this out.'

'Peter, while Amy takes her nap I have to prepare the evening meal, do the cleaning, washing and ironing. In two hours. Anyway, there's been enough talking between us. Too much.'

He said nothing but when she went up to make his bed it was already done, the bedroom tidied meticulously, the bathroom likewise. He appeared while she was feeding Amy and sat down out of the child's line of vision, looking like a recalcitrant schoolboy. She refused to play that game, winding Amy and laying her on her changing mat without comment. When at last he spoke Amy appeared to have known of his presence all the time and ignored him.

'May I come with you this afternoon?'

Meg glanced at him without approval. 'I think you should get some air. But—'

He interrupted swiftly, 'Amy won't mind. I talked to her while she was having her nap.'

Meg tried to conceal the shock she felt at this.

He said, 'Did you think I might harm her, Meg?'

'Of course not!'

'You see, I thought you would understand. About Meredith. I wanted to tell you – before I knew about Amy. Because I thought you would understand.'

'I did understand. Of course I did.'

'Then let me come with you for a walk. You, me, Amy.'

'All right.' But she could not keep the unwillingness out of her voice.

* * *

He took the pram handle; Amy did not object to that either. They walked along Sunday Street and up to the next level, then took the path to the top of the cliff. The one that would branch off to Prospect Villa.

She said very calmly, 'Do you think this is a good idea, Peter?'

He did not reply immediately, but when they reached the turning he stopped and looked at her.

'It's up to you. But remember this. You're not very good at facing up to things. But you started coming back to Fish Cottage for Miranda's sake and gradually it has become a second home for you. The heartache has gone. For Miranda's sake, shouldn't I face up to Prospect Villa again?'

'I . . . don't know. Could you go alone?'

'No. Sorry, but no. We'll carry on up to the top road. It doesn't matter.'

'Yes. It does to you.' She turned left. 'Come on. For Miranda's sake then.'

She marched stolidly along the dirt track. It was already the second week of May and the weather, often capricious that year, was glorious. She looked out across the expanse of the Atlantic and wished with a sudden painful intensity that she was in Artemia.

They came to the front gate, still sagging on its hinges. The house seemed to have given up. Brambles masked the downstairs windows and there were loose slates everywhere on the roof.

Peter halted and stared at it. Meg stood close by the pram and reached for Amy's hand. The child cooed happily, unaware of the atmosphere.

Peter said eventually, 'Right. Now down the steps to the cove.'

'We can't take the pram down those rickety steps, Peter!'

'No. I'll carry Amy.'

He hoisted her out of her cover and held her close. She looked at her mother and then accepted the situation and pointed vigorously out to sea. Peter started down the 'private way' to Lannah Cove. Meg followed perforce, really frightened now. It was a steeper path than the one down to Mutton Cove and Peter did not have the strength of Charles. Nor the reliability. Her longing for Artemia evolved into a longing for Charles.

But there were no accidents. Peter put Amy down very carefully in the dry sand beneath the cliff and sank down near her. She bounced experimentally, then took a fistful of sand and shook it far and wide.

He laughed. 'Look at her, Meg. She's beautiful, isn't she?'

Meg too sat down. She said tremulously, 'Yes.'

'You haven't forgotten that we made her together?'

Meg did not answer. She kept her mind on the image of Charles carrying Amy. Charles, who could be trusted to the ends of the earth.

He said, 'I'll never forget. I mustn't forget. I thought all I would remember was that Meredith killed my child but then . . . as we stood there just now, and as I carried Amy down here . . . I realized that I had another child. Another daughter. I mustn't forget that, Meg.'

Meg kept her head down. She swallowed.

He said, 'Don't cry. It's all right. I know you don't love me. I can't explain what happened to us . . . that night. Perhaps it was as simple as Miranda said and we just had to get each other out of our systems.'

She looked at him. It was as if her defences were melting in the face of his sudden enormous effort to rational-ize the irrational. She had forgotten that besides genius and the crazy impulsiveness of his nature, he had courage. It seemed petty to maintain her busy, matter-of-fact front just to hold back a fear that was itself unreasoning.

So she forced herself to say honestly, 'I did love you. And afterwards . . . until Artemia . . . I wanted to be with you. Very much.'

'Oh, Meg.' His face worked. 'Thank you for saying that. Thank you.'

There was another silence. Amy pushed herself forward on to her stomach and swam frantically in the soft sand. Peter laughed.

'Look at her. She's going to be crawling any day now.'

Meg cleared her throat. 'She's too young. It says in my baby book—'

He laughed again. 'Oh, Meg! Katie crawled at seven months!'

She said, 'Sorry. I forgot you were an experienced father.' She met his eyes. 'I didn't mean . . .'

'I know what you meant.' He reached across the squirming baby and took her hand. 'Meg. We were such good friends at first. Until I tried to force you into something you didn't want. I'm sorry.'

She smiled somehow. 'In Artemia, Amy – Amy Smithers I mean – called us a mutual admiration society. You and me – we sound like a mutual apologetic society!'

'Yes. I suppose we shall always be sorry. Full of regrets.'

She shook his fingers. 'No. We mustn't be. Regrets are negative, pointless. We must be full of . . . thankfulness. We've got so much, Peter. In spite of everything, we've got so much. More than we started with!'

He sat there, thinking.

She persisted. 'I am thankful for Amy. Therefore I must be thankful for . . . that night. Mustn't I? As Alex always says – it stands to reason!'

'I suppose so.'

She held his hand tightly. 'Perhaps . . . I can be thankful even for Uncle Cedric. Has Miranda told you about Uncle Cedric?'

'Yes. He was the reason that Meredith happened in the first place.'

Meg had not realized that. 'Was he? He was the reason I could not talk to you all those years ago. And I suppose that was why I forced myself on you last year.'

'Meg! You did not force yourself on me!'

She smiled. 'Almost.'

Amy got one knee under her and moved forward six inches. They applauded and she crowed.

Peter said very quietly, 'There's still the fact that I have killed a man, Meg. I don't quite know how I'm going to live with that.'

She had hoped so much that already he had found a way. She had no facile answers and sat very still, thinking about it as logically as she could.

At last she said, 'I really do think you should tell Miranda. I'm not just trying to unload it. I think you should tell her. You see, Peter, Miranda would have done the same for you. It's – it's in your natures.'

'But Meg, you know what I'm like. She'd see in a minute that I'm . . . going mad. It would force her back home. I don't want to do that. She's come into her own now.'

'It wouldn't be like that. It would let her see how desperately she is needed.' She pulled his hand, making him meet her eyes. 'Listen. She'll have to come back home, Peter. For the children. I'm leaving. Definitely.'

'Oh God . . .'

'It's Miranda you need. Not me. I'm a better house-keeper than Miranda, but that will eventually irritate you. You can't be bothered with domesticity any more than Miranda can. And she – she knows all about acting on impulse.' She smiled. 'The only time I acted on impulse, Peter, was when I was linked to her too tightly.' She released his hand. 'You must share this with her. She is the only person who can truly accept it.'

He shifted his position slightly so that Amy had more space.

'Meg. This sort of illness thing . . . it really came to a head when I saw Amy and knew she was mine. If you go, Amy goes with you.'

'Yes. It's the only way.'

'I – I don't think I can take it.'

'You won't have to. Miranda will take most of it. That particular pain is Miranda's.'

He said again, helplessly, 'Oh God.'

'Miranda is very strong. And she has met Charles. She knows he is a good father.'

'Please – Meg—'

'It's true.'

'But there is no love between you! How can Amy possibly thrive?'

She stood up and gathered Amy to her.

'I think you can see how well she is thriving, Peter.' She shielded her eyes against the glitter of sun and water. 'I think the tide is far enough out for us to walk around the point. We can fetch the pram later.'

He scrambled to his feet. 'Meg – don't put up the shutters again! I'm sorry! Of course Amy is thriving – I didn't mean—'

She began to walk down to the shore and when they had rounded the point, she said, 'Actually Peter, I do love Charles.'

She trudged through the pools and between the boats, and above them on the harbour wall Billy Majors drew to a halt and the three older children spilled out and ran down the steps to meet them.

She thought that Edward Bracknell was probably older than Eva Kovacs, which must mean he was eighty. She had tried to make an appointment to see him at home, but he would have none of that and was at St David's station to meet her the next morning.

There was a decorous peck for her and a beaming smile for Amy.

'Such a happy name, Margaret! I met your mother only a few times but there was something about her . . . a gaiety, a joy.'

'Miranda used to be like that.'

'Yes. Miranda had it, spiced with sheer wickedness.' He stood by helplessly while she unfolded the pushchair, then held the handle like a child himself. 'I've got a taxi waiting outside, my dear. I thought we could have an early lunch somewhere and a gentle walk along the Hoe.'

'That sounds nice,' she said doubtfully, wondering about Amy's routine.

But Amy responded well to Mr Bracknell, tugging at the brim of his hat unmercifully.

'Why on earth should she do that?'

He was amused but bewildered.

'Actually—' Meg removed the clutching fingers for the second time and sat Amy in a corner of the taxi. 'Her granny in Artemia wears a similar hat. I just wondered—'

'Her granny?'

'Miss Smithers. I must have mentioned—'

'Ah. The lady who now owns the island.'

It was Meg's turn to look bewildered.

He said, 'Your husband mentioned her when we met at Easter.'

'You met Charles at Easter?'

'Um . . . yes. A question of a will.'

Meg was silent. She had assumed Charles would have his own solicitor; the man who had sorted out Eva Kovacks's affairs probably. But she knew it was no good questioning Mr Bracknell.

She said instead, teasingly, 'I thought you had retired?'

'Just occasionally I go into the office and stick an oar in!' He chuckled. 'I enjoy seeing the dismay of the other partners! Sometimes I know just how Miranda felt when she donated her raw steak to me!'

The tale of Miranda's untouched steak lasted while they got out of the taxi and into an hotel near the sea.

'I call it Miranda's "spanner technique",' he said as he surrendered his hat and coat. 'She smiles and throws one – a spanner – right into the works!'

Meg nodded wryly. Wasn't that exactly what Miranda was doing now by staying away and forcing her to look after Peter?

They had a table near the door where there was room for the pushchair next to Meg's chair. After a plate of the hotel's chicken soup, Amy settled quite happily for a sleep, thumb in mouth. Mr Bracknell waxed sentimental over her.

'Such a short time since you and Miranda were that age, my dear. And now you're both mothers.' He smiled. 'I was delighted to hear about your marriage. Really delighted.' He ducked his head almost shyly. 'I hope you and your husband will have children, Margaret. You're so like your aunt. And she would have been a wonderful mother.'

Meg said soberly, 'She *was* a wonderful mother. If only—'

'I know – I know—' he spoke quickly, still unable to face the fact of Maggie's untimely death. 'Anyway.

Dig into your fish and save a corner for some pudding. They have some wonderful puddings here. Cedric and I used to dine here during the first war when we were on leave. We thought we were no end of dogs, eating turbot and cabinet pudding so near Drake's stamping ground!'

Meg smiled, remembering Eva's reminiscences. She did a quick calculation . . . yes, he was eighty, maybe more. She asked him how he spent his days and he told her with an insouciance she found somehow moving.

'There's maintenance, my dear!' he beamed. 'Personal maintenance! Takes quite a while at my age, you know! That includes a daily walk whatever the weather – look at the sea – that sort of thing. Like to keep tuned in for the meteorological reports. Weekly visit to the theatre – that's Miranda's doing, of course. Traipse around the art galleries – that's your doing. I look in at the office. Dine at the club. And I'm still a governor down at Staple School.'

That was where Aunt Maggie had taught. Meg smiled at him gratefully. 'We have so much to thank you for. Things we don't even know about.'

'Rubbish. After Maggie died, you two girls – you kept me going.' He signalled to the waiter. 'I'm not much good at close relationships – that's what they call it these days, isn't it? Maggie and I . . . never developed. But it was there. I'm not bad at the long-distance stuff.'

He asked about puddings and turned to her to suggest rice. 'Sounds deadly dull, but it's like you used to have with your aunt. A proper rice pudding. Nutmeg, toffee-tasting skin, very creamy.'

Meg nodded, quite unable to speak. She nearly told him that it was possible to learn to have close relationships. Aunty Maggie had learned through her nieces;

Meg herself was learning through Amy. But it hardly mattered now. And he had been happy in his way and was happy now.

She said thoughtfully, 'There are so many *kinds* of happiness.'

Amy slept on so they lingered over their lunch until past two o'clock. He was worried to hear that she intended going on to London that night.

'How will you manage with the baby? Such a long journey.'

'There's a train at four. Gets in to Paddington at nine. I can have a taxi just around the corner to the flat. Or walk.'

'Your husband isn't meeting you?'

'He's away on business.'

'Take a taxi, please, Margaret. I read such awful things about London at night.'

'I'll take a taxi.'

He was slightly mollified. 'And Peter Snow? You said he was ill. Can he manage the children?'

'They'll look after each other over the weekend. I want Miranda to be back on Monday.'

'Miranda?' He was surprised. 'She's in the middle of a long run of *Midsummer Night's Dream*. I thought you knew that.'

Meg leaned back in her chair and began to fold her napkin carefully.

'That's really my main reason for seeing you today. I've been trying to get in touch with her for two weeks now.' She took a breath. 'Mr Bracknell, she has to come home. I told you Peter was not well. He was – perhaps still is – having a breakdown.'

'Good lord!' The old man sat up. 'When I met him – last autumn it was – he seemed such a sensible chap.

Determined Miranda should have her chance with the Arbitrary.'

'He's still determined. She has to break through that determination.'

'Well . . . you can get in touch with her through Miss Pugh at Exeter – you know that.'

'I've left messages. She won't get in touch with me.'

'Perhaps you haven't been explicit. Sufficiently.'

'I've said he's ill. Even Miss Pugh seems to think a few square meals will put him right.' She hesitated. 'As a matter of fact, he is much better, so in one way she's right. But . . . underneath . . . it's like a sore that's healed over but is still there.' She shook her head. 'I can't explain properly, Mr Bracknell. So much has happened between us over the years—'

He interrupted. 'In other words, Miranda knows that this little Amy here belongs to Peter. And she is leaving the field clear.'

She looked at the tablecloth and after a while said, simply, 'Yes.'

'And you don't want that.'

'No.' She looked up. 'I never really wanted it. I was like you. A long-distance person.'

'I . . . see.' He too was silent, thinking. Then he said, 'Margaret, perhaps Miranda and Peter are finished anyway. If you were sure of that, would it make a difference?'

'No,' she said quietly but emphatically.

'I'm glad.' He smiled. 'I like Charles Kovacks.' He did not wait for a reaction but went on, 'I have Miranda's address. I suggest you write to her. But I'm inclined to think it's a waste of time.'

'No. There are other things – terrible things – they need each other. Badly.'

'What about the Arbitrary?'

'It must wait. There's plenty of time for the Arbitrary.'

'I've never heard you being so definite.'

At last she too smiled. 'I've never felt quite so definite before.'

He said, 'I can give you her telephone number. You could ring tomorrow. You'll catch her on a Sunday.'

'Thank you. Thank you, Mr Bracknell.'

He took her back to St David's in another taxi and she hung out of the train window and waved to him, then held Amy's hand and waved that too. Then she settled them both into a seat and they watched the countryside roll past the window and for the first time since Charles left Keyhole, she felt hopeful.

However, five hours later when she struggled into the flat and surveyed its emptiness, her optimism waned considerably. The electricity was on and the fridge hummed from the kitchen, but dust lay visibly on the mahogany surfaces and the flat smelled musty.

It was long past Amy's bedtime and she was tetchy; Meg sat her on the floor and flew around drawing curtains, switching on the heating, putting an electric pad into the unmade cot. Amy flung herself back, found the sofa in the way and held her body furiously rigid while she screamed the place down. Meg found some powdered milk and mixed it somehow with the baby perched on one hip. She talked to her through the racket, at first coaxingly then quite sternly.

'My spirits are fairly low too, but you don't hear me complaining at the top of my voice, do you?'

Amy pressed plump knees together in a pincerlike movement and flung her torso back against Meg's aching arm.

'Also—' Meg adjusted the weight firmly. 'Also I know

a lot of things you don't. Like not only is your aunt in-communicado, but your father – sorry, stepfather though you'll probably never know that either – has disappeared.' She poured the made-up milk into a bottle; half of it went over the table. She struggled with the rubber teat one-handed. 'Now. The question is . . .' She sat down and propped Amy, still protesting, in the crook of her knee like Charles did. The child clamped her jaws on the teat. 'The question is,' Meg said loudly into the blessed silence, 'has he gone for good? In other words, has he had enough? Has he left us?' She smiled at Amy who released the bottle long enough to smile back. It should have been infinitely reassuring, but it was not.

'You see, Amy . . . Little Amy . . . if he's gone to Artemia, I can't very well go there too, can I? And I can't go down to Keele any more. So really, there's nowhere I can go. Because this flat is not my home. It's Eva's.'

Amy stopped sucking and gurgled happily.

'Oh, I know I've got you, sweetheart. I know, I know.' She rocked Amy, crooning the words at her now. And when the bottle was empty she changed her, sponged her, and put her carefully into her warm cot. And then while Amy sucked her thumb, Meg spoke again. 'You see, Amy darling, I've only just discovered that I love Charles. I've probably lost him, and I love him.' She put out the light and retreated quietly. And she said to the big sitting room, 'It's ludicrous, isn't it?'

By this time it was too late to ring Peter so she went to bed. And amazingly she slept very well; and so did Amy.

Twenty

Miranda was with her by mid-afternoon. She was thinner than ever, her eyes made up again as they had been in the old days, her hair piled on top of her head looking just as thick. She stood in the foyer, her face working uncontrollably.

'I didn't think . . . I didn't think I'd see you again,' she said and came into Meg's arms with a rush that sent them both backwards.

Meg had pulled no punches on the telephone.

'Peter is probably going mad and I am not going to look after him,' she had said bluntly as soon as Miranda came on the line.

Miranda had tried hard to make light of the statement; she was set on her course of martyrdom and could see no other.

'Look here, Miranda.' Meg had wanted Peter to be the one to tell her, but it seemed unlikely that Miranda would give him the opportunity. 'Peter did something . . . that awful night eighteen months ago . . . which he cannot now accept. Frankly I find it hard to accept too. For Amy's sake I had to come away. I think for the sake of the other children you must go back.'

'Oh, Meg. What on earth d'you mean? It's for Amy's sake that you must stay with him. You know that. The other children – they'd as soon have you as me and—'

'Stop being so damned selfish!' Meg shouted into the receiver. 'Peter killed a man because of you and all you can think of is your bloody acting! All right, so you're not the domesticated type! It bores you! But you can go back to the stage in six . . . seven . . . years. If you leave Peter on his own down there now, he might kill himself as well as Meredith!'

There was an aghast silence. Meg heard her own sobs and checked herself quickly. She waited for Miranda's incredulous questions and exclamations and general disbelief.

But when she spoke Miranda said, 'I'll be with you as soon as I can.' And the phone hummed emptily.

They sat a long time over tea. Amy, orientated again, practised her swimming techniques on the thick carpet, then rolled on to her back, laughing up at her mother and aunt, quite incredulous that one could duplicate the other so exactly.

Miranda sipped gratefully. 'The landlady at Weymouth stews up her old tea bags. This is heaven.'

'We went for a walk this morning to find milk and bread and stuff. I don't think Charles could have come to the flat at all after he left Keele.'

'You're worried about him too?'

'Not in that way. I'm terrified he might have thrown in the towel.'

'Not if I read him right. You and Amy were his. No way would he let you drift away.'

Meg smiled wryly. 'He's not a bit like that, Sis. He's lost so many people in his life. I think he assumes it is his lot.'

'Oh God. Don't start me off again! First Peter . . . now Charles—'

'You can do nothing about Charles. You can save Peter. You're the only one who can.'

'Meg, he's so gentle. The thought of him actually holding someone under the water—'

440

'A reptile. A mad thing who had almost killed his wife. Peter wasn't sure that first night that you would live.'

'I think the men of Keele must know about it. I've been in the Coastguards when they've clammed up.'

'It's the kind of thing Cornishmen are good at. Making their own justice. We've seen it before.'

'That man who fished on a Sunday. They threw him in the harbour, holed his boat.'

'Yes. And when Mrs Hitler did the washing on Sunday it all disappeared from the line. D'you remember that?'

'No. Washing would not have interested me.'

They both laughed wryly.

Miranda had a natural affinity with children and she played with Amy tirelessly. Then she told Meg of her experiences with the Arbitrary, and how significant it had been to perform in Weymouth where she had done her first proper show seventeen years before.

'In fact everything I do seems to have a sense of *déjà-vu* about it. Sometimes not *my déjà-vu* . . . does that sound crazy? Well, of course it does!' It was wonderful to Meg to hear that young laugh again. 'Sometimes I know it's what Terence did. Or Amy. Or Brett. I'm repeating history. All the time. I'm not putting it very well—'

'I understand. I felt it strongly when my Amy was born in Artemia. Eva Kovacks had given birth to Charles in the same house with her Amy in attendance.'

'Oh, Meg . . . oh, Sis . . . to think of you alone out there . . .'

'I wasn't alone. Actually I was dreading coming back to an impersonal nursing home, the baby having to be a secret from you, so no visitors. Not being able to see you – hiding from you—'

'You married Charles Kovacks so that you could see us again?'

'I can't remember now why we married. When the

441

advantages were all on my side I couldn't bear the thought of it. But then . . . he came to tell us about Eva dying and he seemed so alone. So terribly alone. And he loved Amy. I felt I was able to give him something.' She shook her head. 'Honestly, Miranda, all I know now is that it worked famously when we were on the island. *And* down at Keele. Here . . . it's not so good. Charles works long hours. Of course. And he comes home to Amy. Not to me. Not even to the comfort of the flat. Just Amy.'

Miranda glanced around her. 'He's not interested in this place perhaps? Should you move?'

Meg said painfully, 'I don't know whether . . . it's over.' She too looked around. 'And anyway, the answer isn't in moving. Not really. We have to make something of the past, not shut it off and try to forget it. It happened. And if it hadn't happened we wouldn't be here. So it's important.'

Miranda nodded thoughtfully. 'I'll have to get that across to Peter, won't I?'

'Just be with him.'

'He needs to be painting too.'

'Not yet. At least I don't think so. He spent two weeks in the Kilburn house painting his heart out. He has to learn to live properly again.'

'Meg. You know him so much better than I do.'

Meg closed her eyes with sheer exasperation. 'Sis. We've just said about the past being important. Think about it. What has happened. It's so obvious that you and Peter are right together.'

Miranda lowered her head with a kind of acceptance. And after a long pause she said, 'And you and Charles?'

But Meg would not be drawn. 'Ah. That is a different story.'

She walked round to Paddington with Miranda the next

morning and the bunting reminded her that preparations for the Jubilee celebrations were well under way at Keele.

'There's to be a bonfire on the beach. You couldn't be going back at a better time,' she promised.

But Miranda's mood had dropped overnight. 'I've done all that bit,' she commented. 'The pageant . . . everything . . .'

Meg said, 'The thing is, you won't have to do anything now. It will be happening around you.' She paused, then added, 'Sis, I sort of promised – well, I didn't but he thinks I did—' She stopped, laughing, and resumed. 'Alex – all three children – think I am coming back. Can you get over that?'

'I'll tell them I'm you,' Miranda joked.

'Don't do that,' Meg said and crossed her fingers superstitiously.

Miranda said, 'I can cope with the children. It's Peter.' She turned suddenly to Meg. 'Darling . . . I promise I'll do my best. And I'll bring up the children just as you would. But . . . later . . . when Seb is settled . . . I shall want to go back to acting.'

Meg smiled. 'I know. You don't have to make any promises to me, Sis. I just hope . . . I do hope it will be all right.'

She watched the train draw out and wheeled the pram down Praed Street and into Edgware Road. It was nine-thirty. Charles should be at the office. Her heart beat uncomfortably fast as she skirted the crowds on the wide pavement. There was a little wind blowing at the decorations and the bedecked lamp posts. She shivered suddenly, remembering the Coronation and Uncle Cedric's pleasure at booking 'a window' on the route. Amy, catching her mood, turned down her mouth and started to grizzle.

'Cheer up, darling,' Meg adjured her, leaning over the

443

pram handle to pick up a rattle. 'We're going to see Daddy.'

The words came so naturally, yet it was the first time she had referred to Charles as 'Daddy'. Of course, that's how it was. Charles was more of a father to Amy than Peter ever could be. He might have turned his back on Meg, but not on Amy. Encouraged by that thought she wheeled the pram in an exaggerated semicircle into Brown Street, and Amy sang her delight as if she knew they were on their way to see Charles.

It was more than an anticlimax when Charles's secretary welcomed them personally and settled them in a chair in her office.

'I was delighted Mr Kovacks was writing a *proper* book!' she enthused. 'I've always said to him – he ought to get some of his experiences down on paper.'

'Um . . . yes. Quite.' Meg swallowed a gabble of questions. All she really needed to know was Charles's actual whereabouts.

'I rang last week actually.' Miss McGuire's smile became roguish. 'Just to enquire how it was going, you know. When there was no reply, I did wonder if the whole thing was just an excuse for an early return to your island!'

Meg laughed obediently. It was obvious that Miss McGuire had no idea where Charles might be writing his 'proper' book. She asked if she could collect any new manuscripts for Charles and left immediately. She was angry with herself, angry with Charles. And at a completely loose end.

Back in the flat she put Amy down for her nap and stared around the sitting room. This was her home, bequeathed indirectly by Eva. She had been happy in Eva's other home and she could be happy here too. And if Charles wanted to finish their marriage, then he

444

would have to confront her and tell her so. Until that time, they were still married.

She fetched tape measure, sketch block and pencil. Charles had told her she could spend money on the place; and that was what she was going to do. She was going to make a new home, right here in Sussex Gardens.

That night Miranda telephoned and asked whether Charles was back.

'No. They don't know where he is at the office either.'

'But you're . . . OK?'

'I've brought some of his work home to do. And I'm remodelling the living room here. And spring-cleaning.'

'Steady on!'

'You too.'

It was too late for the children to be around, but there were no messages from them.

She said goodbye to Miranda then dialled Magda's number.

''Allo?'

Magda sounded terrified. Probably phone calls heralded doom for her.

Meg said, 'Magda, it's Mrs Kovacks.' She paused and when Magda forbore to tell her that Mrs Kovacks was dead, she was encouraged to go on. 'I'm back in the flat and I need some help. I want to change things around a little and have a thorough clean. Would you be willing to come in every day for a while?'

Magda said, 'I always clean for Kovacks family.'

That implied that Meg had become one of the family. She was about to confess to Magda that Charles was not there, then held back.

'Tomorrow?'

Unexpectedly Magda said, 'Pronto!'

* * *

She was nearly smiling when Meg opened the door to her the next morning.

'Is good to be home,' she said, taking off her coat as she came through to the kitchen. 'Ah . . . the little one progresses!'

Amy's latest achievement was to roll from prone to supine. She did so several times and Magda applauded.

'I have missed her,' she confessed.

Meg felt an unexpected surge of something akin to affection.

'Have some coffee, Magda. Then let me tell you what I have in mind.'

She passed her a cup of instant coffee and was almost relieved when Magda made a face of disgust; she had not changed that much. Then she told her about the new curtains and chair covers and the big coffee table and low shelves.

'The little one will reach easily,' Magda warned.

'I don't want everything to be out of her sight. I know it will be awkward for a few months but I'd like her to be able to see all these marvellous things. The display cabinets make the room look like a museum. Don't you agree?'

'It is not for me to say.'

'I want you to say, Magda. You are part of this place. I need your opinion!'

Magda almost smiled for the second time that day.

'Perhaps . . . a few higher shelves for the very precious books and *objets*. But it is your saying. And Mr Kovacks.'

Meg led the way into the living room. 'This is a surprise for Mr Kovacks, Magda.' She waited for some serious objections and when they did not come she said, 'Your idea is excellent. Yes. Charles's lovely books and the glass . . .'

They moved around, talking, and then, shocking in its

446

unexpectedness, Magda laughed. It was the first time Meg had heard the sound and she looked round, startled and apprehensive.

'It is the little one!' explained Magda. 'Look!'

Amy had followed them through the kitchen door. At last on her hands and knees she made for the furniture and pulled herself upright. The two women knelt by her, united in their admiration.

After that it was as if they'd been together all their lives. When it was time for Amy's walk Magda made out a shopping list and told Meg where to go.

'I make goulash for your supper,' she promised. 'A proper goulash.'

'Oh . . . Magda. I was going to have an egg. Well, that's fine. If you will stay and have some with me.'

Magda said nothing and Meg took that as grateful acceptance and carried Amy down to her pram.

Two days later the post brought a letter from Amy, forwarded from Cornwall. Meg skimmed it hastily. No mention of Charles. Was Amy covering for him or was she as ignorant of his whereabouts as everyone else? She read carefully for a hint of evasion. Amy was replying to the frantic letter Meg had written from Keele and her advice was uncompromising. 'Let Charles take over. He will find Miranda for you. Probably drive her back home and take you out of the situation. You are not the person to help, Meg. Accept that. Your presence there will make things worse, not better. Peter imagines he is in love with both of you and if you stay it will either increase his delusion, or he will transfer all his passion to you. Then he will hate himself. He might try to kill himself. He might even try to kill you. Or Amy. Sorry to be the voice of doom, but I am far enough away to see things very coldly. Let Charles rescue you, Meg. Lean on Charles. Force him to be strong again. He obviously knew that Peter was offstage somewhere and he has withdrawn. Not good. Force him to fight.'

Meg frowned. *Had* Charles guessed? How? If only she knew where he was. She hated the thought of him alone, unanchored, with no plans.

Magda came with her to choose furniture. She was obviously pleased with the arrangement, though she kept saying that London streets were no place for a small Kovacks and she would have been better looking after Amy at home while Meg did the choosing. Meg said seriously, 'I want it to be a surprise for Mr Kovacks, not a shock. And you are Hungarian like him, so I need your eye, Magda.'

Magda succumbed and gave in unequivocally. Meg had thought of white shelving. Magda pointed out that her expertise with the furniture polish would go unnoticed on white paint.

'Rosewood. The Kovacks have always had rosewood,' she maintained.

Meg nodded. Rosewood would look better with the Edwardian ceilings.

'Also we need playpen. For Amy,' Magda added. 'Now that she can crawl she will be everywhere.'

They chose a playpen, this time with Amy's help. It was wonderful to see that Magda was enjoying herself. Suddenly Meg could understand Aunt Maggie's effort on behalf of the Hungarian refugees.

She said, 'You must be missing Mr Kovacks as much as I am, Magda. You have been so kind.'

Magda flushed. 'It is you . . . I am old and not of your kin. It was difficult.'

'Yes. For both of us.'

'Will Mr Kovacks finish the book before the Jubilee?'

Meg could not remember mentioning the book. She said honestly, 'I don't know.'

'He will come home for that day only perhaps?'

Meg said again, 'I don't know.'

'He surely will! I will cook the goulash again – yes? A special Jubilee dinner!'

'Well . . .' Meg made heavy weather of getting the pram down a kerb. 'I'm not sure . . . he hasn't said exactly when . . .'

Magda nodded understandingly. 'He wishes to be in-communicado. But for such a special day . . . you could go to the house and bring him back. In a taxi.'

'The house?'

'Your house. Where he writes the book.'

Meg gripped the handle of the pram very hard. She said, 'Did he . . . did he tell you he did not wish to be disturbed?'

'Yes.'

'I see.'

They manoeuvred the pram into the foyer and she busied herself putting Amy down for a rest. Later, before Magda left, she said, 'I'll think about your suggestion. For next Tuesday. Thank you very much, Magda. I appreciate . . . everything.'

Magda smiled at her; she almost beamed.

Miranda could not believe she had been away from home a mere three weeks. So much had happened in that time; she had known that Peter had been ill. His attitude to her after Meredith had been that of father to child. She had been grateful in one way, but there had also been a feeling of rejection. He met her at Penzance and greeted her fondly.

'Darling, I'm sorry I took the car that day. Was it very inconvenient?'

She had almost forgotten that. She kissed his cheek; he did not offer his lips.

'It didn't matter at all. Oliver and Marjorie both run cars.'

She stared at him as they walked out of the station. He had a curious smile fixed on his lips and his eyes looked straight ahead.

'Are the kids OK?' she asked.

'I think so. They missed you when you went off on Saturday. They'll be glad to see you tonight.'

She said firmly, 'It was Meg who went off on Saturday, darling. I was at Weymouth.'

'Yes. I meant Meg.'

He opened the door for her. She settled into the passenger seat and watched him in the mirror as he put her case into the boot. If Meg had not told her how ill he had been she would not have known. He had been thin and haggard when she left and he was still thin and haggard.

She waited until he was turning the ignition key, then said, 'Hang on. If we do a bit of shopping here, it would be time to meet the kids. It's three o'clock already.'

'Oh, I don't meet them.' He looked at her as if surprised. 'Billy Majors meets them. And takes them in the morning.'

'But you were meeting them before Easter.'

'Yes. But . . . I've not been very well, Miranda. Sorry.'

She nodded. 'Meg told me.' She smiled full at him but his gaze slid away. She said, 'Don't worry, my darling. Everything will be all right now.'

He said nothing. After a while he put the car into gear and drove out on to the road.

If she had needed a more effusive welcome, the children gave it to her. Sebastian clung to her possessively and asked her twice if she still loved him. Katie said, 'I do understand about you being an actress, Miranda. But you're not off again just yet, are you?'

And Alex shadow-boxed in front of her and said belligerently, 'I got in, Ma! You thought I wouldn't, but I did! And Zach. We need to buy lots of things. They play rugby as well as soccer.'

Peter had disappeared so she drew them to her and asked how he was.

'He's fine,' Katie said sturdily. 'He worked like stink all through the weekend. We hardly saw him!'

Miranda was startled at the thought of the three children more or less looking after themselves.

Sebastian said, 'He was so ill at first, Mummy. Aunt Meg was frightened he might die.'

'Did she say that?'

'No. But you could tell.'

'Poor Meg.' Miranda looked at Katie. 'I've opted out of *Dream* – and the rest of the summer season.'

'So you'll be looking after Dad?' Alex said.

'And Katie and Seb.'

Alex acknowledged that he could look after himself by making a hideous face.

Then he said seriously, 'I promised Aunt Meg I'd look after things. But it's hard work.'

Miranda smiled. 'It is, isn't it?'

She took a sort of high tea up to the attic and sat with Peter while he ate it. He was working on another portrait of Meg. Miranda tried to feel some jealousy, but there was none. She stared at him as he cleaned his brushes and wondered in a clinical way if he had slept with Meg during the last ten days.

He sat on the floor at her feet and forked some pickled mackerel into his mouth. 'Good,' he said through it.

She smiled. 'I didn't realize how thin you were getting.'

'I was at Meg's place in London for a while. Can't remember how long. Didn't bother much with meals.'

'You were working all the time?'

'Mm.'

'What have you done with the work?'

'Still there. When I spoke to you . . . locked up . . . left the keys in Kovacks's office. I'll have to get the agency to pick them up, I suppose.'

'Yes.' She poured tea and passed it to him. 'What were you painting?'

He jerked his head at the easel. 'All of Meg.'

'How many?'

'Don't know. Seven. Eight perhaps.'

The thought of eight portraits of Meg stacked along the walls of the Kilburn house gave her a strange feeling of unreality. She imagined it was how Peter felt all the time.

She stared out of the dormer at the familiar view. Since Meredith, Keele had offered a safe haven; but she had left that haven and found some kind of independence.

She said, 'I'm going downstairs to organize the kids into bed. Will you come and say goodnight to them?'

'Yes.'

But she knew he would not.

That night she brushed out her hair and creamed the make-up from her face and got into her side of the big double bed. The sheets were pristine. Peter must have changed the bed. Why?

It was midnight when he opened the door and stood there indecisively.

'I saw the light.' He seemed to be making an excuse for his presence.

Miranda put down her book. 'I was just coming to see where you'd got to. You mustn't work so hard, Peter.'

He came into the room. He looked like a zombie.

'No,' he said, staring at her, apparently mesmerized.

She said, 'There's some coffee in the Thermos on the table if you—'

'No,' he said again, coming to the foot of the bed.

'Well then . . . come on into bed for goodness' sake. It's almost half-past twelve and I have to be up at seven for the kids!'

He started to strip off his clothes, his eyes still on her, devouring her.

He said, 'I never thought . . . not again . . . I never thought . . .'

And quite suddenly she knew that he was talking to Meg.

For an instant she was still, preparing herself for the violent denial, the anguish of knowing that his passion could still be aroused for her sister if not for herself. And then the incipient violence left her, drained away and replaced by a terrible pity.

She held out her arms. 'Peter,' she said quietly.

He came into them as Sebastian so often did and clung to her as if he were drowning.

'Meg . . . am I really going mad? . . . oh, darling girl. I'm sorry . . . so sorry . . . I shouldn't have told you . . .'

She bowed her head to kiss his. 'It's all right, darling. All right,' she murmured.

And then he whispered brokenly, 'Oh Meg. I can't. I can't even do that . . . I can't, Meg. I can't.'

She stroked his face, murmuring reassurance, kissing him, reaching for a tissue to dry his tears. After a very long time he seemed to sleep and she put the light out and fitted her head on to the pillow next to his. Her questions were answered. He had not slept with Meg. He never would.

She smiled painfully into the darkness. She would have to learn how to love him differently now. And perhaps her few hours in Gladys Pugh's house with Brett had helped.

She kissed her husband's face and closed her eyes.

Meg hardly knew what to do. She felt she had to respect Charles's obvious wish to be alone and tried to take comfort from the fact that he was in her house. That must mean something. Surely if he had decided to end their relationship he would have gone to an hotel?

She tried to question Magda without appearing to do so.

'How on earth is he managing without any domestic help? He's so hopeless –' That was a cruel injustice. Charles might have been uninterested in the London flat, but in Artemia and Keele he had more than pulled his weight.

But Magda approved of men who did not know how to open tins.

'I offered to go each day.' Her shoulders touched her ears in an enormous shrug. 'He would have none of it. That is why it is good to come to you.' She smiled; it was becoming habitual. 'And when I see that you accept his – his –' She gave up. 'When he is doing a book he is like this?'

'I expect so.' Meg relaxed some of her guard. 'You know him better than me, Magda.'

'Oh no. Not so.' But she was pleased all over again and could be heard singing a strange Magyar song as she went about her work. Amy loved it and echoed it with a moon song.

Miraculously, the furniture and curtains arrived earlier than the promised date. The flat changed practically overnight. The low tables and units seemed to lower the ceilings. The Sanderson fabrics gave warmth. Meg thought of Charles all the time; she forgot to phone Miranda; the manuscripts she had brought home with her became vitally important. She read them carefully, made

454

notes. She poured her heart out in a letter to Amy.

'I love him, Amy. I know now how Peter felt all those years ago; his friendship for me developed into a love. Mine didn't. I loved him only through Miranda. Perhaps one day Charles will grow to love me through Little Amy. If only he would come home – yes, it is a home now and becoming more so every day as Amy crawls around it leaving a trail of soft toys, rattles, rag books. Magda and I have been working nearly all the daylight hours to get things shipshape for him, though heaven knows whether he will ever see it. There were three manuscripts waiting for him in the office and . . .'

The phone rang and she leapt for it. It was Miranda. She just stopped herself from sounding disappointed.

'How are you now, darling? Nearly a week. Are things settling?'

'In a way.'

'Can't you talk? Is Peter there?'

'I'm on my own. I persuaded him to go to the Coastguards. The kids are in bed.'

'The Coastguards – that sounds marvellously normal.'

'Yes.'

Meg glanced at the clock. Ten-fifteen. Not late enough for Miranda to worry.

'Well?' she asked.

'Nothing. It's just that . . . we've got to work out a different . . . thing.'

'How do you mean?'

'Nothing. Are you still alone?'

'Yes and no. Magda comes in every day.'

'Oh God.'

'No. It's fine. Really. I'm revamping the living room and I couldn't have done it without her.'

'What about Charles?'

'Well, I know where he is. The Kilburn house.'

'*Your* place?'

'Yes. He told Magda. No-one else knows. Not even his secretary.'

'How strange. Both Charles and Peter. A sort of refuge from us?' Miranda gave a strained laugh.

'I hadn't thought of it like that. I hope – I'm hoping so much – that he will come home for the Jubilee day. Magda is planning an enormous goulash.'

'Have you asked him?'

'No. I have to wait. I can't force Charles to do anything.'

'You could send him an invitation.'

Meg laughed but still said, 'No, I don't think so.'

'Listen, Sis. It's your house. You ought to go and check on it. Nothing to do with Charles!'

Meg continued to laugh. 'Miranda . . . you are still devious!'

'Am I?' the young-old voice sounded sad. 'I think I need to be now.' Meg waited, then said, 'Can't you tell me more?'

'Nothing to tell really. Now and then he thinks I'm you.'

'Oh Sis. I'm so sorry.'

'It doesn't worry me. It's just that . . . well, we were sort of instant lovers, weren't we? We're not lovers any more. We have to learn to be friends. It will take time.'

Meg said nothing; the irony of their situations struck her forcibly.

Miranda said, 'It's OK, Sis. I'm not copping out. He . . . he's worth every second of time.' She paused, then added, 'You should see the portrait of you he's doing. It's different. Wild and uninhibited—'

'Oh, darling . . . it's *you*! He might call it Meg, but it's you!'

Miranda said, 'Well, whatever . . . it's amazing.' She

sighed. 'Meg, don't waste time sitting there. Go and see Charles.'

Meg lifted her head and stared at her new Sanderson fabrics. 'I'll see,' she said.

She went back to her letter. '*The Stone Garden* continues to do well over here. How is it over there? Have you finished "The Devil's Advocate"? I am so looking forward to next month when I hope to bring Amy to see you again. You will be very surprised at her progress. But she still sings her moon songs . . .'

Tuesday the seventh dawned bright but chilly. Magda arrived at eight-thirty as usual and began getting things out of the fridge.

'You have heard from Mr Kovacks?' she asked when Meg carried Amy in fresh from her bath.

Meg just shook her head.

Magda pursed her lips. 'You should telephone. How will he know about the goulash if you don't tell him?'

Meg said, 'He knows it is Jubilee day, Magda! If he wishes to work through it—'

'He cannot work all night!'

'He'll just turn up. You see.'

But by the afternoon there was no sign of Charles and the celebrations were mounting to fever pitch in the city. Magda and Meg watched the television continuously and at three o'clock they carried Amy into Hyde Park to catch a glimpse of the celebrations. Everywhere was packed to capacity and they were jostled and bewildered.

'We see better on the television!' Magda said close to her ear. 'Amy does not like so much people.'

Meg nodded and they fought their way back. It was all turning into an anticlimax for them. Meg looked at Magda's drooping mouth and made up her mind.

She went to the telephone and dialled her own familiar

number. A high-pitched whine was all she got. She raised her brows at Magda and dialled the operator.

'I'm afraid the receiver has been removed, madam,' the girl's voice came back after a while.

Meg replaced her telephone.

'All right. He's obviously there and has taken the phone off the hook. If you will stay with Amy, I'll grab a taxi and go up to Kilburn.'

Magda revived on the instant.

'It is best,' she agreed, smiling again and whisking Amy on to her knee as if for instant protection. 'I take very great good care of Amy. And you fetch her father.'

It sounded very simple and straightforward.

It was not. For one thing, taxis were at a premium that day. Eventually Meg managed to find one outside the very nursing home into which Charles had booked her last autumn. Even so it was five o'clock when it parked behind Charles's BMW outside number seventeen. She paid it off thankfully and walked to the front door feeling unbelievably self-conscious. She had always watched the arrival of visitors from the window; it would have been so much better if she could have sprung a surprise on Charles.

But in the event all her embarrassment was wasted because there was no reply to her knock.

She tried several times, then walked over the tiny front garden to peer through the window. No-one was in the living room and the door to the kitchen was firmly shut. She frowned, suddenly apprehensive. Supposing Charles had been ill – or worse – and no-one knew? She remembered him saying many years ago that it was important to know your neighbours. But her neighbours all thought she was in Artemia and the house let to a series of anonymous tenants.

She scrabbled anxiously inside her handbag and eventually located the keys in a jumble of pens at the bottom. Praying he had not dropped the latch on the door, she fitted the key in carefully. It turned. She went inside.

She glanced quickly into the big kitchen. It was a clutter, but no-one was there. She took the spiral stairs as fast as she could. The bedroom and bathroom were empty. Charles's pyjamas and shaving kit were in the bathroom. She went back downstairs again and looked in the kitchen for signs of a meal.

The pots and pans were shining. There was a cup and saucer on the table and a lot of papers. But what arrested her attention were the pictures. At intervals around the walls were placed eight canvases. She recognized Peter's work immediately. In any case, who else would have painted a series of Miranda or Meg portraits?

She stood very still, staring at them. It was like seeing Miranda and herself being created. Each one, though obviously of the same person, was subtly different. The poses were varied, but whether the face was looking over its shoulder, or coming through a typical Keele mist, or half seen through a cloud of hair, it was an evolving face. And someone – Peter or Charles – had arranged them in order. The first girl could have been seventeen. She was raw, frightened even, hiding something. The last girl had an air of quiet self-knowledge and might have been forty. In between there were girls with half-smiles, cunning, vixen-like; and one, exquisitely beautiful, with hair piled on top of her head, bewildered and surprised.

Meg felt tears on her face. The kitchen started to shake with a passing train and she said aloud, 'Oh God, please help him.' And did not know if she meant Charles or Peter. Or both.

When at last she turned slowly into the living room, the day had lost its brightness; she glanced at her watch. It was half-past six. She had been at the house over an hour. And there was still no sign of Charles.

Outside she stood again, completely indecisive. There would be no taxis going back into town; she would have to walk. It was such a letdown she hardly knew what to do. Magda waiting at home with that goulash; Charles doubtless enjoying the celebrations with someone . . . maybe in this very road . . . or Jill Forsythe. Anyway not here.

She trailed back down the endless road as far as Maida Vale. Her head ached; her legs ached. It was only about four miles; it seemed like forty.

She saw him coming towards her long before he saw her. He was walking purposefully almost in the middle of the road, his eyes on the traffic. She recognized his good suit; he had taken off the jacket and slung it over one shoulder and she thought that was rather foolish because it was quite cold now. She stopped walking and stood by a large plane tree watching him, noting separate things about him that made up the whole person. He'd always had that vigour, but since losing weight last summer it was much more obvious. His long strides were also very fast and he swung his free arm energetically as if pumping himself along. And his dark hair was not dry and wiry like Peter's and Alex's. It was rather floppy and because it needed cutting, it fell over his forehead and made him look younger than he was. She wondered if he took after his father, Androulis. He seemed suddenly more Greek than Hungarian.

And then he saw her and his relief was evident. He waved frantically and accelerated still more as if he expected her to run away.

'Oh, I'm glad to see you!' He arrived at a run and leaned against the tree, panting a laugh, looking very naturally at her as if they'd been together a few hours before.

'I've been to the flat – must have arrived about ten minutes after you left. We waited thinking you'd come straight back in your taxi. Then I realized there'd be no taxis . . .' He shook his head. 'I'm just so glad to see you!' he concluded helplessly.

She realized with a surge of gratitude that it was going to be all right. He had been away working and now he was back. There were no awful undercurrents after all; she had dreamed them up.

She laughed too with relief. 'Same here!' She shook her head. 'I was beginning to wonder if you were ill somewhere. You'd cut yourself off so completely—'

'Magda knew where I was.'

'She didn't tell me.'

'She didn't . . . then how did you know?'

'Well, she assumed I knew. It slipped out. Oh, Charles . . . this is marvellous.'

'Yes.' He turned and put a hand beneath her elbow. 'Let's go back and eat Magda's Jubilee supper, shall we?'

'That would be great. Oh, Charles . . .' She nearly said then and there how much she loved him. Instead she smiled beatifically. 'Just think. In another month we're going to Artemia!'

And he smiled back. 'So we are,' he agreed.

Twenty-one

In Keyhole the harbour was closed to traffic all day and the celebrations began in the afternoon with races and games for the children, fancy-dress parades, and entertainments. There was a bun-and-jelly tea at half-past four, and then a hiatus while everything was cleared for the evening. As the tide went out the lifeboat crew set up the displays of fireworks, and as soon as it was dusk the adult revelry began.

The Snow children were in their element. Sebastian and Katie won the under-ten three-legged race. Zach and Alex won the fancy dress as Batman and Robin. They joined with Miranda and Janis from the Coastguards in a barber-shop quintet. They cheered the Queen and Prince Philip and Prince Charles and Princess Anne and Prince Andrew and Prince Edward louder than anyone else.

Miranda had thrown herself into it all at the very last minute. After her telephone call to Meg on the Sunday, she started on the fancy dresses for the children and then she made repeated batches of small cakes until the whole house smelled like a bakery. Sebastian, Katie and two of their friends crayoned tiny Union Jacks and stuck one in each cake. Janis came up to help and she and Miranda started singing one of the songs from the Newlyn Amateurs' last Gilbert and Sullivan production; the Snow children joined in; the barber-shop quintet was born.

There had not been such a celebration in Fish Cottage before and Peter was forced to respond.

'They could do with your help with the fireworks, boy,' Janis told him, keeping a watchful eye on him as he drifted past the wire trays of cakes. But Peter was not interested in the food.

'I think I'll stay in. It's going to be noisy,' he said in the toneless voice he often used these days.

'Lisen 'ere, m'boy.' Janis had no patience with such lethargy. 'You're on standby crew for the *Solomon*, aren't you?'

'Well . . . I was.'

'No-one told me you'd resigned!'

Alex looked up warily at his father. They all tended to talk to him very gently since his illness. Miranda stooped by the oven, taking out more cakes as if opting out of the conversation.

'I haven't actually resigned. No.'

'Then you'd best give 'em a hand now and then,' Janis said smartly. 'You always used to say you liked to paint 'em when they was working. In which case you'll have to go and work with them, won't you?'

Peter half smiled. 'I suppose I will,' he said.

Magda stayed the night at Sussex Gardens. She had met Charles and Meg in the foyer, Amy in her arms, her face split almost into two by the smile which now seemed a fixture. She then went into the kitchen and produced a tray of tea and scones and watched Charles crawling around the furniture with Amy.

'Is better than that thing,' she pronounced, jerking a scornful head at the television.

Charles lifted his head and grinned. 'You didn't tell me she was crawling!'

Magda spread her hands. 'We know you wish for

463

complete silence from everyone in which to write your book!'

'But something marvellous – cataclysmic – like this!' he protested.

It was all so . . . normal. Meg did not know what to think. She could sense happiness beginning to spread through her. It was almost frightening.

She said, 'She was pampered by the other children down in Keele, of course. And when we arrived back here she was as cross as two sticks. But then, quite suddenly—'

'She enjoyed us doing the changing—' Magda waved an expansive hand around the refurbished room.

Charles sat back and surveyed it all from Amy's viewpoint. He nodded.

'It looks good from any angle. But from here – it's much more accessible.' He met Meg's gaze and smiled. 'Thank you,' he said.

'You're sure?' She looked around. It was certainly different. 'I mean . . . Eva's stuff—'

'I like to be able to see it. Especially that pair of satin shoes. I can remember my mother when she was still quite young. She was very conservative. But when it came to shoes . . . she had what was known as aristocratic feet. Very narrow with – ' he laughed deprecatingly – 'a well-turned ankle!'

Meg wanted so much to put her arms around him. Instead she said, 'It was Magda's idea to put your books and most of the glass higher up.'

'Well done, Magda.'

The walnut face flushed darkly with pleasure.

'I have to turn the heat down on the goulash,' she said and made for the kitchen.

Meg moved a chair to make room for Amy's chosen route and sat down. Charles stayed where he was on the floor.

He said, 'I am writing about Eva. A few illustrations. What I can remember of Buda. And Androulis. And Amy.'

Meg felt her face open wide with surprise and pleasure. 'Charles! I thought . . . I didn't realize . . .'

'Neither did I.' He stretched his legs in front of him and Amy clambered over them. 'At first . . . when I left you . . . I went to the office and sat around like a zombie for the rest of that day. Then I found the keys of your house. I didn't want to come to the flat – it would have been unbearably empty. So I went to Kilburn. After all, you and I have . . . well, anyway, I went there. And found Peter's portraits.'

The bubble of happiness bounced like a stone to the pit of her stomach.

'Charles, they are the work of a man obsessed!'

'Yes. I saw that. They are also the work of a genius.'

She said passionately, 'I hate them!'

'I knew you would. That was why I didn't take them to Peter's agency immediately. I wanted to ask you about them first. But they'll have to be exhibited. Separately they're brilliant. Together they represent a masterpiece.'

'He – he can't tell the difference between Miranda and me any more!'

'Oh, he can. Just because some of those portraits contain both of you, does not mean he cannot see the difference. It is the difference which fascinates him.' He looked at her. 'It was the difference which fascinated me.'

She was silent, unexpectedly close to tears.

He said, 'I'm sorry, Meg. I didn't want to upset you. Not this evening of all evenings.' He rescued Amy from halfway beneath the sofa and set her on course again. 'Tell you what. Let's see if Magda will stay the night. Then we could go out and watch the fireworks.'

She half smiled. 'It would be marvellous.'

'We'll do that.' He leaned forward and pointed a finger at the approaching Amy; she squealed her delight at the new game. He said, 'Meg . . . those portraits . . . they helped me. Enormously. Without them – without knowing your true feelings – I could not have settled down to wait for you and start my book. I hadn't even thought of the book until I saw them . . . lived with them.'

She faltered, 'I don't understand. I thought they would make you terribly unhappy.'

'At first . . . the shock. Then . . . understanding. Your link with Miranda. Sometimes so wonderful. Sometimes so terrifying.'

She nodded. 'Yes.'

'I know so little about you. But you told me once about your uncle. And then the experience Miranda had with the man who turned up last year.'

'Yes.' She had tried to explain Miranda to him and had known he had not understood.

'Miranda's experiences were yours. Weren't they? Maybe if it had not been for your uncle . . . but because of that, the terror of her meetings with that crazy man who committed suicide were yours.'

She said stonily, 'He did not commit suicide. Peter killed him.'

'He . . . what? Oh my God. Did he tell you so?' Charles pushed himself on to his knees, staring at her.

'Yes. He arrived the day you left. Was it only three weeks ago? A bit longer . . . anyway, he was in a terrible state. I thought he might die that night. And I couldn't tell anyone—'

'Meg. I'm sorry. God, I'm so sorry. I thought—'

'Yes, I know. I had an eternity to work it all out from your angle. Only two weeks, but it seemed like an eternity. Miranda refused to get in touch with me. I couldn't contact you . . . it was awful.'

466

'I should have left a message at the office.'

'I wouldn't have rung the Kilburn number. I would have assumed that you did not wish to hear from me.' She got up and went to the window and lifted the curtain slightly. A single firework shot into the darkening sky. She said, 'He told me about a week later. When he began to get better physically.'

Charles stayed where he was on his knees, staring at her back.

At last he said, 'You have to forget it. There is nothing you can do. Miranda—'

'That is what I told her. But from what she said when she telephoned, it seems he still thinks I am down there.'

'He will get over that. It's the shock – after all this time – coming out—'

'I know. He should have professional help.'

Charles said, 'It might push him over the edge.'

She lowered her head and made a sound like a sob.

He said strongly, 'Meg, I cannot tell you how sorry I am. When you needed my help, I wasn't there.'

'You couldn't have helped. Only Miranda could do that. You were the last person, Charles. Amy said in a letter that he might try to kill me. Or Little Amy. He wouldn't have done that. But I think he would have tried to kill you if you'd appeared.'

Charles gathered Amy into his arms and stood up.

'Listen, Meg. I have to say this. You do not love Peter Snow. Because of Miranda you thought you did. You thought he was more than a friend and an admired painter. That was how Amy came about. But—'

She interrupted him. 'I know. I know this very well.'

He removed Amy's thumb and forefinger from his nose. 'All right. Then go one step forward. Because of Peter Snow you are convinced that love and friendship are quite separate.' He shifted the child to his shoulders where she grabbed two handfuls of hair. 'That is not so.' He laughed. 'It is impossible to say more with Amy removing my hair! But will you please think about that? You can be good friends . . . wonderful companions . . . and also be in love.'

She turned at last and saw that his eyes were streaming. She reached up, laughing, and removed Amy from his shoulders, and from the safety of her daughter's clutching arms she said simply, 'I know that too, Charles. What I do not know is whether it works for you too.'

When Magda came in to announce that dinner was served, they appeared to be waltzing with Amy clutched between them and a great deal of laughter mingled with one of her louder moon songs.

Miranda had herded the overexcited children into bed and quietened them with Meg's old moonbeam story, and still there was no sign of Peter.

She rang the Coastguards and managed to get hold of Janis.

'I know it's crowded down there but surely someone has seen him?' she insisted after Janis had explained at the top of her voice the hopelessness of knowing who was in the bar and who wasn't.

'Hang on. I've just spotted Billy.'

There were raucous shouts of enquiry against a constant roar. Arthur was doing a good trade.

'No. He's not bin in. Last anyone saw of him was just beyond the West Pier, setting up the big rockets there.'

'*Beyond* the pier?'

'On them flat rocks. Towards Pezazz Point.'

'The tide was going out. He could have gone to the lifeboat house.'

'Suppose so.' Even at full volume Janis sounded doubtful.

'When you spoke about being a relief crew member, it seemed to get his attention. I wondered . . . he might be sketching the *Solomon* or something.'

'Sounds like him. Listen – I'll give you a ring if he comes in. Or if I hear anything.'

'Thanks, Janis.' Miranda hesitated. It wasn't a good time to thank Janis now, but perhaps there would not ever be a good time. 'Jan, I just wanted to say . . . we haven't always seen eye to eye, but you've been so good to us lately. Thank you.'

'Oh . . . m'dear . . . 'tis a pleasure!' Janis sounded almost shy. Miranda was glad she had spoken.

She waited another hour, boiling the kettle, and letting it cool, then she went upstairs. Alex was sitting up in bed gluing a model boat; something that was strictly forbidden.

'Ma – I'm sorry. It was just that I couldn't get to sleep and I thought Dad might be interested . . . it's the lifeboat. The *Solomon*.'

Miranda sat on the end of the bed where it was comparatively uncluttered.

'Alex, I hate to ask you this. But could you . . . just keep an eye on things for half an hour?'

''Course, Ma. You and Dad going to the pub?'

'No.' She decided on the truth. 'Dad hasn't come in yet. I'm just a bit worried about him. I think he's down at the lifeboat station.'

Alex was instantly alarmed. Since the events of the last eighteen months he had ceased taking his parents for granted.

'I'll come with you,' he said.

'No, darling. Much as I'd like that, someone has to be here. I'd like you to get up, actually. Man the phone.

If you're worried, ring the Coastguards. Janis can be with you in under five minutes. I won't be that long myself.'

'OK. Yes. OK, Ma.' He pushed his model bits into the lid of a box and got out of bed. 'Don't worry. He'll be all right.'

'What about you?'

'I'll be all right. We'll all be all right.'

They struggled downstairs with his model and Miranda slid into a short coat. It had started to rain. She shivered and shoved her hair inside the collar of the coat. It was the kind of Keele weather she hated and Peter loved. Mysterious and ethereal, or damp and dreary, depending on your point of view. She walked along the harbour rail until she came to a flight of steps; the same flight she and Peter had climbed so soggily twelve years ago. She took them carefully one at a time; they were slimy with weed. The coloured fairy lights strung between the lamp posts lit the empty harbour eerily. The boats had all moored out to sea so that there would be room for the firework display. She ran across the empty sand and splashed through the puddles at the end of the piers. She had turned left towards the lifeboat house when suddenly she paused. The tide was a very long way out; as it had been the day she walked around the sand to meet Meredith in Lannah Cove. She turned to her right and sloshed through ankle-deep water and between the rocks of Lannah headland and eventually came into the sheltered cove. She was breathing heavily and the rain no longer felt cold. It was completely dark, the stars hidden behind the low cloud. There wasn't a hope of seeing him even if he were here. It was much more likely he was sketching in the lifeboat house. She was annoyed with herself for her suspicions. She walked up to the dry sand and looked out to the line of surf where the sea was beginning to turn.

And then she saw him. She knew immediately what the flash of phosphorescence meant. They had been out bathing at night before and marvelled at the sudden gleams of light around their moving bodies. And this was the steady repeated flash of a swimmer moving out to sea.

Just for a moment she tried to convince herself he might be swimming for the sheer pleasure of it. But Peter normally swam overarm, ploughing through the water like an athlete. This was a slow breaststroke. Even at this distance with so little to go on, Miranda felt his despair.

She tore off her waterlogged sandals and jeans, threw her coat on top of them, rushed down to the water's edge. She hardly noticed the cold, diving into the first of the waves when she was still knee-deep, arming her way frantically through the water, sucking in air on every fourth stroke, keeping her body as straight as an arrow. Peter was two hundred yards out to sea at the very most and moving slowly, but it seemed to take an hour to reach him. She trod water twice, searching the darkness frantically without seeing him. The third time his shoulders, still in the white shirt he had been wearing all day, appeared to her left. He had not seen her.

She kept him in sight while she got her breath and her bearings. When the swell lifted her she searched for any nearby boats at anchor. They were all too far out; it would be quicker to swim back to the shore. She wondered if she had the strength for the return trip; if he would drag her down with him; she did not want to die.

'Peter!'

She called his name without urgency; as if they might be meeting accidentally during a perfectly ordinary swim. His arms stopped moving and he turned on to his back to locate her.

'Here! Peter!' She held up her hand and then swam

gently towards him. 'I couldn't see you for ages.' She spat water and pushed her hair behind her ears.

He said something. She could not hear separate words; he was far gone.

She said, 'Time to go home, darling. Do you need some help?'

He said in a normal voice, 'No thank you, Meg.' And turned over to begin swimming out to sea again.

She got in front of him easily, thanking God for her early training in this same sea with Meg.

'I'm Miranda, Peter. Not Meg. Miranda.' She spluttered a little on her name. Then spat and went on loudly, 'I am your wife. Stop swimming. Turn on your back. I'm going to take you home.'

He did stop for a moment, dashing water from his eyes, trying to focus her. But then he said, 'No,' and moved his arms wearily.

She came alongside him.

'Darling. Just do as I say. You know I cannot manage without you. I'm responsible for the death of our child and for the death of that man, Meredith. I cannot be responsible for your death too.'

It was said in spurts, in loud clusters of words, against the invasive water. He continued to swim towards the darkness with laboured but steady strokes for so long that she thought he was ignoring her. She swam on her side, facing him, keeping pace with him easily. She began to feel a real fear.

Then suddenly his arms stopped. He appeared to be treading water but only just. Then he tried to speak. She reached out and held him beneath his armpits.

He said, 'I can't even do this properly.'

'Oh, Peter . . .' she was weeping. 'I don't care – I just don't care. Be with me. That's all.'

She turned him on to his back and drew his head on

to her midriff. Slowly they began the long swim to the shore. He did not struggle. Occasionally she could hear him speaking but could not make out the words. She went through all the stages of exhaustion from aching muscles to a kind of limbo. When she thought she must simply stop, he would kick with his legs and send them shooting forward for a few yards. And then he had her hands in his and he was saying clearly, 'We're there. It's all right. We're there.'

They crawled up the beach side by side on hands and knees. It had stopped raining and the air felt balmy after the cold of the sea. They lay beneath the cliff for a long time, panting, sometimes sobbing. Miranda said several times that they must get home because Alex would have called Janis out, but she did not move and neither did Peter.

When they stood up at last, the tide had come around the headland and they could not walk back over the sand.

She said, 'Peter, I cannot go up to the house. I cannot.'

He touched her tentatively on the shoulder. 'Yes you can. I did. With Meg. It's just a house. We both know he's dead.'

'Oh God. If it were that simple you would not be trying to kill yourself!'

'It's because it's that simple. An eye for an eye.'

She reached out and gripped his hand with sudden passion. 'Then it's over! Don't you see that? He killed our baby. And you killed him! It's over!'

He drew her to him. 'I do see that.' He paused and she felt him shiver. 'And then . . . I don't see it. Because of Amy. We've got Amy. The scales are not balanced yet. Darling, am I going mad?'

'I don't know. I don't know anything much any more.'

For the first time she was down there with him, in the

473

pit of despair. Amy . . . she had not seen Amy like that.

She whispered, 'Don't think about it any more. Think about what we'll have for supper. And Alex going to Truro College. Don't think about . . . outside things.' She moved forward. 'Come on. There's no other way out of here. Let's go up the footpath.'

In the event he was right. Prospect Villa meant nothing to her. A horrible, damp, spooky old house. She looked at it and it was as if another person had gone in there, believing herself to be Trilby meeting Svengali. She had another part to play now.

Alex had called Janis and she met them wide-eyed and anxious at first, then deliberately calm and low-key as she realized that their wet clothes could not be attributed to the misty rain. Tactfully, she left immediately and they went to bed. Peter was so completely sane that Miranda thought it would be all right from now on.

But some time in the night he sat up in bed and said clearly, 'Meg, you shouldn't have told Miranda that I killed Meredith. She'll feel she has to stay with me now.'

And then he turned on his side and was asleep again.

Zach joined the Kovacks and young Snows in Artemia that summer, and he and Alex camped on the plateau and cooked their own food over an open fire. Charles spent two hours each morning in Amy's cottage working on his book.

Amy was deeply pleased. 'It's doing him so much good. And it's all due to you, you know.'

They were swimming lazily side by side off Mutton Cove. Amy was still wearing her dilapidated hat. Katie and Sebastian were making a complicated pool for Little Amy who was sitting plumply upright in her two inches of water, kicking her legs and slapping her hands on it for all she was worth.

Meg laughed, turning on her back, this wonderful small world wheeling around her making her the centre of the universe.

'I don't quite see how that can be as I've known Charles for the last twelve years only!'

'One needs to see a pattern before one can write about one's own life.' Amy too turned over and her hat fell off. She let it go. 'I didn't do any decent work myself until after Androulis died. Then I could see straight again.'

Meg reached for the hat. 'Do you still miss him terribly, Amy?'

'Of course. I think I've been more content without him. But I miss him like hell. I didn't always want to be content anyway.'

'You sound like Miranda.'

'Do I?' Amy did not look pleased. 'Give me my hat, I shall get sunstroke and I need to work this afternoon.'

'In this heat?'

'Yes. In anything. I'm probably running out of time and this is the best thing I've done.'

'What is it?'

'You shall see. Quite soon. Come on. There's Charles coming down the path with an enormous picnic basket. He must have done his thousand words early.'

Miranda had dreaded being alone in the house with Peter, but in the event it seemed to be proving his salvation.

'Darling, it's like a holiday for us,' she said as she prepared a very basic picnic to take on the moors. 'D'you know we haven't been for any sketching picnics since . . . I don't remember.'

'Since Alex was born.' He gave her one of the fleeting smiles that filled her with hope. 'Anyway, be honest, you never enjoyed them. You used to be bored out of your skull!'

She took his smile one step further and threw a crust of bread at him. He did not duck. Nor catch it.

'Well . . .' If only he'd pick up the crust and throw it back at her. 'Well, I enjoy them now. I'm older. Or lazier. Or both. And—' she looked at him directly. 'I enjoy being with you, my love.'

His Adam's apple bobbed in his throat. 'I didn't think . . . you did.'

'Oh, Peter, be fair. When you kept thinking I was Meg, it was a bit off-putting. But you haven't done that for ages.'

'Not since Jubilee night.'

'Not since then.' She snapped the plastic lid on to a tub of cold sausages and smiled widely. 'Almost three months ago. A quarter of a year.'

'Yes. And that makes you happy?'

'It's a sign that you're well. And that makes me happy.'

'You saved my life, Miranda. Not only pulling me out of the water but taking my guilt away.'

He spoke the trite words as if he'd read them somewhere. She almost asked him about Amy and was glad she hadn't when he leaned down, picked up the fallen crust, weighed it in his hand for a moment and tossed it back at her.

For some reason it made her want to weep. She took his arm. 'Come on. Let's go. Is your painting stuff in the car?'

He nodded and let himself be taken through the back yard to Sunday Street.

At first Meg thought the sculpture was of Miranda and herself. The two marble figures were intertwined like Siamese twins, the hair of both lying in one long plait over a single shoulder. Amy was strangely uncertain about it and pulled her hat almost over her eyes with unusual embarrassment.

'It's not really finished. And I'm not sure whether the marble should be polished.'

Charles spoke in a hushed voice, almost awed. 'Don't do another thing to it. The roughness, the spiky bits . . . they say everything there is to say about the relationship. It's absolutely right.'

The children did not know what to make of it.

Katie circled it cautiously.

'It's smaller than your usual, Granny,' she observed neutrally. 'You could have it inside the house instead of in the garden.'

'Yes. Yes, I could. But it will be happier outside. And it's small because I'm looking at it from a long way off. Things get small with distance and time.'

Sebastian said, 'May I touch it, Granny?'

'Yes.'

He placed a hand on top of the massed hair. 'There's a book called *The Moonstone*,' he remarked, seemingly irrelevantly. 'I saw it in your bookcase the other day.'

Amy peered at him from beneath her hat. 'That is so,' she agreed.

'This stuff – marble – it's like moonstone, isn't it?'

'I suppose it is. Yes.'

'P'raps these ladies here come from the moon? D'you think they do, Granny?'

Amy was silent. Then she crouched by the small boy and put her hand next to his on the stone. 'I hadn't thought of it before. But, yes. You're right. They were children of the moon.'

Meg cleared her throat. 'Were?' she asked.

Amy looked round at her. 'I know I'm still here, but by myself I'm no moon child. Only when Eva was with me.'

Meg held Little Amy close to her shoulder so that no-one would see her face. Of course, the sculpture was of Eva and Amy. Not of Meg and Miranda. She had never completely realized how close they were.

Alex made no comment, smiling and nodding when the others did. Zach was frankly bored. But on the way back to their tent for what they called their cook-out, Alex lagged behind his friend and said to no-one in particular, 'It's not that I don't love it here. It's the best place in the world. It's just that . . . I'd really like to see Ma and Dad again. I hope they're all right.'

Meg said comfortingly, 'We'd have had a cable if anything was even slightly wrong. They promised.'

It was Charles who said, 'I ought to look around the office, actually. How about if I took the four of you home first?'

Alex's face showed his gratitude. 'It's not that . . . I mean, can we come next Easter and all?'

'Of course.' Charles grinned. 'With Amy's permission, I should add. It's her island.'

Alex grinned back as if Amy's permission were a foregone conclusion. But then he said thoughtfully, 'I think Amy is a bit of a genius. Like Dad. Geniuses are very difficult to understand.'

'You didn't like the sculpture, old man?'

'Well, I did really. But it made me . . . frightened.'

'Frightened?'

'Not frightened. But uncomfortable. I mean . . . I'm pretty close to the kids. And Ma and Dad. And you three of course. But not all twisted up. Like the sculpture.'

Charles put a hand on his shoulder. 'Keep it that way, Alex. Adults are very apt to twist up their feelings into corkscrews. It's better not.'

Alex nodded vigorously. 'That's why it's so easy with you and Aunt Meg.' And he ran off.

Charles took Amy, now asleep, and held her in one arm while he draped the other around Meg's shoulders.

'Little does he know,' he commented dryly.

Meg shook her head. 'That's the best compliment we've ever had, darling. And it's true. Oh, we've had our twistings perhaps, but not now. Not any more. And Alex can see that.'

She stopped and turned within his arm to kiss him. He made the most of their spurious privacy and then straightened and took a deep breath.

'I can't believe all this,' he said wonderingly, looking around him and then down into the baby's sleeping face. 'Meg, is it true? I had nothing. And now . . . everything.' He pulled her against him hard. 'You're real. They're real. A real family. My God.'

She put her head into his spare shoulder and wrapped her arms tightly around his waist. 'Charles . . . you're so generous. And you don't even know it – you think you're taking, and all the time you're giving.' She tipped her head and she was smiling. 'Darling, your family is on the increase. I'm pretty certain that we're having another baby.'

She said 'another' without thought; it was so obvious that Amy was now Charles's child. And his reaction was all she had hoped. He literally shook with joy. She put a finger to his lips.

'Let's keep it to ourselves for a little while,' she whispered before he could shout aloud. 'It makes it even more exciting.'

He stared at her, his dark eyes too loving for her to bear.

She thought of the Charles Kovacks who had met her in the Royal Hotel at Paddington nearly thirteen years ago. She had revered his renowned talent and business acumen, and had been in awe of his dictatorial ways. And now . . .

She whispered, 'Charles, don't look at me like that.

I'm still the twisted girl you've helped over the past years. Just because we're having a baby doesn't make me anything special, you know.'

He smiled suddenly and his face lightened and became young again.

'I know all that. You must be crazy linking up with an old grouch like me. But . . . you did!' He shifted Amy into a more comfortable position. 'Meg, with luck she'll go straight into her cot. Katie and Seb are exhausted. So we could have an early night too.'

It was a suggestion which at one time would have filled her with fear.

Now she smiled blissfully and moved on after the others.

Alex settled well into his new school. Miranda sometimes marvelled that none of the children appeared to realize that Peter was walking a psychological tightrope. That this was to her credit did not occur to her. She sometimes wondered how long she could go on herself. She was married to an impotent genius who painted as if his life depended on it – which perhaps it did – and who could be a wonderful companion and father one minute and a reclusive neurotic the next.

She read books on depression and suggested that he should see a doctor. He always dismissed such suggestions.

'Once I've finished this series of portraits, I'll be as right as ninepence,' he said like the schoolboy she had first met.

He refused to let the agency show the eight pictures he had done in Kilburn.

'Wait until the set is complete,' he insisted.

Miranda crept up to the attic one afternoon in late October when he had fallen asleep, and looked at the piece of hardboard on the easel. He had blocked in the background; it was dark as usual but she thought it consisted of panels of wood. Perhaps the joists of a roof. The face did not so much emerge from the darkness, as appear to be silhouetted against it.

A week later, on a Friday, the two younger children were gathering driftwood from the shore for their Bonfire Night celebrations. Alex had not arrived home from school. She was at the sink peeling potatoes for their evening meal and Peter came downstairs at a slow plod and went to the Aga.

Automatically she forestalled him. 'Cup of tea. Sit down, I'll make you a pot. You look done up.'

He did as he was told and sat heavily at the table, spreading his hands flat in front of him.

He said, 'I've finished.'

'Finished? Your portraits, d'you mean?' She stared, frightened at what might happen now. She put the teapot near him and fetched milk and a mug.

He nodded. 'Yes. The portraits.' He poured and sipped. 'Aren't you having one?'

'I . . . no, I don't think so.' She could not have borne to drink tea then. She sat opposite him, potatoes forgotten.

'Well . . . good. Congratulations.'

'Thanks.' He finished the first mug of tea and poured another.

She tried to tease him. 'Anyone would think you're thirsty!'

'I am. I feel . . . withered.'

She swallowed on a dry mouth, staring at him.

'What . . . what happens now?' she asked at last when he continued to drink.

He looked through the steam at her and frowned, concentrating on the question. But then he asked irrelevantly, 'Where are the kids?'

'On the shore. Getting wood. It's Guy Fawkes night tomorrow.'

'What day will that be?'

'Saturday.'

'That's handy.'

She did not know what to say. He finished his tea, got up and fetched his duffle coat.

'I think I'll join them. Fresh air. Like the day we went on the moors in the summer.' He smiled at her suddenly; it was somehow quite heartbreaking. 'I enjoyed that day, Miranda. That was a lovely day.'

'Yes, it was.'

There was a rush of cold air as he opened the door. She put her head on her arms and wished that she could send for Meg as she'd always done before. Or Charles. But they were the last people on earth to help Peter now.

The door opened again and Alex came in.

'Where's everyone?' he asked immediately.

She stood up. Her back ached, her legs ached, she felt so old.

'Down on the shore getting wood for tomorrow. D'you want to go and tell them tea will be ready at five?'

'No. It'll be too dark for them in a minute. We've got all tomorrow to make the bonfire. D'you think it'll rain?'

'Yes. The forecast says it will.' She removed his cap and poured him some tea. 'How did today go?'

'Triffic. I'm getting quite good at rugby. The only thing is . . .'

He hesitated and she prompted him. 'Well?'

'Ma, we're doing a play for Christmas. Can't remember what it's called. But – don't dare laugh – I'm cast as a bloody girl!'

She told him off for swearing while she laughed helplessly.

'I told you not to laugh! I wouldn't have mentioned

the bloody play only I thought you might give me some coaching.'

She stopped laughing. 'Me? Give you some coaching? I didn't think . . . I mean, I hardly remember that I'm an actress these days!'

He said stoutly, ''Course you're an actress, Ma. It's just that you've got to mark time for a bit.'

'I suppose it is. OK. I'll coach you. Bring me the script tomorrow. And no more bloodies.'

That evening they sat around the big table and laughed as they'd done in the old days. Peter had colour in his cheeks and ate two helpings of cottage pie. She felt a surge of pure and unadulterated happiness. It was going to be all right.

The last portrait was without mystery. The face was open and rather anxious; the eyes not quite blue, not quite green; the hair pushed behind the ears and fraying slightly across the forehead. The drooping mouth and lined eyes told their own story.

Miranda looked at it for a long time without speaking. Then said, 'This is me. Meg's gone. This is me as I am now.'

'Yes.' With loving care he covered the hardboard. 'It's the best I've done. The very best. I need not go on.'

She felt her heart jump as it so often did these days.

'Not go on? Painting, d'you mean?'

'Oh, of course I'll paint.' He put another canvas on the easel. 'In fact I've started. Look.'

It was the view from the moors. She could see Zennor Head and Gurnards Head and the long contour of Cape Cornwall.

She drew a long breath. 'Peter, it's wonderful. It's . . . like . . . I don't know. I can't find words.'

He said quietly, 'It's got a lot of Scaife in it.'

'Gerald Scaife? From St Ives?'

'Yes. He was a painter Meg loathed. She was frightened of what he was trying to say. Just before his wife died he painted this huge mural. It was like their lives. Like their love.'

'Oh God.' She knew suddenly why Meg had been frightened. It was too much. It was eternity.

He said, 'Don't you like it?'

'Yes. I like it. It frightens me that you've painted it. But I like it. It makes me want to stand on tiptoe. Just to understand.'

He put his arms around her and held her tightly.

'Darling Miranda. I'm . . . sorry,' he whispered.

She said fiercely, 'Never be sorry. Never. D'you hear me?' She took his head in her hands and held it away from her. 'Listen, Peter. You are a creator. I think . . . darling, I think you created me.'

He kissed her tenderly, without passion.

Alex's voice could be heard calling up the stairs for them to go and see the bonfire.

'But it's raining,' Miranda objected, not wanting to lose this precious and wonderful moment.

Peter laughed into her hair.

'That's the best weather of all,' he said. 'Come on. We'll pour some petrol over the wood and it'll go up like tinder!'

It did. And all the children from the village screamed and shouted their ancient rites around it. Peter stood back and watched through narrowed eyes as the smoke whirled everywhere. Miranda knew he was seeing the darkness and light, and the faces coming and going, with an intensity that she herself would not fully realize until he painted it.

She wrote to Meg soon afterwards, 'Until I see Peter's work, I am half blind. His last painting of me made me see myself. Art must be special if it can do that, mustn't it, Sis?'

Meg read the letter over a riotous breakfast and passed it to Charles without a word. He read it and reached over the marmalade to take her hand.

He said, 'She knows what she has to do. Will she be able to do it? How talented is she?'

Meg shivered. 'I don't know. I don't know what is happening to her down there.'

His grip tightened on her fingers. 'I'm glad,' he said. 'I'm glad you no longer have to suffer with her.'

'I am too,' said Meg.

Twenty-two

In 1981 there was the royal wedding and a repeat of the celebrations of '77. Peter did not just get through it all, he seemed to enjoy it. He was now a regular member of the lifeboat crew; his paintings were no longer of people. He had produced three seascapes which were received with enormous acclaim.

In the September when Sebastian was accepted at Truro, he insisted that the three children should be weekly boarders there and that Miranda should do a season with the Arbitrary.

That winter the Players took their stock repertoire of Shakespeare into the Midlands for the first time, and found a new and appreciative audience. They rested for the pantomime season; Oliver and Olwen went to Gladys Pugh's for Christmas, but Zoe and a newcomer called Jack Sturgess went to Keele with Miranda. Peter had had the children home each weekend and worked hard in between. Janis cleaned and cooked for him; his spare time was spent with the lifeboat crew.

Miranda hugged him with all her old passion.

'You look so much better, darling!' Her voice was higher, lighter; it could carry to the back of the most makeshift theatre.

He held her to him, burying his face in her hair and closing his eyes as he smelled the familiarity of her.

'I am better,' he said with conviction. 'And you – you

486

were superb! You've got something really special, darling. A sort of restraint – a kind of mystery—'

'Oh, you and mystery!' But she was pleased if puzzled. 'How do you know anyway? Has there been a review I missed?'

'I came twice to see you,' he confessed. 'Leamington and Wolverhampton.'

She was thrilled and dismayed. 'Darling! Why didn't you tell me – where were you? What nights? Oh God—'

'Shush – shush—' he was laughing as he'd always laughed at her outbursts. 'I'll tell you everything when we go to bed.'

She stared into his eyes for a moment, but they told her nothing, so she kissed him on the cheek and whirled around the kitchen getting to know it all again. Janis had found new places for things, provided a new tablecloth, put sprigs of holly along the deep window ledges. There was a time when Miranda would have changed everything back; not any more. She admired everything. Zoe came down from her room and announced that Katie was a born actress. Peter laughed and said, 'We've always known that!' and Miranda hugged him again. He *was* better.

It was the sort of evening Miranda adored, with people packed around the table, the children chattering freely, the visitors laughing, impressed by the family atmosphere, telling Miranda she had the best of both worlds, and, perhaps best of all, Janis doing all the food. Zoe and Jack drifted off with Janis to the Coastguards later, and Miranda concentrated on being with the children and catching up on all their news.

Amazingly, Sebastian had settled in at Truro from the first day.

'It's because I can tell stories, Ma,' he said. 'I'm like Aunt Meg, you see. Last summer she sort of showed me the knack of fitting a story together. A drawing, then something happening, and another drawing.'

'I saw Meg last week,' Miranda told them. 'She came up to Birmingham and we had a whole day together.'

Katie said, 'Did she bring our presents?'

'Yes. And I gave her that swing-thing you wanted me to get for Andrew.'

'Is Amy all right at school? She didn't want to go. She told me she wanted to live with us all the time.'

'Well, she's fine. And one of these days Aunt Meg will bring her down here.' Miranda had always thought that Meg would never risk bringing Amy – or Charles – to Keele again, but things were changing. Perhaps time really did heal everything.

'What did she do with Andrew?'

Miranda smiled. 'Magda had him, of course. Anyone would think he was Magda's son. She's the funniest old thing – like someone out of a pre-war film.'

Alex, fifteen, very tall and serious, waited until Katie was in bed and Sebastian in the bathroom. Then he spoke in his incredibly deep hoarse voice.

'Ma . . . you and Meg haven't had a row, that's obvious. Is it Dad Aunt Meg can't stand?'

She looked up from turning down Sebastian's bed. She supposed this question had to come; Alex was intelligent and had always been close to Meg. She gnawed her bottom lip, pulled her hair, finally clasped her hands tightly.

'It's not that she can't stand him, darling. It's . . . when Dad was so ill, he could not tell the difference between Meg and me. And Meg thought it would be best . . . not to confuse him any more.'

It was so simple when she put it like that. And true.

She smiled, reassured by her own words. 'Dad is better now. I'm sure it won't be long before we can get together again like the old days.'

Alex said acutely, 'But not Uncle Charles.'

Miranda pulled her hair again, some of her assurance dissipating. 'Perhaps not. I just don't know, Alex.'

'Sorry, Ma. But it's such a pity. Meg won't come without Charles. And the two little kids . . . they'd love it here. And Uncle Charles is a good man to have around.'

Miranda turned briskly to the bed again. 'Yes. I think you're right. I'm sure you're right,' she said.

Peter held her close as if he'd never let her go again, but that was all.

'You see, Miranda . . .' He kissed her hair, his eyes closed as before. 'I wanted you to – to do your thing. Ever since Brett St Clare died and I saw . . . how it must have been for you . . . like my painting . . . I'd die without my painting . . .'

'Yes, I know, darling. I know.' Her arms tightened around him. His sense of reality was there, but it was fragile, so vulnerable.

'Ever since then I've wanted you to go back to the theatre. I felt – you knowing about . . . you know . . .'

She said calmly, 'John Meredith?'

'Yes. I felt that was a sort of imposition. I told Meg and I wanted it to stop there. I wanted you to go on acting then. But . . .'

'Peter, it was better the way we did it. These past four years have been wonderful. We know each other. Properly.'

He kissed her hair again. 'We're old, old friends, Miranda,' he whispered.

'Yes. And like old, old friends, we can trust each other, can't we?'

'Of course.'

'So if I give this a whirl for a year, then decide to come home again, you'll know it's the right thing for me?'

There was a pause. She loosened her hold on him and tried to look at his face, but he reached beyond her and switched off the light.

'All right. I'll trust you,' he said.

'Thank you, darling.' She kissed him on the lips and held his head on her shoulder as she had done so often in the past four years. When he relaxed against her, she closed her eyes and waited for sleep to come.

In July of the following summer Amy Smithers put her tools carefully into the wooden boxes in which they had arrived from Athens in the 1930s, tidied up her spare stone as best she could, and settled down in her old folding chair which she set in the sunshine on the plateau. Spiro found her the next morning when he came to tidy up Eva's garden ready for the arrival of the Kovacks. She must have died the previous evening, probably just after sunset when it became quite chilly. She looked very happy.

Charles and Meg left the children with Magda and flew out immediately. They found the letter she had left for them and arranged for a quiet humanist funeral on the island. She was buried in her own garden among the stone pieces she had chiselled for so many years, and her grave was marked by the marble work she had completed in 1977 of herself and Eva Kovacks.

Meg's sadness was intense and poignant, unlike anything she had experienced before. Charles had finished his book a year ago and she had read it carefully and knew more about Amy than perhaps anyone had ever known. Charles had consulted Amy throughout, and there was so much of her in the book.

After the service they went into Amy's cottage and began the business of clearing up. It was amazing how little there was to do.

Meg said, 'She's been sorting out for ages. I expected a dozen uncompleted figures around the place. I remember the first time I ate here . . . everything was covered in stone dust.'

'She was over eighty. She knew she wasn't immortal.' Charles stacked books on the table. 'We have to go through these, but then let's put them back, Meg. It'll always be Amy's cottage, so her stuff might as well stay here.'

'You don't know that. We haven't found a will. Perhaps she's left the island to someone else. She might have long-lost relatives in Australia or something!'

'Darling – she asked me to deal with that. She left the island to Amy and Andrew. But . . . well, Meg, I'm afraid I hoaxed her when my mother died. I should have told you ages ago, but it didn't seem important. The island didn't belong to my mother. Or Amy. Androulis left the island to me.'

'But why on earth . . . why did you lead her up the garden path like that?'

'What could I say? If Amy had ever known that Androulis left her out of things, her life would have been wasted.' He smiled ruefully. 'Amy loved that old reprobate more than my mother ever loved him. But . . . you see, Meg . . . my mother gave Androulis a son.' He waited, looking at her. 'I'm not a Kovacks, Meg. I should be called Charles Androulis.' He gave a helpless shrug. 'Sorry, darling. Some of the staff call me a bastard, but—'

She said, astonished, 'Amy told me ages ago! You weren't supposed to know!'

It was his turn to be astonished. 'Amy knew? Oh God. D'you think she guessed about the island too? I told my half-sister to fob her off with some story – but Amy was so bloody intelligent—'

Meg said, 'Except where Androulis was concerned. No, she wouldn't have guessed.' She looked at him with new eyes. 'Oh Charles . . . you're – you're – ' she sighed, exasperated at her lack of words. 'You're such a nice man!'

He laughed and hugged her and said over her shoulder, 'D'you hear that, Amy? I'm not such a bastard after all! I'm a nice man!'

Meg punched his shoulder lovingly.

'Oh . . . my love. My dearest love. That was why you needed a family . . .' She drew back suddenly. 'But you had one! Kristina Androulis your half-sister? I can't believe it!'

'They've never recognized me, Meg. I *was* a bastard. They were terrified I'd try to claim half of everything.'

She was silent, digesting the enormity of the past. He put his arms around her.

'Meg. It makes no difference, surely?'

'Not to how I feel about you. Idiot. How could it? But it explains so much. Dear Charles. I do love you.'

They held each other thankfully. Then Charles said again, 'But Amy . . . d'you think she was fooled? Really?'

Meg considered. 'Yes. Because she would assume that Androulis – your father – would leave half of the island to your mother in the certainty that it would then come to you.'

Charles wanted to be convinced. 'Yes. Perhaps. I do hope so.'

'And anyway she believed that you were ignorant about your real father. She definitely believed that. She told me only as a precaution. In case one day you had to be told.'

He nodded slowly. 'And if I'd known that the island was mine, then I would have guessed about my parentage.' He laughed suddenly. 'My mother told me quite soon. When I was about ten, I suppose. She had to explain why we lived with my grandparents and why they treated me with such enormous reserve.'

'So then you behaved like a spoiled brat!' Meg smiled roguishly at his surprised face. 'Amy's expression, darling!'

'I can imagine. She told me one or two home truths. I didn't see her for a long time.'

'Then you sent me over as your ambassador.'

'I suppose I did in a way.' He kissed her tenderly. 'It worked, didn't it?'

'It did.' She looked around the cottage. 'Dear Amy. I'm so glad I knew her.'

'Me too.' He opened a book at random. 'This is a sort of diary . . . no . . . she's copied verses . . .' He read aloud, '"By night on my bed I sought him whom my soul loveth: I sought him, but I found him not."' He looked up. 'The Song of Solomon. She's copied out verses from the Song of Solomon.'

Meg's face contracted. 'Oh, Charles.' And then she looked through the door at the sculpture garden. 'Oh Charles, I do hope she has found him now!'

He closed the book gently and went to her. 'I think she must have done,' he said.

Miranda came out for two weeks of the long school holidays. Peter would not come with her. She took over Amy's cottage and worked on it like a demon, cleaning windows and scrubbing the stone until the place shone.

They all went back together on the first day of September. Alex was staying at Truro for another two years and the three children had asked to continue to board there in spite of Miranda being back at home. She and Peter settled into a routine of such contentment it was hard to imagine their early tempestuous years together.

Peter painted a picture called 'The Calm after the Storm'. It was modelled on an Edwardian narrative painting and showed the long front at Penzance awash with flotsam and jetsam of all kinds, lamp posts leaning, boats upside down hanging from railings, the lone figure of a woman surveying it all.

People from the art world wanted to interview him; it was suggested that he should feature in a late-night television programme called *Ringside Seat*.

'They want to peep through the keyhole at our private lives,' he explained to Miranda when he turned it down.

She shook her head decisively.

And then something surprising happened. A man arrived at the door, unannounced, and introduced himself as Huw Devereaux. Miranda had seen him on television and had read about him in the newspapers, but still had difficulty in recognizing the gaunt battered face and stooped body from the virile man of the media she recalled.

He had knocked at the top door and she took him into the sitting room which looked over the roofs of Fish Street to the harbour. He stood by the window, holding on to the ledge, drinking it in.

'I'm glad Peter Snow lives here. Settings are vital for very special gems.'

It was the sort of flowery remark she might have expected and she said tartly, 'Actually he's up on the moors walking today. He likes the rain.'

He looked round at her and smiled. 'It was you I wanted to see, Mrs Snow. I was a friend of Brett St Clare's.'

She held herself still against a childish gasp of surprise. The renowned Huw Devereaux, critic extraordinary, a friend of Brett's? It was 1982 and a great many homosexuals had declared themselves publicly, but many others had not.

She deliberately dropped her shoulders and said, 'I expect you could manage a cup of tea. Unless you want to go on looking at the view, come downstairs into the kitchen and I'll make some.' She gave a small smile. 'I'd like to talk about Brett.'

They went down into the big old fish cellar and he wandered around while she assembled tea things on the table.

'This is a marvellous place,' he commented, running his fingers over a section of the granite wall. 'It's good that you've left it in its natural state. Too many of these places are tarted up ridiculously.'

'Oh, we've done our share. You should have seen it when we moved in.' She refused to enter into one of those conversations that verged on the precious. 'We've had to bring up three children here, Mr Devereaux. It had to be dry and it had to be warm.'

He sat down. He looked frailer than ever leaning on the table. A few wispy hairs trailed over the top of his head. She knew suddenly with terrible insight that he was dying in the same way Brett had died. That was why he was here. To ask her about Brett's end.

She pushed one of Janis's Cornish heavy cakes towards him. 'Have a slice of this. And perhaps when Peter gets back, you'll stay for supper?'

He smiled again. 'That's decent of you. I've booked in at the Coastguards but if it wouldn't put you out I'd very much enjoy eating here.'

At one time an unexpected guest would have been just a bind. Now she smiled back and poured tea and asked him what train he'd come on and how Arthur

Bowering looked these days. And they made small talk easily until the teapot was emptied.

Then he said, 'I've written a play, Mrs Snow. It's about a woman who discovers her husband is gay. How she copes with it. Her name is Martha Cutforth. The play is called *Martha Cutforth*. I'd like you to play Martha.'

She felt her mouth open and snapped it shut quickly, but her face was uncontrollable. If Huw Devereaux had written a play it would be performed in London, in the West End. He was that sort of man.

She cleared her throat. 'Me? Well, of course . . . what an opportunity. I . . . why?' It was hopeless, she had to be honest with him. She simply did not have that kind of experience.

He shrugged slightly. 'I saw you in Birmingham. You were playing Portia. You gave it something special. Very controlled. Almost hard. Martha Cutforth has to be controlled and hard.'

'I've never done anything contemporary.'

He shrugged again. 'You're an actress.'

'I don't know.' She was unexpectedly nervous. 'There's Peter. And the children. I thought I'd got it out of my system – I have got it out of my system. We're so happy.'

He stared at her for a long unnerving moment. Then he said, 'In that case, I'll say no more. Happiness is everything.' He stood up. 'I don't think I will stay to meet your husband after all. He might well see me as a threat.'

'Oh no. Not a bit. In any case . . . did you want to hear about Brett? I was with him just before he died, you know.'

He stood holding the edge of the table, head down. Then he straightened.

'I knew him in the army. We met at intervals over the years. I was going to feature his rep company in a programme once. It fell through. He was angry with me about that. I apologized and said I'd resurrect the idea and he said it was too late, he'd got cancer. But that I was to keep an eye on someone called Miranda Patch. Because one day she'd be a great actress and he'd like to think that he'd helped her get there.' He looked at her. 'Does that make any difference to your decision?'

'So you're offering me the part as an apology to Brett?' she asked straightly.

'Maybe I was. But since I've met you . . . no, that's not true. I'd never jeopardize my play by giving this part to anyone I didn't admire. I've seen you several times. You are good.' He leaned forward. 'Listen. I've already had film offers. If you've done the part on stage, you will be in the running for it on film. And . . . it would please Brett.'

Peter would not hear of her turning it down. She went back to London with Huw Devereaux and stayed at the Sussex Gardens flat while rehearsals were under way. *Martha Cutforth* opened in the West End on 8th November. Peter brought the children up to see it and made certain they sat between him and Meg.

Miranda took half a dozen curtain calls. It was obvious that Huw Devereaux's play was going to be the event of 1982.

Back at the Kovacks' flat they improvised beds and laughed a great deal and Charles opened champagne.

'At the age of thirty-eight, I've made it!' Miranda said, hugging Peter's arm protectively. He was smiling, coping marvellously.

They slept in Meg's old room. He said fondly, 'It's what I wanted for you, Miranda. I can't believe it's happening. It's exactly what I wanted for you.'

She could not understand her own unease. Surely it was what she wanted too? They were all under the same roof;

it was the start of them being a family again. And when he reversed their usual positions and took her head on to his shoulder, she was certain all was well.

'You were amazing, darling. And you know, you couldn't have done that part if you hadn't known Brett St Clare.'

'True.' She was terribly sleepy. The last six weeks had been very hard.

And then, out of nowhere, he said, 'Darling, do you think one day we should tell Amy the truth?'

Sleep was gone. She said carefully, 'Why on earth should we? Surely that would be Meg's decision?'

'I simply thought . . . she and Seb are so close.'

'Of course they are.' She realized what he was saying and drew a breath. 'Oh. I see. Well. Perhaps.' She raised herself on her elbow and looked at him in the darkness. 'One step at a time, darling. Let's wait and see.'

She kissed him tenderly and slipped her arm beneath his neck. He lifted his head slightly so that he could feel her hair over his eyes. And she stared at the invisible ceiling and tried to think about tomorrow's performance.

The storm started on Saturday 19th December. The children had broken up for the Christmas holidays and had gone to London to stay with Meg. As Peter was now on the official lifeboat crew, he went straight to the lifeboat station and waited with Billy Majors and the others. The call for help came just after eight o'clock in the evening when the wind had reached hurricane force. The *King Solomon* was launched to go to the aid of a coaster of 1,400 tons registered in Panama. It reported engine failure eight miles off Wolf Rock. There were no survivors from either vessel. A report was issued by Trinity House and was read again and again by Peter's family during the weeks that followed.

'The wind was blowing from south by east and increased to force 12 at eight o'clock, gusting to 90 knots. There were mountainous seas, reported to be 60 foot high close to the coast. In the driving rain, visibility was very poor. The *Atlantic Star* was caught in the maritime trap of Mounts Bay in a southerly gale, drifting towards the cliffs four miles southwest of the lifeboat station. Eight people on board. A Sea King helicopter from RNAS Culdrose reached the scene half an hour after the first rockets were sighted. It was blown back over the cliffs three times, but managed to get into position at nine o'clock. The rotors missed the ship's mast by 76 feet. It was impossible to make a lift. The *King Solomon* arrived at nine five; twice it was lifted on to the deck of the *Atlantic Star* and slid stern first into the sea. Four people were seen to jump aboard. The last radio message was received at nine twenty-one and confirmed that four people had been rescued. There was no further radio contact and the *King Solomon*'s lights disappeared ten minutes later. At that time the *Atlantic Star* was overwhelmed and laid on her side between Pezazz Point and Tater-du. The Coastguard Cliff Rescue was on the scene and a member was twice lowered over the cliff in an endeavour to spot any survivors. Fragments of the *King Solomon* were washed up in Lannah Cove during the following week. Local fishing fleets searched all next day in heavy weather. Penzance sea front was a scene of storm wrack and desolation, shingle cast on to the road, helicopters overhead.'

That Sunday afternoon before they knew more than the fact that all those lives had been lost, Meg and Miranda surveyed the littered sea front from the safety of Charles's BMW.

Miranda could not stop shaking. 'It's like his last picture. It's as if he knew.'

Meg held on to her tightly and said nothing. Charles turned in the driver's seat. They had received a phone call from Janis just after last night's performance and had left London at midnight. Then there had been the service that morning led by the RNLI branch chaplain on the sea front and afterwards in Keyhole itself. He wondered how much more the girls could stand.

'I think we should go to Fish Cottage now and spend the rest of the day with the others,' he said quietly. 'Miranda's got a long day tomorrow.'

Miranda said fiercely, 'If you think I'm going on stage tomorrow night—'

Meg rocked her. 'Of course you're going on stage tomorrow night, Miranda. You're going on stage for Peter. It's what he would want. What he would expect.'

Miranda started to weep. She had known even as she spoke that she would make the long drive back tomorrow morning and be in the theatre by six o'clock. She hated herself for the force which would drive her there. But if it were indeed for Peter . . . if she could now act for him . . . if she could draw on the strength that was Meg . . .

Even as Charles drove slowly along the harbour and up to Sunday Street, she controlled the shaking; she took on some of the characteristics of Martha Cutforth.

Christmas came too soon that year. Charles brought all the children down to Keele and Magda looked after Miranda until Christmas Eve and then travelled with her by train.

They opened their stockings on Christmas morning and found things bought and wrapped by Peter. Katie was white-faced and still disbelieving. 'I don't think I can bear this,' she said. 'First Granny in Artemia. And now Peter.'

Sebastian said fearfully, 'You don't think he did it on purpose? He seemed to have finished everything.

There are no new paintings upstairs. And everything is so tidy.'

Alex was definite. 'He didn't know the *Atlantic Star* was going to founder that night, you idiot. Anyway he was better. We all know that. He wasn't ill any more. He was *better*!'

Sebastian looked at the electric typewriter, unwrapped but labelled with his name and found beneath the stairs.

'I'm going to write a story about Dad,' he said suddenly. 'But it won't have Dad in it.'

Katie sobbed suddenly. 'What are you talking about?'

Sebastian looked beyond her and said, 'It's going to be about twins. Twin moonbeams. And how they looked after someone. Someone special. And there was always one of them there. To look after him.'

Charles, halfway down the stairs, overheard this.

'How would you like it if one of them looked after you, Seb?' he asked, coming over to the table. 'Just a thought. One you could talk over between yourselves. If Miranda's going to be in the film of *Martha Cutforth*, she's going to be busy for a while. And you know that is what your father would have liked. It crossed my mind – hearing what you said then – that Meg and I could live here and work and Amy and Andrew could go to the school where you were.'

The children looked at him without speaking for so long that Charles wondered if he'd gone too far. He did not want to be seen as usurper.

Then Alex said, 'We always hoped one day, you'd come and stay. But we didn't think it would be like this.'

Charles held up his hand. 'Don't say anything more. It's your home. You need to talk about it.'

'It's Meg's home as well,' Katie said. 'And you're Meg's husband. And we're all used to each other because of

Artemia.' She paused and raised her eyebrows. 'We'd still go to Artemia in the summer?'

'As long as you want to,' Charles said. He went to the Aga. 'I think your mother could do with a cup of tea now. How about cutting the Christmas cake, Katie?'

She went to the pantry. She was as tall as her mother now and very slim. It crossed her mind that at her age Miranda had been an orphan for some time. There had just been Meg and Miranda. And Katie had this enormous family.

She said, 'I'll cut some sandwiches, shall I? We can all eat upstairs. And watch the Christmas lights.'

And so they did.

Epilogue

The film première of *Martha Cutforth* was held back because of the death of its author, Huw Devereaux.

1984 had come and gone and nothing special had happened, though many thought Britain was already in the hands of a Big Brother somewhere. At the end of 1985, on the day that Mikhail Gorbachev became the new leader of the USSR, Miranda Patch made her curtsy to the Queen Mother and knew that she had fulfilled her destiny. She was forty-one, an actress of considerable standing in this country and America. And somehow it was all because of Peter.

Afterwards at the reception, she stood with her family and talked expertly to critics and press. Her son, dark and thin-faced, did his duty for a while and then retired to a corner of the room and began to draw on the back of his programme. Her daughter, a younger edition of herself, held the hand of a nine-year-old girl and led her slowly along the table of food. Miranda Patch watched them, smiling, and was glad that what she had told her children about this same small girl had seemed to bring them closer than ever.

At a table, her younger son sat with her nephew. Her sister and brother-in-law came and went between all the children. Miranda felt her smile deepen and realized with a shock that she was happy. Truly happy.

Sebastian said, 'When you're a bit older, of course you

can use it. But my father gave it to me, Andrew. I can't let you muck it up.'

Andrew said fiercely, 'I wouldn't muck it up.'

'You just do, old man. You're at that stage. Sorry.'

'I could write stories too. Only I haven't got a typewriter.'

'You don't need a blasted typewriter – I've just told you that!'

'Well, you use a typewriter!'

'Not all the time! My God, I can see why Amy loses her temper with you! All you do is argue!'

'I have to. I'm the youngest and no-one listens to me if I don't argue.' But Andrew smiled as he spoke. He knew Sebastian would never lose his temper with him. Sebastian was the best person in the world. And one day he would let Andrew use his typewriter and Andrew would then be able to show him that he too could write marvellous stories.

Meanwhile he dropped the subject of the typewriter and wheedled, 'Tell me a story, Seb. It's so boring here. Tell me a story about the Devil's Advocate.'

'Your own mother wrote that story!'

'Yes, but I like to hear you tell it.'

So Sebastian began to tell the *Stone Garden* story for the umpteenth time.

Katie said, 'If I tell you something, will you promise never to tell another living soul?'

'I promise,' said Amy.

'I've got an audition next week.'

'But Miranda said not till you'd finished college!' Amy was wide-eyed, apprehensive.

'That's why it's got to be a secret. Miranda will be thrilled to bits if I get the part. Really.'

'She wants you to go on the road with the Arbitrary.

504

I heard her say so,' Amy maintained stubbornly.

'Following in Mother's footsteps,' Katie parodied scornfully. 'Not on your life! If she thinks I'd knuckle under to that old queen, Oliver Freres—'

'You shouldn't say that!' Amy announced righteously, knowing it was an insult, not knowing why.

Katie shook her head slowly. 'You don't seem to have much of your father in you,' she said sadly. Then hugged her. 'You're my alter ego. D'you know what that means?'

'No.'

'Sit down with that cake then, and I'll tell you.'

Charles said, 'Do you miss him, Meg?'

Meg smiled up at him, knowing exactly what he meant. 'No. Because it's working out as he wanted it. Miranda has got her fame, the children are wild and wonderful—'

'Amy's not.'

Her smile went. 'Charles—'

'I didn't mean that as it sounded, my love. I'm thankful Amy hasn't got his nature. She's like you.' He pecked her cheek. 'I'm human enough to be glad of that.'

'It's strange, Charles. In some ways, she's more like you than any of us. She's got your courage and your drive—'

'You think you haven't got those things.' He laughed. 'Thank God Peter did those portraits! Go and look at them, Meg. See yourself.'

An elderly woman standing nearby turned at the words and stared at Meg. They would have turned away, but she was smiling as if she knew them.

'I couldn't help overhearing. About the portraits. I went to see them – three years ago now, wasn't it? I was talking to a gentleman who told me they were of two girls, not one as everybody supposed. I've just realized that you are one of the girls. And Miss Patch is the other. She darkened her hair and cut it short for this part, but she is your twin, isn't she?'

Meg normally hated to be 'found out' as she put it. But there was something about this woman. She nodded and returned the smile.

'Yes. I can see that now.' The woman laughed frankly. 'D'you know, I've been haunted by the 'Girl with Red Hair' for the last three years. If those portraits were of two girls, then they had to be twins, and I am very interested in twins. Two sides of a coin.' She dived into the pocket of her suit and handed Meg a card. 'I'm a writer. I wonder if I might talk to you some time?'

Charles waited for Meg to give a polite refusal. But Meg did not. She knew why she felt so at ease with this stranger: she was reminded of Amy Smithers. The woman was suitably dressed for an occasion like this, but there was a carelessness about her that was Amy's. Meg wondered what she would look like in a man's trilby hat. It was possible.

So she returned the smile. 'Of course. I'll leave you my address. I work at home so you can nearly always find me there.'

The woman took Meg's card and drifted off without any small talk. Meg liked that too.

Charles said, 'Will you let her write about you, darling?'

Meg shrugged. 'I don't know. Depends.'

He said, 'I had thought of making the two of you into a book.'

'Really?' Meg hugged his arm. 'I think you should do a proper biography of Peter. I think you are the only one who really understood him.'

'I'd like to do that, actually.' Charles glanced over at Miranda who was posing for photographs. 'I'll ask Miranda what she thinks.'

'She'll be all for it. Those last few years when she nursed him back to life made her realize that they were meant for each other. Whatever you said in a biography . . . she could take it now.'

'And you? Could you take it?'

She smiled up at him wordlessly and he shook his head as if to clear it, then said, 'Come on. Let's round up the brood and go home for supper.'

He signalled to Alex and walked towards Sebastian and Andrew. As if they were joined physically, Miranda looked over at them, cut short the photographic session and began to make her exit.

The sisters linked fingers for a moment as they walked out to the waiting limousine. Then they made room for Amy and Katie. Charles followed with the three boys. People paused on the pavement beneath the neon lights displaying Miranda's name, and ogled the little group avidly.

It had been Miranda's evening, and now it was Meg's.

'Guess what Magda has made for supper?' she said as they packed themselves into the car.

And the concerted cry of 'Goulash!' sounded like a cheer.

THE END

TOUCHED BY ANGELS
by Susan Sallis

They were just schoolgirls – evacuees – when they first met the Reid brothers. Berry was the one who dazzled them – handsome, funny, sexy, he somehow symbolised that golden summer of the war when they all worked together on the farm. Then their world collapsed around them.

Morag, the strongest and quietest of the three girls, lost everything she held dear in one savage bombing. Vallery's beloved brother was killed in the desert war, and Jannie – well, Jannie had never had much to start with anyway. With a father away at war and a succession of 'uncles' passing through her mother's bedroom, she grew up both insecure and promiscuous. But still, she had Morag and Vallery.

When the Reid boys returned from the war it was Berry, the vibrant one, who had changed. Crippled, both in mind and body, he held the dream of Morag in his heart, even though it was Vallery he married. As they settled to a life in the remote cliffside abbey, away from everyone, so the old ties between the three girls and the Reid brothers grew more intense, more confused – and Morag, Vallery, and Jannie discovered that Berry still had the power to draw them all to him.

0 552 14466 5

BY SUN AND CANDLELIGHT
by Susan Sallis

They discovered the empty cottage in 1940 – when they were still at school, four teenage friends from wildly different backgrounds and with the war casting its shadow over their lives.

It was to the cottage that Monica came, pregnant, alone, frightened, and it was there that their story really began. For Bessie, born secretly and shamefully to one of them, raised by another, and loved by them all, came to represent what was the very best in their lives.

A huge and powerful novel – of four friends and the lifetime bonds that held them together.

0 552 13545 3

SUMMER VISITORS
by Susan Sallis

Madge was four years old when she first saw the Cornish sea and fell in love with it, and it was there that her family grew and suffered and loved. It was there that she and her mother went to recover from a heartrending tragedy – there she was forced reluctantly into marriage – there she fell into a wild and passionate wartime love.

And it was there she saw her children grow and love and cope with the secret legacies the years had left them, until finally they became more than just Summer Visitors.

The magnificent story of a family and the woman who held them together.

0 552 13346 9

AN ORDINARY WOMAN
by Susan Sallis

When Rose was four the scandal broke about her head. She was really too young to understand what was happening – only that her mother was in disgrace and that they were leaving Aunt Mabe in America and returning home to England. The following May, Joanna – 'Jon' – was born.

Rose and Jon were totally different. Jon was vivacious, fun, liked a good time, and always got what she wanted, even when what she wanted happened to belong to Rose. Rose was reserved, controlled, never wanted to leave her home or Gloucestershire, and was – well – an ordinary girl who grew into an ordinary woman.

But as Jon raced from disaster to disaster, from one violent relationship to another so Rose, in her quiet way, salvaged the family, held them together, pasted over the cracks of tragedy and emotional upheavals whilst at the same time fighting her own personal crises.

It was much later – when the children were growing up, when life at last seemed tranquil and settled, that Jon precipitated Rose across the Atlantic and into the most extraordinary event of her life. When Rose finally returned from America no one could ever again think of her as an ordinary woman.

0 552 13756 1

A SCATTERING OF DAISIES
THE DAFFODILS OF NEWENT
BLUEBELL WINDOWS
ROSEMARY FOR REMEMBRANCE
by Susan Sallis

Will Rising had dragged himself from humble beginnings
to his own small tailoring business in Gloucester – and on
the way he'd fallen violently in love with Florence,
refined, delicate and wanting something better for her
children.

March was the eldest girl, the least loved, the plain,
unattractive one who, as the family grew, become more
and more the household drudge. But March, a strange,
intelligent, unhappy child, had inherited some of her
mother's dreams. March Rising was determined to break
out of the round of poverty and hard work, to find
wealth, and love, and happiness.

The Rising girls are introduced in *A Scattering of Daisies*,
and their story continues in *The Daffodils of Newent* and
Bluebell Windows, finally reaching its conclusion in
Rosemary for Remembrance.

A Scattering of Daisies   0 552 12375 7
The Daffodils of Newent   0 552 12579 2
Bluebell Windows   0 552 12880 5
Rosemary for Remembrance   0 552 13136 9

A SELECTED LIST OF FINE NOVELS
AVAILABLE FROM CORGI BOOKS